Charlie Courtland

Dedicated to my family and my dog, Ruby.

The Hidden Will of the Dragon

Sequel to Dandelions in the Garden
A Novel

Edited by Linda Boulanger
In association with TreasureLine Publishing
http://treasurelinebooks.com

This is a work of fiction. All of the characters, organizations, and events portrayed in this novel are either products of the author's imagination or are used fictitiously.

THE HIDDEN WILL OF THE DRAGON

ISBN 1452890056
EAN 9781452890056

CRS Registration 1048915203

First Edition: August 2010

Rose Hill Sanitarium

T he nurse's crisp white skirt swept through the doorway of my room. "It's time for your medicine," she said, bending over the night table. Her perfect posture matched the staunch twist of her bun.

The sanitarium was a sadistic place, with its whitewashed walls and natural light. The days seemed to last forever, and the birds outside my window never ceased their incessant singing. I had arrived a few days earlier after I'd had my spell. That is what the doctor called it, a *spell*, and my voluntary admittance was a precautionary measure. He recommended I admit myself so I could have around the clock care by professionals. He told me not to worry, reminding me over and over again that it was temporary. His knitted brow revealed how distressed he was by my relapse. I knew the look. It was the fear of death—not his, but mine.

"Are we feeling better?" the nurse asked. She was now drawing the curtains. I braced for a burst of sunshine, but instead I was greeted by a familiar overcast. "Oh dear, looks like rain," she said. "It was sunny earlier, but it seems those big clouds overhead have chased the cheer straight away."

I glanced at the bottle of medicine centered on the tray. I could taste the bitter burn already in my throat, and the thought of choking down another course caused an instant gag reflex.

The nurse rushed to my bedside and poured a cup of water. "Oh my, are you choking? Having trouble breathing?" She sat me up and gave a hardy thud to my backside.

I coughed and shook my head. I swallowed a mouth full of water. It was like trying to force a wad of cloth down my throat. I took another sip, and this time the liquid moved smoothly.

"There, there," she cooed, giving me a pat as she released her firm hold on my arm. "Just needed a bit of water, didn't you?"

I wanted to spit in the basin, but I knew there'd be blood. I could taste it, the metallic taint playing on my tongue. I didn't want the nurse to see it; I didn't want to alarm her. I knew the difference between concern and a trace amount, and I was certain this was just a trace that settled over night.

"I'm not dying," I said. I tried to fix my hair, but it was a mess from rolling around on my pillow all night.

"Of course not, milady. You've caught a chill, but at your advanced age the doctor wants to make certain it doesn't turn into something more serious."

"I'm not that advanced," I grumbled.

"Oh, of course not. I didn't mean to imply," she explained. "I only meant that as years pass we become susceptible."

"I was always taught the young were susceptible, and the old wise," I said. I sneered at the nurse, knowing full well that any look I shot her would be intimidating.

"You're quite right, quite right," she said, giving an agreeable nod.

This woman was no fun, no fun at all. I wasn't going to get a rise out her today, so I decided to let it go.

"Shall I pour your medicine?" she asked, pointing to the vial.

I rolled my eyes. "Very well." I knew she wasn't going to leave until I drank.

"Your friend across the hall got the most lovely bouquet of flowers from her family yesterday. Did she show them to you?" she asked as she shoved a spoonful into my mouth.

I had a choice: either spit it out or swallow it quick. Down it went, burning all the way, right into my gut where it warmed and bubbled.

When I stopped shuttering from the awful taste I said, "She's not my friend. I don't even know the woman."

"Oh, I thought she visited."

"More like she wanders in," I said. I waved at the door. "She doesn't even know where she is. She just lets herself out and roams up and down the hallways. Perhaps, you should put a lock on her door."

The nurse pulled a face. "She might be a touch out of sorts, but she's harmless."

"The woman's an imbecile," I grumbled.

"Milady!" she exclaimed.

"Oh don't look at me like that. I'm old and dying. I can say what I want. Who's going to tell? Are you going to tell?" I asked.

To my annoyance, she planted her broad hips in a chair. I was hoping she'd pick up the tray and leave, but apparently she took my remarks as an invitation to engage in further conversation.

"Some people can't take a hint," I mumbled.

She pretended not to hear me. She looked around the room. Not a single letter, framed picture, or even a vase of flowers decorated the space. Nothing personal showed except for the dressing robe thrown over the end of my bed. "Do you have family?" she asked.

What a presumptuous question I thought. "Do I look like I have family?"

"Well your condition came on suddenly, and perhaps you did not have time to pack all the things you might want to have with you." She folded her hands in her lap. "I see all you've brought is a bundle of papers. Are you writing a journal?"

"Don't you have other patients to tend too?" I asked.

She pressed her lips together and made a face like she'd just eaten something terribly sour.

"Oh all right, if you must know, I'm writing a story for my great god son."

Her eyes lit up. "A story! How wonderful. What's his name?"

"I was once in love with his grandfather, Count Drugeth," I said.

"Oh my, I bet that *is* a story," she said, interested.

"It is indeed."

"I'd love to hear it," she said. Her posture slacked. I took this as a clear indication she wasn't going anywhere.

"Your patients," I reminded.

"Oh, you're the last on my route. I don't have to make rounds for a few hours."

Just my luck, I thought.

I looked toward the window. The gray cast hung as if the world were stuck in perpetual dusk. "I'll make you a deal. If you take me out there, I'll tell you a story," I said.

She glanced at the window. "I don't know. I'm not sure the doctor would approve."

"How am I to recover if I can't get a breath of fresh air?" I asked.

"I think it's best if we stay inside. I'll sit here, and you can remain comfy in bed," she said, treating me like a child.

I crossed my arms and closed my eyes. "In that case, I'm feeling sleepy. Perhaps you should go bother someone else."

There was silence for a few moments. I kept my eyes pinched shut. I heard the scrapping of her chair and her distinct footsteps march out the door. I peeked to see if she had gone. The room was empty. I grabbed the basin and spat a bloody string of spit. I looked around for a place to hide the bowl. There weren't many options, so I shoved the evidence beneath the table.

A noise broke the silence and echoed down the hall. As the sound grew closer, my breathing quickened. I heard a squeak and then a curse as the nurse wiggled the contraption through the door. "If we're going outside you're riding in one of these," she said.

I couldn't help grinning as I kicked the covers from my feet and dragged my dressing robe around my shoulders. While I fumbled with the ties, she got my cape from the bureau and wrapped it around me before lifting me into the chair.

4

"I'm not helpless," I said. "I can walk you know."

"I know, but I don't want you having another episode and blacking out again." She folded a blanket over my legs and fixed a hat upon my head.

I felt such joy as she wheeled me away from the sick bed and toward the doors. "I feel like a child sneaking out," I whispered. Once outside, the fresh air burned my tender lungs as I sucked in a breath. I didn't care. It was a good hurt; an alive hurt, and I welcomed the discomfort.

"Where shall we go?" she asked, pausing for a moment on the walking path.

I told her I wished to rest by the park bench. After she had me situated, she arranged herself beside me. I noted she took special care not to soil her starched white skirt. Her uniform was a symbol of independence and she was prideful of her Christian duty.

When she was appropriately postured, I spoke. I began to tell her my story. Not the story I was writing for Count Drugeth concerning the truth about his ancestry, but my story. I told her about my mother falling ill and how I went to serve as a lady in waiting to the Countess Bathory. I spoke of my love for George and how it was not meant to be. She was sad by the news, but brightened when I introduced Draco Lorant to the conversation. In a way, I shared Elizabeth's story while I shared my own because it was impossible to tell one without telling the other. I found it refreshing to talk and have someone listen. At the time, I didn't know if I'd ever leave Rose Hill, or if I'd fulfill my promise to Count Drugeth, but I was going to try. I wasn't ready to die, not yet.

"So Elizabeth's grandson just appeared one day on your door step?" the nurse asked.

I nodded. "He was seeking answers about his family. There is so much he doesn't know, so much he doesn't understand because history has it wrong, well, not all wrong, but distorted." I leaned forward, placing my hand on her knee. "I feel that before I leave this world I must set it straight. I owe it to him. I owe it to Elizabeth," I said.

"I must know," she said. "Is it true? Did the Countess Bathory really do all the horrid things they say?" She lowered her voice even more. "With the blood, did she do those things with the blood?"

I patted her leg. "That's the question, and I'm afraid it requires a complex answer. It is not one I can give with a simple yes or no. It's much more complicated, and that is why I must write it down. It is the singular reason I will get well and leave here to return to my home. You see I am determined to finish the story for Count Drugeth. After all, I made him a deal. If he follows his heart and marries his beloved Kate, I agreed to share the truth about his grandmother, Elizabeth Bathory. I suppose I can be accused of forcing his hand to choose his heart over tradition." I paused. That was exactly my intention. "Admittedly, I blame tradition for all the wrongs Elizabeth suffered and this is my way of making it right. At the time when I fell ill I still hadn't received word of his decision, but I am hopeful and determined. I cannot help but fantasize about trading my written gift for a wedding invitation; a symbol of sacrifice for love." I took a deep breath. A violent burn branded my lungs causing my eyes to water. "I wish I could tell you more my dear, but I made a promise. A promise to my mistress and a promise to Count Drugeth, and I intend to keep it." I discreetly wiped my tears while blaming them on the breeze. "However, I can tell you this much, there are both truth and lies in every rumor. Trying to decipher which is which is the delicious part. Remember nothing is exactly as it seems. Nothing!"

She nodded, taking my words seriously. She was listening so intently that I hardly think she noticed my extreme discomfort.

A few raindrops hit the ground and rustled the leaves above our heads.

"We'd better get inside before we are soaked to the bone," she said, taking hold of the handles on the chair and giving me a hardy push toward the doorway.

"How soon do you think it will be before the doctor will see me fit to leave?" I asked.

"Since there is no blood in your spittle and you are complying with treatment I will make a positive recommendation regarding your recovery."

I smirked. I had befriended the nurse and with little effort she was already imagining a bond. The poor dove was naturally good-natured. "I'm very eager to get home. Very eager," I repeated.

***

I continued to hide the basin of bloody spittle from the nurse and within a week the doctor lacked reasons to keep me confined. He mixed several vials of medicine for me to take home including strict instructions to follow and recommended dosage, which I assured him repeatedly, that I would do. I had every intention of complying because I did not want to return. If I were to die, I wanted to do it at home, and only after I finished my story.

The nurse gave me a big hug after she packed my belongings and ordered my trunk to the carriage.

"I've personally sent word to your household in Vienna. Everything will be in order when you arrive. I am certain they'll be thrilled to have their mistress home," she said, with a brave smile. She was a bit choked up, but pleased to see me leaving under my own will and not by way of a wooden box through the body chute.

"Let's just hope I still have my silver," I said.

She laughed heartily.

"I'm serious, the servants will rob you blind when you're not looking."

"Oh milady, you are too much!"

I gave her a quick hug and adjusted my hat. I was ready to go home. Each step I took down the hall required considerable effort, but I was determined to exit under my own strength. My breathing labored and my hands trembled as I gripped the side of the carriage and heaved myself up the footholds. Once inside, I let the tickle building in my throat out. I covered my cough with my handkerchief. A small spot of pink soiled the delicate white linen. *It's just a trace*, I thought. It's just a tiny trace. I tucked the handkerchief in my pocket and rested my head against the seat cushion. I was going home, probably to die, but still, I was going home.

Home Sweet Home

Everything was properly arranged. The house was in order, and the cat was still fat and lazy. The post sat heaped on the service tray, and my tea waited in the drawing room.

"We're so glad to have you home," the maid said, as she pinched the skin of my underarm as she helped me to the chair.

I was too weak to climb the stairs, so the servants carried down my writing desk and shoved it in front of the window. It hit awkwardly, the top rising above the sill and cutting the pane in half.

"Can I fetch you anything else?" the maid asked.

I waved her off. I was already lost in my own thoughts and didn't want to be bothered with formalities. Besides, there lingered my half finished book. The truth was staring at me as the past spilled out line-by-line and permanently soaked in the parchment. I could burn it, bury it, or even hide it away, but I could never erase it. I just wished the others had come to the same epiphany before their deaths. Since I was the last, I was going to purge it all upon the page and give it to Count Drugeth. He could do with it as he pleased. Perhaps, set it a fire or drown it six feet under, even conceal it in a tomb. Whatever precaution taken, it could never be destroyed. I knew that now. Why...why couldn't the past just be forgotten? Superstitions were embedded in the stone and crumpled in the dirt. Whether we liked it or not, evidence of our lives was in every little crack. I could sense it. It was the uneasy feeling I got when a strong wind blew, or the tingle I felt when my hair stood on end. It's that little something that nags.

***

There it was, the beginning of my story that started with my mother's death. I was eleven when I met Elizabeth. So much had occurred since then; the birth of her baby, her marriage to Count Nadasdy, the affairs and the workshop. Elizabeth's retreat into her private underworld was growing, and so were her collections of devices and bottles of brewed concoctions. Her dabbling was increasing, and her appetite for release was mounting. I remembered our troubles bubbling up from beneath and seeping through the castle. It was like water rising, and it seemed as if I were forever moving to avoid being consumed and dragged down.

At last our escape came when I discovered a rare painting of Elizabeth's kin, the *Impaler*, Vlad Tepes hidden in the catacombs beneath the monastery. Fascinated, I hauled the treasure from the bowels and presented it to the heir, Elizabeth. I thought she'd be discreet, but why I assumed she'd have a change in character was beyond common sense. Elizabeth did exactly what her nature demanded; she insisted on displaying the portrait. This caused quite the disruption and did nothing but stir rumors and gossip. The whispers streamed around corners and floated on the dust. The tension in the castle was heavy and with each utterance I overheard, I quivered. When it became too much and my nerves could take no more, I begged Elizabeth to stow the painting. I hoped that if out of sight, the restlessness I felt in the household would settle, but she was stubborn and refused all my requests to restore peace.

Ill-fitted and unstable, I exploded. I tried to steal the painting from her chamber. We struggled, each wrestling with it, both trying to take it from the other, and in the fight the backing was torn. Something slid and poked out from the injury. At the climax of our feud we inadvertently uncovered a secret document. Penned in fading ink was scribed the singular name *Mihnea*, the eldest son of Vlad Tepes.

Elizabeth unsealed the letter and found several military maps and a document referring to property rights in Brenta just outside of Venice. As she read on, she learned Vlad Tepes commissioned a mansion to be built. Apparently, there was an agreement established between Vlad and the city of Venice that was secured through the Ministry of Finance. Immaculate instructions outlined how the funds were to be dispersed to maintain the Brenta estate. A man going by the name *Issachar* was executor over the property. Upon his death, the chore passed to his next of kin who would always go by the code name of *Issachar*. It was simplistically complex and perfect.

At the time I did not know a lot about history, but I knew enough to understand that all of Vlad Tepes wealth and properties were confiscated. Surely, this abandon retreat was no longer in existence. I expressed my concerns to Elizabeth. I will always remember the pause that lingered, and the bright lightness that cast over her eyes as she raised her head and exclaimed, "He was a genius!"

Vlad Tepes took this man Issachar into his confidence and together they plotted a protection over his assets. She was convinced that somewhere in a vault located in Venice housed the last of Vlad Tepes, or rather *Dalvia Sepet* legacy. Elizabeth dipped pen in ink and scratched the name on a piece of parchment. I did not see it immediately, but as she broke it down and wrote in reverse it became apparent. *Dalvia Sepet* was Vlad Tepes with the feminine 'ia' added to the end.

She folded the papers and returned them to the envelope. "There is only one thing to do," she stated. "We must go to Venice and find this Issachar!"

This was our salvation. This was the escape and the answer to our sinking. Suddenly, all the weight that had been gathering and pulling us down seemed to recede. When the last horse was secured, Felix, Elizabeth's manservant assisted us into the carriage. Already waiting inside was an armed royal guard. It was strange to have our privacy invaded, but I understood it was necessary to ensure our safety. The driver snapped the reins, and the carriage lurched. With the driver flanked by two armed men, our envoy was steered through the drawn gate and over the hill's crest. We rocked along the winding hillsides before picking up speed as we ventured south. It would be several days before we reached seaport, but I didn't mind. I was just glad to be free of Cachtice, the dreaded castle we called home.

I stared out the window watching the farm pastures roll by. Elizabeth smiled at me, and I returned the enduring gesture with the same loving courtesy. As we crossed the miles of land, I thought about the vellum documents stowed in her trunk and the reference to the name Issachar. It'd been nearly 130 years since Vlad Tepes arranged the secret agreement. Was it truly possible that the kin of a previous advisor was still carrying out the contract, or would we soon be sadly disappointed by a ruined and forgotten plan?

Uncovering Issacher

Nicholas waited on the boarding plank. His profile and ginger-streaked hair gave the impression he was Venetian, but his traditional dress was unmistakably Hungarian. We were from the far north where customs clashed and alliances occurred between barbarians and aristocrats. Although defined oppositions, I never understood how the two worlds, those of the barbarian and gentry, differed in practice. It was all a masquerade, men parading beneath disguise.

Nicholas slipped the captain a handful of gold coins. Bribery was part of the grim business of securing passage. It had to be done. It was common practice. I tried to appear unimpressed by the sheer size of the vessel docked before us but found it difficult to conceal my amazement. While living along the Danube, I'd seen my fair share of barges transporting cargo, but none compared to this ship. Five white sails flapped in the breeze as sailors rushed about the deck wrenching ropes and securing shipments.

"The captain has agreed to drop us at our lodgings before sailing out to sea," Nicholas announced.

"We're boarding this ship?" I asked, looking around for other passengers.

"It's the only boat sailing today," Nicholas answered.

I was amused by his authoritative tone since he'd barely reached the age when whiskers shaded the chin. I presumed the responsibility of the chore had something to do with his inflated confidence.

"It will do," Elizabeth said. She adjusted her hat to protect her eyes from the bright sun.

"How long until we sail?" I asked.

"Not long. The captain's eager to get underway," Nicholas replied.

The smell of day old fish mixing with seaweed overwhelmed the afternoon air. I had the urge to wash the taste from my mouth, as well as the dust from the journey. I watched as a pelican squatted on a dock pole envying a seagull that had just swooped down and snatched a limp fish from an unguarded crate. A fisherman scolded the monger for neglecting his job. He threatened to deduct the cost of the lost cargo from his earnings. The monger cursed beneath his breath. However, he did not argue. *How could he?* I thought. It was his fault the fish was taken. Or, perhaps it was our fault for distracting him from his work. He was preoccupied with ogling Elizabeth. It was obvious by his leering that women of wealth and importance were a rarity at port. I got the sense we were attracting too much attention, and it appeared we were drawing a greater audience. I nudged Elizabeth. I thought it was a good idea if we boarded the ship as soon as possible and disappeared.

Taking hold of the braided ropes, we steadied ourselves along the inclined plank. The captain was less than hospitable. He grumbled good day before calling for his cabin boy. He informed our party that a platter of fresh fruit, steamed fish, and a decanter of the finest Italian wine wait below.

Just as I turned to make my way, I spotted a thin pink tail hugging the edge of a shipping crate. I watched the fleshy string wrap around the boxes. I was certain I knew what it was, but I asked anyway. "What is that?"

"Tell Lucky we've got ourselves a wharf rat aboard," shouted the boy.

"Where's the bugger at?" someone yelled back.

"Right here by this crate."

The tail slithered away disappearing somewhere behind the cargo. I shivered. I hated rodents. I absolutely despised the creatures.

"He's on the run," a man shouted.

"Keep an eye on it boy. Lucky's on his way."

Before I could utter another complaint, Lucky appeared on deck. He lumbered toward us carrying a fish spear in one hand and a burlap bag in the other.

"He's hiding behind that crate," the cabin boy said.

Lucky grunted, "Ey."

Bam! The spear jammed between the wall and the crate.

"Did he get him?" I asked, backing away.

"I'm going to scare that bugger out," Lucky said.

Lucky was whacking the spear back and forth, and above the clamor of the attack I heard the hissing and scratching of the hunted. I knew the rat was trying desperately to claw its way to escape.

"Gotcha now you vermin," Lucky shouted.

"Is it dead?" I asked, hoping he had killed the rat.

But before anyone could answer, the rat shot from its hiding spot and scampered by the hems of our skirts. I screamed as I pedaled backwards. I bumped into Nicholas who was also keeping a safe distance from the action. I scrambled to put more space between the nasty vermin and myself.

Lucky swore something awful. A string of naughty words I never knew existed rolled across his tongue. Meanwhile, the rat was making a run for it. Someone else shouted, and things crashed in the rat's path sending the creature in several directions as it fled for its life. Lucky pursued, and amazingly he managed to get a second and third chance. The last strike penetrated squarely in the fatty part of the rat's backside. The spear sliced clean through impaling the critter to the deck. Facing death, the rat fought. Squirming and unable to free itself, it bared its protruding teeth. A deckhand tossed Lucky a club. With a single blow to the head, Lucky finished the rat off.

"It's over," he said.

"Do rats often come aboard?" I asked. I was frightened that I'd see more of them. I stared at the rat's sharp teeth. They horrified me.

"Ey, they're part of life on the ship. They wreak havoc by eating holes in the salt bags and ruining all kinds of things. If you see another, I'll get 'um." He yanked the spear from the deck with the impaled corpse of the wharf rat stuck to it and dumped the body into the burlap bag, tied it, and tossed it overboard. "No worries, he can't bother you any longer. How's 'bout you eat your lunch. I bet you're famished."

Our cabin was the finest accommodations on the ship. It was a cramped space with a low-beamed ceiling, but it provided a place to sit and a table to enjoy the food the captain promised. Unfortunately, the encounter with the rat killed my appetite. Although it had been some time since I ate, I still could not bring myself to taste the fish. I poked at the arrangement deciding I might be capable of choking down a nibble of fruit and washing my throat with a drink of wine.

Through a tiny porthole I saw the dockworkers going about their business. They were tossing ropes and shouting orders. A deckhand sounded the horn announcing our final departure. Slowly, we drifted. We were officially detached from the mainland. In comparison to the sea, I felt small and helpless. We were now at the mercy of the Adriatic Sea as it steered the ship to the island of Venice.

We sailed through the Canal della Sacca. Along the horizon, I viewed the white-washed silhouette of San Michele. The structure erupted from the water cutting into the vast sky like a monument amidst the sea. The birds circling above hovered for a moment before swooping for a meal. I wondered how it was possible for the birds to see anything lurking in the waves. I found the turbulence of the wake confusing and hypnotic. Mesmerized, I watched as a bird dove fearlessly into the water. It vanished for a second, and then to my astonishment, soared upward with a silver fish pinched in its beak.

"Who lives there?" I asked, appreciating the seaside estate of San Michele.

"No one living resides there," Nicholas answered. "San Michele is the island of the dead."

"The dead?"

"It's where the Venetians' bury their people. San Michele is a church which oversees the cemetery."

I thought it was such a waste to devote an entire landscape to rotting corpses. It was nothing more than an isolated island littered with graves and never receiving visitors. As the ship came about, I lost sight of San Michele. It was as if the place simply disappeared. It was there one minute and gone the next.

The ship continued onward, cutting through the Canal Colombola before entering the Grand Canal, which would take us into the very heart of Venice.

"Come on deck," Nicholas said, sensing we were nearing our destination.

The brims of our hats caught in the wind as we stepped into the crisp breeze. The scene was a fantastic dance of sailors calling out orders as they moved from one side of the ship to the other, each pulling ropes to swing the boom of the sails. I could hardly believe my eyes, coming to life all around me was a living painting. The dull gray was replaced by the delight of character and color. What a strange and marvelous wonder? How could I trust that I was not dreaming? I clutched the railing. I was in awe of the floating city where the streets were waterways, and the passengers rode in funny-shaped boats instead of horse drawn carriages. I had so many questions. Like how was it possible that water could hold up the enormous structures? I laughed at the buildings mocking the balance of nature by kissing the waves lapping from choppy wakes. Passing by were men wearing wide-rimmed hats. They seemed to enjoy their work because they serenaded the supplies as they moved from one dock to the next. Over there, a boat bobbed in front of an arched three-story building where a gondolier escorted two gentlemen. He indiscreetly presented his open hand gesturing for a tip. I fixated on the gentlemen, watching them until they disappeared into a shaded archway. It was just in time too, because a splash of water soaked the stones where they were once standing.

"This is the business district. Trade commissions, financial exchange and rulings on trade matters happen in those buildings," Nicholas pointed out.

"What is housed over there?"

"Those are storage houses. All kinds of supplies are put in there and then later distributed. Venice is a complicated metropolis."

"Oh my, look at the beautiful mansion," Elizabeth said. "Do you know who lives there?"

"It is the Palazzo Vendramin Calergi. It belongs to the Codussi family," a sailor answered.

"Is the family home for the season?"

"I'm not privy to society. Just know who owns the house. Not my business to know their whereabouts."

The sails flapped as the wind lessened under the protection of the Grand Canal. Ahead I spy two small boats rowing toward us. As we drew closer, a deckhand tossed an oarsman a rope.

"The boats will take us to our accommodations," Nicholas announced. He gestured for us to follow him to the boarding plank.

"How are we to get down?" My excitement was quickly turning to seasickness as I stared at the swirling water below.

Our trunks were lowered through a pulley attached to a pole secured to the mast.

"You don't expect us to climb over?" I asked. The trunks lurched with each release.

"No, of course not."

After the last trunk was secure, Nicholas led us to a giant crate that had ropes tied to all four corners. He opened a hinged door on the side. Reluctantly, I stepped in. The deckhands hoisted the lift making sure first to clear the railing of the ship before lowering it down toward the boats. The cage swung viciously as the deckhands tugged, maneuvering it over the side of the ship. I shut my eyes fearing we would plunge into the canal, but not seeing added to my disorientation and only made me feel more nauseous. I tightened my grip as we swayed like bait suspended above the water. The motion from the ship churned the water into thick gravy making the clear blue look more like sewage. It was utterly distasteful, and I could taste the wine and fruit I just consumed push up into my throat.

"Oh my God," I said, my voice low as if I were praying.

"It's nothing," Elizabeth said. "We're almost there."

I heard the men in the small boats speaking to one another. It was Italian, but did not resemble the formal dialect I'd been practicing.

"Stand back. The boat is a bit rocky because the ship is giving off wake. We'll try to hold it steady, but you'll still have to make a leap. Don't worry, we'll catch you," Nicholas instructed.

I shook my head. "What do you mean we must jump?" I asked, my voice shaking and my stomach reeling.

"It's only a short distance, but it's impossible to line the floor of crate with that of the boat. We are on unstable territory," Nicholas said. "An oarsman will hold out a hand. All you have to do is reach for it when the wave goes down."

The waves crashed against each other in chaotic rhythm. The boats bounced up and down as the crate rocked. The jagged motion caused my vision to blur, and I could not focus on any particular object. The deckhands labored to keep us steady. Nicholas was the first to leap. He stumbled a couple steps before regaining his balance.

"All right Countess, when the boat meets the crate you'll need to reach for our hands and jump. I assure you, we will catch you."

"Are you going?" I asked.

"Unless you want to go before me," she said, gripping the door. Water was splashing on the toes of her shoes.

"This was a fine idea Elizabeth! You never mentioned we'd have to leap out of a box into a boat!" I snapped, still clutching a makeshift handle.

"Well, I didn't know!"

"All right Countess, on my count. One, two, three..." Nicholas counted.

Elizabeth jumped from the crate and into the outstretched arms of the oarsmen. Her hat was knocked sideways, but she was safely aboard. She let out an elated squeal and hooted how much fun it was.

"It's your turn Lady Amara," Nicholas called.

I tried to will my fingers to release the stranglehold I had on the handle, but each time I loosened my grasp, the crate swayed away from the boat.

"Come on Amara, you must jump. They can't hold the ropes forever," Nicholas shouted.

I edged my feet towards the open door. The waves slapped sprays of water on my dress.

"That's good. Now on my count you must leap," Nicholas instructed.

Unable to speak, I nodded my head. I took a deep breath.

"One, two, three…"

I shut my eyes and leapt with such force that when I landed I toppled over an oarsman and rammed Nicholas into a paddle. In the same moment, the wind snatched my hat and dropped it into the canal. It surfed the waves as it waited to be rescued. A kind guard dove overboard to retrieve my silly hat before the current carried it out of reach. It took two men to pull the guard, who was now weighted down by wet layers of clothes, into the boat. I did not have the heart to tell the man that my hat was not worth risking his life for, but I was grateful he retrieved it.

"See, everything is just fine," Elizabeth said.

I was shaking uncontrollably as we rowed toward the boarding dock outside our hotel.

"Leon Bianco is the finest hotel in all of Venice," Nicholas said.

Although the Leon Bianco was entirely square, nothing else about it appeared symmetrical. The first floor had three archways; two identical, while the third was much wider. From a distance the entry looked slanted, but as we neared I saw that the ramp offered a function rather than added an aesthetic appeal. The second floor had skinny windows, two were alone, while those in the middle were squashed together and caged by a thin iron balcony. I supposed the balcony was purely ornamental since no door provided access. The third story was simply a larger reflection of the second and lastly, the top floor was separated by a masonry ridge covered in seagull droppings. That was Leon Bianco; or at least my first impression of it.

The boat bumped into the dock causing me to check my balance. When all was secure, we followed Nicholas beneath the shadowy arch over the tilted floor and into the grand entry. I immediately recognized that the face of Leon Bianco was deceiving. Behind the boxy structure was an airy cathedral interior decorated in rich greens and Italian artistry. A loggia overlooked the grand entry where the stairway crawled along the brick walls cutting through the balconies above. Intricately carved grilles provided intimacy, which would otherwise be impossible to achieve in a typical spacious interior.

Our apartment was on the second floor. There were double doors leading from the main room to a balcony that overlooked the atrium. I called for Elizabeth to join me. She was enchanted with the view and commented on the tiny yellow birds that fluttered beneath the glass canopy. I agreed that they were much more appealing than the bluebirds looming around Cachtice. In Venice the sound of babbling water mixed pleasantly with clacking petite chirps. I was pleased that they were nothing like the menacing creatures squawking in the trees at Cachtice. I did not care for those birds, but these were comforting, and I was determined to enjoy listening to their songs.

"Ah there is an orangery," Elizabeth said, pointing to a clump of leafy trees with green and orange fruit.

The scent rising from the atrium was a pleasing change from those lingering along the canal. Although the odor of fish and salty spray first offended me, I soon came to welcome the familiar scent. There was something exotic about foreign smells. It shocked life and adventure into my dulled senses. Colors became more vibrant, food more delicious, and the sun was like a friend's embrace after years of absence.

I leaned over the balcony railing to get a better look at the beauty below. Elizabeth yanked the back of my bodice. "Careful!" she giggled. "Wasn't it only moments ago you were as white as the sails on the ship and scared to death to leap a few feet? Now, you're swinging from the railing?"

I laughed. I lifted my feet from the stone floor and allowed the iron railing to crease my stomach. A man walking below noticed our liveliness.

"You're making a scene," Elizabeth said.

"Good afternoon ladies," the man called.

We nodded in unison.

The man removed his hat and held it over his heart. He sang something in Italian, and as he did, his deep voice resonated off the glass ceiling of the atrium. When he was finished, we applauded eagerly, shouting cheers and bravos that drew attention from a neighbor on the third balcony. Before the man continued on his merry way, he blew us a kiss.

"He's very bold," I said, still laughing.

"Shocking!" Elizabeth mocked.

Our neighbor cursed, mumbling something about young girls making mischief.

"If she only knew the half of it," Elizabeth said. She playfully dragged me inside the apartment where we talked for hours about all the things we would do and the sights we'd visit.

***

The instant my foot met with the stone tiles of Leon Bianco, I was charmed by Venice and seduced by the defiance of the sea swelling at the city's door. Each edifice, whether original Byzantine or renovated Renaissance fashion, was a unique menagerie where I imagined men serenading lovers. As I walked, I pictured the courtyards transforming into artist studios and becoming a poet's muse. Just beyond the arch and sitting beside a pot of overflowing foliage, was an elderly Italian gentleman. He was the only audience to the improvisation of daily life.

Today I could hardly contain my enthusiasm because I had learned how Venetians skirted conventional manners. I'd found it was acceptable for citizens and visitors to don masks and wear clothing not intended for the wearer. Originally, I had been skeptical, but now that I saw the mystic of the city, I knew the rumors were true. Even though it seemed surreal that such folly was encouraged, I embraced it, for I was seeing it with my own eyes.

In Hungary, such foolishness would draw the severest punishment. Neither imposter nor tailor could escape judgment. It was a terrible crime to portray something you were not, but here in Venice, pleasure was permitted.

In time I would learn that despite the playful games, Venice still maintained the custom of class and rank. Even in the silliness, everyone knew where he or she stood in the order of things. They bestowed privilege to those most worthy. However, the line of separation was slightly more blurred when a person of social importance benefited from an arrangement. A lesser person could not take advantage on one's own, God forbid! No, a person could only advance when accepted members of polite society blessed them with an approving nod and invited them into the inner circle.

Even though masquerading was an amusing past time of the upper crust, what Elizabeth and I were plotting would never receive approval from our equals. If discovered, we'd spark glares so wicked that not even the king himself would be able to save us from being ostracized or worse. I shuddered to think what the worst would be, but was certain it included exile. I did not want to leave Venice, but I also had to remember why we came here in the first place. We were on a secret mission to find the lost estate of Vlad Tepes. That alone was not so scandalous, but the plan Elizabeth conjured to obtain information was worthy of the most devious charlatan.

Nicholas spent the days prior to our arrival casing the city. He knew the business district and acted as an adequate escort during our stay. He even supplied Elizabeth with a detailed layout of the Ministry of Finance. He described each floor, what official occupied what office, and the necessary course taken to inquire about inherited property and monies. As I listened, I realized the process was more complicated than either of us originally thought. Fortunately, Nicholas was patient and did not mind repeating himself several times until finally we nodded with understanding.

Once I memorized the layout of the Ministry of Finance, I progressed to learning the jargon of gentlemen. I was schooled in the daily dealings of trade and finance, which in this case included property titles and vaulted funds. Even though Nicholas was a guard and certainly no expert, he was the only source we could afford to retain. His duty was to linger around the business district eavesdropping on conversations until he found a common language most of the gentlemen spoke. That way when the opportunity presented, we would not raise suspicion. Thankfully, I learned I would not have to say much. In fact, Nicholas discovered the most respected gentlemen visiting the district said very little. Idle chitchat was frowned upon and considered a complete waste of time. Niceties were for parlor rooms and card tables and had no place in the world of finance. Although Nicholas never admitted it, I suspected he had figured out what Elizabeth was up too. It was not until much later that I realized he was completely off the mark.

While Nicholas gathered useful information, we kept busy by exploring the plaza and crossing the Rialto to visit the market. Here, we too observed the daily habits of gentlemen. We watched how they walked, talked and handled their dealings with one another. In the evenings, Elizabeth insisted I practice my role over and over. It was critical I get it correct – I absolutely had to be convincing.

Dressed in a borrowed gentleman's suit, I sauntered across the floor practicing my habits and formalities.

"You're walking too light of foot," Elizabeth said. "Let your hands hang by your sides."

I tried again.

"Don't divert your eyes! Hold your chin firmly in place."

"It feels unnatural," I whined, tugging on my padded doublet.

"Well of course it does, but you must maintain character if we're to pull this off."

"I'm too small to be convincing. I haven't seen any men as tiny as me."

"Nicholas is ordering a higher heel be added to the boots. It should give you enough lift."

"Heels? Won't that draw suspicion?"

"I hear they are becoming fashionable, especially with the French. You know how tiny they can be," she said.

I agreed. If we were in France, I'd easily pass for a man. "Should I do a French accent?"

"Heavens no! Now walk across the floor again, but this time try not to look like a woman dressed as a man."

I scowled. I'd been trying to get this down for days and with little success. Just as I was taking my fifth trip across the room, Nicholas entered carrying a sack.

"I've got your boots," he announced, wincing at the sight of me dressed in men's clothing.

I took the boots and slid them on. The heels did add to my height. I gave them a whirl. The heels clopped against the flooring. "It's impossible to be masculine in these things." Frustrated, I laced my hands on my hips.

Elizabeth cocked her chin. "Take the boots off Amara and give them to Nicholas."

"Me, why me?" Nicholas complained.

"We have to see how a man walks in the heels."

Nicholas hesitated. "I don't think they'll fit, but I'll try." After cramming his feet into the boots, he stood up. His arms flung out from his sides and flapped around like a grounded duck trying to take flight. He regained his balance and then teetered before his ankles buckled. I burst into hysterics. It was the funniest thing I'd ever seen and as hard as I tried, I could not quit my laughing fit.

"Come on Nicholas. Stop messing around," Elizabeth scolded. She thought he was poking fun.

"Trust me countess, I'm not making a fool out of myself on purpose," he said, with one arm straight out while the other clung to a chair for support.

"Have you found your center?" Elizabeth asked.

"Center?"

"Your balance?"

"I'm afraid not," he said, trying once again to steady himself.

I don't believe Nicholas ever found his center; more like slightly left of center, but it would do. Eventually, he was able to walk across the floor without rolling his ankles. Elizabeth ignored the wobbles even though it was agonizing to witness. Finally, when she'd seen enough, she dismissed Nicholas from the humiliating chore.

He dabbed his sweaty brow with a handkerchief. "Terrible fashion. I don't know how you ladies do it or the French for that matter."

I stood before Elizabeth and Nicholas. Just for amusement I wobbled a few times mimicking Nicholas's trial. It sparked a slight smile from Elizabeth; however, Nicholas did not find my antics funny.

"You've no sense of humor," I muttered, brushing off his mood.

I proceeded across the floor. Actually, it was more like I stomped.

"Yes, that's it," Elizabeth cheered. "I think you've got it!"

"What are you going to do about the hair?" Nicholas asked.

Elizabeth contorted her face as she considered.

"Don't even suggest I cut it." I bundled my hair protecting the strands from impending doom.

"How about a wig?"

"A wig?"

"I saw a shop in town that sells them. They're for masquerading, but they do look rather realistic," Nicholas said, delighted by his ingenious suggestion.

"Even in daylight?"

Nicholas raised a brow. "Daylight? Why would you be wearing this in the daylight?"

Elizabeth made a fatal error. Until now, Nicholas thought all of the effort he was making was to pull off the finest charade at a formal masquerade ball. He knew Elizabeth well enough to understand she'd be amused by any liberty and up until this point he was willing to go along with the perverse disguise.

"What do you have in mind?" Nicholas asked; his voice dropping and becoming very serious.

Elizabeth pressed her lips together forming a thin line. "Why Nicholas, what made you think this was for a ball?"

"I just assumed."

"Well that was silly of you," she said, standing up and smoothing out her skirt. "That's all for now Amara. I think you've got it."

Poor Nicholas was more confused than ever. His mouth went slack as another question formed in his head, but he shied away from Elizabeth and settled his eyes on me. He was hoping to discover the truth in my expression, but I was a quick study. I smiled as if I hadn't a singular thought in my pretty little mind. I presumed Nicholas figured it was best if he did not know what Elizabeth was up to, and for now he dropped the inquisition. Often, I worried he'd demand an explanation, but he never did. Being a good servant, he continued to run errands. He purchased a brown haired wig and a pair of tanned pigskin gloves to complete my outfit.

One day, while we were alone, Nicholas announced he knew I was up to something. He was looking out the window overlooking the Grand Canal. "I know you're not going to tell me, but I just want you to know I'm worried."

I did not answer.

"You've asked for the layout of the Ministry of Finance and the costume," he said. His eyes moved to the items on the bureau.

"Nicholas," I began.

"I do not demand to know, but I think whatever you are planning is flawed," he interrupted. "You'll need a manservant, most gentlemen have an aide."

I admit I was surprised. It wasn't what I expected to hear. "It's best you're not involved," I said, protectively.

"I'm already involved."

"No, you're following orders."

"So are you."

"True," I said. It was a good defense.

"The two of you are going through an awful lot of trouble. Whatever it is, you're willing to take quite a risk. The last time you did such a thing, you saved a man's life. Now, I'm not saying I'm condoning your behavior, but it does seem you do things for good reason." He was justifying. I recognized it because I often took the same approach.

"I hate to disappoint you, but we're not planning on saving anyone's life."

He stroked his chin.

I bit my lip. I wanted to tell, but I knew Elizabeth might kill me if I spoke about the plan without her permission. "I tell you what, when Elizabeth returns I will mention the manservant idea. We'll include you if she feels it is critical to the plan."

"Very well," Nicholas said, returning his attention to the view of the canal.

Nicholas was observant, very few gentlemen traveled around the city without a manservant. Those who did were not of significant wealth. Reluctantly, Elizabeth agreed to include Nicholas in the scheme. He listened to the whole story nodding along as we explained the discovery of the portrait, the servants' superstitious beliefs in the legend of Vlad Tepes, and finally, the hidden envelope.

"Why not tell your husband?" he asked Elizabeth.

Elizabeth looked at me and then at Nicholas. "Why, so he can claim it for himself?"

"Rightfully it is his," Nicholas noted. He spoke like a true man.

"And who determines these rights?"

Nicholas became uncomfortable. He knew he'd hit a raw nerve.

"Men, that's who," she continued.

"Well, yes but…"

"What if there is a turn in events? What if the sultan pushes forward, and gains ground until he's banging on our door?" she asked. "Then what? Shall I just let him take me and all my possessions?"

"Surely, the king will not allow that to happen, and besides the guards will protect you, I will protect you," he said.

"And why will the king protect me?"

"Countess, you do not need to concern yourself with such things," Nicholas answered.

"Let me ask you this, Nicholas. Please tell me what happened to Vlad's mother, his mistress and not to forget his wife?"

Nicholas tensed. He knew his answer would support Elizabeth's argument.

"That's right Nicholas, they all died by the hand of the sultan or in fear of him. They all thought themselves safe, protected by the most powerful men, but in the end they were imprisoned, raped and killed or jumped to their own death to avoid capture. I do not wish to endure the same fate."

"But you are protected," he protested. The claim was weak considering the argument she presented.

Elizabeth let out a cynical laugh. "Oh yes, perhaps today." But, before Nicholas could retort, Elizabeth said sternly, "You volunteered for this mission. I must have your oath you will take whatever is discovered to your grave."

Nicholas stiffened beneath Elizabeth's penetrating stare. "Yes Countess, absolutely it is my sworn duty to do so."

"It will be entirely by your own doing if you choose to either keep the secret in old age, or meet suddenly with a horrific death." She allowed the words to penetrate. "Am I understood?"

There was no mistaking the seriousness of the situation. Nicholas understood this was not an idle threat. Elizabeth had already proven she was capable of dishing out fatal punishments. Some of them were so gruesome it made being captured by the Turks and sold on a ransom block seem a favorable alternative.

From here forward, we spent most of our time rehearsing exactly how we intended to pull off the caper. I determined Elizabeth could not play any actual role in the scenario, which left Nicholas and me to do the deed. We could not risk Elizabeth being recognized. If anything should go wrong, it was best that she was not connected with the scheme.

***

Early Tuesday morning, I dressed in the gentleman's suit. I adjusted the itchy wig and clutched a leather-bound portfolio under my arm. Inside were the documents believed necessary to prove heir to Vlad Tepes' estate. Nicholas and I were to take a gondola to the Ministry of Finance and Affairs, while Elizabeth remained at Leon Bianco. Together, we boarded the boat and headed towards the business district.

When we arrived at the dock, I instinctively offered my hand to Nicholas to take. He coughed loudly to distract the gondolier. Quickly, I yanked my hand away and cursed beneath my breath. I sighed. I knew I must gather my nerves and take some coins from my pocket to pay the gondolier.

"Remember, stick to what we've rehearsed," Nicholas encouraged. "If you get in trouble it's better to say nothing than the wrong thing."

"Sound advice," I mumbled. "Do you know where you're going? Remember I can't lead, only follow," he said.

"Up the stairs on the left," I answered.

Just as he predicted, a staircase ran up the left wall leading to a second balcony. Upstairs there was a long counter behind which a man with a black beard and curled tresses idled.

"May I assist you?" the man asked.

So far my disguise was convincing. "I'm looking for a gentleman who goes by the name of Issacher."

"Issacher?" he asked.

"Do you have anyone here that goes by such a name?"

He maintained eye contact as he paused to recall. I steadied myself. I swore he was peeling off my disguise and seeing the woman behind the mask.

"Let me inquire on your behalf," he finally answered. He scrawled Issacher on a piece of paper. My knees shook and I balled up my hands into fists to control my nervousness.

"It's working," Nicholas reassured.

"How did you hear of Issacher?" the man asked.

"Is there anyone here by that name?" I replied, ignoring his question. I remembered it was better to say less than more.

"He is a specialist of sorts. Your inquiry is most curious."

I thought I might faint, but I managed to remain calm. "Ah, I see. Perhaps I should explain my reason for inquiry?"

Nicholas coughed again. The man grinned at his rude habit, which revealed he had a missing front tooth.

"I've inherited documents that have led me to your establishment. It appears they were misplaced for some time, well, until recently discovered."

"And, this Issacher is mentioned?" he asked, still grinning.

"A relation made a special arrangement with a man going by the name. Upon Issacher's death the favor transfers to his next of kin, I assume going by a similar name," I said.

"Ah, I see. This is most curious. May I ask why you seek Issacher?" Obviously, I had not made my errand apparent. He was asking the same question over and over again. He was trying to trip me up.

"It's concerning entitlement to an estate," I said again.

"Ah property, you'll need to go up two floors. Give the man behind the counter this note. He will direct you to where you'll need to go next."

Annoyed, we climbed two more flights of stairs. A man almost identical to the one two floors below stood in a similar fashion behind yet another counter. Without a word, I gave him the note. He lifted a glass piece to his eye and examined the scribbled writing. He glanced up at me, and then over to Nicholas.

"Name please," he asked.

"Vladis Sepet," I answered, in the most manly of voices.

"Sepet, you say?"

"Sepet," I repeated.

He tucked the note in his jacket pocket and excused himself. A surge of panic tingled through my body. It began in my belly and spread all the way to my toes, which were crammed in cloddy boots.

When the man returned, he was carrying an oversized book. He scanned several columns of names before glancing at us one last time. "Ah, here it is, Issacher."

I experienced a hint of relief. He scribbled something on the piece of paper.

"Go down to the first floor; you'll see four doors on the right side. You don't want any of those. You want to continue along the corridor until you come to a dead end. Turn right and go all the way to the last door on your left," he said.

"Last door on the left," I repeated. "I will find Issacher in this office?"

"You go there, the man will help you."

"Are you sure?" I asked.

The man used his index finger to mark the spot on the page that listed Issacher's name. He tapped it. "The book refers to this office. This is where you must go if you want information concerning Issacher."

I thanked the man and followed his directions down the corridor and to the last door on the left. Inside was a tiny office with a single desk.

"I'm told you can assist me," I stated, upon entering the room.

The man behind the desk rested his quill pen in the inkwell.

"I'm looking for a man by the name of Issacher. I've been directed to your office."

"Issacher? What is your business with Issacher?"

"It's a matter concerning entitlement." I was growing tired of repeating this information.

"You claim to be entitled?"

"I believe I have business with Issacher."

"You do, do you?"

I found his sarcastic tone irksome. The complex bureaucratic system was wearing on my patience. "Yes, I do. Now can you help me or am I to be routed to another room?" I asked.

Nicholas folded his arms across his chest.

"Can you produce documentation requesting Issacher's services?"

I took the items from the leather portfolio. After thumbing through the pages, I retrieved a single piece of paper containing the reference to the man named Issacher. I set it on the desk and pointed to the line with the name.

"Where did you get this?" the man asked.

"If you are not Issacher, I do not see how it is any of your business," I stated, sharply. I removed the document from under his nose before he had an opportunity to pry further.

He took out another slip of paper and scratched something on it.

Good lord, I am being sent to yet another office! I thought. I did not know how much I could take. I wondered how any business was ever conducted in the building.

31

"You'll find Issacher at this address," the man said, giving me the paper.

"He does not have an office in this building?"

"No. He is independent."

I thanked the man and quickly exited the room, and then the building. Outside, several gondolas were tied to the dock. I showed the gondolier the address. "Can you take us here immediately?"

He ushered us into the boat. I wished I had the means to send a message to Elizabeth about our progress, but that was not possible. We could not risk it, not now. We'd just have to explain the circumstances when we returned to the hotel.

The gondolier guided the boat towards a narrow water route. We turned several more times, winding deeper into the watery labyrinth. In the belly of Venice was where true Venetian's lived; it was far from the novelties that attracted visitors. Overhead hung laundry from drying ropes. Loud women nagged their children, while wrinkled grandmothers idled on brittle balconies. A young girl blew Nicholas a kiss and then flashed her breasts. I gasped, utterly appalled. Nicholas grinned, his eyes never leaving the topless girl beckoning from the railing above.

"Is she a courtesan?" I whispered, apparently not soft enough because the gondolier answered instead of Nicholas.

"No, not in these parts. That's a different kind of woman altogether. Perhaps after your errand, you'd like to explore for yourself?"

"Good lord, no!" I exclaimed.

Nicholas chuckled at my blunt rejection.

"Too good for that sort of company are you?" the gondolier asked.

Being too good had nothing to do with it. I was completely the wrong sex.

"Ah you noble types are all the same. You always refuse, but after you've been here a while you'll manage to find your way back. I see your kind coming and going. Nothing to be ashamed of, men are men—we all have the same desires you know."

Wearing a sheepish smile, Nicholas shrugged. I hated that he was enjoying this.

"Ah, here we are," he announced. He let the boat drift towards the dock.

I paid the fee and then asked if he'd kindly wait for us to return from our errand. I baited him with a little extra if he agreed.

"Do you see the path? You go that way until you reach a reddish colored building with a wooden sign. Are you with me so far?" he asked.

I nodded, clenching my hands in fists again. I felt the surge of nerves rising up.

"You can't see it from here, but once you're around that corner there's a row of houses. Just look for the number. That's where you'll find who you seek."

"You'll wait for us?" I repeated.

He counted the monies. "I'll be right here," he answered.

We followed the directions. Along the way we passed a drunk slouching with arm wrapped around a clay jug. I noticed he had dirty nails with sores around the edges. I tried to disregard his incoherent ramblings, but he was so menacing. His begging was difficult to ignore. He reminded me of the pathetic peasants near Cachtice. How sad and starved they had looked. Playing just beyond the vagrant was a group of filthy children. Their bare feet slapped the stone path as they circled.

"Get on, now!" Nicholas yelled.

"Nicholas, they're just children," I said. I did not see the danger they presented.

"No such thing as children in these parts," Nicholas said. "Wolves, hunting in a pack. That is what they are. They want to rob us blind." He swatted at the air in an effort to shoo them away. They giggled and scattered.

"That's 24. Over there I believe is 26. It seems we're heading in the right direction," I announced.

The alley was nearly vacant except for a man exciting a nearby building. I noticed that the collar of his long coat was pulled up to conceal his features and his chin was tucked deep inside. The silver embossed design along his pockets was familiar, but not immediately apparent. I admired the gold buckles on his boots, which were peeking out from the hem of his jacket. I deduced from his dress that he was a foreigner and quite out of place. "I dare say that gentleman is just as transparent as we are," I said to Nicholas. I'd hardly spoken the words when I was suddenly struck. I'd seen those gold buckles before, and that coat. They were unforgettable. I tried to get another look, but the man had disappeared around the corner. "What the hell is George doing in Venice?" I blurted out in disbelief. I noticed there was no sign on the building from where he came.

"Are you certain?" Nicholas asked. He paused and touched my arm. "Did he recognize you?"

I replayed the brief encounter in my mind. "I don't believe so," I said. "What business could he possibly have here?" I asked.

"Perhaps, you are mistaken. Let's not worry ourselves right now. First, we must find Issacher."

I agreed with Nicholas we couldn't be distracted from our task. When this was over I'd have him get to the bottom of things. If George were in Venice, Nicholas would uncover it.

Nicholas unfolded the piece of paper. "Number 39," he said, looking up at the building. This is the place."

Nicholas knocked on the door. It was quiet except for the rattling of dishes, and then I heard the creaking of approaching footsteps.

"State your business," a voice said from behind the door.

"We're here to see a man who goes by the name of Issacher," I answered. I felt ridiculous speaking to the door.

"What business do you have?"

"It's concerning entitlement." It was strange having a conversation through a wood, and I hoped my choice of words would give me entrance.

"Entitlement of what?" the voice asked.

Before I answered, I wondered if I was in the right place. "A property I believe is somewhere in Brenta."

"Brenta? There's no property in Brenta." I heard footsteps moving away.

"What do we do?" I whispered.

Nicholas knocked again. Again, the footsteps returned. This time the door opened a crack.

"Go away, I can't help you."

"I've got documents. I wish to show them to Issacher."

"Documents?"

"I believe they prove an estate exists, an estate I have rightfully inherited." I waited anxiously for an answer. My knees wobbled and my mouth went dry.

"What is your name?"

"Vladis Sepet," I croaked.

"Sepet?"

"Yes, Sepet."

The door opened and I could see the old man had a black beard. His blue eyes were cloudy and floated in dingy orbs. There was a yellowish tinge, like the color of urine after sitting too long in a pot. His eyes searched unscrupulously, roaming about as if they were looking for something solid to settle upon.

"I'm Issacher. Please come in," he said.

The apartment was larger than it appeared from the view in the hall, but that was how things were in Venice – nothing gave a proper perspective. The furnishings were old, but in pristine condition. Figurines decorated the shelf above the charred hearth, and a fluffy white cat with a scrunched up face purred by the window. Traces of fur littered Issacher's clothing and rugs.

"You say you have documents?"

I presented the portfolio to Issacher. Using an eyeglass, he examined the fine print. The lens distorted the writing and his eyeball. I wondered how the device worked since it took him a great deal of time to read the papers.

"May I ask how you came in possession?" He set down the eyeglass and looked at me.

"I found them hidden in a portrait of a deceased family member."

"A portrait?"

"There is a painting that has been recently discovered, as well as the contents hidden inside," I informed.

"And who is the portrait of?" he asked.

"I don't see how that is relevant," I said, hesitantly. I was not certain I should trust this man.

"Oh, but it is." The limitation of his sight was becoming apparent. He fumbled along the table until his fingers found the handle of the teapot. "May I offer you some tea?" The pot trembled as he poured the hot brew.

"It is a painting of the Prince of Wallachia," I divulged.

"Hum, there have been many, which is your prince?"

"Vlad Tepes," I answered. I took a hearty gulp of tea. It was soothing and I enjoyed the warmth.

Issacher's bulbous eyes widen, his lips twisted into a curious smile. "Interesting. Now where did you say you found this painting?"

"I didn't say, but if you must know it was in a catacomb beneath a monastery."

"Which one? Which monastery are you referring?"

"Ah, that Mr. Issacher I'm afraid I cannot reveal. You do understand I'm afraid I've said too much."

"Such a shame, but yes, I do understand." He eased into the soft cushion of his chair. "You are a descendant of the prince?"

"Yes," I stated. I wanted to further explain, but I knew it was best to keep quiet. Again, Issacher let several moments pass by before speaking. The cat stretched in the window seat, spreading her paws before settling back to sleep. "What do you wish to know?" he asked.

"Well, I gather from the documents the prince intended for this information to reach his son, but it appears it never did. Also, I believe he wanted to keep the estate a secret. It was to be a refuge for the royal family."

"But it is not in Vlad Tepes name. What makes you believe it belonged to him?"

"I believe the name on the document is code for Vlad Tepes. Sepet, is Tepes in reverse. He used it for the same reason I've chosen to use it. If this were ever found out, the property along with everything else would be confiscated. Besides, the name Tepes is not one many choose to be associated with these days, or back then for that matter. It carries…well, I'm sure you're familiar with the legend."

"Ah yes, Dracula, the Impaler, or whatever one wants to call him. He inspired much fear, this legend," Issacher noted.

"Tales and old superstitions," I said, dismissively.

"You do not believe the stories?" he asked, surprised.

"Are you asking if I believe the man they call the Dragon is undead? No, I'm afraid I do not believe that particular tale."

"Ah, this is very convenient. May I ask why you've come to claim the entitlement? I'm aware of other descendants, how do I say, more noble and from a direct lineage."

Heat flushed my cheeks. I figured Issacher was referring to the Bathory family. "It's a reasonable question. It is evident Vlad Tepes intended for it to be kept a secret; surely, a more social figure would be recognized. It'd be impossible for any other members of my family to make inquiries without drawing questions, which hardly could go unanswered. You do understand my position?"

"Humm…" Issacher said, his eyes wandering around in their sockets.

"Although I am a descendent, let's just say I'm not one who has much claim."

"A bastard?" he asked.

I cleared my throat indicting this was the truth. I winced at the ease with which he used the term, and how indiscreetly he threw it into the conversation.

"Just the type of person the royal family wouldn't mind hiding away in a remote estate?" he added.

"Issacher, I do believe you are beginning to understand." In fact, it was me who was beginning to understand.

"I do see. Tell me, what is it you want, exactly?" he asked.

"Nothing at the moment. I wish for the current arrangement to remain intact and that the estate continues to be managed by you or your kin. In the event the royal line needs preserving, I'll leave specific instructions to seek Issacher." I gathered the documents. "If you ever need to contact me," I placed a sealed envelope on the table. I'd said my peace and now arranged to take leave from his company.

"What's this?" he asked, stopping me.

"It is where you may send a message and to whom."

Issacher nodded. "As you are aware, this estate, or the care of it has been in my family for over 100 years."

"As I said, I'd like that to continue."

Issacher was pleased.

"May I ask if there are adequate funds to maintain the property?" I asked.

"Be assured, the prince made certain."

"And your family, are they sufficiently provided for?"

"Times have changed, things are more expensive," he said, sadly.

"I imagine they have," I answered, looking around his apartment.

"I will see if I can increase your allowance." Regretfully, I set down my teacup and headed to the door.

"You have my deepest gratitude," Issacher said, bowing. "I have a son. His wife has many expensive needs, and his children, ah, don't get me started on them. Spoiled, every last one of them, spoiled. They've no respect for the value of things. They think coins fall from Heaven."

"Children, they are naive creatures," I laughed.

"Ah, don't get me started."

Before I took permanent leave I asked Issacher if it was possible to see the estate while I was in Venice?

"This can be arranged," Issacher said.

"And the vault? The funds are secure?"

"Extremely. Issacher is an honored keeper over the Ministry of Finance," he said, referring to himself in the third person.

We said our goodbyes, and I thanked him for the tea.

When we were safely in the street Nicholas addressed me, "By God, we've done it!"

We did not waste a moment. When we got to the dock we found the gondolier squatting on a crate eating meat stuffed between two pieces of bread. He jumped up when he saw us coming and untied the boat. "Business goes well?" he asked, lending a hand.

"Yes, thank you."

The gondolier shoved the boat away from the dock. He navigated the narrow waterways leading toward the Grand Canal.

"Good thing you're a generous fellow. After you disappeared another gentleman made me a generous offer, but I stayed true to my arrangement and waited for you. Maybe you'll remember this and give me more business in the future? You can refer me to all your rich friends?"

I was annoyed to learn that the man I thought was George had tried to bribe our driver.

"I told him I was waiting for some other gentleman who'd already paid. Well, he didn't like hearing that! It seems he was in a bit of a rush. You'd think the city was on fire or something," the gondolier babbled.

"I appreciate your loyalty," I said.

"Ah, got nothing to do with loyalty, but everything to do with money. A man's got to feed the family, keep the wife happy."

"So, this man couldn't make you a better offer?" I asked, curious.

"Seems he'd already spent his lot up there in the lady's room," he said, with a wink.

"What makes you think he was with a woman?"

"As I was saying earlier, your kind comes around more than you think. All for the same reason, to see a woman." He pushed the oar deep in the water. "It's always about a woman," the gondolier chuckled.

We passed beneath the balcony where the topless girl had been standing. She was gone now. I spied Nicholas sneaking a glance. "Thinking of ways to spend the reward Elizabeth is sure to give you?" I joked.

The Grand Canal was ahead. Gondolas passed one another, and rowers shouted out to potential customers waiting dockside.

"Where to?" the gondolier asked.

"Leon Bianco."

As the gondolier guided the boat to the hotel, I felt I was finally able to relax. The worst was over and I'd been successful. I did my duty, I got the information Elizabeth sought and fooled everyone in the process. Not a single person suspected I was anything but a gentleman. As we neared, I saw the silhouette of Elizabeth standing in the window. I fought the urge to wave my arms. I must resist the desire to celebrate my victory. "There she is," I said to Nicholas. "Probably going out of her mind."

However, before we could reach our room and share our news with Elizabeth, I was stopped by the hotelkeeper. "Excuse me, I can't allow admittance without announcement," he said.

"Ah, of course, but we are expected," I answered, remembering my disguise.

"Whom is expecting?" the keeper asked.

I thought it unwise to be connected to Elizabeth. Who else in the hotel could I offer as a name, which guest might I be acquainted? I stuttered caught off guard and unable to think quickly.

"Thank you Miguel," I heard Elizabeth call out. "I forgot to announce I was expecting guests."

"Forgive me," Miguel said, bowing to the countess. "Just doing my duty."

"Yes, yes…" she said, waving him off.

"How did you know?" I asked. Elizabeth escorted us upstairs.

"Miguel's been hovering all afternoon. I thought you would return while he was lunching, but you're very late."

"A detour was necessary and there was no time to waste."

We took turns recanting the whole tale for Elizabeth. We told her about the various offices, the ride to Issacher's house and the near encounter with George.

"George? What is George doing in Venice?"

"We spotted him coming out of a less than respectable building in the district."

"Your George, what's he up to?" she asked.

"Sampling the services of Venice," Nicholas joked.

I did not find the jest funny. I pictured the young girl showing her wares to the gentleman and wondered if George was supporting a mistress.

"You're teasing!" Elizabeth said. She was intrigued by the scandal.

"We don't know for sure," I interrupted. "He could have other business in the area."

"Oh come now, Amara. You heard the gondolier. What else would a man of George's position be doing in a place like that?"

"Honestly, there are other possibilities."

"You dress like a man, but you do not think like a man."

"I'm flattered," I said. "But, if you recall we were doing other business."

That reminded Elizabeth. "So you found this Issacher fellow?"

I told her all about the man and what information he offered. "I'm to send a note announcing when I'd like to visit the estate."

"It really exists!" she exclaimed.

"Oh yes, and the prince secured a vault which Issacher draws from to maintain the estate and a little sum for his troubles. That reminds me, Issacher seems to be a man of honor. He hinted the sum settled years ago for his service is no longer adequate."

"Did he say how much was kept in the vault?"

"No, not exactly, but he did lead me to believe it was a significant amount." "Incredible!" she said, clapping her hands.

"When shall I go to the estate?" I asked, removing the itchy wig.

"I'd like to visit this Sunday after mass if it can be arranged."

We were all in agreement. We'd venture to Brenta on Sunday.

However, Sunday came and went. An unforeseen circumstance prevented us from carrying out our anticipated errand. The encounter was totally unexpected, as most chance encounters often are; however, this rather peculiar diversion detoured our plan and prolonged our visit to the secret estate of Vlad Tepes. It was pleasant enough, but I often think about how different our part in history would be if such a distraction never took place. I suppose it is futile to consider such things because one cannot undo what is done. It is what it is, and we all must play our role.

The Detour

Raphael Petrucci was a man of little consequence to anyone other than his employer, and perhaps his mother, if he had one. He was alone in the world except for his sole companion, his art, and if he didn't hurry he'd miss his chance. On this day and for him, time was precious. The purple hue blending across the sky was the perfect backdrop, and if he dawdled a second longer, he'd miss it. He yearned to smudge the sharp lines of San Marco, preserving them for eternity with his grease paints. It was not a commission, but a compulsion that beckoned him to do so. Today, he determined he had no patience to dance with people in the crowded lane. Instead, he darted down a narrow cobblestone alley. It was a dreary refuge where thieves hid and squatters slept. The waste of emptied piss pots collected in the corners of connecting buildings. As he hurried toward the square, he tried to avoid the rank puddles from soiling his boots while chiding himself for messing with detours and waltzing through mazes. He knew the other artists would take the favorable vantages, and he'd be out of luck.

Meanwhile, Elizabeth was nearby complaining the campo was too stuffy and urged me to avoid the clustering of busy bodies by cutting through an unfamiliar alley. In Venice everyone knows there are no short cuts. There is only another route leading you back to exactly where you were. I too knew this, but I did not wish to upset Elizabeth. So, I obliged her whim. However, this particular blunder changed our course and led us in a seemingly different direction, but had it? Was this a random meeting, or was it destiny? I thought it was a coupe that Elizabeth had decided to divert from the mainstream and wander along the cobblestone leading to the heart of Venice, but maybe it was not a whim at all, maybe this was exactly what was suppose to happen. All I know is what occurred and what came to be. What happened next was the result of her decision.

We were strolling in one direction when a man carrying an easel rushed at us from the other. Elizabeth did not see him until it was too late. They collided. The force with which they hit sent the possessions he was protecting flailing to the ground.

"No. Oh no, no, no!" Raphael cried. He dropped to his knees.

Elizabeth stumbled. She was stunned by the collision and cursed the man's ill behavior. Fortunately, I avoided the rubbish by tiptoeing over the splintered leg of the tripod. Raphael moaned as he assessed the fracture of his instrument. Beyond the roofs the sky faded from lavender to gray, and a translucent half moon was appearing overhead. The vibrant colors were abandoning the square with each moment he spent kneeling on the ground and this greatly irritated him.

"Pardon you!" Elizabeth snapped. At first, she did not offer to help him with his things.

Raphael ignored her royal decorum. He muttered a string of curses while pathetically gathering his art supplies. He was speaking Italian, or rather something resembling the language. He ranted in choppy hackneyed phrases accompanied by broad gestures and punctuated by a disparaging sigh.

Elizabeth shoved me out of her way and retrieved a bag lying on the path. One-by-one she placed curled tubes of paint and mangy brushes inside; then thrust the bag at Raphael. "There, everything

43

seems to be in its proper place." She dusted her hands. "I'm fine by the way. Thank you for asking."

"*Grazie*," Raphael said. He tucked the blank canvas beneath his arm.

"*Prego*," Elizabeth replied.

"*Va bene?*" He pointed to the part of her body that took the brunt of the impact.

"*Bene, bene*," she muttered.

"*Mi dispiace.*"

"My Italian is not very good." She figured she'd better say something before he carried on.

"Where are you going?" he asked.

"Leon Bianco."

"This is no place for you, especially with night falling." Raphael sighed dramatically as the light disappeared from the sky. He'd missed the mysterious prism, the exquisite moment when light reflected from the angles of San Marco and held it briefly before letting it go.

I felt sorry for Raphael. He wanted so badly to capture the city's essence and preserve the beauty of the place for prosperity. Like so many artists he'd keep trying, but if he continued to run late, he'd fail to capture anything but darkness. It was an innocent enough mistake, but one he couldn't afford to repeat.

Most people believed that San Marco was where the city's pulse began, but I disagreed. For me, the mystery of Venice hid in a deeper, seedier place where raw passion fed the people who claimed it as home. I thought to myself, this is what Raphael should paint. He should sketch the hanging lines of laundry and debris littering the ground. He should bring to life the cracks in the cobblestone and the apple rotting on a weathered crate. It was from this very alley that Venice breathed, and it was from here that Elizabeth's path took a fateful turn.

Mastery of Artful Play

Nicholas took the list and retrieved all the necessities Elizabeth insisted on having for the ball. The masks she commissioned hung from a knob on the bureau drawer. The black outlined eyeholes of my mask slanted at the corners and an arch cut just above my nose, perfectly following the line of my cheekbones. Brushed strokes of white, orange and gold feathered across the smooth surface layered by thin charcoal lines fanning out on both sides. It gave the impression of whiskers. Not those dirty things found on rats, but the elegant kind bowing on the cuddly faces of kittens. Elizabeth's mask was an elaborate collection of feathers and sequins made unique by the symmetry of rivaling color. Depending on the perspective, the mask was either dramatically black twinkling with silver, or a soft opulent white.

Elizabeth put on the mask. It covered her entire face except for the pair of red lips and definitely feminine chin. She faced the mirror and admired her reflection. She enjoyed looking at herself, especially when in costume. "It's precisely what I wanted. My design exhibits two opposing forces, clashing. One eye remains in the dark, while the other playfully dances in the light." She admired herself from every possible vantage. "Clever, is it not?" she asked.

I took my mask from the knob and tried it. I desired to appear as stunning in my disguise as she did in hers. My eyelashes batted against the peek holes. I adjusted the mask trying to find the most comfortable spot for it to rest on the bridge of my nose. I tipped my head down to see where I was walking, which caused the mask to slide. This masquerading was not as exciting as I imagined. It was actually quite uncomfortable and irritating, much like the horsehair wig I wore when I dressed up like a gentleman. "I look like your pet," I said, standing beside Elizabeth in front of the mirror.

Elizabeth turned so she was showing only the dark side of her mask. "Of course you don't. Don't be sour."

"Yes I do. I look like a cat." I pawed at the unruly locks of my hair.

"You're a lioness," Elizabeth corrected. "It's very exotic."

It was not as exotic as opposing forces. I fussed with my mask, so it would not pinch my nose. Her mask reminded me of something I couldn't quite place. Something I'd seen before or perhaps read about, not a living creature, but something mythical. I tried to recall where she got the idea for her design, but nothing presented.

That evening, a private water taxi took us to our destination. A light breeze from the sea caressed the canal, and I found it a welcoming change that refreshed the night air. Several boats rowed in the same direction toward the Doge's Palace, each shuttling masked couples eager to reach the party. Torches lit the entrance, and musicians noisily tuned their instruments as we arrived in the courtyard. Of course I expected the event to be impressive, grandeur. Where royalty was involved always was, but I was not prepared for the scene set before me. The glitter of sequins and feathers and flowing dresses coupled with men buried beneath ruffles and velvet was magnificent. I delighted in watching the people milling around arm-in-arm near the outlandish fountains and epicurean buffets. Their decorum was amusing and their practices less formal than I expected. I found the guests to be an odd mix of

English, Italian and what we'd become to be known, the *exotic*. The exotic was a generalization of indiscernible races lumped together for the purpose of discussion. The English were the English, the French, French and so on, and everyone else was foreign. It was our accents and color of skin that gave us away, but tonight we were all masked together and prancing about in outrageous costumes. The only difference was that some women chose to emphasize their bust lines while others modestly concealed their natural shape.

Above the chorus of conversation, Elizabeth heard the clanking of the gaming table. I swore she could sense risk, and from the moment her brocaded slippers touched the stone walk she was on her way to tempt chance. She did not bother with the customary ritual of meeting polite society by greeting the ladies in the parlor. Instead, she latched onto an aristocrat, chatting him up as she led him astray to lose his fortune. He had plenty of riches to spare, and she was ripe for the taking.

This left me on my own. My only protection being the anonymity of the cat mask that concealed my identity. I could hardly be so bold as to intrude on the ladies in the parlor without a proper introduction, so I lingered on the fringe of conversations, smiling stupidly at passersby while sipping a glass of wine. Rescue from my uncomfortable situation finally came in an invitation to dance. I realized for the first time since I'd been in Venice, I missed Draco. I didn't like being alone and even though I was surrounded by hundreds of people, I felt like an uninhabitable island.

"You must be bored because I know I am terribly bored. How many of these things can a person stand before they completely reject the invite? It is rather grim, don't you think?" A gentleman wearing a fool's mask asked.

I knew the voice, but I couldn't be sure. "George? Is that you?" I asked, reluctantly.

His lip curled in that familiar playful way it did when he thought he was being cute. "Don't you look delicious," he teased.

I detected a hint of brandy on his breath. He'd already been dipping into the spirits and was half way to drunk. "I didn't realize you were in Venice. Are you and your wife here on holiday?"

"I'm on business and she decided to tag along for the season."

"Where is she?" I asked, eyeing the crowded room. I supposed she was not too far away.

"Oh bother! Who cares where she is. I hardly doubt you are truly interested."

"George!" I exclaimed, shocked by his disregard for his wife.

"Let's take a walk, shall we? It's too loud in here and I think I need some air."

"I don't feel inclined to walk," I said.

"I'll behave," he said, sensing my uneasiness. "I promise I have no ill intent."

He offered me his arm. I adored the smooth line of his clothing, the way the lace cuff folded around his manicured hand and how the tailored coat elongated his stature. I swooned, my head suddenly becoming dizzy and my knees weak. My bold attempt at appearing strong was shot and I was wilting like a cut flower in the heat of the room. I had to get out of there before I made an ass of myself. "Very well, but don't you dare trick me. I'm in no mood to deal with your games this evening."

He agreed, and together we strolled from the ballroom to a spacious hall. I was relieved that the air flowed better in this area of the palace, and within moments I felt more like my usual self, which gave me confidence.

"Where's the countess this evening?" he asked.

"Where else, but in the gaming room."

"Spending the count's money is she?"

"Unlikely. I imagine she is spending a lord's or a prince's."

"Ah! I see. Speaking of lords, I saw a friend of yours earlier tonight."

"Did you?"

"Lord Buckley. Is he traveling with Elizabeth?"

"Lord Buckley? He's also in Venice?" I asked, surprised.

"Ah, you didn't know?"

"Lord Buckley departed from our company some time ago. I can't imagine what he's doing in Venice?"

"Courting a dowry I assume. He's keeping company with the daughter of a wealthy Italian family."

"Is that so?"

George offered a seat on a divan. He reclined beside me crossing his legs before leaning in, his lips inches from my ear. "That reminds me, I'm not in danger of being challenged to a duel am I? I'm no good with jealous husbands. They're such a bother."

I did not wish to give him the satisfaction of learning I was alone. It was better if he thought Draco was looming nearby.

"I take it that your silence means the valiant knight is not in attendance?" He fiddled with the lace on his sleeve. "I suppose it is lucky for me that he enjoys romping around the country instead of escorting his lovely wife to the Doge's ball."

I should have remembered George always knew the answer to a question before he asked it.

"Draco is patrolling…" I began, and then stopped myself. I'd fallen right into George's snare. If he didn't know the answer, I'd just told him.

"And you have no idea where, do you?" George asked, amused.

"No, not exactly, but it isn't because he doesn't wish to tell me. It's because he can't tell me. It's for his own safety and mine." I was making excuses.

"Ah yes, of course it is, I see, I see." George's fingers touched the nape of my neck.

I resisted because he was hitting a nerve. He was enjoying the notion that I was not blissfully happy in my marriage.

"How long are you in Venice?" he asked, backing away, but only a bit.

"It is not up to me."

Again, George tried to flirt with my neck.

I scooted out of his reach. Just because I was injured by my husband's absence, it did not mean I was ready to throw myself into another man's arms or allow certain liberties.

He frowned at my frigidness. Frustrated, he tapped his fingers on his knee. "There's no need to pull away like that Amara."

I gave him one of my looks, but it was lost behind my mask. Who was he to tell me what I could and should not do?"

"Just because you're married doesn't mean we can't still be, well friends," he said. "Actually, it is rather convenient that we are both attached. Oddly, it provides freedom for us to do whatever we wish."

"I'd like very much to be your friend George, but I don't think we share the same definition of the word."

George smoothed back his hair. "Amara, I'm afraid I do not wish to give you up. I think you've always known that, but I will tell you over and over if I must."

"I'm afraid you already have."

"It doesn't have to be so, does it?"

"Yes, it does. We're both married, we've taken vows."

"Vows!" George laughed. "My marriage is one of convenience. My father invested in dealings where all the parties prospered. It was merely a social arrangement."

"I suppose to you that is precisely what marriage is, but to me it is something quite different."

"Really Amara, I'm sure Elizabeth had something to gain by making the arrangement for you to marry Draco. He is Francis' chief comrade. It was an advantageous deal. Certainly you realize this to be true?"

"Is that what you think? I married Draco because of an arrangement Elizabeth and Francis made on my behalf?" I was deeply wounded. How dare he think such a thing! "I married Draco for one reason, and one reason only," I continued.

George rested his elbows on his knees. "You did, did you and what was that for?"

"For the reason everyone should marry. Because I love him, and he loves me."

He pushed the mask from his face. "You *love* him?" The concept was shocking.

I removed my mask and set it in my lap. "I do."

He played with the ribbons dangling from the side holes of his mask as we sat in silence. It was terribly awkward remaining in that space while both of us did not know what the other was thinking or what to say.

"Where does that leave me?" he finally asked.

"As my friend." I paused thinking I better clarify. "By my definition." I noticed the foyer was deserted. Everyone was in the grand hall dancing. Only George and I lagged behind, the two of us exposed, neither wearing our disguises while we talked on the divan. We were vulnerable and unguarded and at any moment a couple could stroll by and spy our intimate posturing.

"What am I suppose to do with this?" he asked, pretending his heart was in his hand. "What am I suppose to do with the feelings I have in here for you? Toss them aside? It is not that easy Amara. I can't simply forget, make it all go away as if what we shared or what I feel doesn't exist. How could you Amara, how could you go and give your love to another man when you promised it to me?"

I was shocked by his outburst and angered that he'd turned the fault on me. "It was a promise *you* broke when you married Lady Doczy!" I flung back rather cruelly.

"I did no such thing. I told you that night, the night we met in the garden that my heart would always belong to you, and it has Amara, I swear it has."

"Ha! You expect me to believe you? Not a word George, not a single letter sent to give me any hope. I waited for months to hear from you, then a year went by, and still not a single note." I hated the emotion I suddenly felt. I thought I was over him, but it was obvious I was not. My feelings were flooding back and my ability to hide them was becoming very difficult.

"I tried. I wanted to write to you every day. Please, you must believe me. Each time I planned a trip, Fruzsina became ill or made another commitment on my behalf that I could not break. I figured it was just a matter of time before things would settle down and I'd be able to take leave, but Fruzsina was much more clever than I gave her credit. She was calculating, and always one step ahead of me. When I planned a trip to Pressburg, she notified me she'd already accepted an invitation to Prague. Not only did I have to go along, but while I was there she made certain I was engaged every dreadful moment. There was no hope of slipping away, not even for a few days. She held me so very tight in her puny little clutches."

"It is for the best then since you do not have freedom." I did not care for his excuses, they meant very little to me and I found myself less forgiving than I imagined.

"No, it was a horrible mistake – an unforgivable error. I took for granted you'd wait, be patient as I worked something out and found a means to gain my freedom. I figured once an heir was born and when I was established in the trade business, I'd be allowed more liberty. I am the man, after all. I am the provider and what I say should go."

I pictured the pregnant Lady Doczy and it made me queasy. The thought of them coupling was disgusting and I didn't want to think about it a second longer. "Ah, yes, that does remind me, how is your child?"

"Oh, the little bastard is just fine. He's staying in the country with his nurse and grandparents."

There was that word again! How easily he tossed it into the conversation and about his own child, no less! "George what a horrible thing to say! How can you be so callous?"

"It would be a horrible thing to say, if the child were mine, but it's not, even though I must pretend it is. Pretend to be a loving husband, pretend to be a caring father. It's all a charade." He chuckled as if the joke was on him.

"Perhaps we should return to the ball," I suggested, slipping on my mask.

"No, please let me spend tonight with you even if it can only be as my friend. I need to be near you. I can't part from your company, not just yet. I swear I'll throw myself into the canal if you leave me alone tonight."

"Don't be so dramatic. You'll do no such thing!"

George stood and offered me his hand. I liked the warmth radiating from his palm. He held my hand tight as if he were saving me from something. I caught my breath praying he would not come any closer. His eyes meet mine from behind his mask. I waited for him to speak, but he remained silent. I wanted to know what he was thinking. I hated that I could not read his expression. He was too good at being mysterious, a practiced skill he'd mastered, and although I'd admired it in the past, I was at the present time greatly annoyed. However, it was George who looked away first. He tucked my hand around his arm and led me from the Doge's palace. I did not resist, nor did I ask where we were going.

We walked along the streets, crossing over bridges and down properly lit alleys. The people passing by did not give a second glance at our masquerading costumes. It was not extraordinary for a fool and his cat to wander the streets of Venice at night. Disguises were common enough that they did not raise alarm. If the people knew who was behind the masks, then our stroll would be a juicy scandal, but that was what was so wonderful about Venice. It was too easy to avoid detection and anonymity was a luxury that came in a plaster covered with glitter and paint. If only I could wear it wherever I went, but that was not the case – it could not be that simple.

"Do you want to know about the child?" he asked.

I tightened my grip on his arm.

"It appears Lady Doczy is a favorite of King Rudolph. They grew quite fond of each other while she was attending the Imperial Court. Well, being a maiden and under the hawk-like protection of her father, King Rudolph could do little but admire the fair Fruzsina from afar." He gazed up at the stars where they scattered across the cloudless sky. "Romantic, isn't it?"

"King Rudolph wanted Fruzsina?"

"Desperately," George answered. "But, dear Fruzsina would be ruined if given to the king before she was married. She was of some worth and could be used to further advance her family. King Rudolph understood Lord Doczy's concern for his daughter and offered a solution from which all could benefit."

"I take it this plan involved you?"

"Ah, you are an astute confidante. You see, the king suggested Fruzsina marry the son of a wealthy tradesman holding several estates and access to important routes. The alliance of our two families would create a trade empire. After we were married, we'd return to the Imperial Court. Of course, I'd have to follow for appearances sake, but the king intended to devise a way to compensate me for the absence of my wife in the evenings. Lord, I felt like such a dope! I knew everyone was gossiping behind my back while the king cuckolded my wife."

"The king arranged the marriage?" I asked, shocked.

"Like a fool I believed my bride would be waiting for me in our bedding chamber on our wedding night, but I found it empty. I was told Fruzsina drank too much wine and was feeling ill. Night after night excuses were made and I grew impatient. I was so angry that I allowed myself to be used in such a fashion that I finally decided to leave my wife and visit my mistress," he said, patting my hand. "See at that time, I still believed I had one."

"What happened?"

"I ordered my trunks packed. I tried to explain I planned a trip, but Fruzsina begged for me to postpone my journey and join her at court. My father added further pressure scolding me for even thinking of deserting my new bride. After some thought, I folded, reasoning it was best to accompany Fruzsina to Vienna for the sake of appearances and to put an end to the gossip. I suppose I cared too much about what others thought and I was determined to wait it out. Eventually, the king would grow bored of my wife and return her to my company."

"Why did you not write?"

"To say what? That I planned to visit but had changed my mind because my father and wife demanded I do as they wished? I couldn't bring myself to write such a letter so, instead I said nothing. I hoped once I was settled, I'd be able to break away for a time. During the entire journey to Vienna I was scheming up excuses. I was so torn, so conflicted in what I should do. One moment I was packing my things and the next I was chatting like some leashed monkey at a dinner party."

I felt guilty for thinking George gave not a single thought about me. I had no idea he was suffering so.

"It was all a scheme, a big sham so the king could get what he wanted. When we arrived in Vienna we did not share a bedchamber and when I questioned the arrangement, I was told the princess requested Fruzsina's company as a lady in waiting. Fruzsina apologized repeatedly swearing she knew nothing about the request, but I suspected she had a hand in it. She spoke often about missing the princess and couldn't wait to be back in her company. To soothe my suspicions, Lord Doczy made sure I was busy during the day and kept company at night. As a distraction he obliged my drinking and allowed my gallivanting around town. Of course it was not what I desired, but it had to do for the time being."

"Did he ever send a woman to your chambers?"

"It is the life of a courtier," he said. "Oh, this went on for a while. Each time I got restless and spoke of taking a trip, I was reeled back in by a hunting party or a matter concerning trading policy."

"When did you discover your wife was pregnant?"

"Well you can't keep a growing belly hidden for long."

Yes, I knew this all too well remembering the difficulty I had altering Elizabeth's gowns.

"At first I thought she was just getting fat since we hadn't consummated the marriage, but then came the announcement and flurry of congratulations. I grinned, shaking hands like a blind serf being robbed of his last coin."

"Did you confront Lord Doczy in private?"

"There was no need. Following the announcement I was taken to the king's private chambers where a deal was cut. The king confessed his love for my wife and admitted paternity of the baby she carried. He had no rightful claim to the child, even though it was his seed from which it sprung. However, he understood discretion came with a price. Lord Doczy acquired another estate and a promotion in the house of advisor's."

"Her father benefited! And you, what did you get as compensation?"

"The one thing I wanted could not be granted, a divorce. So, I asked for the next best thing. I requested the king grant me leave. I desired to be away from court. I thought about you Amara, hoping to seize something from this nightmare, make something good come out of this horrible situation. I requested a villa in Italy, a place far away from all the fighting and scheming – a private retreat where you and I could live together, not as husband and wife, but as friends." George stopped walking. "Standing in the king's chambers, humiliated in front of my father-in-law, and faced with the news the king's bastard would take my name—I thought only of you. All I wanted was to find a way to be with you. That's all I ever wanted, and in this turn of events, I was being offered just that."

I couldn't breathe. My ears were hearing what George was saying, but my mind could not make sense of it all. If only I'd known.

"The king agreed under one condition. I must stay until the child was born."

"Why did you not write?" Stupidly, it was the only question I could mutter.

"To say what Amara, that my wife was carrying the king's baby? That I'd bought my freedom to save myself from disgrace?"

"Yes, that is exactly what you should have written. I would have understood."

"I had the king's word, but did not fully trust it. I confess I did write you a letter and sealed it in an envelope. I vowed to send it the second the child took its first breath of life, and not a second before."

"I never received the letter," I said. "At the palace following the coronation when I saw you with Lady Doczy, why did you not find me, why did you not tell me then of your plan?" My voice was shaking with each word I spoke.

"I intended, I wanted too, but then Draco showed up. I searched everywhere for you, hoping to find you some place wandering alone. Then my wish came true. One afternoon I saw you from my window. You were walking across the grounds heading toward the king's new bestiary. I made up some silly excuse and hurried from my chambers. I was thrilled to finally find you, finally be able to tell you the good news—how I managed to devise a way for us to be together. I knew it wasn't ideal since it was impossible for us to marry, but it was something. I was certain you'd understand and agree it was the best we could hope for, and in my haste I forgot the letter I wrote which explained it all. I wanted to give it to you, to prove I thought it up and truly planned to carry it out. I wanted you to know that it wasn't a rouse to get you in my chambers." Even in the tensest of moments, George always found a way to relieve it with humor. A smile broke across his face as he stared down at the ground waiting for me to catch on to his last line. "Anyways," he continued, "I cut through the king's rose garden. I was sure it was a sign when the most magnificent red bud caught my eye. It was on the brink of blooming, and drops of dew still clung to the skin. It smelled so sweet; I almost hated snapping it from the bush. Holding the rose I raced toward the bestiary. I hoped to find you strolling along the grounds with the afternoon sun playing on those thick wavy locks of yours. It was a beautiful picture, perfect, as I had imagined it would be."

"But, you never came. I never saw you? What happened?" I choked. I struggled to hold back the sob that was fighting to escape from the pit of my stomach.

"As I neared I heard you laughing, and then I saw you weren't alone. Draco was there, standing beside you, your arm tucked around his. The way you looked at him…oh God, I'll never forget the sight of your smile. My heart stopped beating the second I realized it was not meant for me, but for him. I started toward you, but then stopped knowing Draco would never surrender your company without a fight. I watched the two of you walk away. Draco the valiant champion with you as his prize. I've never seen you look as beautiful as you did that day. I envied Draco, hated him in fact. I was determined to get you alone, steal you away from him the moment the opportunity presented. I returned to my chambers frustrated and angry. It was obvious Draco was courting you, but I believed there was still time. I decided I'd try to get you alone after dinner."

My thoughts raced. "But you never did. You never got me alone to tell me, did you?" I remembered the day and the night he was referring to, it was the evening of the dinner honoring the Black Quintet.

"I was an idiot to assume you were simply flirting with Draco's affections. I never dreamed you'd accept a proposal. When I heard the announcement of your engagement, I was devastated." George could not go on. He could not say another word.

"I saw you look at me. You seemed so indifferent, but then I saw you smooth your hair. You do that sometimes when you're nervous," I said, trying to lighten the mood. "I thought it was my imagination, but you were trying to get my attention, weren't you, George? I missed the sign, I let my stubbornness get in the way."

"You did see, then? I thought I imagined, I thought I hadn't done enough to get your attention."

We had wandered far from the palace and found ourselves outside the Church of Saint Maria.

"I wasn't sure, but I thought perhaps you were trying to…" I trailed off, my thoughts going back to that night and recalling the look on George's face. I thought it indifference, but now I realized it was disbelief. Again, I had misread his countenance and it cost me.

George broke down. A gush of sobs rushed from his throat. He clapped his hand over his mouth. I went to him putting my hand on his back, but he jerked his shoulder away from my touch. He sat down on the church steps. The arch of his back heaved as he sucked in air between cries. I searched the square for onlookers, but no one was in sight. I went to his side. George tore off his mask, his wet lashes blinking away the tears as he took a handkerchief from his pocket. "I won't apologize. This cry has been a long time coming."

I slid closer to him on the steps and wrapped my arm across his back. This time he allowed my comforting.

"I left the hall that night and headed back to my chambers. Lord Doczy saw me leave and followed me up the stairs. He caught me just outside the chamber door. I was furious, and in a rage beyond any I'd ever experienced. My terrible temper was getting the better of me and as you well know, I'd had too much to drink."

"What did you say?" I asked.

"Nothing. I grabbed that wretched man by the throat and pinned him against the wall. I nearly choked him to death. Probably would have if it hadn't been for that damn bishop who just happened to stumble upon the scene. All I remember is the bishop spewing something concerning the name of God and those who judge shall be judged. It wasn't my fear of God that forced me to release my hold, but exhaustion. I dropped Lord Doczy to the floor before slamming the door shut in his and the gawking bishop's face. There sitting in the vase on my table was the world's most perfect rose, just sitting there mocking me. An ordinary rose getting the best of me! I took that rose and flung open the balcony doors. I was just about to toss it over when I hesitated. Instead, I climbed on the railing, steadying myself with the rose in hand."

"You didn't," I gasped.

"Oh, I did. I was out of my mind. I couldn't stand the thought of living without you. It was selfish of me to think you'd wait forever."

"Damn you George!" I cried. "Why didn't you jump?"

"Why didn't I jump?" he asked. My question caught him by surprise.

"Obviously you didn't, you're sitting right here. Unless this entire conversation is some sort of bizarre delusion I've created. Perhaps, you're a spook or undead. Are you undead George?" Nothing I said was making any sense. I was angry and confused and I was rattling off at the mouth. I wanted to hear why he hadn't killed himself? What made him stop? Wasn't I worth the sacrifice? It would have been a tragedy, but it was the proper ending. Instead, here we sat, two hollow souls lumbering through the mid-night mist confessing our deepest regrets. It was pathetic and lame and not at all romantic. There was to be no wedding or a death. This was it—this was our story.

"I'm not a ghost, but I might as well be."

"Tell me George, please tell me what made you get down from the railing?"

"I should have jumped," he said. "But, if you must hear me say it, it is because I am a coward. It was fear that prevented me from taking the dive. I was just about to leap to my death when my own conscience stopped me. As I stood teetering on the railing, I thought about my family and the embarrassment they'd suffer. Suicide, what a scandal! Can you believe I was still worrying about my reputation?" He laughed in disbelief.

"Scandal?" I could not believe what I was hearing. My hero was a coward, but I think I'd always known this to be true. He was just a man made of flesh and blood. What else did I expect? This was my problem. I always expected too much from people and was disappointed over and over again.

"Pathetic isn't it. Even in my darkest hour I concerned myself with what others might think."

The bells of Saint Maria chimed half past twelve. I listened until the last echo of the bells dissipated.

"We've passed from one day into the next," George said, wiping his nose.

I wasn't finished. I had more questions, and George owed me an answer. "The child, you stayed until it was born?"

George stood up brushing the dirt from the backside of his coat. "What else could I do? I'd lost you, and I hadn't the nerve to do myself in."

"What's his name?"

"We named him George. Can you imagine?"

"Even though he isn't yours?" I asked, surprised.

"I'll never have a son of my own. I figure the curse of my name is punishment enough. What about you? Do you have a child?" He blew his nose in the handkerchief and wadded it up, stuffing it into his pocket.

The question caught me off guard. I'd been married for sometime, it was reasonable to assume I'd started a family. "No," I answered.

George could see I had more to say so he waited while I arranged the words in my head.

"I don't believe I can," I said. It was the first time I'd given serious thought to not conceiving a child of my own. I wondered if Draco had already come to the same conclusion, that I must be barren.

George weaved his fingers with mine. It was disheartening how well we fit together. We left Saint Maria and walked in the direction of the Doge's Palace. It took all my will not to give in to the yearning in my heart. It was George, *my* George, finally beside me, holding my hand as we moved through the streets of Venice. He loved me. He'd confessed he always had and I believed him. All this time I'd thought George had broken his promise and given little care to the heart he'd abandoned. Although it had mended over time, my heart would never be the same. Now, it was distrusting, even cynical at times. There was a pain, a gripping twist in my chest as if the blood was pushing in with no way out. Oh God, what was happening? I squeezed George's hand. He slowed his pace as we turned a corner.

"George please stop," I said, breathing heavy as sweat beaded on my forehead. I removed the mask from my face. Everything he said was beginning to sink in and I wished we could go back, but we couldn't – things could not be different and it made me panic.

"Amara, are you all right?" he asked discarding his own mask.

"I'm dizzy," I said. My eyes pleaded for something to focus on. Everything he said I had waited so long to hear, but it came too late. Suddenly, I realized I was the one balancing on the edge of an invisible railing trying to find the nerve to jump, but I could not do it. I was a coward. I threw my arms around George's neck. My tears stained his jacket. He held me tight, the two of us huddled in the shadows just beyond the Doge's Palace. While we embraced, the party continued. It went on as if nothing happened. "Damn you George, why didn't you jump," I cried.

I didn't need to explain my outburst. George understood I did not wish him dead, only that it would have been easier for both of us if he were gone. In truth, until tonight George was numbing my heart. I had managed to cage the part that loved him, leaving the rest to beat only for Draco. But George's confession undid all that, his words the key to unlocking everything I sealed away. Just as I was about to give in to overwhelming emotion, I remembered Draco and the words he spoke on our wedding night. He swore to honor me like no other man ever had. I took a step back from George leaving his lips longing for me.

"I can't," I sobbed. "I can't make the leap."

George tried to protest. He wanted to come up with a clever line to persuade me, but he knew the moment of opportunity had passed. "We've had ourselves a good cry, haven't we? I suppose it is time we return to society," he said.

Together, we walked at an agonizingly slow pace to the Doge's Palace, neither of us eager to visit the world where duty bound and obligation suffocated. It was daunting and heavy, and as long as we remained on the boardwalk masked in our costumes we were free.

"Can you ever forgive me?" George asked when we were outside the palace garden.

"For not writing?"

He waited for a crowd to pass before answering. "For all the wrongs I failed to right."

I wanted to say yes, but I couldn't. It would have been a lie. I was angry with George; disappointed by his shortcomings. I plucked a red rose from a climbing vine and poked it through an eyelet in his jacket.

"Common variety," he joked. He thumbed the drooping head of the flower.

"It is what it is. It is not in its nature to be something else."

He straightened his posture and I tucked a stray piece of hair behind my ear before we enter the grand ballroom, my hand gently tucked in the crook of his arm and our masks secured over our faces.

"Where to Lady Lorant?" he asked.

"I do believe I wish to go to the gaming room. I'm certain the countess will love to see you. Shall we, Count Drugeth?"

"Of course Lady Lorant, as you wish."

The gaming hall was packed with ruffles and velvet pressed together around green felt tables. The changing volume rose and fell on waves of cheers and ahs. The winnings and losses were scratched on slips of credit, for the dealings of gentlemen never involved the exchange of actual money. Gold pieces rarely swapped hands, it was too cumbersome. Rather, fortune was recorded in books backed by collateral held in property and extraneous indulgences such as paintings or sculptures. A true gentlemen refined the talent of gambling, knowing how much to risk and when to withdrawal. Ruin of fortune came primarily by that of a lady whose addiction surpassed her husband's means. When apprised of a wife's extravagance, a gentleman was often inclined to freeze credit lines. George informed me this was fast becoming commonplace now that more ladies participated in gaming rooms. Credible establishments obeyed a husband's wish even though it meant decreasing the house's earnings. After all, reputation was everything. However, such standards forced high-class ladies to take their business to lower class gaming establishments. Such desperate decline was creating quite the uproar.

Gentlemen vehemently protested to the Venetian council stating authorization was never given to the lowly establishment; therefore, any debt incurred while at their house was void. Unfortunately for the upper crust, the Venetian magistrate did not agree. It was a husband's responsibility to oversee his wife; his inability to manage domestic affairs was no concern of the court, or the house owner. George said even a lady with the sternest husband would find ways around frozen assets. Gaming rooms were overflowing with gentlemen of loose morals and it was impossible to resist an opportunity to exploit certain favors from a married lady of nobility. There was something absolutely irresistible about a forbidden woman of wealth offering anything in return for a go at the tables. To ensnare such a lady, to get her indebted, was too tantalizing, and too sinful of a scandal to refuse. These were not courtesans playing a part, but actual women lowering themselves to feed a habit. It was mouth-wateringly delicious.

Across the way I spotted Elizabeth accompanied by a gentleman. He was a fine young specimen barely old enough to pass for a man. Upon seeing us, she insisted we join the couple at the table. The dealer asked George if he wanted to place a bet, but George declined. He raised a glass of brandy and stated one addiction was plenty. He didn't need to complicate his situation with further indulgences. We all laughed understanding George's passion for gold came in the form of liquid, not solid.

Elizabeth was flaming with enthusiasm at the young gentleman's winning streak. She waved at a tab holder authorizing another draw from her account. She nodded to the dealer to place the gentleman's bet explaining if he lost the hand, she'd cover the debt. Three gentlemen dropped out leaving Elizabeth's beau and an Englishman to battle for the pot. She was on edge and could taste the winnings. They were so close to taking it all! She playfully winked at the Englishman who was twiddling with the ratty fray of his mustache. Distractingly, she touched her gloved finger to her bare chest. The Englishman tried to ignore the flirtation but the mannerism was obviously breaking his concentration. She wet her lips as she slowly moved her finger in tiny circles over her skin just above the neckline of her bodice.

"Sir, do you want to raise?" the dealer asked.

"Umm, what? Just a moment," the Englishman muttered. He dabbed his forehead before glancing back at Elizabeth who was innocently blushing as if she was completely unaware of her sexuality.

"Sir, your answer please?"

"No, I'll hold."

The Englishman showed his cards. The group gathered around the table gasped at his hand. It was very good.

"Does he win?" I asked George.

"Well it all depends on what the other man is holding, but it is a difficult hand to beat."

Elizabeth's gentleman showed his hand. The crowd roared, and Elizabeth cheered, congratulating her charge. The tab keeper rushed to his side to tally up the winnings. He licked the tip of the quill before adding the sum to the total.

"We've made a killing tonight," Elizabeth squealed.

"You've made a killing," the young gentleman corrected.

"It's only fair you get a percentage. You did play the cards."

Elizabeth made sure the tab keeper worked out a fair percentage to be paid to the young gentleman; a player's fee, I believe she called it.

"What if he lost?" I asked George.

"Well it seems the indenture of favors goes both ways. I presume the gentleman is one of title and not wealth. Therefore, he can't readily afford such pleasures as gambling away the family fortune where a fortune does not exist. It appears the countess was backing his game."

"Elizabeth could have any man in this room if she so wished," I said.

"Undoubtedly, but as I mentioned the thrill is in the debt. If this gentleman had lost, he would owe Elizabeth. She knew full well he couldn't pay by traditional means, so some other compromise would need to be worked out. He was at her mercy."

"What a terrible imposition," I said.

"Oh, I hardly doubt it is too awful of a fix." He smirked at my blushing cheeks.

If George only knew what Elizabeth was capable of perhaps he wouldn't find the game altogether amusing.

"Shall we find a cozy spot to celebrate?" Elizabeth asked.

She led us to a corner sofa. "May I introduce Lord Dorsey. Lord Dorsey, these are my dear friends Lady Lorant and Count Drugeth."

We exchanged pleasantries and small talk before settling on a conversation. Elizabeth explained the strategy they used which led to the big win. It was exhilarating to hear how the pair played not only the dealer, but also the guests. Elizabeth admitted the Englishman made it almost too easy to win. As we were sharing a good laugh at the Englishman's expense, a note was delivered to Elizabeth.

"What does it say?" I asked, worried it was bad news.

Elizabeth squeezed Lord Dorsey's knee, her hand moving up his thigh before returning to her own lap.

"The Englishman wants to know if I'd be so kind as to meet with him in private. Apparently, he hopes that an arrangement might be worked out in which he can recover some of his loss. It seems he's overextended himself this evening."

"Well isn't that unfortunate." George cupped his brandy and swirled it in small circles.

"Lord Dorsey, what do you think I should do?" Elizabeth asked.

"Take advantage of his dire straits."

"Perhaps I should find out just how desperate our Englishman is," she said.

"What do you intend to ask for in return?" I asked. The Englishman was a beefy fellow with receding hair. I knew she'd prefer a tryst with Lord Dorsey, rather than the Englishman.

"Lord Dorsey, is there something you would like?"

"His timepiece is stunning. I've been admiring it all evening."

Elizabeth excused herself from our party. She whispered something to a servant before disappearing through the doorway.

I thought Lord Dorsey was an interesting fellow. Just as George deduced, he was noble in title, but poor in tangible assets. He'd come to Venice to make a proper match. The details were being worked out and he figured he'd be married before Christmas if everything went according to plan. He told us his future bride was lacking in beauty but had an adequate dowry, which blurred any clarity to her flawed appearance. Thankfully, she'd become instantly smitten with Lord Dorsey and begged for the wedding to take place as soon as possible. He had no doubts the match was made. Her father had kindly provided an advance, which Lord Dorsey used to pay off a large portion of a hefty debt. He'd have to curb his spending until after the wedding; a restraint most cutting and inconvenient. He admitted he'd been close to calling the whole marriage off, but attending the Doge's party sobered his romantic ideals. He'd grown keen to a lifestyle beyond any means assessable to him. A title was worthless nowadays, but it did afford admittance to good society. However, it no longer was very useful in acquiring luxuries necessary to keep up appearances. George sympathized with Lord Dorsey's contemplations, stating how a good fortune could buy a title. The age when title and fortune were synonymous was regrettably long past. As long as you had one, you could have the other.

Elizabeth visited briefly with a tab keeper before returning to our quaint party. She squeezed between Lord Dorsey and me, her hip pressing snuggly against mine. "Lord Dorsey, I've a present for you."

"You do, do you?"

"Now close your eyes and hold out your hand." A gold chain dripped between her fingers, an antique timepiece dangled from the end. "Open your eyes."

Lord Dorsey grinned as he shined the precious metal. Marvelous timepiece isn't it?"

"Oh the best is yet to come. Open it, it has an inscription," Elizabeth pointed out.

He lifted the cover revealing the face.

"Go on, read it aloud," she urged.

"Time is a priceless gift."

Elizabeth roared. "Apparently not!"

Lord Dorsey burst out laughing. "Ironic!"

"Isn't that tart," Elizabeth howled. "I couldn't have written a better ending to the evening if I'd tried."

"Irony is a bastard," George chuckled. He beckoned to a servant to refresh his drink. Just as George made the remark, Lord Buckley entered the gaming room escorting a petite Italian girl.

I had to agree, timing was everything. "George, look who just waltzed in," I said, lowing my voice. "This mig ht dampen her spirits."

"And I thought this party was going to be dull, but it seems like things are about to get interesting. Perhaps, I'll stick it out a bit longer."

Elizabeth and Lord Dorsey were still whooping over the prize piece now fastened to his jacket when I announced I saw Lord Buckley. I asked if they recognized the pretty, young girl on his arm.

"You can't be serious," Elizabeth said, her voice immediately flattening in tone.

"There's no denying it. I'd recognize that ridiculous hat anywhere," George added.

"In fact, didn't you say earlier, George, that you bumped into Lord Buckley?"

"Let me think. Yes, I do believe I did mention that."

"Lord Buckley? Who in blazes is Lord Buckley?" Lord Dorsey asked trying to follow Elizabeth's eyes.

"Over there. The gentleman with the rather passé feather bobbing about his hat."

"Oh him. I met him earlier as well. Didn't check his name, but I do recall he was boasting about you, Elizabeth," Lord Dorsey said. "He mentioned he was an acquaintance of yours. I thought it rude that he should boast about how close the two of you got last season. He said something about escorting you to the coronation? It quite impressed the party he was with."

"That charlatan! How dare he use my name to advance his status."

"I take it he's exaggerated your friendship?"

George and I waited for Elizabeth's answer. How was she going to write herself out of this one?

"What's he doing in Venice?" Elizabeth asked.

George ran his hand over his face feeling the shadow of stubble already forming. He glanced at me before answering. I encouraged him to tell Elizabeth the rumor.

"Fishing," he said bluntly before taking another swig of brandy.

"Fishing? Lord Buckley fishing? Good Lord what for?" she asked.

"A virgin bride with a fat dowry."

"Appears he's hooked one," Lord Dorsey announced. "The girl he is with, and I do mean girl because she's barely fourteen, is the sole daughter of an absurdly wealthy Italian physician who dabbles in the art market for kicks. I hear the man's name gets tossed into the lion's mouth more than any other, but there is never any substantial evidence for which he can be convicted of a crime. The magistrate chalks it up to envy, but I believe there is some truth to the accusations raised against him."

"What is the lion's mouth?" I asked.

Lord Dorsey explained the lion's mouth was a sculpture in the center of Venice. It was the Venetian's way of dealing with increasing corruption. Any person may accuse another of a crime by writing an anonymous note and depositing it in the lion's mouth. Once submitted, the accusation cannot be retracted. An investigation commences. If the court finds adequate evidence to support the charges, the accused is arrested and detained until trial.

"What if the accusation is false, or made out of jealousy by someone seeking revenge?" I asked.

"That's why evidence must be found to support the accusation. Rumors are just rumors based on nothing but hot air, which doesn't float in a Venetian court."

"This girl's father is often harassed?"

"Oh my, yes! The lion's mouth is a nuisance as far as he's concerned. He heads a group of physicians who are making astonishing discoveries in medicine. However, many fear his methods. You know; those who are less forward thinking, namely members of the church. It's a shame, but his practice tends to draw suspicion."

"Is her father in attendance this evening?"

68

Lord Dorsey remembered seeing him before we arrived. Elizabeth suggested we all get some exercise and see if we could find this fine gentleman Dorsey talked about. We'd been idle long enough. It was time we took a turn around the room.

"There's going to be a change of scenery," George said, half unaware of what we were doing. He was rather drunk and his attention was unfocused.

"The gaming room concludes Act I. It appears we're about to be cast in Act II," I whispered to him.

"What role do we play?" he asked, sobering up by the news.

"Extras," I said. "We do not have a major part."

George chuckled. "Well then, I think we are perfectly cast. I say, it should take very little stretch of the imagination to bring the house down."

I had to agree. The company we were in was readily amused. Together, we weaved our way through the crowd taking care to follow closely behind the skirt of Elizabeth flanked by Lord Dorsey. I wondered if Fruzsina concerned herself with the whereabouts of her husband, or was she happy to be rid of him for a few hours.

"She's on the prowl," I snickered, referring to Elizabeth.

"Just look at the way she surveys the room," George noted.

"She's just whispered something in Lord Dorsey's ear. I bet she's asking about the Italian doctor."

"Shall we wager?" he asked.

"On what?"

"Whether she confronts Lord Buckley," he said.

"What's the stake?" I asked.

"If I win, you must spend the night with me. Of course the actual night will be of my choosing."

"You're not serious!"

"I wager she confronts Lord Buckley in a most humiliating manner."

"What if I win?" I asked.

"Name your prize."

I considered for a moment. "I've got it. If I win, you have to strip down to your trunks and jump into the canal."

"You *can't* be serious?"

"Most serious. I wager Elizabeth won't confront Lord Buckley. She's too sneaky—a direct confrontation will never amuse her. No, I believe she will devise another method of sabotage. Something much more wicked."

"More wicked than public humiliation? Is there such a thing?"

"Is it a bet?" I asked.

"You're on!" George said, confident he'd win.

The errand was boring Dorsey. He toyed with his new timepiece as he gazed around the room. Then something captured his attention and he tugged on Elizabeth while delicately gesturing to a small gathering of people on the other side of the room.

"The hunter has spotted the prey," George jested.

"Wouldn't you agree this entire night seems too strange to be real? I suppose I've surrendered to the absurdity of it all. You must admit when you dressed for the ball you had no idea this is how it would turn out."

"Or that I'd get so drunk," he said.

"You're not fooling me. You knew that was bound to happen," I teased.

I saw Fruzsina dancing with a gentleman who had an odd, protruding feature, an oblong knot lodged in his throat. He looked like a gull that had swallowed too large a fish. I asked George if he knew the gentleman, but he did not seem to care. His mind was set on winning our little wager and he was eager to accompany Dorsey to Elizabeth's formal introduction to the doctor, Signor Nadossi.

"It is a pleasure to meet you Countess. I've heard wonderful things," Signor Nadossi said.

I doubted his sincerity, but it was customary to flatter titled society. Elizabeth asked to whom she owed the compliment, and on cue Signor Nadossi mentioned Lord Buckley. The conversation was rather dull and I wondered if Elizabeth was ever going to get to the point of this meeting, but then again I really should not have minded since her bland behavior meant I was winning the bet so far.

"How did you become acquainted with Lord Buckley?" she asked Signor Nadossi.

"Vienna. We were picnicking in the garden. That's where Lord Buckley first spotted my Azalea. It took some doing on his part, but he found a way to arrange to be at the same dinner party as us. I must say, Lord Buckley is a cunning fellow. My daughter is very taken with him. Azalea insisted I give him permission to escort her this evening."

"You say you met in Vienna? Well, that is a coincidence. Vienna is where *I* also met Lord Buckley."

Signor Nadossi leaned in as if he had a secret to tell. "At first, I had reservations as you can imagine. My Azalea is a blossoming young girl. Many suitors are knocking on our door. I am very protective and, often called by my daughter, an old-fashion father. I'm particular about whom I let near my precious flower. When I heard Lord Buckley spent a great deal of time in your company, well, I knew he had to be a fine fellow indeed."

Thankfully, Elizabeth's mask concealed her expression. I imagined what she must be thinking, but nothing gave away her displeasure; unless, I considered the clenching of her jaw.

"If I had my way Azalea would stay locked up for several more years, but as I said, she is smitten with Lord Buckley. Why, just last night Buckley asked for a private audience, which of course I granted. I could tell by the way he beat around the bush trying to discover my plans for Azalea and marriage, well, that he was searching for any hint of a betrothal."

"And is the lovely Azalea betrothed?" Elizabeth asked.

"There've been offers, but none I've taken seriously until now."

"You're considering Lord Buckley?"

George jabbed me in the side. He sensed his luck was changing. "Told you he's gone fishing!"

I ignored his wise crack.

"My daughter is determined to make me consider, but as I said, I am a stubborn man."

George was standing so close to the conversation that his head was practically poking through the invisible circle surrounding the couple. I gently guided him back before he embarrassed us.

"You better hope the water is warm this evening because I think you're going for a swim," I 'teased.

George finished his brandy in a single swig and set the empty glass on a nearby ledge. The glassware teetered, but did not slip and smash to the floor. He looked around for another servant carrying a tray of refreshments.

"You've had enough," I scolded.

Lord Dorsey raised a brow while clearing his throat; a discreet gesture reminding us of our place in this conversation. Obviously, we were being too loud and were drawing unwanted attention.

"Signor Nadossi, I know we've just only met, but I feel it is my duty to warn you about matching your precious daughter with Lord Buckley."

"Warn me? Please Countess, if there is something I should know, you must tell me."

Elizabeth glanced over her shoulder before moving intimately closer to Signor Nadossi. "It's true Lord Buckley spent a great deal of time in my company. As you know my husband is the Chief Commander. Certainly he is not the kind of man who'd approve of his wife keeping company with a bachelor."

"But, you just admitted Lord Buckley spent time."

"Shhh, yes, yes… but as a companion who posed little threat," Elizabeth said in a lowered voice.

"What are you getting at Countess? I'm afraid I am missing the meaning of this conversation." The doctor was growing impatient.

"Well if I must be so forward. Lord Buckley is a sodomite, Signor Nadossi. He prefers his own sex. I hope you can forgive my bluntness, but there simply is no other way of putting it. I can only speculate his financial situation has become so dire that he's looking to marry as a last desperate measure to avoid going to the Black Tower in debtor's chains. You see, if your daughter marries Buckley, not only will she be very lonely, but also childless. Imagine the scandal and humiliation she'll face when the rumors get out, when suspicion spreads about his sexual preference. After all, I'm not the only person who knows."

Signor Nadossi's face whitened. All the blood drained instantly from his fleshy cheeks. "Are you absolutely certain?" he asked.

Elizabeth appealed to the doctor's vanity. "An intelligent man such as yourself must see the signs. Lord Buckley's manners, the fashion in which he dresses, it is a dead give away."

"I contributed the oddities to his culture. He is English. I hear they are rather airy."

"Signor, my husband would never allow a man to be in my constant company unless he was sure the man inspired little concern," Elizabeth assured.

"This is troublesome. My Azalea is smitten. This news will break her heart. Nevertheless, there are laws against such practices, this I cannot ignore. My daughter will not marry a known sodomite. It is unnatural and punishable in my country."

Elizabeth hesitated. The pause was calculated; it was done for dramatic effect. She wanted to give the impression of serious thought to Signor's predicament. "I think it is unwise to draw alarm. It will bring unwanted attention to you and your family. Everyone in society has seen Azalea on Lord Buckley's arm. I'm afraid Azalea is unknowingly entwined in a tangled web. May I ask, because it is a matter of concern, but isn't the church already a nuisance to you and your family? Imagine what they might do with such a scandal? I just don't see how any good can come of the association. You must part company immediately."

Signor Nadossi's face reddened. He rubbed his hands together. "I beg you Countess, tell me what must be done? How do I make this go away, quietly? I do not want anymore trouble for me or my precious family."

"I suggest appealing to Lord Buckley's dwindling pocketbook. I hear you're a collector of art. Perhaps a good cover would be to commission Lord Buckley to go aboard to inquire after some pieces for your collection. Maybe to the Orient to purchase silk? Soon everyone will have forgotten and you needn't bother yourself with his return. I'm certain the Orient will provide many distractions for a man of Lord Buckley's nature."

"What do I tell Azalea when he does not return?"

"Well, I'll leave that up to you, Signor. I'm sure you'll think of something. Fathers always do."

Signor Nadossi excused himself from our company. I suspected he would immediately retrieve his daughter from Lord Buckley and execute a swift plan.

"The noose is tied. He'll hang himself," Elizabeth declared.

I agreed. Nothing more would happen tonight. Elizabeth suggested our small party go to Leon Bianco for a nightcap. Arm-in-arm we followed Elizabeth and Lord Dorsey down the palace steps and through the courtyard.

"It's a shame we don't know how the tragedy ends," George said. He was not sure what to make of the scene.

"Don't be silly George. It ends like all tragedies."

"No one died. It was all rather dull if you ask me."

"Perhaps not literally, but Lord Buckley is as good as dead."

"I have to give it to you—I didn't see the twist coming. Brilliant move. I was certain Elizabeth would confront Lord Buckley before we left the party. I suppose you know her better than I do."

"That reminds me," I said, stopping along the canal. I called out to Elizabeth and Lord Dorsey who had wandered ahead. Except for us, the path was virtually deserted in the late hours before dawn.

"You can't be serious? You intend to call in the bet?"

"A bet is a bet. Time to pay up."

He waited for me to say I was joking, but I stood with my arms crossed. George reluctantly stripped off his coat, and then unbuttoned his shirt and trousers. He swayed, tipsy from drink. He was wearing only a mask and his trunks as he inched toward the water. "It's freezing! I'll catch my death."

"You better get it over with my man. I'm still embarrassed you lost to a woman. You do realize you are a disgrace to the entire privileged sex?" Dorsey chided.

"This is exactly why you should never gamble," I reminded George.

"I'm practically naked. Isn't that good enough? You've won, I admit it, you've won," George begged as he shivered on the dock.

"Would you have let me weasel out of my debt if the outcome had been in your favor?" I asked.

George chose not to answer. He knew he'd never let me off the hook. He edged closer. "I want you to know, I'm leaving on the mask." He bowed to Elizabeth before facing the black waters of the Grand Canal. "I'm going to freeze to death. You do realize it's going to be shear agony?"

"A warm hearth awaits," I joked.

"I'd rather it be a warm bed."

Lord Dorsey chuckled. "Get on with it old man before we all catch cold."

George swung his arms and bent his knees. He sucked in a deep breath and without delay launched himself into the water. A splash sprayed the dock getting us all a bit damp. George's head popped up. He flung his wet hair from his face and cursed something awful as he spit dirty water from his mouth. His mask bobbed a few feet from where he plunged. Being a gentleman, Dorsey offered George a hand up. He flopped onto the dock, his trunks sucking to his body as he rolled over onto his back. His naked chest heaved as he coughed out a lung full of water.

"Dear God did you drink the canal too?" Lord Dorsey asked.

George's mask drifted close enough for Dorsey to grab.

"Went up my nose," George said, blowing water out. "Is my lady satisfied?"

I laughed. I admitted I was satisfied to see George reduced to such a sorry state.

He put on his boots and gathered his clothes. He walked the entire way to Leon Bianco in only his mask, boots and trunks. Thankfully, the lobby was vacant and we passed the stairs without creating a scandal. Luckily, the chambermaid kept the hearth burning and the small fire wads warming the antechamber of the apartment where the four of us collapsed in laughter. Dorsey held up a blanket in front of the hearth to shield George as he stripped his trunks before sliding on his trousers and shirt.

"How am I to explain this?" he asked, holding up his soggy breeches.

I burst out laughing. I tried to refrain, but each time I looked at George I began to giggle again, so much so, that tears leaked from my eyes. I doubled over from pains in my sides. It was pleasurable and cleansing, like the smell of wet grass after a violent storm.

Our folly awoke Nicholas. He entered the room rubbing his eyes as he tried to adjust to the lantern light. He focused on the four us lounging on the sofa and divan. Our masks tossed carelessly on the rug, slippers flung on the floor and a coat tossed over a chair. Elizabeth snorted at Nicholas's expression, the corner of his mouth turned up as his hand scratched his backside.

"Good morning, Nicholas! Sorry to wake you," she said.

"It's morning all ready?"

"Damn near," George answered.

The first hint of the sun was breaking over the horizon. Nicholas stared out the window debating whether to stay up or go back to bed. A bird chirped from its nest perched in a tree in the atrium. "I thought the four of you were the only ones still awake at this hour, but it appears I'm wrong. There're five crazy people in Venice," Nicholas announced. He yawned, smacking his lips together as he tasted the dryness of his mouth.

"Who else is awake?" Elizabeth asked.

"There's a man in the courtyard," Nicholas said, pointing.

"Perhaps we should order some breakfast. My stomach is sour," George complained. He expelled a rude burp.

"Well you drank a lot of brandy."

"And half the Grand Canal," Lord Dorsey added.

"He's setting something up. I think it's a canvas. He's pulled up a chair and is balancing against it. Now, he's opening a bag I think. Yes, it's a bag," Nicholas reported.

"It's just an artist trying to capture the sunrise. Dawn and dusk are full of those people," Dorsey informed.

Elizabeth joined Nicholas by the window. "It's Raphael. The artist I ran into in the alley."

"Who ran into you?" Nicholas asked.

"Well there's only one way to find out," Lord Dorsey said. He opened the balcony door, and yelled Raphael's name.

Raphael looked up to see four faces staring down at him.

Lord Dorsey closed the door. "There you go. It appears he is indeed Raphael." He snatched a chunk of bread and buttered it while warming in front of the fire.

Nicholas yawned again. He scratched his neck taking another look around the room before announcing he was going back to bed. He decided it was too ungodly of an hour and no person right in the head should be up.

"We should all get a few winks," Elizabeth agreed.

George was already snoring by the time I turned the covers in my bedchamber. As I lay beside Elizabeth I thought about the conversation George and I had outside Saint Maria. So much had happened over the course of a single night that George's confession seemed like a lifetime ago. Our tears wiped clean by laughter, comic relief coming spontaneously, but somehow finding the most appropriate moment to interject. Without it, life and all its turbulence would be unbearable. All George and I could do was laugh, not only at another's misfortune, but also at our own. I loved George; there was no denying it. I shut my eyes. The scenes written that night flipped through my mind. Our story was not finished, and as each image burned permanently into my consciousness, I drifted to sleep.

Fruit From the Tree

Dorsey was gone. Left behind was a note pinned to the mantle. It said he woke after noon with a gnawing pain in his stomach and a desperate need to change his attire. George was still asleep and snoring. His arm was draped over his face shielding it from the bright day's sun. I sat on the balcony sipping black tea while warming my tired bones. The night had passed, and all that remained was my fond memories. Not much later, I heard Elizabeth stirring in the bedchamber. The floorboards creaked as she moved from one side of the room to the other. I imagined she felt like I did; a heavy burden to carry. Soon she'd join me on the balcony, teacup in hand, and her hair hanging loose. We'd occupy the same space while remaining silent. We were taking it all in, and it seemed both of us were trying to make sense of what the day might bring. It was always what was to come that concerned us, and I knew she hated the mystery as much as I did.

"A quake wouldn't rouse him," Elizabeth said, referring to George.

"He sleeps soundly, but I find his snoring strangely comforting." Hearing another person breathing meant I was not alone.

She peeked over the railing to see if Raphael was painting below, but he was also gone. I could tell she was disappointed. To break the silence, she asked about George. She wanted a story, but I did not have the energy to entertain. It was a long, bizarre night and I was still sorting out the scene myself. I didn't know what to make of it no matter how many times I rolled it around in my head. It was just a night and in the light of day, I'd see all too soon that nothing had changed. This was life, not some childish fairy tale.

I cleared my throat. "He is in Venice on business. Something to do with trade I presume," I finally explained.

"You're tired?" she asked.

"Exhausted."

She seemed to understand I was talking about the emotional toll love had on the mind and body.

George snorted as he flipped on his side curling his knees toward his chest.

"I see the way he looks at you. He still loves you," Elizabeth said, glancing at George.

I knew this too, but it didn't matter. I drank my tea. As time passed, the afternoon sun moved overhead and while he snored, the day faded. I thought about sending a note to Fruzsina to let her know George was fine and that nothing terrible had happened, but I'd have to explain his whereabouts, an awkward chore I was not prepared to undertake. George would just have to do his own explaining. It was his responsibility to deal with the repercussions. Only he could calm a hostile wife racked with worry.

There was a knock at the door. Elizabeth glanced over her shoulder as the chambermaid received the visitor. Lord Dorsey had returned. He was well fed and dressed impeccably.

When he joined us on the balcony, he nodded toward George, "I see he is still sleeping it off?"

"Like a babe."

He ripped into a sack of fresh pastries he'd purchased from a bakery down the street. "You must try these. They're delicious."

Elizabeth and I sampled the Venetian delights.

"It's too late for anyone, even the fashionable to still be asleep," Dorsey complained. He went to the sofa and gave George a hearty shake.

George rubbed his eyes. He blinked repeatedly as he scouted the room. He was trying to recognize whether the interior was familiar or not.

"You're at Elizabeth's apartment," Dorsey informed. He shoved a pastry under George's nose. "Eat this old man. It will cure your sour stomach."

George took the pastry and asked for a cup of tea. He stretched his back before standing up. He walked toward the open doors. "It's a beautiful day, isn't it?" As he emerged into the sun, he squinted. The direct sunlight was overwhelming and he needed a moment to adjust. Without considering, he rested his hand on my shoulder. I got goose bumps and a warm sensation instantly flooded my belly. I did not move for fear he'd remove his touch. At that moment, I secretly wanted everything to remain just as it was; all of us together in Venice. It was not a villa, but we were in Italy. It was what we had dreamt about and, selfishly I did not wish for it to end. Truly, I was not yet prepared for it to end again.

"Well my darlings, I must be off," George said, his words shattering my perfect picture. The spell was broken.

Elizabeth eyed me with weary maternal concern.

"You're leaving?" I asked. The question sounded desperate and girlish.

"I've got a few things to take care of, not to mention a need for fresh clothes. Ones that don't smell of fish and salty water." He looked rough, his hair messy and stubble peppering his chin and cheeks.

"More like the staunch of brandy," Dorsey added, wrinkling his nose.

Even though it was rank, I rather liked the smell of stale brandy on George. It reminded me of better times.

George kissed my cheek. It was a type of kiss a dear friend gives to another-passionless. It was tender, but cool in touch, stiff with tension and deliberately placed to not offend. I resented the kiss, wishing he hadn't bothered in the first place. "I'll call later," he said, squeezing my hand.

As his hand slipped from mine, I took hold at the last second drawing him back to me. I placed a kiss delicately on his cheek just missing the corner of his mouth. His breath was on my face. He whispered my name unlike any way I'd ever heard him say it before. He sounded far away, as if lost and calling out for me to rescue him. I touched the side of his face with my fingertips. It was abrasive.

"George, I am right here," I assured him.

He nodded, and then excused himself from our company. As difficult as it was, I let him go. I had no other choice than to return my attention to the couple conversing on the balcony. I had to turn my back to the corridor and on George.

It wasn't until later that I noticed in his rush to leave, George forgot his discarded trunks that were hanging on the back of a chair by the hearth. The stiff dried fibers loosening as I hide them in my bureau drawer.

Strangely, I'd forget about them for years. They'd remain stuffed away buried beneath other keepsakes and mementos. But, if experience had taught me anything, it was that nothing stayed hidden forever, and the day would come when I'd rediscover my little treasure. When it did, I'd remember that peculiar night we spent together in Venice. Ah Venice, where alleys were confessionals haunted by declarations of love and the watery canals echoed with laughter. It was where the tide carried out all the pain and despair that colored the scenery of the wondrous city. My very own emotions had been collected and mingled among the lapping waves that were drawn to the Adriatic Sea.

***

Dorsey received word he was officially betrothed. We celebrated the good news by spending an evening in the gaming hall at the Doge's Palace. Tonight, he was not as lucky and found himself quickly in a fix and owing Elizabeth an absurd amount of lucre. Elizabeth was not the least bit distraught over the loss; rather, she was pleased by Dorsey's predicament. Her growing appetite for him and for gambling was becoming insatiable. She really could not seem to get enough of either. Thankfully, he did not find her lewd behavior offensive. He enjoyed her crassness, even applauded the manner in which she asserted power and of course, generously shared monies. She was a fine companion, amusing really, and good for a bachelor who was about to be married.

Therefore, I was not surprised when Elizabeth requested that I make other sleeping arrangements for the evening, stating there was a matter of debt to settle. As I gathered my things, I ignored Dorsey leaning against the doorway, his fingers working to unfasten his shirt. Elizabeth teased him, accusing him of losing on purpose, which he adamantly denied, but the smirk upon his face said otherwise. At that point, I was not certain who was playing whom. He seemed well suited for her and I wondered just how long the affair would last.

I packed a small bag and was dismissed so Elizabeth could enjoy the privacy of the chamber. Seeing how there were no other available rooms in Leon Bianco, I decided to ask Nicholas to escort me to George's. I knew Nicholas would have little problem finding a warm bed to sleep in, nightly comfort was bought cheaply on any side street in the city. I was no fool. I knew ever since our trip to Issacher's that he was frequenting certain establishments.

I paused before knocking on George's door to pray that Fruzsina was not keeping company inside. After mustering up the nerve, I rapped on the door. I heard footsteps, then the lock sliding. George stared at the small bag hanging by my side. I could only imagine what he was thinking.

"Elizabeth requests privacy this evening. It seems I have nowhere else to go."

He invited me inside.

"I know this is most unorthodox, but I didn't know where else to turn. I promise I will make myself sparse. I will leave first thing in the morning." I was relieved Fruzsina was nowhere in sight.

George sensed my concern. "She's dining at the Doge's Palace this evening. King Rudolph has arrived for the season. I don't plan on seeing my wife. She has requested to stay at the palace as an intimate guest. An intimate guest," George repeated. He poured a glass of brandy. "You may stay as long as you like."

I thanked him for the kindness.

He sat in the armchair and crossed his legs while holding the brandy in one hand and drumming the fingers of his other. He was distant tonight, preoccupied by thought. "It's pleasant to have company. I thought I'd be spending the night alone," he said, before taking another sip.

"I hear a man is never alone in Venice." It was cruel, but I couldn't help remembering spying George leaving that seedy building across the canal.

George perked up. "And what would I know about that?" he asked.

"I saw you George. I saw you leaving a building where I presume you had no business other than buying pleasure." I stunned myself by blurting my thoughts.

He fixated on my accusing face.

I had no right to cast judgment, no right at all. His dealings were no concern of mine; however, I was possessive, and jealous of the other woman. Good lord, I had no right to feel this way, I knew this, but nevertheless I was overcome with hatred for the woman, for all women that had shared him.

George said nothing, not a single protest or turn of phrase to justify his business.

I supposed there was some comfort that he did not choose to deny it. My cheeks flushed an embarrassing pink. "Are you angry with me, George?" It was a silly question, but I felt compelled to ask.

"Angry? Why should I be angry?"

"It's the tone you're using which leads me to believe so." I removed my shoes and placed them neatly beside the sofa.

His countenance was drawn and dark circles aged his eyes. His dry lips enhance the fine lines around the corner of his mouth and the neglect of his grooming habits left him ragged and sad looking.

"Are you well?" I asked, noticing his disheveled state.

"Hardly fairing." He tried to laugh, but it was cynical.

"Have you seen a doctor?" I was terribly worried he was truly ill.

"What ails me a doctor cannot remedy. I have a wife I do not love, and worse, a wife who fulfills only the favors of the king.

Never mind a bastard son," George said, pausing briefly before adding, "and a mistress, my beautiful Amara... no longer is it my heart for which hers beats. Could things get any worse?"

It was a cold reality, but not all was true.

"I'd beg for you if I thought it would do any good," he said.

I became nauseated and wondered just how much brandy George drank. My reaction surprised even me. "Have you given any thought to how hard this is for me?" I snapped.

George started at the sharpness of my voice.

"How is it possible to love two men, so completely different from one another? Please explain how I can feel so strongly for both of you? It does not matter whether I give my body when my heart has already committed a betrayal in the most sinister way imaginable. My heart can never be devoted to just one man, George, because the other seeps in taking hold with such force as to never let go. The torment, it is everlasting, you have no idea what I go through!" My nausea worsened and I thought I was going to be sick.

"Then why not give in and have us both? As you say, your heart has already betrayed. What is the difference now?"

I could not argue his point, even if it was twisted and convenient. "I don't want to love you anymore, George," I admitted. "It's not right and it's definitely not fair to Draco."

"Are there any words I can speak? If so, I will speak them! Is there anything I can do, please confess it now, and I will do it. Amara, I cannot survive without you, you must see this is true. I will hate it, loathe it in the worse possible way, but if it is the only way then I will agree to share your affections with another. Please, I beg you, don't turn away from me. Stay with me tonight. Come to me when you can. It is you Amara and only you that I long for. It is for you that I will endure time, those painful never ending hours between touch, my eyes settling on your soft skin, the curves of your body and the scent of lavender in your hair. I've tried to fill the hole in my heart only to be disgusted and finding myself living in a deeper anguish than which I arrived. I've had much time to think on this and I'm resigned, if this is the only way, then I will take it." He fell to his knees in front of me and wrapped his arms around my legs.

I could not free myself from him. I did not have the will power to do so and I hated myself for being weak, but I couldn't fight what was inside of me no matter how wrong I knew my feelings were. "If I agree, Draco must never know. Not even Elizabeth or your closest confidante can have knowledge of our relationship. You must swear George to absolute secrecy. This must be the condition," I said. I could hardly believe the words I spoke, to even consider such a thing was despicable and dirty. If I went through with this, I would never feel clean again – but the longer he clung to me, the more I realized I'd give in.

George raised his head. I sensed his hope. "I swear Amara, I will take it to my grave."

He carried me to his bedchamber where I allow him to undress me. My fingers trembled as I unfasten his shirt. I was excited with anticipation and longing for the man I first loved, a love I'd mourned for so long. A candle burned on the bedside table. The closed window muffled the voices of couples strolling outside. Their conversations lingered slightly before fading into the night. George was eager and took me with a passion I never imagined him capable of possessing. It was elating and I matched his release with equal enthusiasm. Joined together once again, we shared a oneness where the crescendo was heightened by a forbidden union. Cloaked in darkness, our sin was forgiven by love and, despite the wrongness, somehow it felt spiritual at culmination. So many thoughts raced through my mind. I wanted to speak, but instead I let tears of sorrow and joy wet our skin. I collapsed against George's chest. His rapid heartbeat was a steady rhythmic pounding caged beneath damp flesh. I gripped his arm fearing I'd float from his bedchamber like a dream vanishing upon waking. He touched my back and kissed the top of my head. I pressed my body against him, holding tight. I wanted to crawl inside for safety. I wanted to hide forever in a place where no one could snatch and tear me apart. I did not want to be brave. He must have sensed my insecurity because he tightened his hold. Sadly, we both knew trying to hold onto the moment was like trying to prevent grains of sand from sifting through fingers. The tighter the grasp, the quicker it poured.

The hours George and I spent together felt like seconds. I had barely laced my bodice when a knock came upon his door. He waved for me to hide while he saw to the caller. Luckily it was just Nicholas arriving to escort me to Leon Bianco. I collected my things and thanked George for his hospitality. There was a moment when I thought I saw a plea for me not to go. It was fleeting, but unmistakable. I pushed the emotion deep in the pit of my heart. Without another word, or a lasting look or lingering gesture I abandoned him once again. The finality of the door meeting the seal sent a shiver from my neck to the small of my back. The last grain of sand slipped through my fingers. I gave one last look at the door hoping to see George, but all I saw was the hard wood with iron hinges and a number hanging from a rusty nail.

I decided it was best if I entered through the glass atrium rather than through the front door of Leon Bianco. It was too early of an hour to manage a convincing excuse if questioned regarding our arrival. Nicholas opened the gate and allowed me to pass through first. The usual chirping birds fluttered overhead flying from tree to flowering bush. I lifted my hem and hurried through the maze of garden artistry. There, sitting in the middle of the atrium, was Raphael Petrucci. I should not have been surprised; he was sitting in the exact spot he'd been sitting for the past few weeks. Propped up on a chair was a half painted canvas.

"Damnation!" I cursed.

My rude outburst startled Raphael. He dropped his palette before standing to greet me, bowing before I had the chance to refuse the grand gesture. "Pardon milady, I didn't mean to frighten you."

Nicholas discreetly took the bag from my hand and concealed it behind his back as he deliberately moved to the back door of Leon Bianco.

"It's awfully early to be painting, isn't it?" I asked

"I'm capturing the sunrise."

His accent was thick and I could barely understand what he was saying. "May I?" I asked, peeking at the painting.

Raphael allowed me to admire his work. It was a partially painted reproduction of the Leon Bianco's atrium at sunrise.

Everything was miraculously rendered, its likeness astonishing including the dark haired beauty standing on the balcony.

"It's remarkable. Is it a commission?"

"No milady."

"All this work for nothing?" I asked. I was amazed at the detail.

"A true artist paints because he must."

"And the lady in the picture. Why do you include her?"

"She is the muse which inspires the must in the artist." He bit his brush between his teeth. "She is like a ghost. She haunts my thoughts. My mind is restless, day and night. You see, I must capture her. I'm compelled, almost driven to do so."

"But you don't even know her," I said.

"Ah, but I do. Look for yourself." He tapped the canvas with the tip of his brush.

I examined the woman standing on the balcony. Her noble posture fragrant of wealth, her chin turned in a defiant manner with her red lips set firmly in neither a smile or frown. Then I spotted what I presume Raphael hoped I would recognize. The woman in the painting was watching the artist. Even more fascinating was the miniscule reflection of Raphael painted within her black pupils.

"How?" I asked, stunned.

"By using the sunrises casting light."

"I mean her eyes, how did you render the reflection in her eyes?"

"The muse persuades the artist's hand. I can't explain, it is just so. See for yourself."

I glanced at the balcony and discovered Elizabeth was watching us.

"She appears every morning to pose for me. She is wonderful."

"It would please her to view your painting. Shall I tell her to come down?"

"No, please. It is not finished."

"You haven't purchased a new easel?" I remembered the collision in the alley and the shattered pieces of his instrument splintered on the ground.

"A minor inconvenience. I'm saving my money." He dabbed a brush in the paint on his palette. By resuming his work he implied our conversation was finished, so I politely excused myself and returned to Elizabeth's apartment.

Through the cracked bedchamber door I saw the naked chest of the sleeping Lord Dorsey.

"You conversed with the painter?" Elizabeth asked, upon my entry.

"He's painting a picture of the atrium. Perhaps you should offer to purchase it. It is the least you could do. He's in need of a new easel and you are kind of responsible for breaking his."

"He ran into me," Elizabeth said.

"I assume Dorsey's debt is paid?"

"Yes, quite energetically," she said, glaring slightly. "He is a good sport."

"What's he like?" I asked. I admired the glimpse I received of the smoothness of his skin. I wanted to run my hand over his chest to experience the softness for myself.

"Surprising. I figured Dorsey to be a disappointment, but he was rather fun."

"You didn't do anything too shocking?" I asked. I was concerned a gentleman such as Dorsey would find it difficult to keep his indiscretion private. He didn't seem like a man who would spare a single detail of his encounters.

"Whatever do you mean?"

"You know damn well what I mean," I snapped. I was not in the mood for her condescending tone.

Our talking woke Dorsey and shortly he appeared half-dressed in the doorway. "I do hope you're not kissing and telling," he said, sleepily.

"I'm doing no such thing," Elizabeth said.

He kissed her openly on the mouth and with little concern that I was in the room. I diverted my gaze, giving the couple as much privacy as the space allowed.

"Amara, did you know our countess is wickedly delicious? She rivals the most sought after courtesan. I can hardly imagine possessing a wife with such, how shall I put it delicately, unusual skills. She won't reveal, but perhaps you will humor my curiosity, where did she learn to perform such exquisite techniques?"

My worst suspicion was realized and I was appalled that he had the nerve to ask such things.

"Can I presume you are as talented?" he asked, licking his lip.

Elizabeth patted him playfully on the chest. "Don't tease. Amara is a rarity, she is a loyal wife."

"Tsk, most shameful. Speaking of wives, do you think the two of you might be able to teach my virgin bride a thing or two?"

His audacity was shocking.

"Poor child, after what I've done to you, she'll never be able to please you," Elizabeth teased.

"There's a book," I blurted out, trying to be helpful. I had no idea why I said it. I guess I was trying to turn the conversation to a more aesthetic topic.

Elizabeth and Dorsey were surprised.

"Really, a book?" he asked, rather sincerely.

I was afraid I'd done it now. I had to go on. "I saw it in the king's cabinet of curiosities. It's called the, 'Art of Love Making;' it's from the Orient. I could not read the inscriptions, but the illustrations were explanatory in nature. Perhaps, it would be useful to a new bride?"

The mention of the book snagged Elizabeth's curiosity as well. "What did the pictures show?" she asked, intrigued.

"Men and women in positions."

"Naughty girls," Dorsey chuckled.

I didn't like the sound of his laugh. It was suggestive and implied we were harlots masquerading as ladies. His boyish response made me feel cheap and lowly, and I regretted mentioning the stupid book. However, he said no more. He took advantage of the morning meal and promised to call later. Playfully, he teased Elizabeth about having another evening of losing at the gaming table. Unquestionably, he was quite fond of being indebted to Elizabeth and I could tell he was not ready to cut his losses and move on to his new life. It was evident that he was not through with her yet. Although, by the coolness in her voice, I believed she was about finished with him. She'd had her fun, but he didn't possess enough passion to hold her lasting interest.

When she was certain he was gone, she confirmed my assumption. "I'm afraid he is getting the wrong impression," she said.

"Intercourse can do that. I take it you're getting bored already?"

"He is so easily seduced, so willing. Suddenly he is less attractive, annoying really. Isn't that terrible?"

"Inevitable. Always is," I answered.

"You know what else is peculiar? The entire time I was with Dorsey I kept thinking about someone else. It's ridiculous really, seeing how I don't even know the man."

I could relate. I too had thoughts of another man while I was with someone else. I was grateful that Elizabeth was too absorbed with her own revelation to question me about my evening. I didn't want to explain. I wouldn't even know where to begin.

"It's that artist, Raphael Petrucci. The man I saw you talking to this morning in the atrium," she said.

"He is an interesting fellow, but hardly someone you can be seen accompanying around town," I said.

"Why can't I?"

"He is impoverished. You'll draw attention."

"Dorsey is a poor gentleman."

"Raphael has no title," I added.

"But artists are exempt, are they not? For example, King Rudolph surrounds himself with artists lacking riches and titles."

"He is a king. No one dares to question the company he keeps."

Elizabeth despised it when I discussed privilege, especially when it played against her argument. No longer amused, she changed the subject. It was what she did when she was not getting her way. I let it go for now. I knew when she was in a better mood she'd broach the topic again.

Later, the chambermaid delivered water for baths. The warmness relaxed my sore limbs, tiring them into a comfy heaviness. I had difficulty willing them into a clean gown and I had even more trouble tolerating the chambermaid dressing my hair. I did not wish to do anything, but Elizabeth demanded I accompany her on an urgent errand. Again, I was at the mercy of her personal desires and I had to obey. Normally I was an obliging companion, but today I was reluctant. I was bothered and irritable, which made me rather poor company.

To my surprise, Elizabeth's urgency involved scouring the shops of Venice for an easel. She insisted she'd been hit by an immediate sense of guilt that compelled her to replace the artist's tool. I knew differently. It was not guilt that drove Elizabeth to do anything. The easel was an excuse to meet with Raphael. She couldn't get him out of her mind, even when she was with someone else. How could I object? It was not my place, so I went along like I always do.

After several inquiries we came across a small dealer of paints and tools just on the outskirts of the Arsenal, the shipyard housing hundreds of Venetian vessels. At one time, it took Venetian craftsmen a day to build a great Venetian ship. As the demand lessened, so did the immediacy to construct. Now, salt merchants commissioned most of the ships being built in the Arsenal. The sound of pounding nails into wood echoed from the walls as well as shouts of fish mongers tossing the day's catch into crates being wheeled to market or loaded onto vessels heading out to sea. Elizabeth bartered with the art dealer and acquired the easel for a fair price. She also purchased some paints and a new brush. I did think it was kind that she made the purchase, but found her true motive unwise. However, I knew she believed the ploy was clever, even though I thought it transparent. The easel was to appear as an apology, but the paints and brush were to flaunt extravagance and wealth. I hoped Raphael's desperation for supplies would trump any insult Elizabeth's boldness might inflict.

Nicholas lagged behind, carrying the art supplies and easel, while we walked along the canal. I took care to side step the pigeon droppings covering the cobblestone, while the fishmongers worked dockside cleaning, wrapping and bundling packs in crates. Elizabeth rudely commented on the stench. She did not care for the smell of fish guts littering the ground. However, she ceased her complaining temporarily when she recognized one of the men gutting fish. He tore the meat with a silver blade from gill to tail. It was Raphael Petrucci. He politely acknowledged the countess with a respectful nod and waited for her to pass before resuming his craft. I was curious as to what Elizabeth would now make of the monger moonlighting as an artist. Would the discovery of his true occupation hinder the fantasy? I supposed he had to earn a living some way seeing how he'd admitted his paintings were not selling. After all, Venice was polluted with starving artists all hoping for a rich noble to save them from hunger. They all wanted to be sponsored; their passion commissioned and showered with flattery.

Elizabeth was uncharacteristically quiet during our return to Leon Bianco. Once inside our chambers Nicholas retired to his room for an afternoon nap. I desperately wanted to do the same. I was exhausted. The late night with George was taking its toll, but I worried my rest would spark an interrogation. So, for the rest of the day and early into the evening I remained in the company of Elizabeth. She read verses while I wrote a letter to Draco. I took special care to create an up tempo correspondence. I hardly wanted to draw suspicion, but then I realized anything too upbeat was certainly suspicious. I crumbled the letter and began again. This time I decided to include a couple of complaints, details of the Doge's ball and a brief description of the Arsenal. Draco would like hearing about the ships. I read it over several times making certain I excluded everything including Lord Dorsey and George. I was about to seal the envelope, when I hesitated. I still hadn't provided an explanation as to why we traveled to Venice in the first place. Again, I crumbled the letter and begin again. This time I carefully plotted my details giving the invitation to the Doge's Palace as an excuse for our visit and season's activities. I expressed how much I missed Draco and how I hoped he'd visit soon. I fretted over his safety and often wondered where his missions took him. Was he far away or only a day's journey from where I stayed? Did he look at the same night sky, wish on the same stars I had or was he preoccupied with devising plans or worse, finding comfort in the arms of a harem girl? It was ridiculous to think Draco would do such a thing, then again, was it? Hadn't I just bedded his sworn enemy, the man who drove his cousin to death by drowning? How was it possible to love such a man after hearing what George had done? To think what this would do to Draco was unfathomable. He'd never forgive! How could he? I tried to justify my affair by convincing myself Draco misjudged George. He did not know him like I did. Although I pitied his poor cousin, she obviously was young and naive. Perhaps, she was not right in the head. She did take her own life after all. Pathetic, the entire exercise in redemption was pathetic! I was a horrible, horrible woman who did not deserve the love of a single man, let alone two!

When finished and satisfied, I folded the letter and sealed the envelope. I placed it on the silver tray along with the other outgoing posts. I was about to pick up my sewing, which lay abandoned for weeks on a side chair, when Elizabeth closed her book and rang the bell.

"I want to go out," she said to the maid.

"Shall I change?" I asked.

"Stay with Nicholas. I'll be back in a while."

I was apprehensive. "Where are you going?" I asked.

Elizabeth fastened her cloak before handing the art supplies and easel to the guard standing at attention by the door.

"You're not really considering? You'd better take Nicholas. He is the only one who can navigate the streets at night. You'll get lost on your own."

She ignored my suggestion.

"I'm to stay here?" I repeated, in disbelief.

"Unless you have some place you'd rather be." That is all she said before the door shut and she was gone.

I lit a lantern and went out on the balcony. The breeze coming off the canal cast a chill. I thought about Elizabeth's parting words. Was there a place I'd rather be at the moment? Perhaps she sensed my dilemma, the strange paradox of my heart. I heard Nicholas rummaging around inside. Then there was a knock, and because it was unexpected, the intrusion made me jumpy.

"Are you expecting someone?" he called to me.

"No, no one," I answered.

On the other side of the door was a young boy wearing ratty trousers and a felt hat. He thrust an envelope in the maid's face.

"Well who is it for?" I asked, coming in from the balcony.

"It is not addressed, Milady."

"Give it here," I demanded. A rose sketched by a quick hand decorated the corner. I unfolded the paper and read:

Something ordinary seeks to achieve the extraordinary

"Well who is it from?" Nicholas asked innocently enough.

My silence indicated he had crossed a line.

"Pardon, it is none of my business," he said, returning to his task.

I paced about the room thinking of an excuse to leave, but then remembered I did not need permission, not tonight. I hurried to my room and retrieved my cloak. There was a place I'd rather be, and someone whom I'd rather be with besides poor Nicholas. I rushed from my room only to find Nicholas standing with his hat in hand.

"Do you require an escort this evening, Milady?"

"Which way are you venturing?" I questioned.

"Toward San Marco."

"By foot or gondola?"

"Foot, unless you wish otherwise," he said.

"Let's share a gondola. I'll pay for your passage."

It was difficult to flag a boat at that time of night. The gondolier took my hand while Nicholas adjusted a cushion and arranged my skirt to avoid the hem getting dirty. A settling fog dampened the dusty surface of the cobblestone streets muddying the soles of our shoes. I gave the dock address of my destination. We rode together both listening to the water lap against the oar as it cut through the surface pushing us forward before lifting and plunging deep once again. Lanterns illuminated upstairs windows, couples waved for vacant gondolas while an accordion mourned in the distance. The musician played a melancholy jig reminiscent of crueler times.

"Here we are, Milady."

I paid the man making sure to give a bit extra to cover Nicholas's passage.

"Shall I call on you in the morning?" Nicholas asked, his voice shy making it barely audible.

I agreed.

"Are you sure you don't want an escort?" he asked, before the oarsman shoved off.

"I know the way. I'll be fine."

I walked down the alley and through the double doors of the building housing George's apartment. The night guard greeted me with a nod from his station opposite the room. I kept my head lowered as I climbed the stairs. I found myself again face-to-face with the wooden door and the number hanging from a rusted nail. I did not hesitate. I heard voices downstairs and the fear of being discovered rushed the removal of my glove and forced me to rapidly knock upon the door. It sounded urgent, even eager in tone. The voices were nearing. I rapped again, this time even harder; still, no footsteps. Instantly I was overcome with uneasiness and wondered if perhaps I had made a mistake and misinterpreted the note. I contemplated leaving. The voices disappeared. As long as I remained on the landing I was in little jeopardy of encountering a neighbor. I took a deep breath, and decided to wait.

I waited on the steps. A half hour passed. It was strange how time allowed doubtful thoughts to creep in and I began to convince myself that George's absence was a sign I should turn back. I should go home and forget this errand ever took place. I had made up my mind. I was leaving. Just then, the large, double doors of the hotel opened and the night guard greeted someone good evening informing the gentleman that a lady caller was waiting upstairs. I leaned over the railing seeing a man dressed in a long cloak and boots. George rounded the final landing carrying a bouquet of flowers and a brown sack, his hat concealed his face, but I knew it is him.

"I'm sorry I wasn't here to meet you," he apologized, taking a key from his pocket.

"I was about to leave." I glanced down the hallway before following George into the apartment.

"I did not expect you so soon. I actually wasn't sure if you'd show up at all, but I did hope."

"What's all this?" I said, removing my other glove.

"It's a surprise for you, that is, if you came tonight. I wasn't sure you'd be able to get away."

He filled a vase with water and arranged the bouquet. "Please, have a seat."

I thought the ceremony was unnecessary. "George, what are we doing?" I asked.

"The only thing we can -- rendezvous. It does not have to be all bad. It can be romantic if you let it."

"George, last night…" I began, but he put a finger to my lips.

"Hush now, don't say it Amara, I can't bear to hear you say it."

He moved his finger from my lips to the pins holding my hair in a bun. One by one, he pulled them out and set them on the side table next to the vase. Strands of hair fell, the tension released by the tight constraint of fashion. He touched the laces on my bodice. The strings loosened letting my gown slip from my body revealing a lacy shift. I stepped out of my slippers, my toes nestling in the thick rug under our feet. George wrapped a blanket around my shoulders and escorted me to the sofa. It was a loving gesture; delicate and careful. He poured the wine and gave me a box tied with a blue bow.

"Italian wine and Venetian delights," he said. Inside the tiny box were six perfect miniature sweets.

"Where did you find these?" I asked, taking one from the wrapping.

"A shop across the Rialto in San Polo."

I was flattered by the effort. "Are they expensive?"

"Ridiculously so," he laughed. "But, you are worth every cent."

I wanted to believe, I wanted to think I was a precious jewel, like a princess or queen. It was a girl's dream, a dream every woman desperately clung to during the terrible times.

As we drank, I told him about my encounter with Raphael in the atrium and Elizabeth's confession. I expressed my concern for Lord Dorsey's heart, but George reassured me he would not suffer heartbreak. It was common for trysts to last a single night, not long enough for either party to form any serious attachment. However, he did include that Dorsey was certain to take advantage of the arrangement as long as Elizabeth welcomed his affection. To me, George presumed too easily, as if he spoke from experience.

"Where is Elizabeth tonight?" he asked.

"With the artist."

"Raphael, the fishmonger from the atrium you talked about?"

I told him about the art supplies and her intention to deliver them personally this evening.

"And you're certain she will stay all night?"

I plucked another sweet from the box. "I am most confident."

***

Our nightly partings became a habit. Every evening after supper Elizabeth went to Raphael and Nicholas escorted me to George's before moving on to his own affair. George always had something prepared whether it was a private dinner or an evening at the theater. Since it was the height of the season, we ventured out under the guise of carnival masks. Even in costume we took special care to avoid recognition. George paid for a private box entering first while I waited before taking a back staircase used mostly by theater workers and servants. We always left before the finale to ensure a swift exit.

Each morning a knock came upon the door. It was always Nicholas. He'd escort me to Leon Bianco, both of us entering through the route of the atrium instead of by the main entry. However, Raphael no longer occupied the garden. He was occupying a more intimate space. I'd find our apartment vacant or on special occasions Raphael would wave from the railing of the balcony. Elizabeth said Raphael preferred his small rooms to her elegant apartment because he enjoyed painting while she slept. It was less complicated, which he preferred. Raphael's rooms were cluttered with half finished sketches and outlines of Elizabeth that he recreated on large canvases and hung on the walls.

In time, Elizabeth abandoned the season, refusing invitations and passing on the opening night of a new play. The silver tray holding the outgoing daily post sat empty by the door. A stack of letters sagged on Elizabeth's desk. I finally decided they needed to be answered because her absence was drawing attention. It took an entire afternoon to sift through them all, but I managed to sort them into piles of importance. I tried to persuade Elizabeth to take a moment to respond, but a moment could not be spared. She insisted on returning to Raphael as soon as possible. She could not stand being away even for the few hours he worked at the docks. She didn't understand why the humiliating job was necessary. She even offered to pay all his expenses, but Raphael refused. He liked buying Elizabeth gifts and complained he would not purchase them with her money. No man of decent character would do such a thing. It was disgraceful. A real man provided, even if it was just a little.

One evening just around dusk George escorted us to Raphael's rooms. He said it was a surprise and wouldn't give us a single hint as to what we were to expect. Elizabeth took a brass key from her pocket and turned the lock. Raphael was inside setting a fresh canvas on the easel Elizabeth bought him.

"Come in," he said, waving us inside.

There were only two chairs in the room. The table was covered in rolled tubes of paint and bits of charcoal. A bowl of soup rested on top of a can and a washbasin with a shelf holding three worn dishes sat in the corner. A faded piece of fabric hung over a dirty window blocking out the light. Through another doorway I could see the foot of a bed. Hanging on the wall was a painting of two naked forms entwined together in such a manner that it was impossible to tell where the male separated from the female. The only color was a burnt red. I surmised the paint spoiled because it adhered awkwardly to the stretched canvas. It broke and bubbled in places causing the lines of the figures to fracture in ragged edges. Raphael noticed me admiring the painting.

"That is Elizabeth and I," he said, proudly.

"Is it common for oils to create this texture?" I asked. I didn't want to insult the quality of the portrait by suggesting the paint was tainted.

"Oh, it is not oil paint." He was searching for a sketching pencil while he talked.

George picked up a sketch lying on the floor. "What is it?" he asked, referring to the paint.

Elizabeth wandered into the bedroom. She tossed her cloak on the bed before lighting a scented candle.

"It's blood," Raphael said, matter-of-factly.

"Blood?"

"My blood to be precise." He rolled up his sleeve to show a bandage wrapped around his forearm.

"You painted it using your own blood? Why would you do that?" George asked.

Raphael positioned the easel so he could get the best perspective while he sketched me. "Oils can't, how do you say, able to capture the passion I feel when..." he trailed off. He shut one eye, tilting his head before going back to work on the sketch. "Blood, it is passion." He paused briefly, admiring his work. "It is the soul, it is eternal...like my love for the Eliza."

"Couldn't you have just used red paint," George suggested. "Isn't art symbolic, red could represent blood."

"It's not the same. It would be false. You see, I cannot lie when it is a matter of my own heart."

George shrugged. I think he was wondering if Raphael was sane. He was no slouch when it came to grand, romantic gestures but slicing his flesh and writing with his own blood hardly was romantic to a gentleman. To a poor artist, however, I suppose the effort was a true representation of his love. When a man had nothing but his heart, it seemed like a perfectly beautiful and priceless sacrifice.

"Tell me if this pleases you," Raphael said to George.

George gazed at the canvas and then smiled at me. "It's perfect."

Elizabeth showed George her favorite sketches and paintings while Raphael labored on the portrait of me George commissioned him to paint. It would take several sittings to work the portrait to the point where I was no longer needed to bring it to completion.

Each day in the late afternoon the three of us walked to Raphael's. I'd sit for hours while Elizabeth and George chatted or read quietly. Finally, Raphael announced it was done. It was the end of the week and my back was terribly sore from sitting absolutely still for so many hours.

"The painting is finished?" I asked, stretching.

"Not yet, but I can do the rest without you."

"It's breathtaking. Raphael, your talent is remarkable," George complimented.

"Where on Earth are you going to put the painting?" I asked. Surely, his wife would not allow it in her home.

"I think I will hang it in my bedchamber, my wife never comes in there," George joked.

"Stop playing, George!" It wasn't funny.

"Don't fret, I have just the place." He suggested we celebrate, but Elizabeth declined the invitation saying she preferred to stay in. We'd been infringing on her time with Raphael and I could tell she was eager to see us go. George told Raphael he'd be by in a couple of days to pick up the portrait and settle on the fee. I was curious to know how much he was paying for the portrait, but I understood such details would never be divulged to a lady. No amount ever seemed flattering. If too costly, the lady stewed over the expense. If too cheap, she was insulted. I thought about the picture painted in blood. Unlike George, I could imagine how perfect the medium truly was because the price of love or what it was worth could not be determined. I was certain Elizabeth admired it, not because of the remarkable extravagance, but for its uniqueness; the bleeding of one's soul for another captured forever on canvas. To most it might be ghoulish, but secretly I envied the romantic allure.

The following day Nicholas and I resumed our customary walk through the garden gate of the Leon Bianco with my mask dangling from the crook of my arm. Out of habit, I glanced up at the balcony, this time noticing the door was slightly open. I figured Elizabeth had returned or the chambermaid was airing out the apartment. Nicholas paused at the front desk to pick up any messages. Today, the hotelkeeper handed Nicholas an envelope with the Nadasdy seal pressed along the fold. I scowled at the correspondence.

"It appears the count has sent Elizabeth a letter. I pray it's not bad news," Nicholas said giving the message to me.

As we climbed the stairs to our apartment, I debated whether to open the letter. If it was urgent news I should read it immediately, but if it was a letter from a husband to his wife, then it was a blatant invasion of privacy. I decided to ask Nicholas for advice.

"Considering who it's from, I think you should. I'm certain she'd understand."

By the time we got to the landing, I had made up my mind to go ahead and read the first lines of the note. I began working the edge loose as Nicholas inserted the key to spring the lock. He was surprised to discover the lock was already sprung.

I was not paying attention to where I was walking and did not notice Nicholas had halted in the entryway. "Good lord, Nicholas. Why'd you stop so suddenly," I snapped, colliding with his backside.

Nicholas fell into a bow. Standing in the middle of the antechamber was Draco. His coat was off, as if he'd been waiting for some time, and I noticed his sword was unbuckled and strewn over the chair.

My mouth hung unattractively open. "Oh my, what are you doing here?" I asked.

"It's nice to see you too, darling. You look well, as if you've been getting plenty of exercise. Out for an early morning walk?"

I slide my mask to Nicholas who tucked it behind his back. "Yes, you know me. I've been dragging poor Nicholas along for company."

"Good," Draco said, turning away. "Lovely view from the balcony, isn't it."

"It's my favorite place to sit."

"I would have thought you'd mention it in your letters."

"My letters? Oh yes, you received them? I was worried they wouldn't find you for some time."

"They found me just fine."

Draco surveyed the room. "Where's Elizabeth?"

Nicholas's eyes widened.

I had to think and quick! "She's at the Doge's Palace," I stammered, shamelessly.

"Really? This early?"

"There was a party... you know it is the height of the season. The affair went very late so the Doge insisted his company spend the night and join him for breakfast on the garden terrace." It was amazing how quickly I constructed the lie.

"And you did not stay by your mistress's side?"

"Of course I did."

Draco puzzled. Nicholas looked as if he were about to be sick. I felt the letter still clutched in my hand.

"The hotelkeeper sent a messenger very early this morning. He was concerned it was urgent. We decided it best not to wake Elizabeth. We were determined to retrieve the message ourselves. Again, I was thinking fast.

"Ah, yes the message, I nearly forgot," Draco sighed.

I could not tell if he was relieved or distrustful. Was he leading me into a trap or did he truly believe the explanation I was making up?

"I've missed you," he said. His arms closed around me, my face smothered against his broad chest. After he let go I asked if I should read the note. I had already broken the seal, but still had not read a word.

"It's announcing the count's arrival to Venice. I wanted to surprise you, but the Francis thought it proper to send a message."

"When will he arrive?"

"Oh, probably very soon."

I contemplated sending Nicholas to alert Elizabeth, but decided to wait. She had less than a day to spend with Raphael. I wanted her to enjoy the precious hours that remained before Francis arrived and spoiled all our fun.

"Shall I have a bath prepared?" I asked Draco.

He sniffed his sleeve. "Probably a good idea."

While Draco soaked in the tub I jotted a note to George telling him of Draco's arrival. I begged George to stay away, explaining I could not risk a chance encounter. I sealed the envelope and ordered Nicholas to deliver it immediately. I didn't have to emphasize the importance. He understood the urgency of my request.

After his bath Draco joined me in the antechamber for tea and biscuits. He relaxed on the sofa and gazed upon me with those penetrating eyes. Was it my imagination, or did it feel more like an inquisition? I squirmed in the chair while the guilt of my cheating and lying ate at me. I was afraid he could see right into me, like I was absolutely transparent. My mind raced with terrible thoughts and a confession boiled on my tongue. The everlasting torment surged inside as I wrestled with my conscience. I wanted to tear my skin off and dispose of the filthy flesh. I had not the time to wash myself and I feared I reeked of George's scent. I am unworthy of his love. I am unworthy of his love I kept repeating over and over in my head. I am a horrible, disloyal wife, and I do not deserve him. What was even more unbelievable was that I loved him. After all I did, it was true—I still loved him. It was just as true as the declaration I made to George. During the entire time I was thinking these dratted thoughts, Draco continued to drink his tea.

"Are you alright my love?" he asked.

Damn those accusing eyes! "Perfectly well. It's just been such a long time since I've seen you."

"I imagine you must get very lonely."

I chewed on the edge of my lip.

"How is baby Anna?" he asked. He knew how much I adored the babe.

Nevertheless, I was taken back by the question. Anna had not crossed my mind in weeks. Originally, we planned to be gone only a short time so Elizabeth thought it best if Ilona and Anna stayed at Cachtice. "Ilona is caring for her at Cachtice," I explain.

"Have you given any thought to having children?" Draco asked.

"Children?" Had he not sensed anything was wrong with me? And, why was he asking about children? This hardly seemed like an ideal time for such a conversation, after all...

"Do you yearn for a child?" he asked.

Frankly, a child was the last thing I'd been considering. "I don't believe I can have children," I confessed. Well if I had to confess something, I figured being barren was better than being an adulteress.

Draco set down his teacup. I was relieved he had finally stopped looking at me. "Not once have you thought you might be, perhaps, had a miscarriage of sorts?"

"Never," I answered.

"So you believe it impossible?" he asked, disappointed.

I suppose I did. I believed many things impossible. "I'm barren," I stated, figuring it best just to get it over with. There was no use beating around the issue, but the words came out harsh and unfeeling.

"Perhaps it is I who is to blame."

This was unbelievable, a man blaming himself for a childless union. I knew very well it was not Draco, but how could I prove it was my fault, by citing my affair with George as evidence of my infertility!

Draco rose from the chair and paced across the room. I was having difficulty understanding why this conversation was happening. He made no effort to gently lead into it, but then again Draco was never very good at subtle conversation. "I'm told a woman feels empty without a child. She grows restless."

"I'm quite settled," I assured him.

"A physician told me that it could lead to madness."

Madness? What was this? I tried to maintain my composure, but the thought of going mad because I couldn't experience the retching pain of childbirth was absurd. "I hardly think I'll go mad, Draco," I said, trying to contain my laughter.

He turned. Again, those eyes plagued me, they where searching for something. "I want to make you happy," he said.

I wanted to ease his burden so I went to him and put my arms around his shoulders. "A child cannot take your place, Draco. It is you that I want. I know we can't always be together, but a child won't change how I feel when you're gone. There is no consolation, only understanding and tolerance. I assure you, managing Elizabeth is quite a task. I'm never idle in her company." I hoped the jest would lighten his mood. It was a trick I'd learned from George.

"Promise you're not going mad."

"Well if I am, it isn't because of a child," I teased. Then I gave the statement some thought. "Good lord, what makes you think such a thing?"

"Your letter, well, it was unlike you, very unsettling. I read it several times and came to the conclusion something was amiss. Something was troubling you. Something wasn't quite right."

"All this from a silly letter?"

His eyes locked with mine and I froze, unable to turn away in an attempt to brush off the absurd conversation. It was if his fingers were rummaging around in my brain trying to find the secret I hid inside. I could not take it a second longer. I had to say something to make the torture stop. "Elizabeth is having an affair," I announced.

"What?"

I did the unthinkable! I failed my duty as a confidante – I committed a terrible act of treachery, a practice that was becoming altogether too easy for me.

"Where is she now?" he asked.

I had my hand over my mouth trying to prevent anything else from spilling out.

"You must tell me, Amara. Francis is on his way to Venice to see his wife."

I refused to say another word.

"Very well, if you won't tell me then you must go on your own to warn her."

I tucked Francis's message in my coat pocket. It rested alongside the note George sent me several weeks earlier. I left Draco waiting in the chambers in case Elizabeth returned before I did. Nicholas was coming through the front doors when I bolted down the steps. His face was pale from lack of sleep and drained from an exhausting errand. I grabbed hold of him by the arm telling him he must go with me to warn Elizabeth. When asked, I told him Draco did not believe my story. After pressuring me with several questions, he figured out Elizabeth was keeping company with another man. I could not betray Elizabeth to save myself, so I lied, again.

"Elizabeth and Raphael are in mortal danger. We must go to them before Francis arrives and discovers what his wife is up to, and with whom."

Together, we hurried through the streets. I was praying we'd find our way without the help of Elizabeth as our guide. In my haste, I'd forgotten to put on my mask. I was racing through alleys in broad daylight completely exposed.

As we crossed over bridges and huddled along alleys Nicholas informed me he delivered my message to George with little incident. He said the news brought great anguish, but he promised to do as I wished. In return, he asked Nicholas to give me a message, which Nicholas took from his pocket and pressed in my outstretched hand. I hid it away in my cloak with the others. I did not have time for this, right now my chore was clear; I must find Elizabeth before Francis did.

Indebted Web of Fortune

I banged on the door. When there was no answer, I   banged louder. Nicholas's face was turning whiter by the minute. The alley provided no clue as to which direction Elizabeth and Raphael might have gone. Every heap of rubbish, every scattered piece of litter was just how I remembered. With the edge of my sleeve, I cleaned the corner pane of the window. The small studio was pitch black. I squinted, shielding my eyes with my hand, as I tried to make out if there were any figures moving around inside. Resting against the leg of the easel was the outline of George's commissioned portrait draped in a dust cloth. Nicholas touched my arm drawing my attention away from the studio and toward the street that was now filling with shoppers and merchants. Day was pressing forth and concealing my identity was quickly becoming impossible. I had no business being in this part of town and, if discovered, there'd be talk. I withdrew further into the ermine trim of my hood for protection.

"Come on," I said to Nicholas. Together we retreated to the only place of refuge I could think of, George's apartment.

I hurried up the stairs while Nicholas distracted the door guard. I pounded on George's door; there was no time for discretion. To my relief, I heard the crossing of urgent footsteps, then a sliding clip of the lock. George's face peeked through the crack.

I pushed on the door, forcing it open. "George, I need your help," I hissed. I shoved my way in brushing past his shoulder as I entered the room.

"What's the matter?" he asked. He peered out in the hall, checking first to the right and then left, to see if I was alone, or worse, followed by my jealous husband.

"Francis is coming to Venice. I have word he'll be arriving very soon."

"Then you shouldn't be here."

"You don't understand. I can't find Elizabeth. I think she is with Raphael. Well, I don't think, I know she is," I said. "I just came from his studio. It was vacant and dark." I put my hand to my mouth. "George, I don't know what to do or where to look and time is running out."

George paced the floor with his hands clasped behind his back as if he were about to address the high court. "Did you come alone?"

"Nicholas is downstairs distracting the guard."

"And Draco? Where is he?"

"He is at the apartment in case Francis arrives before we return."

"And if this misfortune should happen, what will Draco tell Francis?"

I too, found myself pacing the floor. "I told Draco that Elizabeth spent the night at the Doge's Palace. Perhaps he will go along with this excuse, although, I am not certain he believes me." It was amazing how a tiny, harmless lie grew into a carefully woven web of deceit. Everything that was coming out of my mouth was getting more difficult to keep straight.

"Very well, have Nicholas escort you to Elizabeth's apartments where you will wait with Draco. I will go look for her. When I find her, and I will, I will escort her home. Tell Draco we were at the Doge's Palace—tell him she is keeping my company while I attend to business. Francis will believe me, even if he does not want to believe you.

I listened to George's instructions. "This means Draco will know you are here in Venice. He'll know that you are here," I said.

In the distance the bells of St. Mark chimed, the hollow tone echoing a haunting reminder that time was indeed running out.

"You must determine which is worse. It is a gamble," George said. He was referring to Francis discovering his wife's affair, or my husband discovering mine.

I had to choose between Elizabeth and myself. I risked losing Draco or Elizabeth, neither of whom I could survive without.

"George, please find her," I said. I tugged on my hood making sure it concealed as much of my face as possible before I darted out the door and returned to Nicholas who was doing his fair share of pacing in the entry. Like we'd done so many times before, we snuck back to Leon Bianco entering out of habit through the atrium gate.

Draco was lunching at the table set just inside the balcony doors. "Any luck?" he asked, setting down his fork and rising from the chair. He liked a routine, and despite the commotion, was apt to stick to it.

"No, she does not wish to be found."

Draco tossed the linen he had draped across his lap onto the table. "I'll find her," he said, annoyed with my failure. He shoved the chair out of his path.

"How? You don't know Venice. You have no idea where to begin. There are hundreds of bridges, canals, and alleys, which lead to no particular place. Everything looks the same. You'll end up going in circles for hours."

"I'm more than capable," he said.

I sighed. "It won't be necessary. I've already employed someone," I admitted.

Draco arched a brow. "You should have consulted me first. Is this help credible? Can the person be trusted?"

I felt my shoulders slump just a touch. "Promise not to be angry?"

My request alarmed him. "You know I cannot make such a promise."

"Well then, I'm afraid I cannot tell." Stubbornly, I turned my back to him.

"You're being childish, Amara. If I am to assist Elizabeth I must know to whom I owe my gratitude when she is delivered safely to our door. Please tell me to whom I shall be indebted?"

I collapsed in defeat upon the sofa. My head ached from all the lying and if I got any deeper I was certain to make a fatal mistake. As it was, I was already having a difficult time keeping the story straight. "It's George," I confessed. "I went to George."

"George? You don't mean Count Drugeth!"

"Yes, I went to Count Drugeth."

"What is he doing in Venice?"

There it was; the suspicion.

"Business," I stated. "His wife is with him for the season. He is the only person I know in Venice. The only one besides Nicholas that I can trust and you said yourself, we better find someone we can trust. You must forgive me for asking him, but what was I to do? What alternative did I have?"

"You could have discussed it with me before acting." Draco was obviously irritated. "Indebted to Count Drugeth! Do you have any idea what an awkward position you put us both in? We're now compromised."

"There was no time," I pleaded.

"We will be at his mercy! Who knows when he'll be compelled to use this information."

"George would never…" I began, but then stopped myself. Draco did not know George like I did, nor could I make him understand.

Draco leaned an ear in my direction, but I dropped my protest. He shook his head muttering something beneath his breath as he went to the balcony. There was no doubt he was displeased. His knuckles turned white as he gripped the iron railing, the tension of the situation revealed in his posture. He remained poised for what seemed an eternity. I preferred shouting at each other rather than enduring being ignored a moment longer. I wished for something to fill the vast space growing between us, anything, even if it were cutting remarks.

Nicholas crossed his legs, his foot bounced nervously up and down. I had almost forgotten he was in the room. I tapped the arm of the sofa counting the passing minutes in my head. Where could Elizabeth be? Out of the corner of my eye I saw the chambermaid standing in the doorway. She beckoned to me, secretly. Nicholas made a move as if to join me, but I motioned for him to stay and keep watch over Draco.

"What is it?" I whispered to the maid.

"I believe I see the master's boat."

I pressed my palm against the warm glass, my eyes searching the docks below. A group of small boats rowed toward the royal ship anchored in the Grand Canal.

"Is that them, milady?"

"Dear God!" I exclaimed.

"Shall we alert Sir Lorant?"

I grabbed her by the wrist causing her to jump. To touch a servant so intimately was inconceivable. "Pray, pray for us all," I begged, before releasing my grip. My panic frightened her and she backed away. I collected my nerves before I went to Draco who was still sulking on the balcony. "Francis has arrived," I announced.

Nicholas leapt so suddenly from the chair he nearly knocked it over. "Good lord, now what!"

"Tell me Nicholas, how does my wife fair in scheming?" Draco asked, his tone dry.

"I've had a marvelous teacher," I answered, referring to Elizabeth.

"Ah, I imagine so," he said, snidely.

So this was how things were going to be between us, formally sarcastic and cutting.

Nicholas's head bobbed back and forth as he tried to follow our banter. "This is not doing anyone any good," he interrupted. "Francis is nearing shore. If we're going to come up with a plan, may I suggest we do it now?"

Draco swaggered across the room as if he were the master of my destiny. Any urgency to act was dissolved with the clanking of his boot buckles. The rhythmic slapping of metal mocked each second lost. My last nerve was sorely becoming agitated.

"He has just docked at shore," Nicholas shouted from his vantage point.

Entering the atrium below was a man clutching the arm of a cloaked woman. They hurried through the maze of gardens making their way to the back door of Leon Bianco. I had a sneaking suspicion it was my George. He had found Elizabeth, and was leading her through the familiar path. This time she was following in my daily footsteps, and soon she'd be at the front door.

I bit my lower lip. I prayed the pair wouldn't meet Francis and his party in the lobby. "What's Francis doing now?" I called to Nicholas.

Draco joined Nicholas by the window.

"I can't see him. He's disappeared beneath the shadowed archway," Nicholas reported.

"George has Elizabeth. I just spied them coming through the garden. The timing will be close, but I think they'll make it."

Nicholas and Draco darted from the bedchamber and I from the balcony, the three of us meeting in the middle of the antechamber with the maid standing by the front door. The approaching sound of footsteps heightened the tension forming between us. Someone was coming, but we weren't sure who until the door flew open and in walked George still gripping Elizabeth's arm.

He flung her unkindly towards me. "Get her cleaned up immediately. Francis is not far behind."

The chambermaid and I tended to Elizabeth in the bedchamber stripping her of her evening gown and replacing it with a proper day dress suitable for the weather. The chambermaid quickly sponged her body with rose water while I fixed her tresses into a neat bun. The sound of clanking metal beating leather and boot heels meeting wood rumbled through the hall just outside the apartment door. There was a loud thud, a cough drowned out by muffled voices and then a determined knock upon the door. The chambermaid tossed the sponge into the bucket before leaving the room to greet the guests waiting impatiently in the hall. Nicholas, George and Draco arranged themselves leisurely on the sofa and armchair by the hearth, while I dabbed a spot of rouge on Elizabeth's lips. Not a single word passed between us. There was not time. The curtain was going up and we had to be ready to act.

Francis bellowed a cheerful greeting to his fellow commander, royal guard, and old friend, Count Drugeth. He asked where the lovely ladies were hiding before joining his friends in the sitting room. Draco explained that there was a party at the Doge's Palace that went late and we had slept in, but assured Francis that Elizabeth was expecting his arrival and was making herself presentable at this very moment. Draco did an excellent job of flattering Francis by adding Elizabeth was most excited by the message announcing his visit and was taking special care to make an impression. I thought he was over doing it a bit, but Francis was a sucker for flattery and gobbled up the compliments like sweet cakes.

Even though she sat in the room, Elizabeth was somewhere else. She stared blankly at her reflection in the mirror as if she did not recognize the woman looking back at her. No amount of rouge or rosewater could disguise the sorrow looming below the noble decoration. She'd been ripped from her lover's arms once again to fulfill a duty she was obligated to endure despite all protest. Her determined chin waned as her slow sweeping lids caressed her dulling eyes. I hated seeing her like this, and was afraid a fit was not far behind. It was cruel to think, but I thought death might be a relief. At least it'd snuff out the foul emotions coursing through her veins. Each prickly feeling was jabbing and poking, scaring the vital organ keeping her alive and pumping deep inside. I was familiar with how the lungs squeezed tight, how the heart ached and the stomach sickened with every throbbing pain pressing intolerably in the head. Elizabeth clutched her hands to prevent the trembling of racked nerves.

The chambermaid spoke softly through the break in the door. "Countess, the count is eager to see you."

Elizabeth cleared her throat before speaking. "Tell him I'll be out in a moment."

"Yes Countess, I will inform him."

The skirt of Elizabeth's pure, white gown draped over the edge of the chair. I fidgeted with the bow of the pink sash tied around her waist and checked a hairpin poking from her bun. That's when I noticed the clasp around her neck. My fingers traced the chain to a charm nestled beneath the curve of her bodice. Elizabeth's cherished onyx was replaced with a crystal vial filled with red liquid. She let me hold the token between my fingers and watched as I tipped it from side to side. The liquid coated the walls sticking to the etched lines of the diamond-shaped glass.

"A potion?" I asked, mesmerized.

Elizabeth touched a thin pink scar above her breast that the slight curve of her bodice barely hid. "It's a token of Raphael's love."

The cut reminded me of my own scar. I knew from experience only a sharp blade could cause such a clean injury. I thought about the tattered bandage wrapped around Raphael's wrist, the fleshy palette blotted in blood used to create his own declaration of love. It was from his body that he collected the natural paint to make the soft brush strokes of the entwining bodies forever preserved on canvas.

Elizabeth pried the crystal vial from my grasp. "This substance flowed through the sanctity of his veins, raced through his heart...his entire body, touching parts of him that I am incapable of touching, physically. But now Amara, I hold it in my hands, I hold it close to my own heart."

"And Raphael, he wears a similar token?"

Elizabeth tucked the crystal beneath her bodice. "Always, and forever."

Again, the nervous chambermaid poked her head through the crack in the doorway. "Countess I beg you, the count, he is insistent."

Elizabeth's skin was cool to the touch and I worried she was ill. I squeezed her hands tight to relieve the trembling. Her bones quivered, her lips taunt and something in her eyes pleaded for this nightmare to end. I saw it clearly; I saw the blackness and betrayal filling her up, consuming her right in front of me. What was most frightening was I did not know how to prevent it from happening – I was helpless to act. In that moment I thought all was lost. Everything was about to be undone. She was breaking apart, her sanity cracking. She was slipping away. I tried coaxing her toward the door, but she remained stiffly in place. I begged her to come forth, but she did not response to my voice. I clutched her hand harder hoping the pain would summons a reaction, but when there was no change in her constitution, I tried another method. I flung open the window. A rush of sea air filled the room smacking us like a slap. The biting chill did not shake her from the awful catatonic state.

In desperation I called upon an imaginary force; I did not know if there was a God, but I prayed for some thing to come to our aid. I do not know why I did it, but I claimed eternal devotion if divine intervention occurred. I was just as senseless and in my terror spoke not a rational word. Suddenly the temper of the room changed from sorrow to fear and reeked of weakness. Shamefully, my laminations did not come from a pure heart motivated by true belief in a higher being, but rather from the pit of my stomach on behalf of a vulnerable vessel. As I dropped to my knees I again took Elizabeth's hands into my own. I asked for God to take my strength and give it to her. By saving her, I'd selfishly save myself. Images of the gypsy man and his slaughtered horse flashed in my mind. I thought about the horrible way the old man died. I could not get the pictures of him sewn in the belly of his horse's gut out of my head, it repeated over and over. I could not make it cease!

I grasped Elizabeth around the waist, shaking her a bit as I had done so many times in the past. I quit only when I heard approaching footsteps outside the door. Someone called to us. Someone questioned whether everything was fine. I smacked Elizabeth's hands, but again I inspired no response. "Not now Elizabeth, damn you, not now! You can crack up later – you must fight away the shock. You must snap out of this," I demanded. I poured a glass of wine and put it to her lips. The liquid pooled in her mouth before dribbling down her chin. "I call upon God or the Devil himself!" I said, not caring which one appeared.

Another knock came upon the door – again, a voice demanding Elizabeth.

"To Hell with us both, is that what you want?" I asked, slamming down the glass. I feared that at any moment Francis would barge through the bedchamber door to find his wife in a terrible state. He'd want an explanation; launch an investigation into matters concerning his wife's activities while visiting Venice. He'd want to know what she'd been exposed to, try to discover the cause of her illness.

Out of sheer frustration, I turned my back on Elizabeth. Without warning, I was struck by a forceful wind that nearly knocked me off my feet. The cutting chill blistered through the room straining my eyes, forcing them shut. I fought my way toward the open window. With all my strength I pried the shutters closed, but the wind was an overpowering opponent winning out over my failed attempts. I lost my balance and my hold on the shutter. It whipped free assaulting the wall, the impact cracking the plaster and sending it sprinkling to the floor. At the same time the stationary from the desk caught in the windfall frenzy. A vase of flowers crashed to the floor, another booming knock upon the door. Someone had heard the crash and the slamming shutters. I called out, claiming a sudden unexpected wind was responsible.

Now I was on my hands and knees chasing blank pages across the floor while Elizabeth remained oblivious. She was a ghostly statue, unaffected by the universe swirling around her. How could she be so incredibly unaware of the wind terrorizing the bedchamber? Just as I was about to capture the last piece of paper skidding crossways, the air went still. Eerily still, as if the wind was imagined. The shutter swayed to a standstill and the drapes settled in their place against the wall. "Jesus and Mary what was that?" I whispered.

The only sound I heard was a deep exhale from Elizabeth's throat. Her constitution began to transform. Color returned in her cheeks and the trembling ceased as her strength restored. I set down the rumpled pages on the desk.

"Are you feeling well?" I asked, giving her my hand. A shock ran from her fingertips to mine, the jolt breaking our embrace, causing me to take a few steps backward.

She smiled. The strange hollowness of her dark irises frightened me. She took a white rose from the mess on the floor and broke the stem before tucking the head of the flower in her bun. It was not the colorless flower, but the manner in which she committed the action that mesmerizes me. I'd studied Elizabeth's movements for years, and I easily recognized that this habit did not belong in her repertoire. It was deliberately formal. Even the choice of flower was unnatural, and how she broke the stem cleanly in a single snap before pinning it precisely in her bun was too fluid of a motion. The attentive Elizabeth I knew was nonchalant, never meticulous in approach. Besides, she never wore flowers in her hair. She thought it was bad taste. She turned away from the mirror giving me a proper view to mock her from.

Again I asked, "How do you feel?" suspecting all was not well. Something was going on, something had changed, and if I had not witnessed it, I would never have believed it true.

"Surprisingly alive, as if I've been reborn," she said.

Every hair stood straight up on my arms. I pointed to the flower.

"Do you like it?" she asked. "I think it is a nice touch."

"You never wear flowers," I reminded.

"Don't I?"

"No, never."

"Well that's a shame. I think it is quite becoming."

Someone was knocking again. This time it was George urging us to come out and greet the party.

"We must go, the count is growing impatient," I said, grabbing a wrap from the chair.

"The Count?" she muttered.

"Yes remember, your husband Count Nadasdy?"

"Ah yes, my husband, he has arrived."

I feared Elizabeth was not completely recovered. I went to the door, but before I unhooked the latch I gave one last glance over my shoulder. It sounds mad, but I believe something for which I cannot provide a reasonable explanation had crossed the threshold of her room. Whatever it was, it had somehow taken possession of Elizabeth while she was in her most vulnerable state. The evidence, I was certain, rested in the soulless eyes annulled of compassion. Those same eyes were now beckoning me to the door and begging me to unleash them onto the world. Whatever I was facing was too powerful to refuse. I had let it out because I was responsible for calling it from beyond, and it had answered my command. How could I deny it? I twisted the knob allowing the double doors to swing ajar. Nicholas motioned for me to tuck a strand of hair behind my ear. I stood aside giving way to Elizabeth for all to view. Francis waited by the hearth. He reached out as if he longed to touch her and spoke her name.

I swear time slowed as Elizabeth passed by me and through the archway. I thought I smelled campfire smoke and heard the cry of an abandoned child lost in the city's labyrinth below. Was there a fire burning? I bowed my head as the trail of her gown slithered from the room. I sniffed the air. I was sure something was burning, I smelled a hint of chard wood, but could not detect from where it came. Fires were dangerous in Venice since one building connected to another. I peeked in the bedchamber, but everything was just how I left it. I wrinkled my nose. No one else seemed to notice and I wondered if anyone else smelled the burning? It was not the wood in the hearth or the wax of a candle, but something unfamiliar, something foreign I could not place.

Draco was talking, but I tuned out the words. George laughed. Oh, that horrid courtly laugh, which I'd grown to tolerate, but disliked. The fakeness was full of theatric folly. Fruzsina, someone said, someone was asking about delightful Fruzsina. My eyes waltzed from one person to another as I took my proper place in the chair. The smell was overwhelming and I nearly choked on the sooty taste stuck in my throat.

Maybe it was I that was going mad, or was it a terrible dream? Perhaps, I was overly tired. Draco rested his hand on my shoulder. The heaviness was too real to be mistaken. He inquired if I was feeling ill. I mentioned the crying child and the smell of fire. It was most disturbing and I asked him to listen to see if he heard the babe whining below. He denied he heard anything except the gentle pattering of a shutter slapping the window in the bedchamber. I explained the shutter had come loose when the bizarre wind tore through the room.

"That can happen when there is a sudden change in current. Sea air is unpredictable, torrent and uncontrollable. In an instant it can whip calm water into a frenzied rage capable of devouring a royal fleet," Francis explained, overhearing my complaint.

I asked how sailors protected themselves from the natural force?

Francis shrugged. "It appears no man has solved the mystery." He further explained that it was still unknown what forces brought on such wraths. Therefore, it was impossible to prevent. "We are helpless and the only thing we can do is pray such tragedies happen sparingly, and that God and Nature are merciful," he said.

Elizabeth gave his words careful consideration before she spoke. "Ah Mercy, she is divine," she stated, her rouged lips curling up into a sinister smile.

***

For several days our methodical tempo wore on. The only discerning trait separating one day from the next was the natural rising and falling of the sun. I wanted to enjoy my reunion with Draco, but Francis made it impossible. He insisted on extending invitations to George and his wife Fruzsina. She cleverly made excuses to be absent, however, this left George alone and unoccupied. With as much grace as I could muster, I endured the company of both beloved gentlemen. George's courtly experience prepared him for the discomfort that ensued. How he managed an unflinching constitution during that formless time remains a mystery. I suppose I should have put my husband's feelings above all else, but I believed his ignorance bliss. I was careful to avoid George when possible and during those times when we found ourselves subject to company, I appeared indifferent even when my stomach knotted and my palms went sweaty.

Francis received an invitation from the Doge requesting our company at an intimate dinner party celebrating the end of another season. It was our last hurrah before Elizabeth and I made the long journey home to Cachtice. Shortly after arriving at the palace, our party was escorted into the grand dining hall where we were seated around a well-crafted cherry wood table. In company were the Englishman, Lord Dorsey and his commonly plain fiancé. Also, Signor Nadossi escorted his daughter Azalea, and George properly joined Fruzsina, thus, leaving Francis, Elizabeth, Draco and me to amuse each other. Of course other notables including King Rudolph were in attendance, but the entire list was too consuming to name.

Everyone was arranged in proper place descending down the table in order of rank from the Doge and King Rudolph to a single empty chair at the very end of the table. I wished to inquiry for whom it had been placed, but thought it rude to do so. I noticed George was seated beside a young widow. Guests in the party hinted to the dismal death of the woman's husband, but no one repeated the incident entirely. The Englishman kindly expressed his sincere bereavement for the loss to society and in return, the widow graciously accepted the courtesy. However, she did this with such coolness that I believed the loss for her was really of little consequence. Perhaps, I even detected relief in her constitution. I surmised the marriage, like all privileged society, was arranged. I wondered if she understood the pleasure the lengthy mourning period could provide. It'd be at least two years before her family could consider another marriage. Liberated from chastity and a ruling hand, if managed delicately, the young widow could take advantage of certain freedoms including the charge of daily dealings and own opinions. My delightful contemplation was broken by the announcement of our final guest. Signor Nadossi stood up drawing all attention to the center of the table.

"My dear friends, our last guest has arrived. I'm so pleased to see our party complete. May I introduce Raphael Petrucci."

Raphael removed his board-rimmed hat and tucked it beneath his arm before bowing. Curious whispers exchanged between ear and mouth of the seated guests.

Finally, it was Fruzsina who boldly spoke out. "Signor Nadossi, pray do tell us how you're acquainted with our delightful guest. I'm sure I speak for everyone when I say, we're most curious."

A parade of servants entered the dining room carrying the first course. They lifted silver doomed lids revealing garnished platters. Exclamations of admiration erupted followed by a wave of eager nods and beckoning utensils. The servants served from the right, taking up from the left, a choreographed routine designed to prevent any embarrassing collisions from taking place. Elizabeth did

120

not acknowledge Raphael. Her indifference was not for shame of him, but for consideration of Francis who was boasting about a recent battle. Despite her appearance, Elizabeth secretly expressed her love by touching the vial tied around her neck. Raphael returned the decree with a similar gesture. It was so subtle hardly anyone noticed. They inconspicuously held the soul of the other while the insensible guests devoured entrée after entrée flouting only to add comment to conversation before cleansing their palates with wine.

"Countess Drugeth, I assure you your question has not been lost in the bustle of this grand meal," Signor Nadossi said, while tucking his napkin in the neck of his shirt. "My honored guest, Raphael Petrucci, is a talented artist. I've long admired his works and have several paintings hanging in my villa. However, I do find it curious you ask, because recently upon visiting my friend's studio I noticed the most exquisite portrait resting on his easel."

"Signor Nadossi, what does this portrait have to do with me?" Fruzsina asked, while looking at the other guests who were intrigued to hear the connection.

I imagine she worried the king had secretly commissioned a painting of his mistress.

George glared at Signor Nadossi. He too was afraid his own affair was about to be revealed.

"When I questioned Raphael about the fine portrait he told me it was a new commission for none other than your dear husband."

I braced myself for humiliation.

"Really, my George commissioned a painting?"

My George, he was not her George at all! I felt my cheeks warm.

Raphael did not appear lively. His features were rather gaunt and sallow with cheekbones pronounced, and lips void of color. I gathered it was from the discomforting invitation, which caused his malady. This was a room of neither equals nor friends, but a group of vultures waiting for an opportune moment to peck him apart, spare Elizabeth, who sat castrate at the other end of the room.

"You are unaware of your husband's dealings?" Signor Nadossi asked.

I hated this man. I wanted to stuff his fat mouth with food to shut him up.

George drained his goblet of wine. In his nervousness he slammed the glass down. The bang drew unwanted attention. In the startled silence George and I connected. I wondered what he had done to offend the doctor. I looked toward Azalea and then back to George. He better not have touched that fragile flower! If he did, I could not save him. I'd have to use all my cunningness to save myself.

"Pardon my clumsiness," George said. "I rather misjudged the distance."

"As I was saying…" Signor Nadossi continued.

"Azalea, I'm curious where is your fine companion this evening. I notice he is absent from our company?" George interrupted.

Signor Nadossi swallowed hard.

I was proud of George. He had switched it up and pounced on the opportunity to divert attention. I really should not have underestimated him. After all, he'd been playing this game all his life.

"Companion Sir?" Azalea asked, dumbly.

Ha! Now she was the one who must brace for humiliation. What a terrible little twist of tag.

"Yes, Lord Barkley, Lord Buckle? Oh drat! I can't recall the gentleman's name. Dear Elizabeth, please help me out. Surely you remember the gentleman?" George asked.

Elizabeth raised her determined chin while at the same time lowering the hand resting on her chest, and with narrowed eyes settled on Signor Nadossi. The mark was set—she was locked on her target. "Lord Buckley, Azalea was in the company of Lord Buckley that evening." She accentuated the name for my benefit knowing how much the pronunciation struck a nerve. However, this time it inspired a smile rather than a grimace.

"Lord Buckley! Well he is a dandy fellow," Francis bellowed. "Kept my Elizabeth company for a time before business called him away. I dare say, I thought Buckley was headed home to England. How'd he end up in Venice?"

Azalea's face was turned so far down that I believed she'd bury it in the linen spread across her lap. Signor Nadossi's joules bobbed as he tripped over a witty response. He was dangling on a hook and Elizabeth let him flop about before casting a net.

"If I may Signor Nadossi," Elizabeth interjected. "The doctor became acquainted with Lord Buckley in Vienna. My old friend happened to mention our names and his time spent at Cachtice. Of course, Signor Nadossi has the highest respect for you, my dear," she added, flattering Francis. "If Buckley was suitable company for a countess, then he should be suitable company for his precious Azalea."

"Indeed!" Francis stated. "A very trustworthy young man, isn't he? Although, I can't condone his, how can I put it delicately, escapades, but a person can overlook it if such a companion makes for a happy wife, or daughter in your case Signor Nadossi."

"Escapades?" Fruzsina asked. No doubt she picked up the scent of a delicious scandal.

Before Francis could explain, Elizabeth cut into the conversation again. Her ability to control the subject was fascinating. "Yes, a fine gentleman Lord Buckley is. I'm so pleased he was able to help you with that nasty bit going down in the Orient."

I eyed George who was quietly observing. "What's this, a nasty bit?" George asked, hungry for a good tale. He was perfectly on cue. He knew he must prod the conversation along in order to keep it away from the topic of his commissioned portrait. Besides, everyone knew since Lord Buckley was not there to defend himself, he was the ideal topic.

"Buckley agreed to leave Venice and the season early in order to assist Signor Nadossi's art dealings. I'm sure the ladies know how desirable the silks from the Orient can be – anyways, Signor Nadossi's buyer was incapable of breaking into the market. It's a very sticky business; he did not have the necessary savvy to secure the order. Buckley mentioned a connection in the Orient and for a small, but worthy commission, he agreed to make the trip on behalf of the doctor. The dealings, I'm sure, will take months. So easy to forget in that length of time, isn't it! By the time Buckley resurfaces I say we will all have but forgotten the errand he was on. Perhaps, Signor Nadossi will send us some silks as a reminder," Elizabeth said.

The ladies at the table nodded anxiously. They were already imagining the brilliant colors and softness on their skin.

"Isn't our society an industrious group!" Francis noted, pleased with his wife's explanation.

"Well, I owe thanks to your wife, Count Nadasdy. It was upon her suggestion that I requested Lord Buckley's assistance in the matter. Even though my precious Azalea suffers from the loss of a fine companion, as she knows, my rule is always business before pleasure. As I recall Countess, you made the suggestion on the night of the grand ball?"

"Your memory serves you well," Elizabeth said. She spooned a dollop of creamed pudding in her mouth.

I wondered if George would like another dip in the canal. It seemed I had won our bet, twice.

"Ah yes, as I also recall our countess made out quite well that evening. I dare say, Count Nadasdy, your wife has a knack for the gaming table. Where most lose fortune, it seems she increases hers," Signor Nadossi chuckled.

For the time being it appeared George and I had safely escaped scrutiny. The conversation was turning further away from the topic of art and to other interests, like the evils of gambling.

"Took the house, did she?" Francis asked.

"I hear gaming is a growing concern," Lord Dorsey's fiancé added.

"Quite the concern among husbands," Fruzsina noted. She was such a snob. "Do you worry?" she asked Francis.

"Never. Elizabeth has her own fortune. She may do with it as she pleases."

"Is that so? Well then, your wife is very lucky!"

Elizabeth smiled at Francis.

"She is fortunate indeed," Signor Nadossi grunted. Being a traditional man, he did not like progress unless it was in the field of science.

"Only if we all could be as fortunate," George included. He raised a glass to himself.

"Lord Dorsey was also very lucky playing the tables that night, isn't that correct Lord Dorsey?" Signor Nadossi included.

Dorsey's fiancé's eyes narrowed. Bringing up his gambling was a touchy subject, one that her father had already been forced to cover several times.

"I was blessed, but only because I had the generous Countess by my side. Earlier in the evening I confess I was down a ludicrous sum, but the Countess assured me my luck would return. She kindly spotted me a bid or two until I made gains."

"How much did you win?" Francis asked.

Dorsey pulled the timepiece from his pocket. "Good Heavens! Is it that time already?"

The Englishman tensed at the bold display of his cherished timepiece. He prayed his wife did not recognize the anniversary gift being fondled by another man's hand.

"Oh I don't recall the exact sum, but it was enough to clear my debt to the house and give me a little something to tuck in my pocket," Lord Dorsey said. He shined the timepiece with his handkerchief before returning to its proper place pinned to his doublet.

"So what did you mean George when you said not everyone was so fortunate. It sounds like everyone has made a capitol gain from the tables," Fruzsina said.

I resented her spiteful tone and secretly wished lightening strike her dead on her way home.

"It seems so," George answered, dully. He was looking at Lord Dorsey.

"Well it pleases me to hear all my friends have made out so well. Being indentured is a nasty business," Francis said, jovially.

I felt sorry for the man. He was completely lost.

Dorsey's smug smile fell and his fiancé shifted uncomfortably in her seat. The Englishman cleared his throat while Signor Nadossi poked at his roasted duck and Draco glared at George who raised his glass of brandy to Raphael at the end of the table. "I propose a toast to our new guest and friend, Raphael," George said, saluting the artist.

"Ah yes, to our talented artist friend," Francis said, joining in.

"That brings me back to portraits. I mentioned to your wife my collection and invited her to view it when she returns to Venice," Signor Nadossi said to Francis.

"That is most kind. You say Raphael paints portraits?"

"I do paint portraits and landscapes," Raphael answered. He finally had something to contribute to the conversation.

"I should commission you to paint my wife."

Elizabeth looked nervously at me, then to George. She had not meant for the conversation to come full circle.

"That is a marvelous idea," I said.

Draco winced as he wiped the crumbs from his mouth.

"Raphael, can you repair fresco?" I asked.

"Yes, but of course."

"I was thinking the grand hall and the foyer at Cachtice are in desperate need of repair."

George smoothed the side of his face and thrust his glass at a passing servant for it to be filled. I believe it was his third draft, but perhaps I'd lost count. Fruzsina tried to force his arm down, but he yanked it free and insisted on more brandy.

"I'm sure a talented artist such as Raphael is too busy to make the long journey to Cachtice," Francis said. He spooned another heap of pickled cabbage on his plate.

"Actually Sir, I'm between commissions. That is, now that I've finished Count Drugeth's painting," Raphael said.

I wanted to kick him. He was such a novice and completely out of his league! I could not believe he mentioned the painting.

But instead of distress, joy was building on Elizabeth's face.

"Would the request be a terrible inconvenience?" Francis asked Elizabeth.

"I do believe we can manage. Besides, the repairs really should be made. I don't think it is too much of a bother."

"Then it's settled. Raphael you shall come to Cachtice to paint the frescos and while you're there paint my lovely wife's portrait."

Raphael nodded enthusiastically agreeing as Elizabeth beamed beside her husband.

I admit I had not seen that coming when Fruzsina first questioned the artist. Of course, she was not going to let the subject completely dissolve and to ensure equality she asked George whether or not she should have her portrait commissioned too. He answered by rolling his eyes, which greatly insulted her.

"Draco, shall we have Amara's portrait painted while Raphael's at it?" Elizabeth asked just to further irritate.

"I do not need a painting to remember my wife's beauty," Draco stated, sharply.

The outburst killed the giddiness in the room. George's eyes dropped to his plate. He was embarrassed by my husband's loaded remark. I did not have to wonder if Draco noticed, because he was staring directly at George when he said it.

"Please excuse my comrade he is a hopeless romantic. I fear such idealism is the curse of a great soldier. However, I can vouch for my friend, if ever there was a man who did not need a token of love, it is he. His passion burns fast and vivid, like no other I've ever seen."

The ladies at the table marveled at Francis's speech. Flirting eyes batted in Draco's direction. Every woman wanted to feel cherished.

Suddenly I was dizzy with guilt.

"If what the Count speaks is true, then I believe Amara is the most fortunate lady at the table. Until now, I believed such men only existed in romantic tales," Fruzsina said. "Wouldn't you agree George, Amara is the richest lady in the room? Is she not the luckiest of us all?"

Oh, how I disliked her and if I could have cut out her tongue, I would have, but instead, I had to sit pretty and endure her false compliments.

"She couldn't be more fortunate if she had the favor of the king," George replied. His comment burned and it brought me much pleasure.

I wanted to applaud his response, but that would have been distasteful.

"I agree with Sir Lorant, I think a real man shouldn't need a silly portrait to inspire love or remind him of a woman's beauty," Fruzsina fought back.

"Well not all of us men are blessed with the ability to conjure passion from thin air. I believe Raphael would agree that art is a method used to evoke emotion, which perhaps goes forgotten or becomes weighted down by monotony. Art is a vital necessity to preserve a healthy mind," George countered.

"Yes, but to have the power to call forth the same emotion by one's own will – plucking it from imagination is truly remarkable," Fruzsina argued. The smile she cast on Draco sickened my stomach.

Draco listened to the couple's argument while everyone else became bored and turned to other conversations.

Finally, Raphael seized an opportunity to comment. "Art is vital not only to provoke emotion, but to express it."

"Art is decorative," Draco said, gruffly. "Nothing more, nothing less – it shouldn't inspire anything more than a drape does hanging on a window."

"Draco!" I exclaimed. I was shocked by his rudeness.

"You do not agree, my wife? Would you prefer when I admire a painting I see only evidence of desire, passion or feeling? Or would you have me seek the real model, visit the earthy landscape and determine for myself what truths are evident?"

"Draco, I…" I stammered. I searched for a witty answer, but nothing came immediately to mind.

"Shall I trust the artist's rendering to be absolute?" he added.

"No, art is not absolute, it is interpretive," Raphael said. "The viewer sees what they want to see. It mirrors for them what they desire to feel, what they hope it speaks."

"It is deceit," Draco said, slamming down a fist upon the table. His words singed and the force with which he struck boomed.

"It is hope," Raphael replied, gently.

"Perhaps George can settle this argument. Does your portrait, the one you've recently commissioned capture hope or deceit?" Draco asked.

George straightened his posture while slowly setting down his empty glass, the movement deliberate and methodical. "My painting is neither hope nor deceit, but loss. Each time I look at it I'm reminded of man's failures and the innocent who suffer because of it."

My heart sunk.

"I do not understand why you would desire such a reminder?" Draco asked.

"Because my husband adores misery, Sir Lorant," Fruzsina said. "Misery is his occupation."

"And I have my lovely wife and father to thank for that," George replied. A servant refilled his drink. The amber gold twinkled in the evening candlelight.

"You've had enough George." She snatched the glass from his hand like a spoiled child grabbing a toy.

"One thing is certain," George said, addressing Draco.

"What is that?"

"You are the kind of man who will never need some imprudent portrait to remind him of anything. I envy you Draco. I truly do."

The Doge's manservant rang a bell indicating to all the guests it was time to retire to the drawing room. Flanked at the Doge's side, King Rudolph crossed the dining hall. Fruzsina's display of admiration for the king caused George to flinch with disgust. As a snub, he offered his arm to the young widow instead of his repulsive wife. Fruzsina ignored the rebuff by falling in line behind the king's infamous courtiers. Draco eyed the procession taking special interest in the Drugeth couple. I was certain he felt pity for them. They were the most miserably married pair I'd ever seen. If left alone in a room too long, I was sure they'd tear each other apart. I did not understand how two people so ill suited for each other were forced to remain together. And, although I hated her with every piece of my being, I also felt a bit sorry for Fruzsina and her own misery. It was not her fault she'd been forced to marry my George. She had not had a say in the matter. Still, I wanted to rip her hair and pull out her nails. I suppose that is what love makes me want to do—it makes me think the unthinkable.

"Well, that does explain his drinking," Draco whispered. "I am sorry for the fool. Imagine sharing your wife with the Holy Emperor. No man can compare, the chore must be excruciating."

"I thought the discovery of his misfortune would please you," I said.

"Even I can't pleasure in that kind of suffering. However, I am curious. Who do you believe is the model for the portrait commissioned by George?"

A trickle of sweat ran down the void between my shoulder blades. "I assume his sorrow comes from loneliness. Maybe Raphael painted a landscape or a sunset over Venice," I suggested. "Something symbolic I imagine."

"Man is not miserable alone. The only thing that can cause such bloody pathetic depression is being tormented by love lost," Draco said.

Draco was managing to do it again. He was trying to discover a way to poke his fingers around my mind fishing for that locked box concealing all my secrets. I held fast to my outward appearance of indifference. The musicians began playing while the guests paired on the dance floor. Draco offered me a seat against the wall where he politely stood guard by my side, his hands clasped behind his back.

George was coming this way. I prayed he'd turn away before reaching our company, but my prayers were unanswered. He came towards us without the slightest hint of hesitation. The drink has given him courage.

"May I have this dance?" he boldly asks me.

Before I could refuse, Draco unsheathed his sword and put the tip to George's throat. "No you may not."

I rose from my chair. "Don't you dare answer for me," I scolded.

George smirked. The expression only enhanced Draco's desire to stick the tip of his broad sword through his windpipe.

"Perhaps you should go ask your own wife for a dance," Draco insisted.

"Oh I would, but she appears to be in the king's favor. Can't compete with that, now can I, old man."

130

"Your tangled web is no concern of mine," Draco fired back.

"You're always so dramatic, Draco. I adore how you play the valiant knight. Relax, my friend. I'm not here to steal your wife, I only wish a dance."

"I do not trust your intentions are so pure," Draco accused.

"Touché! I suppose I deserve the insult, but tonight I assure you they are truly what they seem."

A crowd was gathering.

"Please Draco, it is just a dance," I soothed. I placed my hand on his arm and gently lowered the sword away from George's throat. An irritated red indention remained where the edge pressed the tender skin of George's neck.

"Amara is mine… I swear if you try anything, I will cut you down," Draco threatened.

"Death would be a pleasure compared to the wretchedness I suffer. If I am to die, it will be by no other sword than yours, Draco. Don't you see you've already taken my life! It'd be an act of charity to drain the blood from this hollow corpse and deliver it to the river man," George said, through clenched teeth.

"Never! I will never bequeath charity to an undeserving creature," Draco shouted. He shoved his sword back in the holster. "Dance with your friend, Amara. I shall enjoy witnessing the pain your embrace inflicts. I see your touch will cut deeper than my sword."

George conceded, bowing to Draco. The crowd parted as George and I made our way to the dance floor. I keep my head high and my eyes firmly set as George drew me in. The heat of his hand against my back penetrated through the layers of satin. Nestled between our woven fingers was a note. I realized George had suffered the humiliation in order to deliver it personally to me. He had asked me to dance as a means to slip me a message. It was the only way to ensure a bribed servant or loyal guard did not intercept. I desperately wanted to kiss George, for it was the bravest thing he had ever done.

With the letter pressed between our hands we circled the dance floor. The outline of the carefully folded edges protecting the delicate words hidden inside was the only barrier separating us.

When the music died I closed my eyes for I knew our intimacy was finished. I shivered as George's hand across my back fell away. Our fingers were the last to let go. As his slowly slipped from mine, I clenched the letter. I tucked it in my pocket. George's eyes glistened with a watery glaze as he looked intensely upon my face. He mouthed the words I love you, always. I blinked, forcing away the tears welling in my own eyes preventing any from streaming down my cheeks. My lips could not form the sentiment; they could not speak what my heart felt. With Draco's stare fixed on my expression I knew any claim even if whispered might be understood. As George withdrew, his brows creased. He was anticipating hearing me speak a tender word. I wish I could, but Draco waited. George was holding his breath hoping for my lips to utter something for him to hold to, anything he might take away as we parted company. Oh, the pain my silence caused, it was just the blow Draco wanted to witness delivered, the malicious slaying of a gentleman's heart.

I was horrified by what was taking place, but was powerless to change the outcome. It was not Draco's hand by which George died, but rather by my silence, my sealed lips and cool release of his intimate embrace.

Not soon after, George disappeared through the crowd. He made his way from the hall and out into the streets of Venice where he'd wind through the darkness to his cold apartment. Inside, he'd discover his trunks packed and his travel clothes neatly placed on the bedside chair. I imagine he'd demand a candle remain lit in the window in the event that I should pass by. He would wish for my coming to him one last time, but as the late hours blended to rising light his hopes would sadly fade. Tomorrow he'd return as a courtier, joining King Rudolph's procession to Prague. His wife would be seated in the royal carriage while he dutifully followed taking his rightful place in line. It would be as nothing ever was, except this time I had a letter, a reminder that everything that happened was not imagined. I fingered the folded note crammed in my pocket. Whether I liked it or not, it was real, a terrifically woven web, indeed.

Charlie Courtland

Amour Cast Upon the Fateful Heart

Francis also joined the king's procession toward Prague. However, Draco remained behind. He insisted on escorting us homeward. The overcast sky coupled with low-lying fog dampened the view across the canal toward the mainland. In the distance, Venice was a macabre specter socked in by misty dew. I feared the entire city would be devoured by a sinister westerly wind, but I knew in truth only the fog was vulnerable to such natural acts. The buildings with their strong stone and vivid colors caged in iron railings and draped in vine-laced foliage had triumphed for hundreds of years, resilient to the sea that licked the doorways and drowned the walks. The wind would threaten and churn the waters, but the city would be victorious – she was too beautiful to be otherwise.

Once unloaded from the boat, our trunks were secured. I could hardly believe we were leaving the city and that this chapter of my life was closed forever. I did not want it to be finished, but the season was gone, and it was time to return home. Draco's horse kicked up dust as he waited for us to climb into the interior of the carriage. Nicholas sat beside Elizabeth with his hands folded in his lap, and his cap pulled low to conceal his melancholy expression. I

133

wondered for whom he mourned. Was it Venice, or a young girl he'd grown attached to during his stay? Elizabeth was also quiet. Her eyes vacant glazed pools peering out the window and toward the horizon. The driver snapped the reins and the carriage jolted in that all too familiar fashion causing us to rock in our seats. I noticed Draco was riding off to the right; his tall frame postured on his stallion and his visor masking his face. He was a soldier doing his duty, not a husband touring with his wife. I sighed as I shut the curtain. I longed for privacy and to obscure the view.

After crossing miles of land, I decided to retrieve George's letter from my pocket. The crumbling noise of my unfolding inspired a sideways glance from Nicholas. I was annoying the dismal atmosphere. I apologized for the distraction, but Nicholas assured me an apology was unnecessary. He reached into his own pocket and took out an envelope. I saw his name was delicately scrawled in tiny letters on the cover. I gave him a sympathetic nod of understanding. The tearing of the envelopes startled Elizabeth from her daze. She slipped the drawstring of her purse from her wrist. She also took out a folded piece of paper. The three of us remained silent with our letters in our laps, each of us eager to devour the words printed on the pages, but fearful at the same time for the flooding of despair which would inevitably ensue. Together in that moment we shared secrecy, an understanding and sadness. An intimate trust bonded us within the small space we inhibited.

I unfolded my note first, then Nicholas and Elizabeth followed suit. I looked to each of them before dropping my eyes to read the words, My Dearest Amara. Elizabeth sucked in a deep breath and fumbled in her purse for a handkerchief. She offered it to Nicholas who was desperately trying to hide his own distress. He thanked her, but he had his own. He showed us the corner of a woman's silk handkerchief, which he tightly wound around his hand. Tears had not come to my own eyes, but I had merely read the address, the first line of my letter, My Dearest Amara. As I watched my two friends weep over their letters, I hesitated to continue with the note resting in my lap. I was reluctant to experience the pain I knew the writing would drudge up. It had taken everything I could muster to bottle my feelings and I knew I was on the brink of breaking. I wondered if I was even capable of guarding against emotion and, for a moment, I wished I could go completely numb.

Nicholas blew his nose. His eyes reddened and the corner of his nostrils began to swell. He asked why I had not read my letter and I confessed my reluctance to feel. I was so tired of feeling every twinge; absolutely exhausted. Nothing good could come from these words composed on the paper I held. However, I could not escape them because either way I'd be in torment. Torment of the love I lost, or the love I was bound to abandon. When Nicholas prodded for further explanation I said I did not simply love one man more than the other, but rather differently in my own way, and since my love was divided I could not entirely love either man. Nicholas squinted trying to protect his sore eyes from the light streaming through the curtain. He considered my problem, and then nodded with understanding. He imagined the complexity, and talked of the mystery of the heart. He cursed, saying how love was nothing but suffering in disguise.

"If love is suffering, then why do we crave it?" I asked.

"Because it makes us feel alive. The pain reminds us we are human."

"But there are other ways to feel alive, aren't there?"

Elizabeth smeared a tear from her cheek. "Humans, we are sadistic creatures. Is it pleasure we crave? We crave sin and the punishment is pain. Pleasure does not last, it cannot, but punishment, the pain digs deep and right to the very core of our being. It is ensuring we never forget our sins. It is God's way of evoking remorse. Confess our sins, feel remorse, and all is forgiven."

"But we must forget, because as humans we continue to seek pleasure, even when we know there is a chance of pain," I added.

"We are strong, stubborn creatures," Nicholas said. "I'd gladly endure years of pain for a few hours of ecstasy. I suppose this is the crutch in God's plan."

"I don't understand. Why should we have to suffer at all?" I asked.

"It's God's will. I guess you'll have to ask him," Elizabeth answered.

"You truly believe this is his will?"

Elizabeth folded her letter and tucked it back into her purse. "Go on, Amara. Read your letter," she said, before turning her chin to the window to admire another of God's creations, the country landscape.

"Very well, if it is God's will to torment." I sighed before reading the address once more:

My Dearest Amara,

Weakness devours. It strikes all at once burning fast and flaming out just as quickly. I find it inspires a curious after effect, a kind of tepid calm. Love, I've decided after serious contemplation, is fears opposite. It perseveres beyond all other human feeling. Its shape forms slowly as it burrows deep into the human soul consuming the heart, filling each crevasse and every void with an essence impossible to exorcize. Where other emotions wane, love succeeds as the true compass of an otherwise rational mind. I pity those who have not come to know love, for to live without knowing, it is to live without direction, ambition and passion. It is difficult to imagine such a person exists, but Love's misfortune is everywhere.

Oh my dear, what you must think is a curse is truly a blessing. Love sought your vessel because it is perfection. I cannot speak for another, only myself when I say it is an honor that your heart keeps hold of my soul. I must believe we will never be apart and that you will always be with me for eternity. With each beat, Love, she will smile upon us.

Amara, love me and love Draco as well. I see he has also given you his soul to keep. Jealousy, it rears even as I write this, but my love for you wins over. Draco will protect you; he will keep you safe and succeed where I have failed. He is an upstanding man, a respected man, and although I suffer great pains when I say, there is no better man to share your love.

Now, I will pledge an oath! Although it is not before a sacred stage and ministered by a clergyman, it nevertheless is binding. If you shall call upon me, I will come. If you yearn to hear my voice, I will call. If you long for my arms, I will run to your side to hold you. And if your heart aches, I will search the land for a cure to ease your pain. If you wish for me to stay away, I will obey. This is my pledge, my undying friendship forever. I will not let weakness devour!

With all my heart,

~ G

I read the letter again and again. I thought about God's plan for humanity, love and pain, sin and remorse. The pleasure we seek and the punishment we feel. However, unlike my friends, my eyes remained dry. And, because of this, I begin to question my own humanity. I was shocked that I felt nothing – not pain or pleasure. I tried to shed a tear, but nothing came, not a single drop of sorrow fell.

I drew the curtain. Draco was surveying the countryside. He protected against pirates lying in wait to ambush our envoy, their mission to snatch jewels or take a hostage for which they might extort. Elizabeth was valuable cargo. I, on the other hand, was a pretty accessory easily used before disposed. But, I knew Draco would ensure no harm would come to either of us and for that I was immensely grateful. For that, I loved him.

***

Despite my internal conflict, I'd been granted my wish and remained emotionally numb for a fortnight. I was unable to mourn the loss of my George and this created a restlessness that haunted me night after night. During this time, I often wondered what the future held and contemplated how long Draco would stay at Cachtice. I could not allow myself to be too comfortable, because I knew it was temporary, so instead I neglected sleep. I traced the shadows along the wall and listened to the owls hooting in the trees. Eventually, the day came and with it brought a blandness that was paralyzing.

When Draco greeted each morning, my heart softened just a touch beneath his kind demeanor. The long nights had left me tired and I no longer had the strength to put up a hardened front. There was a crack forming in my exterior, which made me vulnerable. How could I deny those eyes, or ignore the way he saw through me. It was then, that I decided I wanted to feel again, even if it brought with it pain. I had changed my mind and cast a new wish – I no longer wanted to be numb, and just as quickly as I determined this, I felt too much.

"I've missed you," Draco said, the words spoken with true sincerity.

Pressure rose in my chest and I choked back a tear. "I've missed you too," I said. I had missed Draco, more than I realized. What had I done? Why had I sought the company of another? I thought of George's letter and agreed I too was weak. I had let my weakness devour and now I hungered for my husband, even if I did not deserve him.

I noticed the fine lines forming on Draco's face. They added rather than subtracted from his distinguished countenance. He fiddled with the handle of his teacup, the roughness of his leathery skin clashed with the finery of white porcelain. I asked him about the regime and his future plans. He happily informed me of political peace and his desire to stay at Cachtice. I was relieved by the announcement. I realized that I'd been purposefully distancing myself out of fear of being abandoned. I dreaded the dark isolation of the Carpathian Mountains and I hated the idea of him leaving me again even more. However, the words he spoke were penetrating my wall and my spirit lightened. The heaviness I'd been carrying for weeks, dissolved. I allowed myself to believe that I was not going to be alone. I let myself think everything would be serene and happiness was possible. Even the most jilted person could change what was deep in their core, couldn't they? They must...they *must*!

***

Sharing a rug in front of a winter hearth with Draco was inviting and reassured me that our intimacy could be rekindled in the privacy of our chamber. The reservations I'd been experiencing waned and a friendly tingle coursed beneath my skin causing goose bumps to rise on my arms and legs. The peace he promised had finally come and with it brought joy.

The appearance of Nicholas in the doorway interrupted our private reunion.

"What is it?" Draco asked.

"A message has arrived. It is for the countess."

"Has something happened to the royal envoy?" Draco asked, alarmed.

"No Sir, it is a message from Venice."

Nicholas let his eyes wander to mine. Draco picked up on the exchange. "Lady Amara you must see to the countess, she is fixing to leave. She is threatening to return to Venice with or without an escort," Nicholas said.

I hiked up the hem of my skirt and rushed from the room. Nicholas did not trail far behind, his footsteps accompanied by the clanking metal of Draco's boots. When I arrived, I found Elizabeth in a heated fit. Her chambermaid watched helplessly as Elizabeth flew around the room tossing garments into a small travel bag.

"Elizabeth, what is it?" I demanded, grabbing her by the wrists and forcing her to sit on the bed.

She retrieved the message, which was stuffed in her bodice and shoved it at me. It was a brief hand-written message from a doctor in Venice. It stated Raphael had fallen ill and was calling for her. Unsure of Raphael's relationship to the countess, the doctor thought it wise to send word. He feared the patient was taking a turn for the worse and recovery was improbable.

"Is there no mercy," I cried.

Draco rushed to my side.

"A friend of Elizabeth's is terribly ill," I announced.

She grabbed her bag and cloak and headed for the door.

"Where do you think you're going?" Draco asked, upset by her sudden attempt to exit.

"I'm going to Venice," Elizabeth answered.

"Not on your own! It cannot be allowed."

"Well how else shall I go?"

"Now, be reasonable. I'm sure this friend has family. They will send word as to the progression of the illness. Doctor's always speak the worst, but often fevers break and people recover. I've seen it a hundred times in the barracks. Please, you must consider your safety."

"There is no family. I am all he has and I refuse to let him suffer alone. If I can penetrate an enemy camp, I certainly can return to Venice."

She had a point. If any woman was capable, it was Elizabeth.

Draco pleaded to Nicholas for support. I met his demand with a cold stare while Nicholas cowered, bowing his head. Elizabeth made a move toward the door.

"Stop!" Draco yelled. His booming voice made us all jump.

"If we are to do this, we must be calculated." In his customary fashion, he began to pace the floor.

"What do you have in mind?" I asked.

Draco shouted to a guard standing in the hallway. "Send word to Count Nadasdy that I've received a report of pirates in the area. Although I suspect the informant to be unreliable, I've decided the countess's safety is not worth risking. I intend to remove her from the residence until I feel the threat has passed. Tell him I believe it is a necessary precaution." He then rattled off a string of orders sending guards on several errands. Nicholas was to leave immediately on horseback to secure water passage. Draco stuffed Nicholas's pockets with coins to bribe captains, keepers and gondoliers. It was imperative we go undetected; we must remain ghosts while in Venice. Elizabeth embraced Draco sobbing a thank you against his chest.

"Are you certain he is worth all our lives?" he asked.

Elizabeth raised her tear-streaked face. She looked over her shoulder at me.

"Yes, he is," I answered. "Just as you were worth risking our lives for in the enemy camp." This was not a cheap ploy to get our way, but to prove to Draco Elizabeth's love was true. Just like no one would have prevented me from him, he realized we would not be able to stop Elizabeth. All we could do was go along and hope for the best.

Draco placed a cloak around my shoulders. He stood before us. "I will do what I can, but if we come under suspicion I will insist we retreat immediately. I will handle all movements and correspondences, is this understood?"

We agreed. Draco led us down a back stairway and out a side door where a small black carriage with equally drab curtains waited for us.

"Where did this come from?" I asked.

"I made a trade."

"Traded what?" I asked.

"Never mind. Now get in," he said.

The small carriage raced with ease across the countryside. The plain color and bland interior blended with others traveling along the trail. No one suspected it was transporting nobility. We shared rooms at quaint inns, arriving late and departing early. Instead of boarding a large ship at the docks, Nicholas bribed a monger to row us across the canal in the morning when the fog was thickest and settled on the water. Carefully, we made our way masked by natural camouflage, the mist rising from the water and beneath the shroud of dawn.

We huddled under our hoods, which were snuggly tied over our heads. I shook uncontrollably in the brisk air on the upper deck of the fishing vessel. The fog was so dense that we could barely see a few feet in front of the bow. A tiny light appeared in the distance. It was a lantern hanging from a dock signaling through the thick haze we were nearing the shores of Venice. Nicholas called to the fishmonger asking him to avoid the Grand Canal and take the entrance leading through the Rio di Battelo in the Cannaregio District. The route took us into the heart of the Jewish Ghetto where we'd disembark from the boat and make the last leg of the journey on foot. The monger hesitated, he was suspicious of Elizabeth but the extra money rattling in his pocket was enough to turn a blind eye.

Once the ropes were secured, we hurried down the ramp. We followed Nicholas along alleyways bending around corners and over bridges, taking special care to avoid the smelling slop from chamber pots splattered over the stone paths and bumping our noggins on cross beams. Even though I'd spent time exploring the city, I still did not know my way around. We rounded sharp left, went up a set of stairs and down the next and through a tunnel, across a campo before veering down two more alleys, which intersected. It was there that I got my first glance at the familiar. I recognized the doorways and the tiny faded sign rocking over a local shop window.

Nicholas rapped on the door. Through the greasy window lighted candles radiated. Someone inside was on deathwatch. An elderly man with a beard whiting from age appeared from the bedchamber and shuffled toward the door. Elizabeth was anxiously untying her hood and stripping it away from her face.

As the latch released, we heard the man ask, "Who is calling?"

"The Countess Bathory."

The lock slid and the doctor allowed us inside. Elizabeth's cloak fell from her shoulders and landed on the floor.

"Take care Countess, you do not want to become infected," the doctor warned.

I busied about the room, not knowing what to say or how to act. As I nosed about, I noticed George's portrait remained covered on the easel. I prayed Draco's curiosity would not provoke him to lift the dustcover. I was in no mood to explain why I posed for a portrait, not now anyways. I was too tired from the chilling journey to devise a clever explanation.

The doctor carried in a tray of tea, which we graciously accepted. The strong brew bit at my throat and warmed my belly.

"Did you say infectious?" Draco asked. His mind was on disease, not the state of the room.

"I can't be certain," the doctor said. "I can only take precaution."

"Is it a plague?" I shuddered at the thought. Even though I tried to appear relaxed, the stench of illness in the stale air made me uneasy. My muscles tensed with each breath I took. I wanted to cover my nose with a handkerchief just in case the doctor's caution was warranted, but I did not wish to be rude.

"I do not believe it is the plague, but that does not imply whatever has infected your friend is not catching."

"Then what ails Raphael?" Draco asked.

"A wound on his forearm has become infected. I've bled him several times, but the treatment is failing. I regret to say the wound has worsened. Redness streaks his arm and the flesh is sloughing. His fever has spiked. I don't know if he will even recognize the countess, although he does call for her when he is conscious." The doctor sipped his tea. "Is the countess a relative?"

"Yes, distant but recently acquainted during our stay in Venice," I said, nervously.

Draco's face twisted into a skeptical smirk. Fortunately from where the doctor was seated he did not note my husband's menacing expression.

"Can anything else be done?" Nicholas inquired.

The doctor was reluctant. He explained recovery was improbable and suggested we prepare for the worst. I prayed silently giving a last stitch effort to appeal to any and all angels above to intervene. Elizabeth's weeping weighed heavy on my heart. I wanted to ease her pain, but was hopelessly impotent.

It was nearly midnight when I finally mustered the courage to enter Raphael's bedchamber. Inside, Elizabeth was curled beside Raphael's fevered body. In her fragile state she seemed peaceful. "We are retiring for the evening," I whispered. "I've left the address of our room on the side table. I will return first thing in the morning with breakfast. Please send word if you feel the need."

"Thank you," she said, without raising her head. "I will remain with Raphael, if you don't mind."

"Of course, we understand."

I turned down the bedside lantern. Shadows from the cast off light defined Raphael's pale face. Elizabeth rested her head against his shoulder, her arm draped tenderly across his shallow rising chest. Raphael's bandaged arm lay atop the gray woolen blanket. Why had Elizabeth's wound healed and Raphael's injury had not? The cut, the very source from which he'd drawn to express his love was now killing him. I could not take the suffering. I did not understand the cruelty of fortune. I closed the door. Draco was standing near the door holding my cloak.

"I believe the doctor. Raphael is dying," I said. "I can feel Death lurking in that room. I think she feels it, too."

"There is nothing we can do. It is a fatal wound," Draco said, wrapping my shoulders with my cloak. "It's best if he goes quickly."

"It's best if he lives," I said.

"It is not meant to be."

"How can you say that! How can you know what is meant to be or not meant to be? Who decides?" I asked. I was so angry that this was happening.

Draco was confused. "God decides," he said, faithfully.

The cool wet air kissed my cheeks as we walked through the poorly lit alleys toward the boarding house. We entered through the side door making our way up the narrow staircase. Nicholas removed a key from his jacket and turned the knob allowing me to enter the chamber first. The rooms were tiny but clean, and I was relieved to inhale the pleasing air. Nicholas washed his face before settling fully clothed upon the cot in the corner. Draco pulled the curtain shut dividing the room in half and giving us the illusion of privacy. He tugged off his boots and traveling clothes before crawling beneath the thin blanket. I too, washed the day's journey from my face and brushed out my hair. I was about to turn out the lantern and begin tracing the shadows along the wall when Draco drew my hand away.

"Leave it for a moment," he said.

"What is it?" I asked, sensing something was wrong.

"Tell me how Raphael got the wound."

"Why do you think I know?" I asked. A confession even to my husband was a betrayal of Elizabeth's trust. I shifted beneath the covers. My body shuddered as I tried to warm the shock from my flesh. "It is a private matter," I said, sharply. I snuffed out the light hoping the darkness would deter further questioning, but blackness did nothing to prevent him from interrogating.

"I'm inclined to believe there is much I do not know."

"I am the wife of a soldier. I too have the impression there is much I do not know."

"You do realize I've compromised my own loyalty, several times," he said, as if this were beneficial.

The moonlight streamed through the paned window providing a distorted view of the cracked plaster ceiling. I turned on my side. My eyelids were heavy, but I knew I'd have trouble sleeping.

There was a moment of silence before he spoke again. "She will be the death of us," Draco said.

I was fighting to stay in the present, but my mind wandered. I knew what he was saying to be true. I thought Elizabeth might be the death of us, too. Far off I heard him talking, but I did not understand a word because I was lost in my own thoughts. I was drifting away, dancing through the soft shadows parading across the walls. They were reflections of the moonlight upon the water, the bouncing waves carrying the joy and sadness out to sea. I felt detached as if I was floating, but still I clung to my bitterness and anger for rescue. I clung to the mania that never seemed to leave me.

***

The next morning, I awoke to the sound of Nicholas rummaging around behind the curtain. I blinked, trying to focus in the new light. I dressed quickly and joined him in the main room where he was warming water for tea and setting out a few rolls on a tarnished tray.

"Not your customary meal, but it will have to do," he said.

The smell of food roused Draco. I brought him a warm cup in bed. He smoothed back his hair and stretched his arms before carefully taking the saucer from my hand.

"Any word?" he asked, squinting in the brightness streaming through the room.

I told him we'd heard nothing and that I thought it was best if we went immediately to Raphael's house. I did not want to leave Elizabeth alone for too long. I did not completely trust what she might do.

When we arrived, the doctor was already waiting in the main room while Elizabeth kept vigil beside Raphael on his deathbed.

"He has lapses of consciousness, but no improvement," the doctor reported. "It is only a matter of time."

"Does she know?" Draco asked.

The doctor nodded. "However, I do not believe she accepts the prognosis. She clings to the hope he'll recover."

Both Nicholas and I had witnessed Elizabeth's fury, where Draco had not. He was unprepared for the storm which threatened. If Raphael died, Elizabeth would rage. Unable to wait for the inevitable, Nicholas busily moved around the room tending to chores by sorting and packing Raphael's belongings. When everything was as it should be he took to the streets fetching meals and running errands.

Draco and I sat at separate writing spaces scribing letters, his to Francis and mine to George. When Draco left to post the letter to Francis, Nicholas and I worked quickly to crate George's portrait and conceal my letter behind the thin brown paper covering the backside. Before he returned, I wrote a second formal letter stating the conditions of delivery and the fragileness of the wrapping recommending the brown paper be removed before the portrait was hung. Thus, ensuring George would discover my secret correspondence. I prayed it did not go undiscovered like Vlad's letter did to his son.

Despite our best efforts, Draco returned just as Nicholas was carrying the crated portrait out the door. He informed Draco that upon considering the circumstances we thought it wise to ship the painting to the person to whom it was commissioned. If by luck Raphael should recover, he'd need the income. Otherwise, the monies collected could be used, God willing, for a proper funeral. Nicholas swallowed hard, the words choking in his throat. Draco agreed, claiming although we shouldn't think the worst; it was practical to consider the situation and prepare for an unfortunate turn in events. Elizabeth would be incapable of making decisions and he was certain to encourage her to depart from Venice as soon as it could be arranged. His only concern was for her protection.

***

The days that followed provided me with ample hours to reflect. The minutes ticked endlessly away while we waited for news. Elizabeth never wavered from Raphael's bedside. And I worried she'd too fall ill. At night, Draco and I warmed by the hearth in our small room. As usual he sat with his feet fixed firmly on the floor, his jaw poised in a tense fashion while his eyes squinted, examining the dancing flames licking the chimney chute. He said nothing as he drank his red wine. I found his habits irksome, like how he made a simple glass last hours. Even at his most reclined state, I noticed Draco was on guard. He was careful never to overindulge. A characteristic I once admired, but now found terribly dull. During this time we exchanged few words and it was in those long moments of strained silence that I realized the complexity of the two men I'd grown to love and the reason as to why I'd never be able to abandon either of them. Perhaps it was the influence of the imperfect romance of the Roman tales I was reading, or maybe it was feminine weakness. Whatever it was, I was stuck in the middle – in a purgatory caught between my two worlds.

After much thought, I came to the realization that I adored George because he mirrored Bacchus, the God of wine and intoxication, mimicking a character fueled by passionate intensity and compulsion albeit self-deprecating in nature. His effeminate courtly charm and playful seductiveness coupled with an amusing humor and romantic notion inspired a fatal attraction, which I was entirely unable to deflect. On the other hand, Draco held his own charms by resembling the hero Aeneas. His muscular statue was blessed by the sacred bronzing kiss of the sun. His quiet mysterious aloofness was irritatingly irresistible, but easily forgiven with a single heartfelt word spoken with such sincerity that even the cruelest heart was moved. It was in these flashes of epiphanies that Draco's true self revealed, and the image burned for eternity. His unwavering loyalty and devotion provided stability and security that every maiden throughout time longed to possess.

The rattle of a key turning the door lock broke my mediation. Nicholas appeared in the doorway, his face drawn and tired. "Raphael...he has gone to God."

Draco jumped to his feet. He was poised to do battle. "Elizabeth, is she alone?"

"The doctor is taking care over her. I ran most of the way. I must insist Lady Amara go to the countess immediately. She is in a terrible state. I fear the worst," Nicholas said. He was nearly out of breath.

Before Nicholas could deliver the entirety of his message I was already tossing my blanket aside and making a break for the door. Draco gave chase carrying my cloak in his hands. I broke decorum running through the streets toward Raphael's dank studio. I did not bother to knock; rather, I burst into the room to find the doctor racked with nerves. Apparently upon hearing Raphael taking his last gasp of life Elizabeth let out a horrifying scream. The doctor was certain it alerted the neighbors. He informed Draco that Elizabeth refused to believe Raphael was lost.

Undone by the scene, all the doctor could manage was a meek gesture to the bedchamber. "The countess, she refuses to let go."

We hurried into the room. We made several pleas to Elizabeth for her to release the death grip, but our request went unheard. She would not let him go. She could not let go of Raphael. When the sun rose over Venice, Elizabeth remained vigil over her dead lover. Draco watched from afar as she wept. He could not bring himself to pull Elizabeth away. She cried for her lost love and I shed my own tears of anger for the wickedness of God's will. Finally, the doctor got the nerve to whisper something in Draco's ear before leaving the small studio. I waited a few moments after the door closed before I went to Draco's side. I dried my eyes and gathered some composure.

"He asks what is to be done with the body?" Draco said. "What do I tell him?"

I thought it best if we continued the conversation in the front room. Nicholas was there, sitting with his face buried in his hands.

"She is in no condition to make decisions," I said.

"I can arrange for a plot on the island." It was a reasonable suggestion; after all, it was what Venetians did with their dead.

"The island?" All of Venice was an island to me.

"The island of the dead," Nicholas reminded.

I was nauseous. I had a weak stomach in times of distress. I imagined Raphael being dumped and buried amongst the masses of unmarked graves of disease-ridden corpses. "He deserves better," I insisted.

"Let's not forget he is a commoner. I will do my best to ensure he receives a dignified burial," Draco said.

"There is an alternative," Nicholas interrupted.

Neither Draco nor I spoke. We were desperate to hear his idea.

"Perhaps we could call upon Mr. Issachar to assist in the matter?"

I was stunned. I could not believe Nicholas mentioned the man's name.

"Mr. Issachar? Who is this Issachar?" Draco asked. He could tell by my reaction that I was familiar.

"Nicholas should not speak so freely, especially when it is of no concern to him," I scolded.

"Please do not be cross, Lady Amara," Nicholas replied with formality in his voice.

"Amara, I'm waiting for an answer," Draco said, impatiently.

It appeared in moments of stress people often failed to overcome rank. I reprimanded Nicholas and Draco demanded obedience from his wife. It was a circle spiraling out of control and headed for disaster.

"He is an overseer," I answered, reluctantly.

"An overseer of what may I ask?"

"Personal matters."

Draco threw up his arms. My skirting of the issue was grating harshly upon his nerves. However, he could not dispute I'd given an answer, albeit cryptic and not very informative.

"Brenta might provide solace for the departed and the mournful. The countess could visit the grave without scrutiny," Nicholas added. Again, he misspoke.

"Brenta?" Draco asked. "Is this where this Issachar is?"

I held my tongue while I contemplated Nicholas's plan. I was not pleased with his bluntness, but he did have a suggestion that just might work. I considered denying any knowledge, but reconsidered my position. "Brenta might just be the fix," I said, finally. "Providing one thing, that Brenta truly exists."

"You heard with your own ears that it does," Nicholas replied.

I agreed. "But, we've no idea what condition the estate is in."

"I remember the way to Issachar's house. I'll call upon him, explain our urgent circumstance and insist he take us immediately," Nicholas said.

Being a good wife, I looked to Draco for approval. He let out an exhausted sigh. "Since I'm ill informed I can't possibly give my opinion."

"Very well, Nicholas. Go immediately and make the inquiry. We will wait your return before any mention of this is made to Elizabeth."

After several hours Nicholas finally returned to Raphael's bleak studio. It had begun to rain and tiny droplets peppered the shoulders of his cloak. He motioned for Draco and me to join him at the table. He lit a lantern before removing the contents of an envelope and spreading it across the paint-splattered surface.

"What's this?" I asked, examining the fine writing.

"A map to Brenta. Issacher assures me if we follow the route, we will find what we are seeking."

"It doesn't look like a map, at least not a map I've ever seen."

Draco bent closer, his finger carefully tracing the written lines. "It's not a map in the traditional sense, but it does provide direction."

"How are we to follow it?" I glanced at Nicholas. The excitement of another mission surged through my veins. It was mysterious, daring, and best of all, would please my lady.

"Issachar will secure a guide. He is to arrive in the morning."

"When shall we tell Elizabeth?"

Nicholas eyed Draco. He paced across the room. "I think you should decide. If she is to listen to anyone, it is you," he said to me.

This was true. I was the only person Elizabeth trusted. I opened the door to Raphael's bedchamber. I was instantly struck by the stench of sickening, decaying flesh. I gagged and clapped a hand over mouth to prevent myself from tossing my stomach. How could Elizabeth bare the foul smell? It was awful and unnatural. The room was dark and it took a second for my eyes to adjust to the gloomy interior. In the corner chair sat Elizabeth. She was staring at the hollow cheeked corpse lying stiffly on the bed.

"Elizabeth," I said, gently. I braced myself to be whipped by a sharp lash of her tongue, but instead was relieved when met by a feeble whimper. Exhaustion had taken its toll on Elizabeth. She no longer seemed to have the will to fight. Perhaps, she was accepting the terrible circumstance.

"It is time to put Raphael to rest." I took a handkerchief from my pocket and held it to my nose.

"I know, but I keep hoping he'll wake – that he will speak to me one last time, but the longer I sit idle by his bedside the further I sink with despair. I will never hear his voice again, or feel his touch. He is lost to me."

I moved towards her, the floorboards creaking with each careful step. "Nicholas has made a proposal and has asked me to discuss it with you."

Purplish crescent moons bruised the skin beneath her eyes. She was haggard and unkempt.

"We think Raphael should be buried in Brenta. He could rest among the gardens of Vlad's private villa. This way you may visit whenever you like and no one would be the wiser."

"Brenta?" she whispered.

"Mr. Issachar has provided a map and a guide to take us."

Elizabeth moaned.

"Tomorrow then?" I asked.

To my relief, she agreed.

"Will you allow the body to be dressed?"

She buried her face in her hands. "Yes, of course," she murmured.

***

Dressed in black, we waited while Raphael was properly prepared for burial. Two men carried the swathed body from the studio and loaded it onto a boat waiting dockside. The guide Issachar provided sat forward in the prow. The rhythmic cutting of the oars through the water lolled us along as we rode in solemn solitude concealed by our hooded cloaks and turned down brims. The usual rolling waves erupted into choppy caps as we crossed the vast canal toward the gaping mouth of Brenta's mysterious swamplands. A greenish hue reflected from the surface as we snaked further into the unknown territory. The vegetative stalks and dense lilies broke beneath our slicing bow proving we were pressing deeper into an unexplored region. I turned to see if our path was marked, but just as quickly as the foliage had been scored away, it had

151

managed to float back together concealing our trail. A strange bird with a long orange bill squatted on a rotting tree stump, its head craning to one side as our foreign vessel passed by. Hanging vines draping from twisted knobby trees formed a canopy above our heads as we journeyed inward.

"Are you certain this is the way?" I asked, nervously. I swatted away a buzzing insect. Draco slapped the side of his neck. I opened my parasol afraid that something crawly might drop from the lush greens bending above our heads.

"Yes, milady. It is not far now," the guide said.

As we neared a condemned dock I could see the outline of a small figure standing on shore. I recognized the bearded man with curled tresses to be none other than Issachar. He made no other movement, except for a lame attempt at a bow as our guide tied the boat dockside.

"A servant will be along shortly with a cart," Issacher said to the gentlemen lifting Raphael's body from the boat.

"Countess, it is an honor." Issacher gave a hand up taking care to ensure we secured our footing before releasing his grip.

"This is Brenta?" Draco asked, looking around the swampland.

"Yes Sir. This is Brenta," Issachar replied. "Shall we make our way to the villa?"

Approaching from a bend around the tree path was a single horse pulling a cart.

"I'm afraid the ground is too soft, it will not support a carriage."

The undertakers carried Raphael's body and loaded it on the flat cart. Their grunts mingled with the deadening thud of the body hitting the cart bed were disturbing. As I watched the wagon pull away with the two men sitting on the back edge with their legs swinging freely as it rocked, I remembered Laszlo. Both of Elizabeth's lovers were dead. Who'd imagine in our lifetime we'd witness each of them hauled away for burial.

"They will go on ahead. We will walk to where a carriage awaits," Issachar said.

The mossy earth felt like a sponge beneath my boots as we made our way toward a solid path. An open black carriage waited by a hitching post, the driver adorned in dated finery riddled with moth holes.

"Where are we going?" Draco asked, guardedly. Something about this place set him on edge. It was the unknown he did not like. He did not know how to defend the ground upon which he now stood.

The slight hint of apprehension I detected in his voice caused me to also become alert to the situation. "We are going to the private estate of Vlad Tepes," I said as calmly as I could muster.

"The Impaler?" He asked.

I shushed his outburst. "The Prince, you should remember he was a prince. He was a relation," I said, nodding toward Elizabeth.

"But he is long dead and everything he owned confiscated. We are on a fool's errand!"

"Of course he is dead, but not everything was taken. There is an estate that still exists and has been passed to his kin. Trust I am no fool, Draco."

Draco did not say another word.

The gravel path was barely visible beneath the carpet of weeds sprouting between the crushed stone. The old trees lining the way seemed to touch the sky. A particularly ugly one bore a scare caused by a strike of lighting.

"Is severe weather common?" I asked the guide, pointing to the deformity.

"It is temperamental."

"How long has it been since you've visited the estate?" I questioned, as we arrived at a dilapidated iron gate. Two ghoulish mythical stone beasts mounted on the surrounding wall guarded the entrance. Their expanded wings looked as if they'd been frozen mid flight.

"I do not recall, but it has been many years," Issachar said.

A tan skinned woman and a young girl stood on the vast stairway leading to an enormous arched door. I counted the villa to be sixty windows wide and several stories tall. The grounds were overrun with native plants and shrubbery. A stray thorny bloom fought to survive despite the strangling vines wrapping around the stems. The cart carrying Raphael's body was nowhere in sight leaving me to assume it was driven to the stable. Issachar offered his arm to Elizabeth who reluctantly accepted his escort to the entrance where we were introduced to the caretakers, Mrs. Katavia and her daughter Rosalyn.

"This is incredible," Draco said, marveling at the expansive villa.

Despite the skeleton staff employed by the bank, the interior was respectably maintained. Inside, the plastered walls were decorated with frescos of heroic battles and lovingly watched over by heavenly angels that covered the ceilings. The golden flakes adoring the wings were cracked and sparse, but not forgotten. Moreover, it gave the paintings a hint of ancient mastery and added a value that cannot be replicated with restoration.

"Yes, quite," Issachar replied.

"The master must have been a visionary. How someone could look at this land and conceive such a place could be built is, well, fascinating," Draco continued. "Tell me, how are supplies delivered?"

"In the same fashion in which we just were," Issachar explained.

"Incredible!" Draco exclaimed.

"No, Sir. Quite the contrary. As you see with your own eyes," Issachar said, with a wave of his arm.

Our party followed Mrs. Katavia into the grand hall. Here too, the walls were decorated with enormous paintings framed by inlaid ornamental gold and spaced between armored statues. The floors were warmed by thick, sun faded Persian rugs and rich, dark wood.

"Past masters of the estate?" Draco asked, admiring the valor on display.

"No, Sir. None of the descendants ever resided in the villa."

"None of them?"

"The only residents have been those born into servitude such as Mrs. Katavia and her daughter and, of course, myself," Issachar said.

"Remarkable. May I ask what keeps them here and you for that matter when there is no mistress or master?" It was a reasonable question given the isolation of the estate.

"Obligation, loyalty and compensation, I suppose."

"I'm familiar with duty, but serving a dead master seems, well forgive me for saying, but ridiculous."

"I take no offense to your skepticism. Some say, Sir Lorant, that the Vlad Tepes still haunts these parts. He is watching to make sure his hidden treasure is cared for as he intended; that this place is never abandoned or forgotten. Some say, he is waiting for his son to join him in Brenta where they will be safe forever." Issachar shuffled across the floor to the huge window and gently hooked the heavy curtain to let the remaining daylight inside. He did not look at us as he spoke. Rather, he continued to stare out the window. "Servants claim hearing the hooves of his horse echoing over the grounds." He lifted his finger and touched the glass. "A maid was spooked once when she heard a piano playing in the parlor during the middle of the night and Mrs. Katavia alleges hearing doors opening and shutting in closed off areas of the house." He sighed. "I suppose it is fear that also chains them to this place. As you well know, many believe the prince is undead."

"Ghost stories, that is all it is, silly superstitious folklore and mere rumor," Draco said, crossing his legs as he relaxed in the deep velvet comfort of the settee.

Issachar vehemently shook his head. "Oh no, not a ghost. The master may not walk the earth in human form, but some believe he still walks. I assure you, if you spend some time at Brenta you will have a change of heart – everyone does, they are certainly always convinced."

I did not like the topic of this conversation and given the vastness of the room we were in, I suddenly felt vulnerable. I wished for more visitors to take up the space that at first seemed so grand, but now left me feeling exposed. I pressed my side into the rounded arm of the chair.

"You can't mean as a vampire?" Draco scoffed. He was aware of the tales of Vlad the Impaler.

"Ah you are familiar with the legend of Vlad Tepes?"

"Like I said, a superstitious myth contrived to scare the rebels into obedience after his death."

"Yes, a frightening myth indeed," Issachar said, with a wink. "And spoken like a true soldier."

I expected Mrs. Katavia to appear with a pot of tea and a tray of biscuits. It was customary to replenish after a long trip and before retiring to our quarters to get settled. When she entered, she came empty-handed. Instead of serving the party she waited patiently on the outskirt of the room for Issachar to give further instructions.

"I've requested we take tea in the garden," Issacher said, gesturing for us to follow him deeper into the house. Draco unfolded his legs and heaved himself from the settee. I must say I was quick to shoot out of my chair and fast to fall in line as the party made its way through the double doors and into the grand foyer and along an open hall. Portraits of men on horseback spaced between large twisted iron sconces lined the way and every so often there was a wood door. Shut tight, closed up to hide what lay behind or merely to seal off unused rooms. I wondered what was concealed. Was it more airy grand rooms, a dining area or a small study? Perhaps, there was a library with a balcony and sliding ladder. We continued further on following our host until we came to a glass atrium where two enormous doors invited Brenta's guests to enjoy the tiered terrace. I suppose it was beautiful once, when it was filled with exotic plants and marbled statues, iron garden tables and fancy candelabras, but now it was sparse. All that remained was seating for two and a wooden box of fresh herbs. Issacher pushed open the door and stepped aside allowing us to continue to where moss crammed the cracks between the stone slabs of the terrace and blackened statues made gruesome by fungus stood blind to our party. I did not care for their vacant eyes, shadowed by grime. Elizabeth and I bunched closely together as we carefully maneuvered down crumbled steps and across the lawn to a secret walled garden where a large apple tree stood alone in the center.

"The historical archives mention this particular tree was a gift from the Russian Tsar. Mrs. Katavia has informed me it still blooms and produces fruit," Issachar said.

"I am no historian but I am unaware the Tsar and Vlad Tepes were friends," Draco said, amazed. I suppose he said this to challenge Issachar's account of history, but his provocation provoked little reaction from our guide.

"I am not implying the receipt of a gift suggests friendship. Quite the contrary, I believe the Tsar was appealing to the prince in hopes of deflecting any wrath that might be plotted to come his way. Fear, Sir Lorant, is motive enough in times of war to form as you say, a friendship."

Issachar turned his attention to Elizabeth. "If I may, I think this garden will provide a glorious resting place."

Elizabeth took it all in, the stone, mossy statues and stoic fruit-baring tree.

"Oh yes, I can imagine Raphael sitting at his easel painting this wondrous scene at sunrise," I encouraged. And, I could.

Elizabeth stepped forward. "We could have the grounds tended to – perhaps have a rose garden planted in his honor?"

I nodded. I was envisioning the possibilities. A good scrubbing of the stone and some tending and the place would be an oasis.

Issachar took out a piece of parchment and began scribbling notes.

I strolled around viewing the terrace from a variety of vantage points. "It must have a bench near the tree and a hedge for privacy," I added. "That is, if you think it should?" I asked Elizabeth, checking myself.

She had barely spoken a single word all morning. "Raphael would adore this place," she said.

With that small statement and the faintest smile, I was hopeful she'd recover in time from her tragic loss. I smiled at Nicholas. This was indeed a wonderful plan. Issachar excused himself, announcing he needed to tend to dinner arrangements and other preparations for our stay. He encouraged us to take tea and enjoy the scenery before we were shown to our rooms. And, so we did. We drank our tea and ate our biscuits. When there was nothing left, Mrs. Katavia cleared the dishes.

I took Draco's arm while Elizabeth lagged behind with Nicholas. Instead of following us inside, she insisted on touring the grounds before rejoining us in the drawing room. I was pleased she was taking in some fresh air, so I did not fuss. I figured a walk would do her good.

"What do you make of this place?" Draco asked, as we entered the grand hall.

"Whatever do you mean?" I paused before a brilliant painting at the end of the corridor.

"How is it that this house hasn't crumbled to the ground? It's only logical to ask since Vlad Tepes fell from power long ago and his heirs were slain."

I hadn't given it much thought. Then again, everyone knew females were not prone to logic. "Many castles remain," I said, as I admired the elegant portrait of the Prince of Wallachia. The curl of his moustache and the elaborate turban decorated with a band of pearls presented a regal leader. However, the eyes were depicted in the same manner as the painting I'd found in the monastery, two bottomless wells incapable of reflecting. Was this Dracula's power, the key to his legend? Had he somehow learned to mask his emotion, had he become so skilled that not even a talented artist could render an expression? It was fascinating in this setting and adding to the mystique of the place.

"Those castles remain because they are known about and passed on to the next generation. You can't tell me you don't find it odd that servants serve a master that is never to return. Why not take advantage of such freedom and seek other arrangements to work in another household?"

I did not offer an explanation straight away. I was too enchanted with the painting. However, Draco had a point. What reasonable explanation was there for the servants to stay? Then it came me. "Perhaps, the servants are like Penates." Breaking my gaze from the portrait I turned toward Draco. "It is just like the story of Penates," I repeated. The revelation made me feel clever, scholarly in fact, and I was excited that I could apply the knowledge I'd learned from my readings so easily to my situation.

"Oh no, not you too! Please do not offer me more mythology and superstition! You think these servants remain because Vlad Tepes is undead? That like Penates, they are bound for eternity as keepers of the household?"

In my head it had sounded plausible, even logical. "Can you offer another explanation?" I asked. "I believe Mrs. Katavia and her daughter stay because they are waiting for his kin to return and claim what is rightfully theirs."

"And when shall this occur?" Draco asked. It was obvious he thought I was ridiculous.

Ha! I had him. I closed the space between us and squared my posture in direct opposition to his. "The day has come, my dear husband. Today Dracula's kin has returned to Brenta." I smirked, relishing the spoils of winning an argument.

"Elizabeth," Draco muttered. He was dumbstruck and for the first time I saw him doubt his conviction.

That night the rain beat violently against the paned window of our bedchamber. The fire in the hearth did nothing to rid the room of chill. Draco read by harsh candlelight while I brushed my hair at the dressing table. I was fortunate to have my husband's companionship and felt a deep sorrow for Elizabeth who was alone in her bedchamber while her dead lover lay enclosed in a pine box on the stable floor. Tomorrow we'd break fast before joining together beneath the apple tree to witness Raphael's body laid to final rest. A marker with a lovely epitaph was being sculpted and Issachar assured us he'd overseer the arrangement and proper delivery.

After I finished dressing for bed I went to the window to watch the droplets cling to the glass before racing down to the puddle forming on the ledge. Wind whistled through the trees causing the vinery foliage to wave like dancing witches around a sacrificial fire. They were not tall and stoic but rather feminine and graceful, swooning in circles as the wind played with their tresses. I listened for the master's horse, for the sound of thundering hooves pounding over the ground as they fled the homeland to a distance retreat where not even the king's tracker could follow. This villa was a refuge where the great Prince of Wallachia would wait until the day came to reclaim his throne and take back his power. Did his ghost make the journey over and over again in hope of changing fate? I longed to believe in such a story.

I was roused from my thoughts by Draco's cold hand touching the nape of my neck. He beckoned for me to come to bed. We needed a good night's rest for tomorrow would be a long day. I'd need all my strength for Elizabeth and the grueling journey home that would follow the funeral. I took Draco's hand and guided him to bed. I kissed his forehead before blowing out the candle. In the silence of night, my limbs weighted heavy against the feathered mattress as sleep cast a spell. As the rigid tension of the day lifted from my body, I felt as if I could slumber for an eternity in the secret hideaway.

Dandelions in the Garden

1628: Present Day Vienna

I agreed to share a coach with Mrs. Landry and her daughter. It was the third Thursday of the month, the standing date of the Burg Garden Society meeting. This month, the meeting was held at Lady Draska's home, which to her misfortune, teetered on the fringe of suitable society. A slight turn in property value and the Draska's would plunge off a cliff. I pictured the Draska's house splintering to bits at the bottom of a dusty ravine while the plum of society leered from atop, peering down at the tragedy, our faces mournful, some shaking their heads in disbelief, but all wondering to themselves when it would be their turn – when would they plunge in societal rank?

The gonging of the front bell announced the arrival of the Landry's carriage. I slipped on my white gloves and retrieved my cloak from the outstretched hands of my manservant before leaving. The Landry's coach was curbside; the velvet curtain tied back revealing the sagging profile of Mrs. Landry. Once inside, and after exchanging polite niceties I did what any lady would do, I commented on Lady Draska's ill-timed property investment to Mrs. Landry. She in turn expressed sympathy for Lady Draska stating the matter must weigh heavily on the poor woman's mind. She surmised if Lord Draska were a kind husband he'd seek another residence and relieve his wife's nerves. After all, gossip was an occupation of women and even though I found it distasteful, I must follow some of the rules laid forth by civilized life.

Mrs. Landry's daughter sat prettily on the bench seat. She was lovely in a pink chiffon gown, the maidenhood trimmed in petite constructed silk blooms sewn to the band. I assumed the special care and monies invested in the smart attire meant the girl was on the verge of entering society. I inquired if any suitors were being considered to which Mrs. Landry replied her husband had several young men in mind, but no meetings were set. However, in the same breath she said her daughter was planning on attending her first season this summer. They were hopeful she'd become better acquainted with some eligible gentlemen. The girl beamed with anticipation, which saddened my heart. The poor dove had little awareness of the constraints of marriage and the loneliness of domesticity. All she could imagine was twirling gowns, love-struck men and romantic ideals; all of which, through my experience, faded the moment the wedding cake was served and a skirt lifted in the bedchamber. She was not the first maiden to be disillusioned—like gossip, it was a customary tradition of women.

The coach jerked to a lurching halt in front of the Draska mansion. Manicured pommed trees set in clay vases decorated the narrow stoop. As we passed, Mrs. Landry touched the waxy leaves of the pom. She said she thought silk ribbon dressings would improve the arrangement. I mumbled only a strike of a match could improve the display. The contorting twist Mrs. Landry's face took suggested she did not approve of my remark. I countered her cross expression by turning up my chin. It was a snub demonstrating I did not care what she thought. I was merely posturing since I was of higher rank. It was what animals did in nature, and why should I be any different? We are animals, after all.

I thanked the lord that we were not the first to arrive. That would be embarrassing and much too eager appearing. I did not wish to make a bad impression, but then again, I didn't much care. We were shown to the garden where several ladies perched on the stone benches that circled a babbling fountain. There was a sculpture of Cupid poised in the center of the small terrace, which I found gaudy, but befitting of the Draska's knowledge. The decoration implied love bloomed in gardens when, in truth, I believed gardens were a measure of semblance; an artful design representing mathematical perfection and the delicate balance of nature—which, in my experience, had nothing to do with love. Love was always, and most certainly, out of balance.

I looked around taking in all of Vienna's cultivated elite as they assembled, cramming billow to ruffle postured with saucers in hand, and smiles rooted on their rouged faces. As I made my way, I caught a glimpse of a gesturing glove.

"Good afternoon, Kate," I said, taking her hand in mine.

"Oh Lady Lorant! I was so hoping you'd be joining us today."

"Well, this is certainly a refreshing surprise." I thought today would be boring, but the appearance of Kate brightened my spirits.

Lady Draska tapped a silver pin against a china bell decorated with rosebuds, the ceremonial symbol of the garden club. It was befitting. "Welcome ladies. It is time to begin our meeting," she announced in a self-important voice. "Our first order of business, as you well know, is to welcome our new inductees. Now, when I call your name please rise so all our members can applaud your acceptance."

Lady Draska's maid loomed outside the circle with a basket of roses hooked on her arm.

"Mary Landry," Lady Draska called. Together Mrs. Landry and her daughter stood. The maid offered her a bouquet of freshly cut roses tied with a small card attached. It was the sacred oath and rules of the garden club, which we all read, but hardly took seriously.

"Miss Landry is coming out this season," Lady Draska added.

Everyone clapped while craning their necks to get a better look at the shining young lady.

"She is without title," I whispered in Kate's ear.

"How does she come by her money?" Kate asked.

"Her father is an extortionist," I replied.

Kate swallowed hard as she tried to maintain her composure. An underlying fear of being held ransom or traded for a Turkish prisoner undoubtedly inspired the baroness's reaction.

"Oh don't worry, dear. Mr. Landry is an agent for the king. He sets ransoms and takes in a percentage for negotiating the exchange. Unless you make yourself an enemy, you're perfectly safe," I explained.

Kate forced a smile and breathed a sigh.

"The Baroness of Orbova, Kate Jakassich," Lady Draska grandly announced.

The group erupted into applause as Kate stood, the layers of her gown rustling noisily.

"The baroness will also be joining the season. Perhaps she will be obliged to chaperone the lovely Miss Landry to some of the balls?"

"I'd love to. It'd be an honor," Kate said, as she received her bouquet of roses.

I thought it was most rude of Lady Draska to put Kate on the spot. Surely Kate had her own plans for the season; none of which included towing Miss Landry around town. No, I imagined Kate plans involved slipping away from everyone to meet the adorable Count Drugeth. Damn Lady Draska and her lowly manners!

"Lady Pimpledore!" Lady Draska boosted.

A pudgy lady wearing a bright blue turban with a peacock feather pinned to the side wobbled. Her cheeks were like two apples and her chin a ruddy strawberry.

"Oh, good lord, you can't be serious," I muttered low enough so only Kate heard my protest.

"Are you acquainted with Lady Pimpledore?" Kate asked.

"Heavens no. She is a beastly woman."

"Really?"

"Well for one, just look at her. The last time I saw her she was wearing that same ridiculous turban. You should take care to avoid her. She is nothing but a meddling gossip."

Kate's eyes narrowed quizzically as I pursed my lips in disapproval.

"Our last inductee is Lady Berinski," Lady Draska interrupted.

A skinny beak-faced woman wearing a revolting teal gown, ill-fitted around her bosom, acknowledged the gathering.

"A Pole? If things weren't grim enough," I sighed.

"A Pole?" Kate asks.

"That horrid Polish woman is friends with Pimplechin," I pointed out to Kate, with a wave of my hand.

"You mean Pimpledore?" Kate corrected, giggling.

"Yes, yes…that's what I meant."

Kate patted my hand. "I knew this would turn out to be an entertaining day."

"Well I'm glad you're amused, but I find it all very dull. What's the point of belonging to an elite society if they're just going to let any old weed in!"

"Lady Lorant, is there something you'd like to add to the ceremony?" Lady Draska asked, obviously annoyed by my whispering.

"No, Lady Draska. I was just wondering how long it will be until we lunched? I say it is half past noon. I do hope there isn't any trouble in your kitchen."

Lady Draska's smirk waned as she impatiently gestured to her maid. I could tell she was worried her guests were being mistreated by such a delay.

Lady Manning flipped open her fan. "I'm absolutely famished," she said.

One thing I'd learned from Elizabeth was how to turn unwanted attention from myself onto others. It was a craft she mastered.

"Very well then, come, come, let's make our way up the stairs to the shaded terrace where lunch will be served." Lady Draska exhaled, the fatigue of being a hostess already revealing in her speech.

To my dismay, I was boxed between Lady Pimpledore and Lady Manning, while Kate was assigned to sit beside Miss Landry. I figured this must be because of Lady Draska's severe dislike of me. Although I was not favored, my presence at most functions could not be denied. I gathered a strange satisfaction from this knowledge, and therefore, I continued to come and irritate.

Even though the quail eggs were runny and the biscuits charred on the bottom, I admitted the sprig of fresh mint on the orange meringue was a clever touch. As was customary, I made polite conversation, taking special care not to say too little, or too much. I did not trust Lady Pimpledore. I'd heard how freely she spoke of others and did not wish to become a topic of entertainment at her next gossip session. I figured the less she knew, the better, so I deflected a great deal of her prying questions.

After lunch we were excused to roam the grounds at our leisure, choosing to pair off in quaint groups, some discussing recent books, while others compared aliments and advancements in treatment. After escorting Miss Landry to Lady Irving's reading circle, Kate joined me on the terrace. I pushed up my parasol and secured it to the backrest. "Oh Kate, you don't need to keep my company. Wouldn't you prefer discussing the latest writings with the other young ladies?"

"I hardly think it wise to take pity on you. I am cautious for I believe you are much like a swan; graceful with a wicked bite," she teased, settling into a nearby chair.

I arched a brow at her boldness. "Well Kate, it is a pleasure to hear a young lady speak so bluntly."

"John also approves of my manners."

"How is John?" I asked. I was aroused by the informal use of Count Drugeth's name.

"Conflicted, I'm afraid. He is very distressed over the loss of his grandfather."

I was not interested in his mourning. "And how are the two of you?" I pried.

"That too, I'm afraid is a perplexing matter."

Men! Always consumed by their problems. "Being a sod is he?"

Kate paused. "Well...he is still very indecisive."

I was hoping for better news, but I concluded dear Count Drugeth was still struggling with family loyalty. Alas, I thought a man with a sense of duty was such a terrible waste. I was disappointed. Our John was going to bore me today. "Oh, never mind. Let's talk about something else." There was no use in prying further. I knew all too well that John was a sore subject. If he were indeed like his grandfather, he possessed an inherited inability to manage his own affairs.

"Since I'm unfamiliar with most of the ladies, perhaps you could…" Kate began.

I put up a hand to stop her. "I'm not one to gossip."

Kate shifted uncomfortably in her seat. "I apologize. I didn't mean to presume…"

I burst out laughing. "Oh, Kate! You're too easy."

"Lady Lorant, that was very cruel," she scolded.

I pointed to the ladies sitting in the ailment group being led by Lady Draska. "Those ladies are only interested in sickness; the obsession itself is a peculiar aliment. I'd stay clear of that circle unless you wish to spend your days bedridden and probed by a foul doctor who jollies in examining beneath women's skirts."

"How vulgar! Why would any woman desire such an invasion?" Kate asked.

"Because their husband's have moved onto uninhibited or unexplored territories."

Again, Kate gasped which inspired another bout of laughter on my part.

"Lady Manning, she is in that group," Kate noted.

"Oh her husband is the worst. Lord Manning is less than discreet and is periodically spotted emerging from disreputable houses. I'm afraid the only thing Lady Manning truly ails from is a terminal case of embarrassment."

I beckoned for the servant to refresh our drinks.

"I dare say, Lady Lorant, you just might scare me into spinsterhood."

"Every last one of them," I waved toward the intimate circles, "married for title and advancement, cursive reasoning leading to debauchery, intoxication, humiliation and dissatisfaction. If you're not careful my dear, that is exactly where you'll end up."

"Why, Lady Lorant, I do believe you are a hopeless romantic!" Kate laughed.

"Take an old widow's advice and get a lover, my dear Kate. For God's sake marry a lover – but never marry for anything else."

"If given the choice." Her eyes locking in all seriousness with mine, "I will do as you propose."

The intense honesty from which she spoke was familiar. I'd seen it before. It was an essence that spoke through the eyes and came from somewhere deep within a woman's belly. I regretted it was only expressed in the presence of one another and never surfaced in its full glory while in the company of the stronger sex. I detested how many times I'd witnessed this intensity suppressed, caged in the gut, and forced to retreat until another day, perhaps another year. Men might wager they'd seen a woman's scorn, been burned by a hateful glare or taken back by a foreign determination, but I assure none have seen the pure vitality, or experienced a glimpse of the true feminine soul. A silver tray piled with confectionary delights was thrust beneath our noses. It completely interrupted my thoughts.

Kate removed her glove placing it across her lap. She chose a seashell shaped biscuit with a hardened coat of chocolate sauce. "You know what I enjoy even more than this scrumptious delight?" she said. "I'd very much like for you to tell another one of your stories."

I chuckled remembering the last story I entertained the baroness with. "You favor adventure?" I asked.

"Oh yes, I adore a fantastical tale."

"I do believe I've already spoken of my biggest adventure."

"I hardly believe so." Perhaps, she saw something in my eyes as well. "I'm sure you have another story just as exciting."

I changed the subject by commenting again on the pudgy lady's poor taste in elegant attire. However, Kate was too clever. She used my diversion to lure me into an explanation of my dislike for the lady, which inevitably led to just the topic she was hoping to braze.

"You overheard the ladies discussing rumors regarding Countess Bathory?" Kate probed.

"It was quite unsettling. They were discussing an odd funeral ritual which they believed came about because of Elizabeth and her, well, particular habits."

"Please do not take offense, but I've wondered about the rumors myself." She reclined on her lounge.

I nodded, understanding Kate's curiosity. My impulse was to restrain, end the conversation immediately, take leave if need be, but never under any circumstance discuss my mistress casually upon a terrace lounge. However, I'd grown tired of restraint and was losing any hold I had over my own tongue; a condition I suspected was an unpleasant side effect of old age and a softening mind.

Although the sun radiated high in the afternoon sky, Kate was in the dark. She did not know what came before the tale I was about to tell, nor did it much matter. Kate minded not where I chose to begin as long as it led to an adventure. She only wished to get a glimpse into the mystery surrounding the infamous Transylvanian countess. I could hardly blame her. Elizabeth was indeed an extraordinary creature.

I smoothed my skirt, adjusted my parasol to shade my face from the harsh rays and took a small sip of my lemon twist refreshment. "Katelin, Elizabeth's daughter and John's beloved mother was born six months after we returned from Venice," I started. "Two years later in 1593, King Rudolf appointed his brother Matthias, Governor of Austria." I rested my cup in my lap. "At the same time Prince Sigismond crushed the noble cause that was secretly supporting the Turks and married Princess Maria Christina of Habsburg." I sighed. "As you can infer, both events earned him a hefty reward. And, if this wasn't unfortunate enough in the same eventful year and to Elizabeth's dismay, Felix, our manservant passed away during the winter. He suffered from a terrible griping chill that refused to let go. It was sad, very, very sad indeed! Elizabeth was rather fond of her old manservant. He was a quiet, loyal man who went about his business asking for very little and expecting even less. However, she despised politics and any harassment it brought to her door. She gave little effort to follow the shifting in the empire. I believe things might have been different if she'd given a hint of care, but it was the death of Felix that most occupied her thoughts. So many duties went unattended, and of course there was the burden of burial and the hassle of finding a proper replacement."

"Pardon Lady Lorant but I do not see the relation in events," Kate said. She was desperately trying to follow my wandering thoughts.

"Oh there really isn't one. I'm just providing a place in time for which my tale begins."

Kate shaded her eyes. "Then I shall not interrupt again."

"As I was saying, Elizabeth dreaded finding another manservant. Several appeared with impressive references, but it was a man we called Ficzko who was traveling with a band of gypsies that captured Elizabeth's attention. Did I mention he was a dwarf? A short fellow, a man in a child sized body. She loved oddity. I think it made her feel more normal, less strange in the world she was born to live. But, it wasn't just his size that she found amusing. She was also mesmerized by his willingness to endure mistreatment. Everyone knew gypsies were a scrounging band of people, misplaced and untrustworthy. They were the lowliest form of human walking the Earth. I suppose Ficzko's malformation put him on the very bottom of the pile. Nevertheless, he appealed to Elizabeth in a way a puppy delights a child. To tell you the truth, I found his deformity a bit disconcerting, but Elizabeth adored the gypsy dwarf. She thrilled in dressing him in silly courtly costumes. Why the man never made a fuss, is beyond me, but he never complained of humiliation even when audiences chuckled and pointed at the squat man trailing at the hem of Elizabeth's gown. He worshiped her ladyship with eyes of an infant son who sees only an angel rather than a woman. I believe he'd do anything to please her.

It was this desire that aided Ficzko in gaining a reputation. Even though he was only a few feet tall, everyone greatly feared him. Not because of his physical strength but because that little man could squeeze his form into the smallest of spaces. He was Elizabeth's chief informant and was rewarded for each scandalous and often profitable snippet he delivered. She never doubted the validity of the rumor and those who were found to speak ill of the countess were punished severely."

"Punished how?" Kate asked.

"Racked, chained, whipped or..." I trailed off remembering the gore of Elizabeth's workshop chamber.

Kate dangled on my next word. I sucked in catching the menacing words in my throat. I took a sip of my drink. After giving a hard swallow I said, "Perhaps I should skip ahead a few more years. Yes, I believe it was in 1597 when Elizabeth received a letter mentioning Prince Sigismond's intention to concede his throne in promise of being named Duchy of Opole in Silesia. You see Sigismond was losing his scruples. He'd been caught ranting obscenities regarding his forced coupling with a Habsburg, which greatly humiliated the cherished princess. Of course, these rants weren't the cause of his resignation, but rather came about after pressing the physicians who provided advice to his advisors. A flood of reports littered the royal offices stating Sigismond was becoming increasingly mentally unstable. Poor Sigismond, only a few years earlier he'd been deemed a hero and now he was proclaimed a madman. Funny how the wind changes course, isn't it?" Again, I imagined a cliff. I saw all the faces of those who took the fateful plunge from society. I glanced at Lady Draska who was hovering over the ailment circle.

"You do not believe the allegations were true?" Kate asked.

"Oh it isn't for me to judge! History says it is so, so what can a person do?"

"What did Elizabeth do?"

"She sent word insisting any decision be delayed until members of the Bathory family could receive an audience, but it was too late, the concession was done. The news sparked concern within the household causing Francis to return to Cachtice. Shortly after his arrival, I followed Ficzko to a lattice board placed over a small hole in the wall. We listened intently to an argument between Elizabeth and Francis. Their voices echoed in muffled tones beyond the wall. You see, she was nearing 37 years in age and had failed to produce a male heir. With the house of Bathory vulnerable, the absence of a male infant was indeed troublesome and was the source of the couple's distress. After several days of closed doors behind which arguments repeatedly erupted, Elizabeth did the unthinkable – she conceded to the will of Francis and her family."

"What else could she do? I imagine she had no choice," Kate said.

"One evening after Draco and I had returned from a ride along the back acres Ficzko informed us a private dinner had been arranged in our apartment. When I asked about Elizabeth and Francis, Ficzko, with down turned eyes, announced they were not to be disturbed. I thought his delivery a matter of discretion but upon reflection, I believe it was out of jealousy. He hated sharing his ladyship's attention. I later learned that Elizabeth willingly and unprotected submitted to coupling with her husband."

Kate tipped her head to the side as she tried to understand the phrasing 'unprotected,' but I waved it off indicating I'd give no further explanation.

"The chore was a success. I recall Elizabeth and Francis had a male heir, their son Paul," Kate said.

"It was a miracle Elizabeth conceived considering her advanced age. Paul, the true Nadasdy heir was born nine months later. With the swell of Paul's first breath the Bathory fortune changed. In a twist of luck, a final push from King Stephan's armies brought victory. He defeated the Russian Tsar, which resulted in the Bathory family regaining all the power lost by the demise of Sigismond. The noble babe and the defeat of the Tsar swung privilege in favor of the Bathory's, which I imagine greatly displeased the house of Habsburg."

Kate reviewed the events out loud. "Sigismond and Princess Maria provided no heir, but the Habsburg's superceded this inconvenience by placing a member of their own house on the throne from which Sigismond was forced to concede. However, Elizabeth's giving birth to a male heir provided a direct bloodline descendant while at the same time King Stephan crushed Russia gaining territory and, I assume, an army. What a turn of events!"

"Semblance of symmetry," I answered, "Like a garden."

"Or a scale," Kate suggested.

"Oh, but a scale can tip," I pointed out.

"Yes, but harmony is achieved when there is balance," she replied.

"What makes you believe harmony is the goal?"

"Is it not the ultimate achievement of mankind?"

I laughed. "Laminations of poets, my dear! Perhaps, you should join the reading circle after all," I teased.

"I prefer the story telling circle, if you don't mind."

"Of course, as you wish. After Paul was born a few changes arose in the household, including the addition of Dorothea Szantes, a nursemaid employed to serve Countess Anna who was now thirteen years of age. Anna was thrilled to acquire her own service and could barely contain her growing enthusiasm regarding her coming out ceremony at King Rudolph's court.

Rumors were swirling that the king recently employed a mathematician by the name of Tycho Brache along with his young apprentice, Johannes Kepler. It was believed the pair possessed a special powder which some say turned ordinary metal into gold and, to Elizabeth's intrigue, Brache was also rumored to hold the secret to a potion that could restore youthful beauty. Upon hearing this second marvelous wonder, Elizabeth granted Anna's pestering requests to attend the season. Anna was a convenient excuse to breach the court."

"Surely Elizabeth did not need an excuse to attend?" Kate asked.

"Oh, but she did! By this time, King Rudolph despised the very sight of Elizabeth. He'd rather see her dead than dancing at one of his grand balls. Unfortunately, he found himself in a rather shackled position when it came to her daughter Anna. He could not deny his chief commander's eldest daughter the opportunity to seek a noble suitor. By pushing Anna forth, Elizabeth gained access to the royal guests, including Tycho Brache."

"Anna was the key to her entry," Kate added.

"Precisely. All Elizabeth talked about was that damned potion Tycho was rumored to possess. For weeks, no, I think it might have been months Elizabeth worked out a scheme. She'd stop at nothing to get her hands on the youth potion. I was skeptical, but Dorothea urged Elizabeth on by telling her the rumors were true. Elizabeth was inclined to believe Dorothea because she had served at the court of the Queen of France and told us Catherine de Medici went mad trying to get her own hands on the magic dust. Dorothea told us the story of how Queen Catherine sent spies to find Tycho Brache. One night, the mathematician was dragged through the halls of the castle and delivered to the private chambers of Queen Catherine. No one ever saw Tycho, but a tray of food was delivered three times a day to the tower. Dorothea claimed that after a fortnight Catherine's beauty magically began to return. There was no other explanation other than Tycho Brache's magic elixir. However, misfortune struck when Catherine used it all up. Tycho specifically instructed her to apply the cream sparingly, but once Queen Catherine saw the power of the potion she ignored the orders and began using more and more until nothing remained in the small jar. Distraught, she demanded another jar, but Tycho refused stating he did not have the proper ingredients to create the potion. Catherine flew into a rage threatening to kill Tycho, but he was a clever man and struck up a deal. He boasted he could not make more if he were dead. He proposed Catherine give him monies and a horse. He would ride out to collect the secret ingredients and then return to France once everything was retrieved. Desperate for another vial of elixir, Catherine de Medici reluctantly agreed. Tycho, with a pocket full of French gold and a strapping horse, fled the country trailed by his wife and band of children."

"What did the queen do when she found out?"

"Tycho was a brilliant man. He sent word often to Catherine convincing her of his inquires and troubles of obtaining the rare ingredients. When in truth, he was looking for someone equally powerful under which he could seek protection. I do believe this is how he ended up in King Rudolph's court. Once King Rudolph heard Tycho had turned some of King Henry's ordinary metals into gold, well, he granted Tycho, his wife and many children a place and the protection of the court."

"What did the queen do when she found out she'd been tricked?" Kate asked.

"Dorothea said she went mad. All the servants ran for their lives, spreading across the countryside or fleeing the country entirely. She said with each day Catherine did not use the elixir; she grew twice as old until she was gray as a mare and swiveled like a prune. The frightening transformation had the townspeople shouting the Queen of France was a witch. They suspected such, but now most everyone was convinced."

"Was there really such a potion?" Kate gasped.

"Magic potions restoring youthful beauty and turning metal to gold!" I laughed. "If there were do you think I'd look the age I do now my dear?"

Kate frowned. "You hardly look your age!"

"You are most kind, but it is the Vienna air, not a magic elixir which keeps me fair," I said. "Anyways, learning nothing from the lesson told in Dorothea's story, Elizabeth was determined to get the potion. I remember it was that year the mood changed at Cachtice. It wasn't the usual bleak existence despite the forlorn storms whipping at the walls. The interior of the castle, for the first time, was a warm festival of preparation. Gowns were sewn and lessons learned. Each day Anna refined a dance, practiced a song on the pianoforte or mastered a courtly mannerism befitting a lady of her station. Unlike Elizabeth at thirteen, Anna was receptive to the customary ritual practices expected of her. I dare say, darling Anna bloomed beneath the cold winter frost."

"I imagine she was very lovely when she appeared at court for the first time."

"I think she would have been, if we'd ever made it," I replied.

"You don't mean…oh, poor Anna! What happened?"

"Disappointment, that is what always happens," I said. "Before the season commenced, Prince Sigismond was thrust back upon the throne only long enough to announce the setting aside of his wife. Imagine what a blusterous uproar this created for both families! The scales were rocking back and forth as royalty blackmailed each other into taking sides. Then Prince Sigismond delivered another blow, this time hitting the royal house squarely on the chin by renouncing his throne to the Cardinal Andrew Bathory. A decision which soon reversed with the help of Stephen Bocskay, a parasitic opportunist whose chief goal was to ensure Transylvania and other territories remain vassals of the Sultan Muhammad."

"Good Heavens, what a nasty business!" Kate exclaimed. She looked puzzled for a moment then added, "But I thought Prince

Sigismond was an enemy of noble pro-Turks? Why would Bocskay want him on the throne? What advantage could it provide?"

"He was an enemy, but an easily controllable foe. Prince Sigismond was merely a pathetic puppet on a string. Of course, that is another story altogether."

"So King Rudolph's court was nettled in all the fighting?"

"Oh heavens yes! Sides were being taken and young maidens pushed forth and bedded only to be discarded. It was disastrous!"

"Elizabeth thought it best to conceal her scheme for the sake of Anna?" Kate guessed.

"Oh no! It was an entirely separate event which prevented our attendance," I exclaimed.

Kate shook her head in disbelief. She snapped opened her fan as the afternoon sun burned overhead. The garden party was breaking apart as groups dissolved and ladies filtered through the double doors where they graciously thanked Lady Draska for hosting this month's party and traded invitations for meetings and luncheons. Kate shifted restlessly in her seat.

I closed my parasol and finished my refreshment. "It appears the party is coming to an end," I said.

"There are still a few guests." Kate looked around the nearly deserted garden.

"We shouldn't linger, dear."

"Oh, but I so want to hear the rest of the story!" Kate pleaded.

I rose from the lounge while encouraging her to do the same. She followed me into Lady Draska's home where we said our goodbyes. I gushed about the lovely dessert and accepted an invitation to dine in a fortnight. My acceptance caused a rise in Kate, which I met with a slight shrug. What was I to do, refuse? Kate saw our party out to the awaiting carriage. She promised to visit Miss Landry in the coming weeks.

"And when will I meet with you again, Lady Lorant?" Kate asked.

I paused to consider extending an invitation. The early departing of the party saved me from continuing my tale. I could board the carriage and escape the curious eyes of Kate. This was my chance to preserve the tale for another day, or another chapter in the history I was recording, but instead of a wave of relief, I felt a pang of disappointment. "Kate, would you like to have dinner with me this evening?"

"Tonight?"

"I apologize. It is terrible to extend an invitation on such short notice. I just thought perhaps you wanted to hear how the story ends. I don't know about you, but I hate cliff hangers."

"What time shall I arrive?" she said quickly.

"8 o'clock," I said. The footman closed the door.

"Until tonight!" Kate called as the carriage pulled away.

I leaned into the window watching Kate wave farewell from the sidewalk.

Mrs. Landry slapped her daughter's leg with a yelp of delight. "How fortunate to meet a fine lady like the baroness! Imagine the introductions, not to mention the invitations! Tell me Lady Lorant, who are the baroness's eligible suitors?"

"I'm unaware of any except for one," I answered.

"And who might he be?"

"Count Jonathan Drugeth."

"Oh my. A count!" Mrs. Landry salivated. "See Mary, an attachment to the baroness will only benefit, you shall rise and so on."

The only thing that was going to rise on Mary was her skirt. "But, eventually one will fall," I muttered, "Or if blessed, merely wilt away."

"Don't be silly Lady Lorant! Can't you see your pessimism frightens my dear Mary?"

I apologized. An acquaintance with Kate was advantageous and in truth, could only improve Mary's position. I asked if this was what she wished.

"Of course it is what she wishes," Mrs. Landry sneered.

Mary's petite frame rocked back and forth in the seat as we turned the corner onto Spiegel St. toward Lobkowitz Square. Her natural smile was replaced by a feigned expression as my words burrowed into her mind. Until now, it had been precisely what she wished.

"Pardon, Lady Lorant, but what do you mean by fall?"

My choice of words apparently caused Mary, and now her doting mother, distress.

"She means nothing, dear," Mrs. Landry hissed.

I thanked the Landry's for the ride. Poor Mrs. Landry was worked into a fit. She was probably wondering how she'd exorcize my harsh words from the infected Miss Mary. Perhaps a smart new gown or an elegant jewel bought with money extorted from an affluent Turkish family would clear the dark clouds looming over her thoughts and the words I so callously planted there.

Upon entering my townhouse, I informed the maid I was expecting a dinner guest. The announcement sent the robust woman skittering through the house. Passing by the front window I spied the kitchen apprentice racing down the street carrying an empty basket over her arm. Market was closing soon and she'd have to hurry to acquire the necessary ingredients for tonight's meal. As she jotted down my orders the cook grumbled that she already had dinner prepared and now it would go to waste. I instructed if the meal could not be preserved, then the servants should dine on it. My kindness delighted the cook. Suddenly, she was more obliged to prepare a wondrous meal for my guest. She rattled off a choice of courses, which I mulled over for a few minutes before announcing my selection.

I retired to the drawing room for a spot of tea while I sorted through the daily post. As I shooed Ferocious from the sofa I crumpled my nose at the patch of hair left behind covering the cushion. I rang the bell for the maid. When she appeared in the doorway, I pointed to the trail of hair clinging to the cushion. The maid worked vigorously trying to pluck each thin piece, a tedious task, which I found unnerving to watch. I demanded the cat be kept off the furniture and only allowed to nap in the cat bed placed on the window seat. The maid assured the order be carried out, but kindly reminded me that it was spring and domesticated animals tended to shed their underlying layer of fur.

"What does Ferocious need an underlying of fur for?" I asked. "He lives in a house, not in the wild."

"When God created the creature, he did not intend for it to live in a house, milady," the maid said, picking the last tiny hairs from the velvet cushion.

Ferocious mewed as he kneaded the feathered bed on the window bench.

"God may not have intended it, but Ferocious seems to enjoy the adaptation," I laughed watching the overweight beast settle into the pillow.

"Yes, indeed," the maid said, giving a curtsey before taking leave.

About an hour passed before I saw the kitchen apprentice hurrying once again past the window, this time heading in the direction of the servant's entrance with her basket filled with fresh greens and fruits. Not long after, sweet smells floated down the halls pricking my senses and warming the atmosphere of the cool room. I took note of the time and decided I should retire to my chambers to freshen my appearance for my dinner guest. I did not intend to appear terribly formal, but thought it a good idea to make myself presentable.

After dressing, I went down the hall to my writing room. Inside, shoved against the wall, was an old cherry wood bureau, the edges carved and inlaid with tiny leaves of golden flakes and the initials AL branded into the top drawer. I took out a box and placed it on my writing table. It had been years since I thought about the keepsakes, but my meeting with Kate jarred the memory and sparked an interest in the contents of the little case. Inside was a tattered collar with an engraved charm lying beside a small portrait. I held the collar in my hands, my fingers running over the frayed imperfections and tarnished charm. I closed my eyes as a piercing twinge forced me to clench my stomach. A pain squeezed at my heart, the strangle hold taking my breath for a moment and sending a well of tears into my eyes. I returned the collar to the case and shut the lid. I sucked in a deep breath. I must regain my composure. This was no time for sentimentality. I had a guest arriving soon. I looked around the room. Different things began jumping out at me. Each conjuring a memory, but none so dear as the item stored in the case I now held in my hands.

The Dinner Guest

Later That Evening...

The bells of St. Augustine tolled eight times. I closed the door to the writing room and made my way downstairs. The doorbell gonged just as my foot touched the landing. The deep, resonating sound announced the arrival of my dinner guest. She was precisely on time. I gave the maid the case and told her to take it to the drawing room. For a moment, I thought about calling her back. I was having second thoughts about sharing the intimate contents of the box with Kate. Perhaps, it was wiser to return the box to the recesses of the bureau draw. However, something stirred within; something was spurring a desire to attach myself to Kate. Maybe it stemmed from never having children of my own, from not having a daughter to whom I'd offer advice or pass on the wisdoms I learned throughout my life. My cheeks flushed thinking of what a foolish old woman I was becoming. Was Kate merely a surrogate for what I failed to produce? My manservant unlatched the door and swung it open. There stood Kate huddled beneath an umbrella with her collar pulled around her face to block the wind from chaffing. The vision of her framed in the doorway aroused a response. No, Kate was not a surrogate. Elizabeth's daughters had filled the barren void. I believed my growing fondness for Kate aspired from a strange familiarity I saw in her posturing and a relation in the reflection of her eyes which spoke directing to my heart. She hurried inside. Beads of water dripped from her umbrella. She thrust the soggy mess into my manservant's outstretched hand.

"Heavens, when did the weather change?" I asked, peering through the door before it closed.

"It took a turn for the worse about an hour ago."

I thought it strange I hadn't noticed. "What evil carries this in for the evening?"

"I've no idea, Lady Lorant. It is quite mysterious. It came on so suddenly. I feared it'd keep me from arriving on time. My driver maneuvered excellently through the ruts pocking the streets.

That was how nature was, tranquil one moment and turbulent the next. "Come in, dear. Dinner shall be ready soon."

The wind whistled through the cracks in the windowsills as the maid stoked the hearth. The fiery blaze illuminated the creamy swirls traced in bronze flecks around the mantle and ceiling. Kate removed her gloves, placing them on the table beside the sofa arm. Her eyes wandered around the room examining every trinket properly displayed for the observations of curious guests. I was amused nothing particular captured her attention. I let the silence linger while she settled herself on the sofa.

"You spend a great deal of time in this room," she noted.

"What makes you think so?" I asked, taking up a saucer of tea.

"The room is well lived in and the décor is eclectic rather than fashionable. I imagine each piece a cherished acquisition which was hand selected and most likely imported to this residence."

Perhaps I was mistaken. She did have a keen eye, which I found intriguing. "Imported?" I asked.

"This is not Vienna," she said, waving her hand in a circle referring to the room. "Foreign. Definitely a foreign air."

I cocked my head to the side, "Certainly you're aware I'm not originally from Vienna?"

"Of course," she said taking a sip of tea. She shuttered as the warm liquid pushed away the cold chill. "From where did you acquire the pieces?"

"Not I," I said.

"Elizabeth?" she asked.

"Yes, Elizabeth," I smiled.

The mention of my mistress compelled Kate to rise from her seat and move to a small vase balanced on the mantle. "Curious piece. I can't seem to place the origin," she said examining the vase.

"Russian," I said.

Kate turned, her eyes wide.

"A gift from the King of Poland," I said.

"Ah, and this?" she asked, pointing to a bronze horse sculpture.

"Constantinople, I believe."

Kate looked down at her feet. The tips of her satin brocade shoes were still blotchy from splashes of rain.

"Turkish. Taken from a private chamber in the sultan's court," I said.

"Taken by whom?" She twisted her toe over the rug.

"Francis, if memory serves."

"He stole from the sultan?" she asked, stunned.

"That does sound romantic, but more likely, he bartered."

The maid returned. Her presence indicated dinner was set in the dining room. Kate seemed disappointed by the announcement, the corners of her mouth drawing to a faint pout.

"The dining room is a bit chilly this evening, would you mind terribly if I request dinner be served here, by the hearth?"

"I certainly would not object. I think it is a fabulous idea," Kate exclaimed, the smile returning to her face.

She moved around the room, her hand running over objects of interest. She paused occasionally to ask from where an item came and then moved on to the next until she settled on the small wooden box I'd retrieved from the bureau in my writing room. "This seems out of place."

"I wondered if you'd notice. Please, bring it here."

As Kate handed me the box, more servants entered carrying two trays of warmed platters. I motioned for her to join me at the table now conveniently set for a party of two. The maid lifted the domed lids releasing a sweet smell of candied meats into the air.

"Umm. This smells delicious." She took up a fork.

I spread a linen cloth over my lap. "I hope you enjoy roast duck with plum sauce."

Kate took several generous bites before kindly reminding me about the box.

"Ah, yes. The box. The contents go along with the tale I'd like to tell you tonight." I ran my fingers over the carved lid.

"I must confess, the suspense has been killing me all afternoon."

"Well then, perhaps I should not keep your nerves waiting a single moment longer," I laughed. Although I didn't seem to have much of an appetite these days, I took a few bites of my dinner so Kate wouldn't feel as if she had an audience rather than a dinner companion. "Now, where did I leave off?" My memory was not as sharp as it once was. Oh, sure. I could recall details that happened long ago, but I had trouble remembering simple mundane events from the present day. I spooned plum sauce over a piece of stringy meat.

"You were about to tell me what prevented Elizabeth from taking Anna to King Rudolph's court," Kate politely reminded.

I nodded. "Ah, to have a young mind. What followed was a terrible circumstance, which I'm afraid was orchestrated on my account."

"You? What did you do?" she asked.

"I'll get to that in a moment," I said, offering Kate a warm roll and whipped cream. "First, as I was saying this morning, Paul, the true Nadasdy heir was born. Winter arrived at Cachtice and with it came Francis and Draco. Although I was pleased by the birth of a baby boy, I believe Draco sensed a hidden sorrow which I'd grown accustom to concealing and, quite frankly, did not detect myself. As you know, women have a way of dismissing unpleasant feelings, so much so that even our own selves cannot realize their existence."

Caught with a mouth full of food, Kate nodded sympathetically.

"Draco had the natural ability to sense my troubled soul. Of course when confronted, I denied any unhappiness, but the pained smile he shed always suggested he did not fully believe my protests to the contrary. You see, it was determined I'd never have children of my own. I tried to find joy in being a godmother and faithfully visited the nursery daily. Once, I caught Draco spying on me holding baby Paul. At first, I thought his sad expression was from the realization he'd never have his own son, but later I learned he was concerned for my happiness. He was always and forever the guardian of my heart."

Kate swallowed. "It must have been very difficult."

"At times, but let's not dwell on the issue. You came to hear a tale of adventure, not a lament of sorrow. However, the details I speak of do serve a purpose. During his retreat to Cachtice, Draco often led hunting parties into the woods in search of game," I continued. "He was a superb tracker and a good shot. When other noble families dined on roots and boiled potatoes, we ate heartily on smoked venison and rabbit stews.

"I remember one winter day there was a violent storm blowing. The snow created a white curtain over the land shielding the forest from visibility and dressed the castle in a veil of ice. Sleet pelted the wooden shutters and the eaves frosted with icicles. It would have been a beautiful sight if it weren't for the torrent winds frightening the horses in the stables. That night, we were roused by a knock upon the door. A servant demanded Draco come quickly to the stables to aid in calming the stallions, which he reported were thrashing about and in jeopardy of hurting themselves. However, before Draco could reach the barn, a horse broke from the stall and ran into the woods. I urged Draco not to give chase, but he did not heed. Draped in layers of thick furs, he mounted his own horse and pursued the stray stallion. I swear in a mere breath that horse disappeared into the forest. The snow was falling so hard that the tracks were filling quicker than Draco could track, but he refused to give up and allow the horse to freeze to death. Unable to tolerate the piercing cold, I retreated back to the castle. I sat, waiting all night beside the hearth, listening to the icy blizzard raging outside and praying Draco would return safely.

I must have drifted off, because I awoke to the sound of Draco shedding the layers of furs by the fire while the bedchamber maid tended to pieces of his frozen hair with a warm bucket of water and a rag. He winced with pain as the tingling returned to his numb, red hands and feet. I bolted upright throwing off my blanket. I threw my arms around his neck peppering his cheeks with kisses. It was silly to be so concerned. He was a man who'd survived battles, but for some reason I feared he would not survive that winter storm. After returning my loving affection, he began to laugh, his deep resonating chuckle bringing a smile to my face. Once I was convinced he was unharmed, I inquired about the horse which he informed was also being doused in warm water in the stables. I scolded Draco for always being the hero and that one day he just might not return; the very thought sending an awful twinge to my already anxious heart. He assured me this would never be the case, joking about the legendary myth that he was an immortal warrior, a true descendant of the Gods. I let him know I knew better and would not stand for silly heroic antics. Before I could rant another word, Draco put his fingertips to my lips hushing me.

"I've something for you," Draco said, the softness of his voice soothing my nagging.

My attention was drawn to the maid tending to something swaddled in a fur wrap.

"My heroics saved two lives tonight," Draco said. He asked the maid to bring him the swaddling.

All I could do was stare.

"I've seen your sadness, although you attempt to hide it from me," he said. He gently unwrapped the bundle. "It is an orphan in desperate need of a mother."

I looked down at the tiny creature sleeping in Draco's arms. "How do you know it is an orphan?" I choked.

"I found the mother close by, frozen to death, her paw wedged between a rock. The injury was severe. It appears she lost a great deal of blood and likely lost consciousness and died."

I sat in a chair near the hearth and held out my arms into which Draco placed the infant wolf. I stroked the damp fur between its ears. It let out a deep sigh, gave a slight shiver and moaned before nuzzling its head against my chest.

"He will make a fierce companion. He will love, protect and comfort you. He belongs to you and you to him now."

Draco bent down and kissed me on the forehead before also kissing the small fuzzy creature as well.

"What shall you name him?" he asked, taking a step back.

"Lykaios. *Lyk,* for short. It is Greek, meaning from wolf."

Draco grinned approving of my choice in names for our new addition.

I sat up all night rocking Lyk in front of the fire. I ordered fresh milk delivered for his breakfast and as he regained strength and a set of sharp teeth, I included pieces of meats and fish to his diet. Although Lyk loved playing with Elizabeth's children, he was rarely far from my heels. The hems of all my skirts had tiny tears from where Lyk latched on tugging and twisting the fabric as he warred with the irresistible swishes of my dresses. Elizabeth often scolded me for allowing the beast to destroy my finery, but I found the play amusing and continued to allow my pet to play at my hems.

"You raised a wolf!" Kate exclaimed.

"As my own," I said, placing the domed lid over my empty plate. I waved for the maid to clear the trays.

"Weren't you afraid?" she asked.

"Of Lykaios? Oh, never! He grew up just as Draco predicted, into a fiercely protective and loyal companion. I trusted Lyk above all others. He was," I hesitated for a moment.

"He was what?" Kate prodded.

"I loved him very much," I said, folding my napkin and setting it on the table. "As I was saying, everywhere I went, Lyk went. When spring arrived, Draco and Francis were called away to tend to courtly business and political unrest, which inevitably always seemed to occur over the long winter months. Anna and Elizabeth were busy making arrangements for the season and tending to the daily orders of Cachtice.

One day after having all I could take of talk of lace and dress, I decided to go riding; an activity I often did when I felt the strangling concern of feminine duty. Unfortunately, Lyk had behaved badly the previous night. Truly, it was my own fault because I failed to latch my bedchamber door properly. The error allowed him to nudge it open and sneak out into the castle. From there, he managed to escape into the courtyard and eventually found the hen house. Understandably, it was in his nature to kill a hen. Nevertheless, it was an egg producing hen and the tragedy could not go unpunished. With a heavy heart I caged Lyk in his pen for the day and set out alone. As I rode over the crest I heard his cries, a symphony of shameful howls. My heart sank in my chest. I knew how sad he was, but he'd been wrong to kill the hen and needed to learn a lesson for breaking the house rules."

The maid poured Kate a glass of wine. I opened the carved wooden box and pulled out the frayed collar and tiny painting no larger than a hand mirror. The rest of the items I left concealed snuggly in the satin lining.

"This is his collar and a painting of Lyk in the garden at Cachtice," I said, presenting the items to Kate for her to admire.

"It must have driven you half mad to leave him behind." She handled the cherished pieces with great care as she gazed at the picture.

"Oh it did! I often wondered what would have happened if I'd only allowed him to accompany me that day."

Kate gave me back my token memories. "What did happen?"

"I rode out over the crest and down the hillside and into the woods like I'd done a thousand times before. There was a spring stream that I enjoyed wading in near the edge of the forest. I tied off my horse and moseyed down the beach shore. I waded in up to my knees in the cool water while inspecting the bottom for glittery stones. I should have known better, I'd once before been caught off guard while doing the very same silly exploration. While collecting several stones, I suddenly felt overcome with the strangest sensation I was being watched. I stood still, my ears listening carefully for the slightest noise when I heard the sound of male voices coming from somewhere in the woods. I knew better than to run; instead, I turned around and began to wade upstream to where my horse was tethered. The cracking of branches startled me to pick up my pace. I pushed through the water lifting my skirt as I splashed toward the shore. The foreign voices grew louder and were approaching quickly from behind. I looked over my shoulder to see a band of Turks closing in. Instinct propelled me to run, my toes digging hard into the beach as I tried desperately to prevent my bare feet from slipping in the sand. My wet skirts slapped against my legs as I scrambled toward my horse. The Turks were shouting and laughing. A few dropped off giving up the pursuit, but two men continued to chase me. One was gaining on me, and I feared I would not reach my horse in time. My pulse raced and I recall trying to scream but nothing came out," I said. I rubbed my neck remembering the painful strain of a scream stuck in the throat. "In my haste, I tripped, stumbling a few feet before hitting the sand hard," I continued. "Then I felt a man's hand snatch at my ankle and take hold of my skirt and tearing the lacing around the hem."

"Oh my!" Kate gasped.

"I fought to scramble to my feet, but the Turk was on me. I rolled and tangled with him, throwing him to the side and refusing to allow him to pin me to the ground. I kicked and gouged while hurling curses and threats. He ordered for another man to help, but once he recognized the noble colors displayed from the reins of my horse he backed away yelling something to his comrades. They did not come any closer, but they also did not immediately retreat. Instead, they watched as I wrestled with the nasty Turk. Despite my violent efforts, the man won out and eventually I was pinned to the ground. He and the other man exchanged several more words as I laid there praying my attacker would be convinced to flee, but it was the other man who abandoned the scene leaving me alone with the heaving Turk, his eyes filled with lust and hate. When he tried to kiss me, I whipped my head to the side avoiding the revolting advance and that's when I saw the leader sitting high on horseback down shore. The commander shouted out something, which must have been amusing because it caused the group to erupt into laughter. Again, I thrashed beneath the man giving him no option but to tighten his grip on my arms. The pinching pains caused my body to tense and my back to arch. The Turk turned me over shoving my arms beneath the weight of my own body and pushing my cheek in the sand. Grains stuck to my lips and my face as tears poured from my eyes. I'll never forget what he whispered in my ear as his dirty brown hands fished beneath my skirts, he said, 'Commander says I can have you, if I make it quick.'

"I knew it was probably futile, but again, I kicked and squirmed. I remained determined to free myself from the bastard's hold. I struggled to retrieve the dagger I always carried from the secret pocket sewn below my bodice. I spit sand from my mouth as I scrapped to grasp the ivory handle. I let out a scream when I felt the sensation of the Turks fingers meeting with my exposed sex. With his other hand he fumbled to free himself from his trousers. I hesitated, my hand on the handle of my knife. When he lifted his weight to pull down his clothing, I thrashed with all my might throwing him off balance and to the side. I rolled out from under him and liberated the dagger from my pocket which was torn open in the struggle. The Turk cursed, as he lurched forward at me, one hand making an effort to regain his hold. I let him, knowing the moment he reeled me in, I'd stab my dagger into his body," I said. I jabbed at the air as if the ghost of the Turk was standing in the room.

A flash of lightening lit up the room, a boom of thunder rattled the windowpane. Kate jumped in her seat. She let out a nervous laugh as she settled back into her chair. She smoothed out her skirt as if she were brushing bothersome crumbs from the folds.

"Oh I don't think I could have planned that stroke of lightening any better," I laughed. "Are you all right?"

"Oh yes, just a bit startled by the storm. I say, it sounds like the worst of it is just outside the window."

"Yes it does seem so. Hardly anytime lapsed between the flash and the boom," I noted.

"Never mind me. I'm afraid I've always been a little frightened by storms. Please continue with the story. Tell me, did you stab the Turk?" she asked, wide-eyed.

"Just as I hoped, he reeled at me. He was heaving, short of breath, and cross with frustration. The moment he pushed my thighs apart with his knee, I drove my dagger into his groin. I pushed it deep letting him suffer the pain of being penetrated by something foreign. Then, I yanked it out just as violently as I had thrust it in! He toppled backwards, his trousers soaking with blood from the wound. I did not hesitate. I scrambled to my feet making a mad dash for my snorting horse still tethered to the tree. The wounded Turk's scream mingled with the shouting orders of his commander and troop members." I closed my eyes recalling the sounds, letting them rush up from the recesses of my memory. "They were an invasion of natural noise, a cracking and thundering, like hooves pounding against the earth in numbers greater than the mind can imagine," I continued. My eyes opened to find Kate sitting rather still, her own eyes moistened with consternation.

"I mounted my horse and rode fast ripping through trails and over the hillcrest toward Cachtice. The band of men pursued, but halted at the break where Cachtice was visible on the horizon. I shouted for the gate to be drawn, never slowing my pace until I was safely inside the protective walls. Guards rushed from every corner of the castle to greet my skidding abrupt entry in the courtyard. The very sight of my torn and bloody attire inspired gasps to escape from their otherwise constrained mouths. I dismounted, thrusting the reins of my horse into the stable boy's waiting hands. Nicholas, a friend and trusted guard, approached from just beyond the courtyard with his hand ready to draw on the hilt of his broad sword. He demanded a recount of the entire ordeal, which I gave him in explicit detail. My recantation caused some of the men to squirm, their eyes shifting toward the ground as if the Turk's act disgraced all mankind. Nicholas insisted something be done. He began yelling orders to assemble. Little did I know Elizabeth was listening from the shadows of her balcony, but before Nicholas could carry out his plan, Elizabeth sent word to cease.

"You nearly escaped!" Kate exclaimed. "Tell me, why did Elizabeth prevent the order?"

"She demanded nothing be done in haste. She had no intentions of losing good men due to poor strategy. The men tried to argue assuring her they would not receive a single scratch in the skirmish, but she would not consider their pleas. She reminded them retaliation came by her orders and when she saw fit. In the meantime, the men would sharpen blades and shine armor while I took audience with Elizabeth within the privacy of her chambers."

"Was word sent immediately to Sir Lorant?" Kate asked.

"Oh, heavens no! There was no reason to incite a war over my recklessness. Hearing the wife of the king's favorite knight was violated by a Turkish rouge, well, I cringe to imagine what battles would have been fought and lives lost in the name of my questionable honor," I said shaking my head.

"But, surely you believed your husband should be told?" she said.

"Eventually, but I've learned one must choose when to reveal secrets and when not too."

"What happened next?" Kate asked anxiously.

"I'm trying to tell you, but you keep asking more questions," I laughed.

Kate sucked in her lip forming a tight straight line.

"Dorothea, Anna's attendant, Ilona, who was Katelin and Paul's nursemaid and Ficzko, Elizabeth's manservant were also called to Elizabeth's chambers. While I washed behind a dressing screen in the bedchamber and changed my clothes, Elizabeth sought the advice of her most trusted albeit, unorthodox council. By the time I rejoined the group, a scheme was forming and servants ran errands," I said. Before I continued, I paused to acknowledge my manservant lingering in the doorway.

"Pardon milady, but the weather appears to be worsening. I urge the baroness to consider taking leave, for the streets are beginning to flood."

I rose from my chair and went to the window. In the lamplight I saw water spraying from the wheels of passing carriages. "Yes, it does seem the roadways are becoming quite severe," I said.

"Oh no! I can't leave. I must hear the end of the tale," Kate blurted. The childishness of her own voice inspired her cheeks to once again flush.

"Please, Baroness. The driver expresses his concern for your safety," said my manservant.

"I suppose I must, but I'm dreadfully disappointed," Kate said sharply still unable to check her temper at the interruption.

A crack of thunder sent Ferocious bolting from the window seat toward the dark corner behind a chair. A few seconds of silence passed before three distinct flashes of light snapped across the sky.

"The Gods are angry," I laughed. "Oh, you don't scare me!" I called out to the night sky. "I've seen worse things."

Kate began to collect her things.

"If you'd like, Kate, I could send word with your driver that you'll be spending the night. The storm is quite wild and I believe your family would prefer you don't venture out this evening," I said turning from the window.

"Are you certain my presence won't be an imposition?" she said trying to contain her delight.

"Certainly not! I hope you do not mind bedding in my writing room. I'm afraid it is the only room suitable for a guest at the moment. The servants won't be able to air another chamber with this storm raging outside."

"Oh no, I do not mind at all. It pleases me you should make the offer. It is very kind," she said with a smile.

Before I dismissed my manservant I whispered in his ear to retrieve the carpet I had removed and return it to its proper place covering the stain on the floor. I detected a slight cringe at my request. The presence of the stain haunted every servant in the household. Although it was their duty to enter the writing room daily to carry out chores, none of them delighted in doing so, and now on this stormy night, I was requesting they return the ancient carpet to its original purpose—to cover up the mischief of the past mistress. The very idea sent apparent chills down his aging spine.

"Well then, that is settled," I said turning away from my pale-faced servant and returning to my guest.

Another log was tossed on the fire and hot water delivered for more tea. Overhead I heard the heavy footfall of men moving the carpet into the room followed by a lighter set of feet hurrying back and forth between chamber closets. No doubt they were those of the maids freshening bed sheets and laying out a nightdress for the baroness.

"The house is a flutter," Kate noted.

"It's refreshing to hear someone stirring besides Ferocious," I said. I craned my neck to spy the skittish feline huddled beneath the chair.

"I see Ferocious and I share a likeness for storms," Kate teased.

"It appears so!"

"I hate to be a nuisance, but perhaps now that all is in order we might continue with the story," she urged.

"Of course, if you'd be so kind as to remind me where I left off – my memory is not always the sharpest these days."

"Oh, I disagree! I find it very sharp, but if you insist I do believe you'd just entered Elizabeth's chambers while she and the others were devising a plan of action," Kate accounted.

"Oh what a scheme it was! Instead of sending guards to raid the Turk camp, Elizabeth sent them an invitation to dine at Cachtice."

"What! After what they'd done she asked them to dinner?" Kate exclaimed.

"It was brilliant. As all of Elizabeth's schemes were," I said. "Elizabeth composed a letter expressing the incident was undoubtedly a misunderstanding and that she was certain if the commander believed I to be of noble lineage he certainly would never have allowed his soldier to exploit my honor. To further appeal to the commander's masculine pride, she included it was my own fault for setting out unaccompanied and had I followed proper protocol, I would never have been mistaken for a common peasant in the first place," I said.

"How dare Elizabeth insult you in such a manner to imply you brought on the attack!" Kate said, outraged.

"Just words my dear, to lure the commander – it was all part of the ploy to entrap him. It worked, too. The commander sent a reply stating he too believed it had been an unfortunate mistake and was much obliged to dine with the countess at the next moon. The following evening the sky was dark as chimney pitch, not a single star or hint of moon shone. It was just our luck too because the absence of a moon gave the guards more time to carry out Elizabeth's plan. Cachtice was a clatter with servants and guards working through the night and all the following day preparing for our foreign guests. Each dutifully following the specifications set forth by Elizabeth. By the time the sun descended and the moon rose on the following night, Cachtice was ready to receive the commander and his band of inauspicious trespassers.

I remember listening from my balcony for the horn blower to squawk out the notes signaling the approaching band of Turks. The northerly breeze did not bring sweet smells that spring. Instead, dry particles of dust and weed pollen clung to the parched air. The red sky hinted the dry spell would hold another day. I sat for some time alone in my chamber before I heard the horn ring out the notes, each burst echoing off the stones of Cachtice. In the distance, I spotted the commander and the soldiers trotting behind. The chains of the draw gate churned, iron folding upon itself, grinding as the guards cranked the wheels opening the mouth of the wall to swallow the Turk's whole," I said.

"Swallow them whole?" Kate asked with a shudder.

"Forgive me dear; I suppose that sounds a bit morbid. I've always had a fascination with the dramatic," I said. Just then a gust of wind forced the rain into the windowpanes creating a sinister rattle. The fire in the hearth flickered, inflaming brightly before retreating to a lolling lick. "I fear we are in for it this evening," I said, referring to the storm.

"Yes, it doesn't seem to be letting up," Kate said with a sideways glance.

A cough rattled up from my throat. "The damp air," I said waving off Kate's offer of her handkerchief. "Makes for a dreadful congestion. Nothing another warming of tea won't cure."

"The sight of the commander must have enraged you," Kate said, prodding me back into the story.

"Oh yes, I had great difficulty steadying my nerves. I recall Lyk grumbling by my side sensing my uneasiness. I'm certain he must have fought the temptation to tear through the corridor and down the stairs to where our guests were now entering. Instead he protectively hugged my leg, his shackles casting up behind the collar on his neck as his lip quivered exposing the sharp edges of his canines.

194

"Elizabeth ordered our guests be lead into the great hall where musicians waited to entertain the soldiers. A juggler danced around the room while ladies wearing flowing silk gowns and veils concealing their faces swooned to the rhythm of the beat. I waited for Elizabeth in the foyer, my hand stroking the top of Lyk's head in a consoling motion. Elizabeth appeared a few minutes later dressed in a silk gown she'd once worn while attending Klara Bathory's court. I disliked the dress. It conjured unpleasant memories. I braced myself to be rebuffed by Elizabeth for Lyk's presences at the party, but was pleasantly shocked when Elizabeth crouched down to take Lyk's tense face in her hands. She cooed he was a good boy who deserved a sweet treat. The attention from our mistress eased Lyk's anxiety, ebbing his growls to soft whines. Elizabeth and I exchanged looks as the page announced our arrival to the awaiting men.

"The sight of Elizabeth and me parted by a wolf jolted the commander to attention. His squeamishness delighted Elizabeth who spared no opportunity to poke fun at his expression. The commander retorted the wolf merely startled him, but now that he saw the animal domesticated and of little threat, he found Lyk's presence to be as benign as a house cat. While Elizabeth charmed the commander my eyes searched the room for the man who had violated me. At first glance, I did not see the soldier. It wasn't until my eyes swept the room a second time that I recognized the man who dared to take advantage. He rested reclining on a soft pillow beside the hearth with his head tipped back and his fingers keeping time with the music on his bent knee. I knew it was he because just above his knee was a bandage wrapped around his thigh. The tightening of my grip on Lyk's leash sent a silent message inspiring a revived series of low snarls. I bent down whispering in his ear to hush, which he immediately obeyed," I said.

"Oh how you must have wanted to release Lyk and let him snatch that man by the throat!" Kate exclaimed.

I raised a brow. "My, my, Kate you do possess a wondrous spirit!"

Kate checked herself. "Excuse me, Lady Lorant. I don't know where the outburst came from. I've never wished harm to anyone."

"Certainly you have," I said with a wink. I took a sip of tea, the hot black liquid pinching the back of my dry throat. I continued with my story. "It seemed like years passed as I sat still in the corner of the room while Elizabeth and her ladies entertained our guests. I must confess the chiming of the dinner bell was a welcoming sound to my ears. I gave Lyk's leash to Fickzo before following the party into the great dining hall. Before we entered I overheard the commander inquiring about a member of his party. A soldier had been assigned to escort the stable boy with the horses and had not returned from the errand. Elizabeth insisted the soldier was likely sharing a pint of ale with the stable hands. The commander agreed, but before we took our places at the dining table, he ordered another soldier out to the barn to retrieve the man.

Elizabeth and I sat near the head of the table while her ladies lined one side and the commander and his soldiers sat across along the other. Wine colored the goblets and silver platters garnished with vegetables and fruits decorated the table. Bread was broke and laughter mingled with conversation filled the dining hall. The commander did not question the absence of Elizabeth's adoring children since he was not appraised any resided at Cachtice, a detail Elizabeth gave strict orders to conceal. All evidence of the children was swept away and stored in pantries and cabinets.

Just in time to lead the parade of main courses was Ficzko. I spied his little form slipping discretely through a side door. On his order, the servants began dishing generous portions of the steaming meat onto the men's plates while a maid dished a rabbit strew into the bowls set before the ladies.

'Why do your ladies drink stew when the choice of this game is presented?' the commander inquired.

'I'm afraid this time of year game is scarce. We eat what wanders onto our land. We must make due with the portions we catch. I'm informed there is not enough of the meat to go around, but do not worry, the ladies adore the cook's rabbit stew,' Elizabeth answered. A barely detectable smirk hid beneath her reddened lips. Elizabeth eyed the commander and his soldiers as each gorged on the meat set before them.

'This is a most tender meat and seasoned to perfection,' the commander said. 'Is it elk?'

'Similar. A legged creature, but not often found in these parts, although it does wander uninvited from time to time and when it does, my men are certain to snare it,' Elizabeth replied.

'Well, I am blessed you share such a rare catch with my men,' he said, beaming with cheer.

'It is my pleasure,' Elizabeth remarked.

I leaned close to Elizabeth's ear, 'the commander's man still has not returned. He may notice.'

'Oh, but he has. I have seen to it that he be intimately reunited with his commander,' she said. She spooned a mouthful of rabbit stew.

I followed Elizabeth's dead gaze toward the remains of the game, now mere scraps littering the silver platter. Lyk appeared carrying a large bone in his mouth. He had squeezed through the same side door through which Ficzko had entered earlier. I watched him settle into the corner and begin gnawing on the fleshy knob end of the bone. It cracked and splintered in the grip of his strong jaw.

My eyes snapped back to the empty platters and then to Elizabeth. Her expression remained that of a patient host, but the tapping of her toe beneath the table indicated she was growing restless and wished to progress to the next stage of her scheme.

The commander wiped his mouth. He eased back in his seat rubbing his satisfied belly. Again, he surveyed the table noticing neither of his soldiers had returned from the stable.

'My men have probably intrigued the soldiers with a game of dice,' Elizabeth replied, when again the question arose. 'I'll send a servant to fetch them.'

The commander rattled off something in his foreign language, which instantly caused a soldier at the far end to spring from his seat. 'He will go,' the commander ordered.

'Very well, if you insist,' Elizabeth said. She knew exactly what the commander would do, she knew he would indeed insist one of his own men retrieve the insubordinates from the stables.

'Three down and several more to go,' she whispered between a clenched smile.

Trays piled with sweet desserts arrived accompanied by the enticing swoons of dancing girls. They moved close to the soldiers tempting them by winding silk scarves around the men's necks and tickling the skin above the collar.

'Bewitching, are they not?' Elizabeth said, charming the commander with honeyed voice. It was almost too easy getting them to drop their guard by enticing their desire.

'My men have been away from the sultan's court for some time. I see they are in need of feminine comforts,' he said with a heavy accent.

The soldiers barely ate the desserts. They were terribly distracted by the women cooing compliments in their arrogant ears. Their eyes pleaded to be released from duty to pursue the offerings of the hostess in a more dim, discreet setting. Annoyed with his men's inability to shake temptation, the commander finally dismissed the group. In a chorus, chairs scrapped harshly against the stone floor as the men moved away from the dining table to follow the giggling veiled women down the corridor. Only three soldiers remained: the commander and his second and third in command, neither of which was the man who took liberties against my person."

"Forgive me, Lady Lorant," Kate interrupted. "Elizabeth's ladies in waiting agreed to the scheme? They willingly dressed as harem girls to seduce the soldiers?" Kate asked stunned. "It put them at great risk. What if the ladies were unable to prevent the men's advances? Surely they were not expected to go through…" Kate trailed as she searched my expression.

"Ladies in waiting? Elizabeth had no such thing! Well, besides me, of course. Ficzko had gone out the day before and paid handsomely for the girls. Peasants playing dress up, that is all they were. An illusion, a scheme, a deceptive diversion which I might add, worked beautifully!"

"Ficzko traded gold for the girls?" Kate asked.

"Well tidings were owed. I'm sure the girls were pleased to pay off an entire year's debt with a measly night's work," I said.

Kate looked as if she'd just eaten something sour.

"Are you alright, dear? Shall I continue?" I asked.

"You must think me a prude." Her eyes dropped shamefully towards the linen covered table.

"No, I think you very lucky. It gives me hope to know a woman of your age is not as tainted of heart as I once was," I said. "But, I must inform you the story gets much worse in detail. I'm not sure it is proper for you to hear– I'm afraid you'll be unable to tolerate it," I said.

This sparked Kate to collect herself. I bit the corner of my lip to prevent the escape of a smirk. I knew questioning her tenderness would be irksome. She was proud and believed herself to be modern. She did not want me to think she was so fragile.

"I'm no shrinking violet, Lady Lorant. I apologize for my momentary weakness. I shall not let it happen again, now please continue," she stated.

"If you're certain."

"I am," she said.

"As I was saying, only a small party remained in the dining hall. While I was being ogled by the second in charge, Elizabeth flirted with the commander. Eventually, even his tough exterior began to soften to her charms.

Elizabeth rang the bell summoning Ficzko who appeared again through the side door. 'Is my private chambers prepared?' she asked, giving a playful sideways glance to the commander.

'Yes milady, everything is set for your pleasure,' Ficzko announced with a bow.

'Countess, you keep a private chamber?' the commander asked.

Elizabeth leaned in, 'I have a secret,' she said, her voice very low.

'A secret?' he asked. He obviously liked the sound of this.

'I'd like to show you.'

The commander's face reddened as he cleared his throat. He glanced at his second and third in command.

'They can come too. Amara and another of my ladies will keep them comfortable,' she assured the commander.

The second in charge cocked his chin and gave me a wink. Thankfully I had not eaten much stew and was able to keep the contents of my sickening stomach down. Our party rose from the table and followed Ficzko who led us by torchlight through the poorly lit corridors. We did not walk along the usually route, instead, Ficzko took us through a maze of twists and turns to ensure the Turk's could not memorize the path."

"Where were you taking them?" Kate asked.

"It was not a total lie. Elizabeth was leading them to a private chamber."

"Elizabeth was telling the truth?"

"For the most part," I said. "There was a secret chamber, but not the kind I believe the commander was hoping for. Ficzko, that devilish little dwarf, slide the iron latch to the side allowing the heavy double doors of the chamber to swing open. I remember our senses being hit by the aroma of burning wax mixed with the scented perfume Elizabeth misted her pillows with, which I found nauseating, but the men seemed intrigued by the odor and eagerly passed beneath the threshold to get a better look at the antechamber. Dark burgundy drapes covered the stones walls and concealed all other doors leading into the main room. Most of the fixtures were removed; however, one object remained. Displayed in its usual position was the ancient painted sarcophagus. The piece immediately captivated the commander. He asked many questions, all of which Elizabeth willingly answered. While she was entertaining the commander, Dorothea slipped into the room and to the side of the third ranking officer. She took him by the arm and disappeared behind the thick velvet curtain. Elizabeth took note of Dorothea's exit and requested Ficzko show the second in command to another room, which too was concealed behind a heavy drape. She told him I'd be along shortly with a canter of wine and some delicious fruits to cleanse his palate. Then she whispered something in the commander's ear. By his expression I assume Elizabeth suggested they too excuse themselves for the evening. After the commander was led away, Elizabeth hurried to my side.

'Take leave and find Nicholas. He is waiting for you. Show him the man, show him the soldier who took liberty upon your person,' she said to me.

'And what will become of them,' I asked, referring to the three men now locked in Elizabeth's chambered workshop.

'What happens to all who trespass!' she said.

I did as Elizabeth asked; I took leave in search of Nicholas. Once the iron-planked doors of Elizabeth private chamber were latched shut not a sound could seep through. I found the sudden deafening silence created by earth and stone unsettling. I removed a torch from the wall. The firelight reached out touching the crevasses in the walls just far enough for me to find my way out of the labyrinth through which we'd come. For a brief moment I felt pity for the men now ensnared in Elizabeth's hold. I shuttered to think of what demonic pleasures she'd gain from their slow painful suffering. Then I remembered the Turk's dirty fingers probing my sex. I recalled the smell of his panting breath and the feel of the sand against my cheek as I struggled to free myself from his unwanted advances. What would have become of me if I'd not been carrying my dagger that day? How many men would I have endured, how much pain would my body have writhed with once they were finished? A retching sensation sprung from my stomach. I steadied myself by pressing my hand against the damp stone as I caught my breath and waited for the wave of sickness to recede. Somewhere from above I thought I heard a scream. I pushed on knowing I could not be far from the door through which we'd entered. I continued to feel my way along the tunnels until I came to the door. I turned the latch and swiftly crossed through. The lit sconces made the hall much brighter than the corridors below and I had to blink several times in order to adjust my eyes to the change in light.

'Amara, it's me,' I heard someone call.

'Nicholas?'

'Yes, take my hand and come quickly,' he said.

It seemed the castle was deserted. The musicians were gone, the plates cleared, and there was no sign of the veiled ladies.

'It is awfully quiet,' I said still clutching Nicholas's hand.

'Be glad for it, milady. Come, we have a few men in the courtyard. I am certain one of them is the man who dared to take liberty.'

As we rounded the corner I saw the reason for the sudden silence. Several half naked male bodies lay contorted across the hall. It appeared they had tried to run but failed in their attempt to escape. As I lifted my skirts and stepped over one of the soldier's I noticed his exposed sex had been slashed clean off and he had bled out all over the floor. The closer we drew to the courtyard, the more naked corpses I saw; their ripped trousers soaked with blood pooling between their spread legs. Their dead expressions frozen in wide-eyed surprise as their mouths were permanently held in a lasting scream. Also, near the door lay two deceased ladies, their own bodies slung over a bloody Turk. The soldier had tried to use the women as shields in his escape. Little did he know the ladies were of little circumstance to anyone.

'Do not pay much attention, milady. Remember they were bait and nothing worth bartering for,' Nicholas reminded.

'Still, it is unfortunate they had to perish,' I sighed.

'They served their mistress well. Their families will be compensated,' Nicholas said.

The night air slapped my face as we breeched the door leading to the yard. Forced down on bended knees squatted four Turkish soldiers stripped clean of clothing and from the looks of it, the last men of the commander's troop remaining alive.

'Do you see him?' Nicholas asked.

'Order them to stand.'

Nicholas was puzzled.

'I wounded my attacker,' I informed. To me they all looked alike. The only discerning feature separating them, in my opinion, was the bandage around his leg.

Nicholas signaled for the men to rise."

"Did he give away his horror?" Kate asked in a hushed voice.

"Oh yes, I shall never forget what I saw in those menacing orbs. Sometimes just his eyes appear in my nightmares, as if he is still watching me. Thankfully it doesn't happen very often. However, it does give me a frightful jolt upon wakening," I said.

"Did you accuse your attacker?" she asked.

"I pointed my finger and named him as the one who sought me harm and in turn, unleashed the fury of my mistress upon his fellow comrades. The man standing beside him broke into a sniveling whimper as I backed away from the line of exposed men.

Nicholas stepped forward. 'I seek justice in the name of Lady Amara Lorant. Let it be known, the Countess Bathory has determined punishment will be the slashing of the male organ for all who attempt to or do not prevent the raping of our women. To defile means certain death,' Nicholas shouted. With a ripping slash of his sword he sliced off the male organs. One by one searing screams followed by collapsing bodies smacking the stone disturbed the starry night. Scarlet pools spread between their naked legs as the men twisted into curled balls with their hands clutching what was left of their manhood. All but one waned unconscious. I watched as the man tried to crawl away, his struggle written in blood trailing down his hairy thighs. I knew Elizabeth never showed mercy by ordering a swift execution. However, Nicholas weakened by the pathetic sight of the suffering of his sex, and he decidedly took matters into his own hand and lobbed the man's head clean off. A spray of blood shot from the gapping hole as the limbs twitched before dying against the cold slab stone. The man's head lay not far from his body, his lips and tongue already bloated, his hair like a ratty wig stuck around his damp flesh."

A booming clap of thunder rattled the windows but was not followed by a stroke of light.

"The storm, it is moving away," I said.

Kate sat still, her mouth moving slightly as if she was trying to form words.

The drawing room door slid open. "Milady, do you intend on retiring soon?" my manservant asked.

"Just a few more moments," I answered.

"Very well." He closed the door again.

"I suppose you're wondering what became of the commander and his ranking officers?" I asked.

Kate gulped. "I am curious."

"I wish I could say they experienced the same fairly swift death as the foot soldiers, but I must report they were not so lucky. As I suspected, Elizabeth showed little mercy in carrying out punishment. She insisted the commander be the last to die. It was only befitting since he was the leader and the one ultimately responsible for the actions of his soldiers. Although we never spoke in detail, I heard from Nicholas that Elizabeth kept the commander alive for sometime in an iron cage hidden in her private chamber. I believe he eventually died from an infection; however, the servants claim it was from loss of blood. They whispered the mistress drank the life fluid directly from his vein. Of course, this is nonsense, but it does make for a morbid tale, don't you think?"

Kate's face was as white as her gloves draped across the sofa armrest. "She really killed all those men?" she muttered in disbelief.

"She devised the attack and gave the order if that's what you mean," I said pushing myself up from the seat. "I'm afraid I must retire now. My bones tell me there is more rain in sight and if I don't get a proper night's rest I will be creaking like a half hinged door for weeks." I stretched my legs.

Kate rose from her chair. The color began to return to her pallid cheeks. I slid the drawing room door aside to find my manservant slouched in his chair against the wall. The clearing of my throat startled him awake. He grumbled a few incoherent words as he swayed to his feet.

"Please show the baroness to her room." I wished Kate a goodnight.

I had only taken a couple of steps when she asked, "The bodies, what did they do with all the bodies?"

My manservant shook his head as if to ward off a bad dream.

"Ah yes, this is an interesting question." I glanced at my manservant. "For which an answer must wait until morning. Shall we pick up where I left off at breakfast?"

Kate agreed to retire the story until morning. I waved goodnight as she crossed the upper balcony, her regal frame following the dim light of my manservant's lantern. I touched my temple, a searing pain was pressing against my tired eyes. A cough rattled in my chest. Now with everyone retired for the evening I allowed my weary shoulders to roll forward as I made my way to my private apartment. The chambermaid awoke upon my entry. She worked quickly to unlace my gown and remove my swollen feet from my slippers. She commented on the purple bruising around my arch insisting I soak my feet in cool water before sleeping. I dismissed her advice stating I only needed a good night's rest and an appointment with a master shoemaker. I took a drink of water to quiet a coughing spell before pulling the downy blanket up over my shoulders. I adjusted the pillows to form a support against my backside.

I missed my bedfellows; I dearly missed the weight of a warm body next to mine. With each sunrise I wondered how many more I'd endure before I'd meet with any of them again. Although in my youth I balked at any belief in Heaven, I found in my old age I often prayed that a place where souls reunited existed. I closed my eyes picturing Draco's face, as it once was, youthful and strong, bronzed by the sun, and his loving eyes with a flicker of stubbornness. In my vision he sat upon his stallion with his broadsword strapped by his side. He was speaking to me, but I could not hear his words. It was always the same; I could not hear what he was saying to me. He'd close the visor of his helmet before tightening the reins and riding off. I'd shout after him, but he was gone. He was gone and it was my fault.

***

"Lady Lorant, Lady Lorant," I heard my chambermaid calling from somewhere far away.

My lids were heavy as I pried them from sleep. I sat up in bed, my hips sore from remaining curled on my side for too long.

"What is it?" I asked still trying to gain orientation.

"I've been informed the baroness is stirring. She'll be expecting you at breakfast," the maid said.

"The baroness?" I asked. Everything was hazy.

"Yes, milady. Your guest from last night. You do recall the baroness spending the night?"

I rubbed my temple. The searing pain in my head from the night before was now reduced to a dull ache.

"Of course I do," I snapped. "Now retrieve my robe."

I discovered Kate waiting for me in the library. I stood in the doorway admiring the way the morning sun broke through the stained glass window landing in a prism of color over her pressed skirt. *The bodies,* I thought. Kate would certainly ask about them at breakfast. I had not known her long, but did know her curious mind would not rest until she heard the tale in its entirety.

Once we sat down to our eggs and hash my suspicions were realized. Not two bites into our meal did the words cross Kate's lips.

"Lady Lorant, last night you were about to tell me about the bodies," she reminded wasting no time.

"Hardly a proper topic at breakfast," I answered tapping my plate with my fork.

"Forgive me, but you did say you'd continue this morning at breakfast. Tell me, did the news of the event anger the king?" she pressed.

"Anger the king?"

"I just assumed this was the reason Anna never made it to King Rudolph's court for the season."

"Ah...it played a part. It wasn't so much the event, but Elizabeth's handling of it. She was never very good at restraint or diplomacy."

"The king was enraged by not being apprised?" she asked.

"Oh no, he would never let a little trifle ruffle his enormous feathers. It wasn't so much being informed, but rather Elizabeth's insistence she be recognized for the slaughter. Imagine if news spread that a noble woman of rank commanded the execution of a Turkish brigade. A woman ordering royal soldiers and conquering a highly decorated Turkish commander in the sultan's ranks! Elizabeth's arrogance infuriated the king. He had enough intriguing and scandal swarming his court; he did not need another coal thrown on the imperial fire. He immediately dispatched an advisor to Cachtice to reason with Elizabeth. In the letter King Rudolph demanded Nicholas be promoted to captain and honored for escorting the sultan's men by sword point from the territory. If pressed for further information about the missing band of soldiers, the king would insist the Turks were alive when last seen and must have perished in the woods after losing their way, most likely fallen sick or tragically eaten by wolves." I took another bit of my eggs. "He had the eaten by wolves part correct anyways." I chuckled.

Kate scrunched up her nose. "Lyk ate the bodies?"

"He gnawed on a few bones. The others parts burned, buried and…" I trailed off distracted by footsteps in the hallway. The servants were eavesdropping.

"And what?" she asked.

I lowered my voice. "Well that is where Elizabeth made her fatal mistake." I pushed back my plate. "The king's demands insulted Elizabeth. She chased his court advisor, the poor man appointed the duty of delivering the letter, screaming from Cachtice with her less than polite response nailed to his hand." I shook my head recalling her fit. "After removing the letter from the tortured messenger, King Rudolph determined Elizabeth suffered from an inherited family aliment known to plague the Bathory bloodline. He called a conference with Francis insisting a physician be sent immediately to Cachtice to attend to the countess. The letter written in Elizabeth's own hand along with the advisor's crippled palm was evidence enough to convince Francis to obey the request. King Rudolph ordered Elizabeth be confined to Cachtice indefinitely or until word of recovery was received."

"Was she insane?" Kate asked. Her fork dangled between forefinger and thumb.

"No not insane, just obstinate, which I suppose some feel is the same thing. It is a dangerous flaw in a female. Many of the great ones have been put to death for possessing the trait."

"Obstinacy is surely not in league with insanity?" Kate said.

"Be careful, Kate. The line between the two is a fine one."

"And who draws such a line?"

"Ah, this is the question. Who determines indeed!"

"But there are laws, there are definitions written in books," she continued. Her logic was adorable.

"And who writes the laws, who determines the definitions and who pays for it all?" I asked.

"The king," Kate stammered. She closed her eyes and bowed her head like a child who'd just been horribly disappointed.

I nodded, although I doubted she noticed.

When she raised her chin I leaned forward placing my elbows on the table and folding my hands in front of me. "In response to her confinement Elizabeth ordered several bodies including the mutilated corpse of the high commander to be carried to the secret tunnels joining Cachtice with the neighboring monastery. In those tunnels were hundreds of pine boxes built presumably by Vlad Tepes for the bodies of slain soldiers and then forgotten, trapped for years beneath layers of cobwebs until I discovered them quite by accident."

"What was the purpose?" Kate asked.

"Evidence. Elizabeth wanted to preserve evidence, which she intended to use to prove to the world her power and to embarrass the king and expose the cover up. Of course, she couldn't do it immediately, but Elizabeth despite the temporary suppression was not going silently into the good night. By keeping Elizabeth away, his majesty simply allowed her time to scheme a new plan," I said.

"Had she not learned anything? Did you not try to persuade her, try to convince Elizabeth she was compromising her life and those of her children?" Kate asked.

"Until I was breathless! But, she would not hear it. I warned her it might come back to haunt us, and that, I'm afraid, is exactly what happened. If she had only listened!" I slapped my hands on the table. "That evidence which Elizabeth intended to use…well, it was used, but not in the manner she intended. Those corpses, those spoiled bodies mutilated beyond discernible recognition with their sex slashed off were a curse. Eventually, they were all exhumed from the bowels of Cachtice." I stopped. I let the tension relax from my face and limbs. "However, my dear Kate that is another story entirely," I said.

A House Condemned

1628: Present Day Vienna

As I sat at my desk with fresh ink dripping from my pen tip, I thought of Kate. I glanced at the manuscript piled in front of me. I ran my finger along the stack, admiring the work I'd accomplished. I got a peculiar rush from seeing it collected in a volume. It was therapeutic, like a soak in a salt bath. I could feel every part of my being, which meant I was still alive, and that was refreshing. I was doing what I set out to do, tell the truth—the truth as I remembered it. There it was; my memoir bound and twined, preserved for centuries in the pages on my desk. Since my dinner with Kate I'd written several more chapters including the days following that fateful night, the night Elizabeth slaughtered the Turks and hid their castrated corpses in the tunnels beneath Cachtice.

The walls of the royal house were crawling with scandal. After receiving word of Elizabeth's untimely revenge, the royal advisors convinced King Rudolph he could not survive another slanderous blow. If word spread about what Elizabeth did, the monarchy and all those involved would suffer terrible embarrassment or worse, the disaster might spark a war. This was something King Rudolph did not want. He was already having difficulty managing the annoying border skirmishes and was in no position to defend against war. Surely he could muster the men and weaponry if pressed, but it was the financial drain he did not wish to consume.

However, the chore of hushing Elizabeth was no simple task. After all, she was proud of what she'd done. It would take an iron hand to gag the countess. I imagined a private meeting took place between King Rudolph and Francis where it was determined the best course of action was to confine Elizabeth to the remote recesses of Cachtice and deny all rumors of the affair. That's what they called the slaughter in the letter, an affair, a bloody unfortunate affair!

The king's scheme to explain Elizabeth's withdraw from society involved an illness, a faux blood disorder. As a twist, his majesty included hallucinations and hysteria as symptoms of the sickness. It was the surest way to safeguard against further gossip. It was a cruel method to guarantee any words uttered by either Elizabeth or her loyalists would be instantly dismissed. However, although he thought citing an illness was clever, it was a common scheme used by men throughout the ages to mask undesirable feminine traits or actions otherwise not acceptable in polite society. Despite my own opinion regarding his creativity, his story was effective and certainly believable. To solidify his plan, the king whispered the rumor in his mistress's ear. He said Elizabeth hallucinated Turks were invading the halls of Cachtice. He claimed the guards often found the countess roaming the corridors wielding a sword and screaming at the apparitions to get out. It did not take long for the account of Elizabeth's mythical misfortunate to travel from bedroom to ballroom until finally settling in the drawing rooms throughout the kingdom. All those, even women who suffered from similar fraud, fell for the farce.

For the second time in Elizabeth's life, society was misinformed about the true reason for her absence. Two celebrations denied, the first a birth, and then a well executed victory, both doused by scheme and cover up to protect position and political scandal. Anyone of importance was briefed about the countess's ailing symptoms. Physicians arrived to tend to her along with letters of sympathy and condolences, which she did not read but rather shred and burned. The lengths by which they carried out the plan were insulting and with each accommodation, she grew more spiteful.

Unfortunately, the benefactors of the sentence were the undeserving children, especially Anna. Disappointed, she stowed her party dresses and retired to the drawing room. Her dreams of coming out to meet a charming suitor were dashed. She'd spend another season reading by day and in the evening strumming a mournful tune along the keys of the pianoforte. If all went well, in a year's time Elizabeth would be cured and recovered. Of course, this depended on satisfying the demands of King Rudolph, for he was the only person who could grant an invitation to attend the following season's festivities. For permission to be arranged, the king insisted on securing an oath of silence from Elizabeth regarding the distasteful affair.

I'll never forget the expression on Anna's face when the conditions were read aloud to us. She bit her lower lip to prevent it from quivering, her chin dropping toward the floral design on the rug beneath her feet. I turned to Elizabeth who was too consumed with anger to notice her eldest child's grave disappointment. If ever I regretted a single moment in my life, it was that one. I should have stood and spoke out demanding Elizabeth see past her own selfishness to consider her children, but I did not. I remained fixed to my chair, my hands gripping the edges while I braced for the inevitable, a full-fledged tirade beginning with the hurling of a Russian porcelain egg against the wall.

Don't misunderstand; I too was outraged by the proposition. I found it most unfair. We'd been abandoned in the castle, left alone to defend against God only knows, and when we succeeded, we were punished. Our choice was death or exile, neither of which seemed rightfully deserving. My moment of weakness came from the fleeting illusion I had for Anna – a hope for happiness. I wanted a life of ballrooms and pretty gowns, of storybook romance and marriage. The smashing of the egg was like a slap across the face snapping me back to reality. I knew the tears welling in Anna's eyes were only the first of many to come. It was best she learned now the cruelties of the world. The sooner she accepted the truth, the sooner she might harden herself against it further penetrating her soul and eating out her heart. I smoothed my skirt and straightened my back. Oh, we'd endure another year confined to the dreary castle, just as we'd endured the previous years.

I watched the maid crouching on the floor with a dustpan and whisk sweeping up the pieces of the broken ornament.

"Dorothea!" Elizabeth screamed.

Dorothea was Anna's lady in waiting and was becoming a trusted member of our intimate circle.

"Dorothea!" Elizabeth called again.

She appeared in the doorway precisely at the moment the maid cleaning the floor squealed. The blood trickling down her wounded wrist horrified her. She snatched up her apron wrapping it around the injured hand to hide the red ooze from Elizabeth, but she did not succeed in hiding the wound from Dorothea. The maid whimpered as a red stain spread across the woven threads. Elizabeth's head twisted around at the sudden silencing of the room, her eyes moving to the crimson pattern seeping through the starched apron. The maid's boots stammered against the floorboards as she hesitated, deciding whether to flee or wait for dismissal. Everything seemed to slow as we watched a single drop break through the saturated cloth and land on the toe of the maid's scuffed boot. Her jaw went slack as the droplet plunked on the leather, her knees buckled, and her limp body thudded on the floor. Dorothea pulled the rope ringing the bell for Ficzko who came immediately followed by two towering guards. The maid's sagging body was lifted, her soiled apron draped over her hitched knees as her lolling head swung from the guard's cradled arms. In minutes another maid swooped in to take the injured girl's place. She worked vigorously cleansing the pool of blood mixed with broken glass from the floor and into the dustpan. She labored until no trace of the incident was evident. Everything was just as it was supposed to be, clean and neat.

I began to think about blood. After all, it was a fascinating substance, priceless in fact, without value, but also possessing the most worth. Like gold, blood came from nature and held its appreciation for generations. I must confess I never quite understood Elizabeth's preoccupation with the ruby ooze. It was curious, but never captured my interest like it did hers. She found the mystery of natural science spellbinding.

During her convalescing, if one should call it that, Elizabeth's interest in experimentation grew. She took pleasure in discovering what reaction various concoctions had on the human body. While I withered away in boredom, Elizabeth disappeared with Dorothea for days on end to her workshop. After lags of time passed and neither woman surfaced, the servants became anxious. That's when the rumors began to leak from their lips and with each passing breath the story inflated two fold.

One evening while I was dressing for bed, I overheard my chambermaid whispering to the laundress that Dorothea was a black magic witch. It was believed among the servants that prior to serving the infamous Queen Catherine and before appearing at Cachtice, Dorothea dwelled in the forest of the French countryside where her grandmother tutored her in the darkest form of witchcraft. They also accused Ficzko of being accomplished as well. It was his gypsy upbringing that led them to the inevitable conclusion that he too was cursed. What other explanation could there be for his deformity? His dwarfism was punishment from God for meddling with things he should not. It was a sin to desire unnatural power. His desire stunted growth and twisted his spine.

The servants scattered like cockroaches from a lit flame every time the unlikely trio emerged from the bottom recesses of Cachtice. I tried as gently as I could to persuade Elizabeth to abandon her experiments in the cellar. I explained the increasing distress within the household and suggested giving up her hobby, which was heightening unrest and worse, drawing unnecessary attention, namely from King Rudolph's henchmen. I reminded Elizabeth she was confined against her will and the only way to regain freedom was to appear recovered. It was all smoke and mirrors – a fake recovery from a false disorder. As careful as I was in choosing my words, the reaction was always the same – Elizabeth raged. She'd spread her arms above her head flapping them in violent circles shouting all the while that she'd get her revenge on those who wronged her. She'd slam her fist hard against the table sending maids scampering for cover behind folded linen and into broom pantries. My own heart fluttered when she leaned close, her voice catching in her throat as she whisper, 'I've a plan, my dear Amara. Just you wait and see.' Yes, it was undeniable—Elizabeth always had a plan.

I sighed thinking about it even now. Perhaps, things would have turned out differently for Elizabeth if only she'd been more suited for abandonment. However, this was not the circumstance. Despite many attempts, I failed in convincing her. A person does not need a sixth sense to foresee no good could come from Elizabeth's underground dealings. A slip of the tongue in the ear of the wrong fellow and all would be lost. It did not help matters that Elizabeth sought the assistance of the most unwilling kind, her servants. After several months of painstaking secrecy, Elizabeth's overwhelming desire to witness the effects of her labors took over.

On an unusually dark night in late January, Elizabeth asked me to join her to spy outside the servant quarters. It was here that we first observed the brutal outcome of an ailing potion. The servants cried out in retching pain as they withered in curled balls, hands gripping at their squeezing stomachs, their legs twitching on the cots as the bedpans over flowed with the contents of regurgitated suppers on the floor. They cried it was a curse placed upon the household, but I knew better. They were merely victims of curiosity, unwilling test subjects for a larger scheme. Elizabeth, Dorothea and I watched from the shadows as the chaotic masterpiece exploded to life upon a living canvas. It began with a droplet deliberately plunked in the mulled wine. Many times the rendering ended badly, resulting in our entire service falling ill for several days, and the weaker ones dropping dead.

Do not misunderstand, I had little sympathy for the subjects, but rather feared for my own safety if Elizabeth's experimentation were ever discovered. Nevertheless, Elizabeth pressed on despite the many undesired outcomes. She was, after all, a most diligent scientist. She never let a poor result sway her determination. She took many notes documenting symptoms and preferred, or in most cases, not so preferred results and reasoning a conclusion as to why a particular result occurred. Some of her notes on the topic were extensive, others simply read, 'girl was unfit, weak constitution with little tolerance.'

On occasion, days and nights passed without a single person catching sight of the trio. Then the threesome would again surface from below covered in awful smells permeating from their soiled clothing. Elizabeth hinted my participation would complete the square. Although I did not mind observing the experiments on the Earth's surface, I hated the thought of spending time in the damp confines of the dungeon Cachtice. I was a lover of light and beauty and, as more time passed, I learned to find all things beautiful, from the newly blooming flower in the garden to the dying milkmaid with greenish vomit crusting on her chin. From this experience I drew my own conclusion; birth and death at just the precise moment were virtually indiscernible.

I also wrote, but my notes were more poetic than scientific and after I had set them permantently upon the page, I'd burn them in a fire. I never wanted them to be found—they were my private thoughts, and no one was going to read them.

However, I am compelled to mention there were periods of reprieve. Sometimes after getting the same dreary result Elizabeth along with Dorothea and Ficzko emerged from the workshop. She was often discouraged, a bit bored and in a most impatient temper. Instead of taking in a deep breath of fresh air and retreating to the backstairs, Elizabeth retired to her bedchambers before reappearing bathed and dressed.

Upon seeing her, I thought perhaps the worst was behind us. For several weeks she joined the table for meals and even took to accompanying me for walks in the garden making sure to slow our pace so we could laugh at her children playing a game of bowls on the castle lawn. In the evenings she dabbled with a tapestry scene while Anna practiced her lessons on the pianoforte. During these peeks of normalcy the remaining servants edged uneasily around the countess, for her temper was still very much unstable. Often, and for no good reason, she'd burst into a cruel fit lashing out at a servant, the injury suffered so severe a doctor was called to attend. Other times, the servant was dragged away by the guards and never seen again.

I decided to secretly write Draco. I sent several letters pleading for him to speak with Francis and King Rudolph. I begged him to find a way to allow Elizabeth a pardon from Cachtice. Although I did not go into detail, I explained the confinement and silly treatments prescribed by the doctors were doing more harm than good. Draco's reply was sympathetic. He assured me he'd speak with Francis as soon as they met in Pressburg. I learned that upon departing from Cachtice, the Quintet had separated. Draco received orders to lead his own troop, while Francis who was getting on in years, was inclined to remain in the king's service at court.

The letters were always the same, full of promises never acted upon. Eventually, I grew despondent with Draco's nonchalant responses to my pleas. Frustrated by my husband's lack of urgency, I turned to an old friend, my George. I scribbled the order of events, which lead to our confinement and requested he use his influence to aid in changing our circumstances. In the early morning hour I rang for a courier to take my letter to Humenne. I waited. It did not take long to receive word from my dear friend. He had kept his promise; he'd come if I called.

Dearest Amara,

I find myself greatly distressed by the urgency of your letter. I, like many others admittedly confess to hearing the rumors of Elizabeth's illness and under the circumstances had no reason to believe them to be false. Be assured I will do whatever is in my power to bring you comfort, but I fear my influence is not as it once was. My duties are limited due to my excess diet of spirits and stubbornness against reform. However, I will find a way to come to you at once. If all I can offer is a shoulder to weep on and the amusement of my company, then it is yours. You should expect my arrival by the next full moon.
G__

I set the corner of George's note to the candle flame and held it until it threatened my flesh. I tossed it in the hearth and watched it burned. A pang of guilt pinched my stomach as I tightened the blanket over my legs. Perhaps I was too hasty in involving George. What if Draco found out? He had every reason not to trust me in the presence of George, although I was still certain Draco did not know this. I began to pace about the room contemplating whether I should compose a second letter telling George to postpone his visit when I heard the pattering of approaching feet. The door flew open just as I was swinging a wrap around my shoulders.

"Amara, come quick, we must find mother," Anna said grabbing my arm and dragging me toward the corridor.

"What is it?" I asked.

"I fear something is amiss."

She hurried me down the staircase and toward the servant's wing of the castle. A single ghost lamp lit the shadows of the kitchen. Anna tugged me toward the familiar door leading to the dungeon. I hesitated at the top of the stairs.

"Must we go down?" I asked.

Through the darkness I felt the spying eyes of the kitchen maid burrowing in the back of my head. I turned around squinting in the pitch black as I tried to catch the reflection of a figure near the closet, but I saw nothing. I held my lantern out in front of me swinging it side-to-side trying to illuminate the corners of the room. The floor creaked beneath our feet as I shifted in place. Anna grew impatient. She tugged on my sleeve urging me down the dank staircase. The smell of musky earth rushed in my nostrils as we sank deeper underground.

"Why are you taking me down here?" I asked. I wondered how much Anna knew about this place.

Anna slide open another shutter on her lantern. The two of us accompanied by only our own slim shadows crawling along the walls pressed onward as we winded through the narrowed passageway.

"Mother's taken a girl."

"How do you know?' I asked. I coughed trying to clear the rotten taste of decay from my lungs.

"I was just about to douse my lantern for the night and retire to bed when I heard the sound of carriage wheels slowing near the house. A few moments later chains rattled beneath my window. I saw Ficzko and the guards followed by mother. They were escorting a prisoner, a petite girl draped in a white robe shackled in chains. She was very young, about Katelin's age, I think. I decided to follow them," Anna informed.

"To the dungeon?"

"That's where I thought they were going." Anna stopped. She held the lantern up exposing a curtain of cobwebs bridging overhead. Together we ducked safely beneath the veil before continuing on. "There's a secret room."

I touched Anna's sleeve. "Perhaps it is best we return to our rooms," I said.

This time Anna raised the lantern to my face, the blinding light forcing me to shield my eyes. "You know about the room?" she asked.

I pushed down her arm, deflecting the light. "Yes, Anna. I know."

I started to turn back. I took a few steps before I realized Anna was not following. "Anna, it is not wise," I warned.

"I'm old enough to know," she said, her voice deadening in the wall.

I trailed behind Anna as she navigated the final bend. A tiny crack of light revealed the entrance to Elizabeth's workshop. Anna's hand gripped the latch. Slowly, she eased the door ajar, her face pressed against the edge to peek at what was hidden inside. "I don't see anyone?" she said, her voice low.

I waited. Nothing. I heard nothing stirring from within the room.

"What's that smell?" she asked. She scrunched up her nose, twitching it like a rabbit sniffing the scent of the vegetable garden.

The earthy musk carried a hint of tainted citrus, like the smell of rotten fruit molding or a man's breath thick with cheap ale.

I shrugged, wrinkling up my nose at the pungent odor. It was familiar, in an unpleasant way.

Anna tilted her head to adjust her eye for a better look.

Impatient, I shoved the door open exposing the spying Anna. Anna's jaw slacked, as she stood stunned and staring at the back of Elizabeth's long ermine cuffed robe. Elizabeth turned at the sound of the door scraping against the uneven stone floor. Her surprised expression gave way to annoyed complacency. She said nothing, only waved for us to enter the room.

"So glad you could join me this evening, Amara, but what possesses you to bring my daughter?"

"It is she who brings me, Elizabeth," I said moving toward the blazing fire in the hearth.

A cauldron hung across an iron rod, the smell of boiled fruit and herbs rising in the steam.

"Is this true, Anna?" Elizabeth asked.

"Yes Mama. I heard a commotion outside my window. I dressed and followed you and Ficzko into the kitchen and down the cellar staircase. I did not dare enter alone so I went to Amara's room and asked her to accompany me."

"And why would you do such a thing, Anna?"

"I wish to know why you brought that young girl here. I want to know what has happened to her. I hear things, noises sometimes late at night, and then I overhear the servants talk," she said.

"Do you, and what do the servants say?"

"You know very well what they say, Mother," Anna snapped.

I was shocked by Anna's tone. So was Elizabeth. Her lip twitched as she gripped the edge of the table.

"Careful, Anna," I whispered.

Ficzko appeared through a side door carrying a white robe over his infant arm.

"Is everything ready?" Elizabeth asked.

"Yes Countess."

Elizabeth pointed to Anna and me. "We have an audience this evening. It seems my daughter is interested in my rather, how shall I put it, royal duties. I suppose she is old enough to see the darker side of our existence. Someday she may find herself in a similar circumstance, although I pray for her sake, she never does."

"What is she talking about?" Anna asked me.

"Come dear, come see what I must do to protect my children and myself," Elizabeth said.

Anna and I obeyed Elizabeth and followed Ficzko into the adjoining room. There, suspended from the ceiling hung an enormous iron cylinder cage. It reminded me of a birdcage, but this thing was big enough for a small human, but too narrow to sit and too squat to stand. Trapped inside was a naked girl grabbling with the bars. Her body crouched half bent as she whimpered for forgiveness. The sight of Elizabeth approaching sent the girl into hysterics. She squirmed trying to find a means of escape praying there was a secret door in the rear through which she could shimmy down the rope, which was now moving her upward. Ficzko was cranking a wheel bolted to the stone wall. The ropes slid through a pulley toward the top of the chamber where barely visible in the torch light hung a dozen short spikes jutting, like icicles after a deep freeze, from the ceiling. Trapped with no way out, the girl began to cry. "No, please mercy, no!" she screamed. She twisted and turned contorting her body in all kinds of positions to avoid the claws poking through the bars.

Ficzko pulled harder on the ropes swinging the cage in circles trying to catch the bars on a spike. The apparatus clanked spinning the girl closer to death. She screamed each time the cage banged against the sharp metal. I heard a scraping then a squishy sound as the girl's skin was pierced. Blood ran down her arm and smudged across her small breast as she jerked in pain.

"Force her closer," Elizabeth ordered.

Ficzko yanked on the ropes, his feet leaving the floor as he used his own weight to thrust the cage higher. I jumped at the loud sound of a cracking snap, the girl wailed as a metal spike split her chest. Blood trickled from her mouth, her eyes rolled back into her skull as her hands pawed at the stake driven clean through.

"Mercy," she muttered. "Forgive me…"

The cage swung like a pendulum rocking from the ceiling. Anna stepped forward, her face turned upward, her eyes fixed on the death chamber. A mist sprinkled the cream shawl protecting Anna's shoulders, a few droplets freckled her face. She blinked clearing them from her eyes not realizing what was raining down on her. More fell, and she mindlessly wiped her face with her nightdress sleeve, a pink smudge dirtied her fingers.

"Come away, my dear. You're getting soiled," Elizabeth said. He voice soft with motherly concern.

Anna spread her palms open in front of her. She shook, not from a chill, but from knowing the mist kissing her pale skin was blood. "Dear God," Anna said.

"Ficzko fetch a cloth," Elizabeth ordered. She wrapped her arms around Anna. "It's alright, dear. We'll get you clean again."

"That girl...she, she is dead."

"Almost," Elizabeth said tenderly. There was a faint moan coming from the cage. Elizabeth escorted Anna to a nearby chair. "Now listen to me darling, that girl sought to betray us. Oh I know she is young, but that should not be confused with innocent. I had on good authority she meant to do our family harm. The guards captured her not far from here. She was fleeing to the lower village where she intended to bribe a driver and visit the governor."

"Why did she seek the governor?" Anna asked.

Elizabeth dabbed the blood splatter from Anna's pale cheeks. "To tell him I am a witch."

"But that is absurd. She has no evidence. Who will believe a servant girl? She is no more than a child?" Anna asked.

Ficzko handed Elizabeth a dingy knapsack, which she untied. She took the contents out and laid them on the table before Anna. There were two glass vials, one containing a red liquid and the other a golden-flecked substance. Also, she displayed a dinner pan of rotten food and a wooden goblet rimmed with a mulled wine residue. "This is her evidence. She was going to give the governor these items," Elizabeth said, waving a hand over the contents as if she was casting a spell.

"What is the significance?" Anna asked.

Elizabeth pointed to each item. "Medicines, spoiled food and peasant wine."

"I don't understand," Anna said. She was trying to make sense of the arrangement.

Ficzko placed two pails beneath the cage to catch the spilling of blood now running in a stream and pattering on the floor.

"I've been brewing medicines. I do not trust the doctors the king sends. The medicines I make are mostly to heal, but some are for darker purposes – for protection."

"Mother, you do not mean poison?"

"It's a prickly science my darling. I'm still learning the craft, trying to perfect my potions," Elizabeth explained.

"And the food, it was tainted?" Anna asked.

"I can't very well test on myself or on you and your siblings. However, I must experiment. All good scientists do. It is a necessity."

"It's true then, you are practicing?" Anna could not take her eyes away from the objects.

"If you must call it that. It's not what you think, the servants, they are ignorant. They are very superstitious and do not possess the intelligence to decipher science from myth. For them, what cannot be explained must be evil. What I am doing is not so simplistic." Elizabeth strolled across the floor with her hands locked behind her back. It was as if she were a teacher giving a lecture to a room of students. "Men have been using poisons to protect against enemies for centuries. What I am doing is no different." She paused. "Why should I be any different?"

"But why kill the girl? Why not lock her in the dungeon?" Anna asked. "I do not understand why she must die as punishment."

The room was quiet, not even the ping of blood droplets pattering in the bucket beneath the cage disturbed the conversation.

"I've learned fear is the ultimate power. Our subjects must know if they betray us, they will die – no mercy…never."

Anna nodded in unison with Ficzko who was washing the grime from his child-size hands. Elizabeth's straightforward explanation was all Anna needed. She understood it was a matter of survival.

"Like a hunter killing a deer to survive. I do not enjoy the thought of killing a creature, but I must eat in order to live." Elizabeth touched Anna's shoulder. "Self-preservation can be a dirty chore. In the absences of your father, I am afraid the welfare of the family and the burden of taking care falls to me, my dear."

"At least we can give the girl a Christian burial. We can do that much," Anna said.

The dead girl's arm twitched and flopped through the bars of the cage. The motion sent a shower of fluid onto the floor. The splash sparkled with hints of bronze gold as the blood momentarily captured the firelight radiating from the lit torches before disappearing in the dark pool collecting in the buckets.

Elizabeth flinched. Attaching any significance to the carcass hanging above our heads was silly, but Elizabeth, like any good mother, wanted to please her eldest daughter.

"Mother, you must," Anna said gripping Elizabeth's sleeve.

Elizabeth twisted away, gently. "Very well, if it pleases you."

Anna tugged her blood-speckled shawl tight around her shoulders. She was satisfied for the time being.

"Amara, please see that Anna returns safely to her room."

"Of course," I said. The formality of the order almost forced me to curtsey, but I held my position giving only a curt nod.

Anna was silent during our walk to her chamber. What she saw was gruesome, what she felt was uncertain. This was her gutted horse with a gypsy man sewn inside, a tragic spying of vigilante justice.

Anna paused outside her room. "I do not think I could ever do what mother did tonight." She was ashamed to admit weakness.

I brushed a strand of loose hair from her blood-smeared cheek. "If ever the time should come, you will do what you must to protect your family," I assured her.

"I don't think I'll have the courage," she said, her eyes turning downward.

I looked her squarely in the eye, "You must find the courage Anna, or you will die. You will not survive in this land if you are not willing to do what you must." The words I spoke were harsh to hear, but she needed to know the truth about the world in which she was born.

"What if she is found out? What if mother is tried for murder?" Anna choked.

"For murder or as a witch, neither is better than the other. Burned or quartered, it makes no difference," I said. "You see she has no choice, but to take the risk."

Anna's eyes searched mine for more answers, but found none. She was hoping to discover another alternative, something more benign. She wanted a solution that would settle easily upon her young nerves.

"She is a good mother. She protects you – I cannot say all mothers would do the same," I said, hoping my words brought courage. "She is a strong woman and I know you will grow up to be the same."

Anna nodded. I turned the latch on her chamber door pushing it open just enough for her to pass through.

"Try to sleep," I said.

I shut the door. I hesitated for a moment listening to the sound of my own blood pumping through my veins. My mind pictured the gypsy man sewn in the gutted horse, and then I saw the dead girl's arm twitching between the iron bars. Anna had seen something she was not ready to witness. Like Elizabeth so long ago, Anna snuck from her bedchamber to spy. Tonight, Anna got her slaughtered beast.

I rubbed my temples as I walked through the twilight of the night to my chamber. I knew Anna would never be the same. This would change her, but I did not yet know how. Upon entering my room, I poured a glass of water. The cool liquid washed the smelly dungeon dust from my throat. I thought about Anna's request for the servant girl, that she be given a proper Christian burial. It was a way to repent the sin. I drew back the velvet curtain from my window and gazed upon the thick crescent moon overhead. No clouds floated by giving depth to the vast universe. I let the drapes fall. I could not bear looking at the world. I did not fully understand just how serious Anna's request would become. Like Elizabeth, I assumed granting her wish was the least we could do if it'd make her happy. Elizabeth was the strongest woman I knew. Her only weakness was pleasing her children. Unfortunately, it was this weakness, this very act of kindness, which would lend to her demise.

***

I wrapped my arms tightly around George's shoulders, my nose nuzzled against his tied scarf. The sweet smell of damp cedar trapped in the rich animal fur was comforting. I fought back the tears threatening to wet my eyes. I was relieved no one witnessed our embrace. If anyone had, they'd know it was too long and intimate even for old friends. I gripped the back of his coat pressing my elbows against the bulk of his arms. He tensed, drawing me in and closing the space separating our bodies. Tears escaped, running down my cheeks as I exhaled, then just as quickly, I breathed in tasting the memorable scented oils and gentleman odor belonging intimately to George.

"It's you," I said smiling.

"Of course it is," George said softly.

I released my hold easing away from George's embrace. Reluctantly he let me go.

"You must tell me, does Draco know I'm here?" George asked.

"No. And Fruzsina?"

"No."

"Won't she miss you?"

George gave a hearty laugh. "Doubtful. She is traveling this season."

"Shouldn't her husband be escorting?" I asked.

"I'm afraid I've been behaving badly. I'm quite the embarrassment these days."

"Was there an incident?"

"Several," George said removing his riding gloves. "My services, I've been told by my dear wife, are not wanted. Although she is no longer the king's favorite, he still adores Fruzsina and is making sure she is properly cared for during her travel aboard."

"And the children?" I asked.

"Properly placed with tutors. Yes, everything is most proper."

I noticed George's hands trembling.

"Are you chilled?" I asked taking his hands in mine.

He sighed. "No, but I wish I were."

"Perhaps we should go inside for a drink," I suggested.

"Yes, I think that should do the trick."

I led George to Cachtice. I deliberately navigated the halls to avoid a chance meeting with other members of the household, not because I was afraid of his discovery, but for the selfish reason, I was not ready to share my guest. I wanted George all to myself. George removed his thick, fur coat and pulled the scarf from his neck placing it on the back of the chair. I uncorked the brandy bottle and poured a glass. After George settled near the hearth, I handed him the drink. His hands quivered as he raised the glass tipping it to wet his lips. He closed his eyes as he swallowed hard. "Thank you," he said crossing his legs.

"Feeling better?" I asked, taking a seat beside him.

"Yes, much." He took another drink of brandy. "How long has it been?"

"Almost seven months."

"I presume you wrote to Draco?" His eyes caught mine before I could look away.

"Yes, of course."

"And still, he is not here. Tell me, what does he have to say?" George was pleased to point out Draco's fault in failing to tend to his domestic responsibilities.

"He assures me he will talk to Francis and King Rudolph when they next meet. He's written they are no longer traveling together, the Black Quintet that is, they are on different assignments," I said.

"Yes, I'm aware of the split, but I'm sure he's told you the reason?"

"Only that he's been assigned his own troop," I answered.

George raised a brow. "Is that all he has told you?"

I did not like George's tone. I thought of the recent letters from Draco. I could not deny I had detected a strange vagueness and a nonchalant tone. I dismissed the inconsistency to lack of time during his tour. After all, he did not have the luxury of witling away the hours by penning letters. However, I should have paid more attention.

"You've heard about poor Sigismond?" George asked.

"Gone mad," I said.

"Oh quite mad, raving, ranting mad. The poor man declared a public separation from the archduchess. Imagine not wanting to remain married to a woman you never wished to be married to in the first place? Scandalous!" George laughed. "Of course the prince must be insane to be repelled by a Hapsburg. The audacity!" He took another drag from his glass.

Charlie Courtland

I chuckled. "Yes, the audacity."

The Bathory's were never short on delivering their share of insults. However, the incidents of certain family members committing public offenses were becoming more serious. The logical conclusion for unruly decorum was determined to be a tainted bloodline. The Bathory's were cursed by a plague of inherited insanity. What other explanation could there be for their error in judgment besides a birth defect polluting the bloodline? In reaction, a royal cleansing was taking place by streaming out the undesirables of the family to remote estates along the fridges of the Empire. Elizabeth was confined to Cachtice and Sigismond...where was Sigismond?

"Sigismond is enjoying the peaceful scenery of Silesia," George answered as if he had read my mind.
"Silesia?"

"I hear it is lovely this time of year," George laughed. "Maybe it will be an added stop on the seasonal tour."

"Oh I'm sure just like Cachtice. Tell me, does Silesia have a beautiful view equal to Cachtice and the sporting wildlife, like bears and wolves?" I asked, sarcastically.
George gave it some thought. "I can't say it does," he said in all seriousness.
"What a shame."

"A terrible shame," George muttered. Sigismond's pitiful existence no longer seemed funny. He poured another drink. "If we can't go to the party, perhaps we should have the party come to us. I dare say there are more of us excluded than invited. Our halls will be more festive than the king's for certain," he said, saluting and trying to lighten the mood.

"But, you've forgotten a detail. Our guests are beleaguered by blood disorders and haunted by specters," I joked.

George waved his hand. "Posh, it is no different from carnival."

I laughed. "Oh George, your sinister humor brightens even the dimmest rooms."

George set down his drink and knelt beside my chair. "It is you who brightens the room, my lady."

227

The ceremony of our performance was regretfully broken by a presence looming in the doorway. "You did not tell me we were expecting a guest," Elizabeth said.

George rose from bended knee and went to Elizabeth greeting her with an affectionate kiss to each cheek; a custom he acquired from the French court. "Countess, you look stunning," he said.

"I wear illness well. You do know I'm quite mad, don't you?" she said.

"I hear it is an epidemic, but you hardly appear infected. You must be very resilient to survive a condemned house. Pray, do tell. How do you do it?"

"The secret is to maintain a proper perspective," she said.

"Ah, mine is typically distorted," he said, lifting his glass of drink. "Won't you join us?" George asked.

"Thank you for the invitation, but I've only come to tell Amara about our plans for tomorrow. I've arranged for a morning ceremony in the small plot by the monastery. Anna requests you join us," she said.

"Has someone died?" George asked, surprised.

"A servant girl," I informed.

"A servant?" He was bewildered, and rightfully so.

"My eldest daughter Anna believes it proper to give the girl a Christian burial," Elizabeth said.

"That is a lot of trouble for a servant." He was aware masters had little obligation.

I shrugged.

"It won't take long. Amara will return in time to join you in the dining hall for an early lunch," Elizabeth said.

"Will Anna be offended if I do not attend the ceremony?" he asked.

"I think it's best that you don't," I said. The thought of explaining was too much to endure.

"Very well, as you wish," he said.

Elizabeth said good evening and retreated from the room. George and I stared at one another. It was obvious neither knew how to break the sudden silence hanging over us. I finally broke through the awkwardness by suggesting I show him to his chambers.

"She's aged," he said, as we walked through the castle.

"Shhh! Keep your voice down. She'd be very upset to hear such a thing. She obsesses about her appearance daily."

"Her cheeks are pallid, her hair dull," he said, ignoring my request.

"She does not exercise. She no longer goes for walks or rides her horse." We were now outside his chamber door.

"What does she do?" he asked.

I thought of the tainted smell of the musty workshop. "Rots. She is rotting away here," I said.

George reached for the latch of the door. I stopped him.

"And I? Tell me George, how do I look to you?" I asked.

He touched the side of my face, the shakes warded off by warmed brandy. "Just as I remember; your lips red as a demon's tongue and your eyes virgin gold." His finger twisted a piece of my hair. "The color of cloves and ginger and smelling of lavender," he continued, bringing the lock to his nose.

"Follow me," I said. I took George by the hand and led him away from his chamber door and toward my apartment. We were just about there when a small figure appeared in the corridor. I immediately recognized the hobble of Ficzko coming toward us.

"What is that?" George whispered. It was apparent he found the deformed man repulsive.

"Elizabeth's pet," I answered. I kept my voice low so Ficzko could not hear my comment.

Ficzko's pace quickened as he drew near. "Good evening, Lady Amara," Ficzko said with a tip of his felt cap. Given the surroundings his appearance was comical.

"Don't bother running to her, Ficzko. She already knows Count Drugeth has arrived."

Ficzko crinkled up his face, his round eyes and bulbous doll nose contorting in a grotesque manner making him look like a menacing joker. "She does, does she?" he said, cocking his head.

I resisted the urge to kick him in the buttocks booting him like a rag doll down the hall.

"Shall I wake you for the peasant funeral or will you be sleeping late?" he asked, his eyes roaming over George. I could tell by his tone he also thought the procession ridiculous.

At the moment, everything seemed ridiculous. Like a fragmented dream with things appearing, which were evidently out of place. "I will be there," I snapped pushing the little man aside. Ficzko grunted as he stumbled to regain his balance. He gave a hop and was on his way.

"Strange twist of nature," George said once Ficzko was out of earshot.

"You must be careful of him. He hides in the tiniest of places and Elizabeth absolutely adores him."

"I thought she adored you," George said.

"She does – but Ficzko serves another purpose," I said. I opened my chamber door to find the hearth stoked, wine poured, and scented candles lit.

"Well this is pleasant." George loosened his shirt, making himself more comfortable.

"That little sneak! He knew I'd invite you to my room." I went to the bedchamber and found fresh linens on the bed and flowers on the dressing table. I supposed keeping me happy was also advantageous.

"What purpose does he serve?" George called from the other room.

"Who?"

"The dwarf."

I heard the outer door creak followed by a low grumble.

"Amara…come here please," George said nervously.

I had almost forgotten about Lyk. He was another character quite out of place in a noble residence. "Come here, my boy," I said. Lyk stalked forward with his teeth bared and ready to attack George if he made any sudden move.

George braced himself against the sofa with his foot raised in guarded defense. "Is that a wolf?" He did not take his eyes off the snarling beast inching closer.

I slipped my hand beneath Lyk's collar. "This is my pet." I ordered Lyk to sit and when he obeyed, I stroked the fur between his ears.

"Wouldn't a cuddly feline be a preferable companion?" he asked.

I covered Lyk's ears. "I wouldn't say that if I were you. Lyk does not care for cats."

"His name is Lyk?"

"Lykaios. Lyk for short," I said.

"First a dwarf and now a wolf?" He shook his head. "Where on Earth did you get a wolf?"

"He was a gift."

"From whom?"

"Draco found him orphaned in the woods when he was a pup," I said. I motioned for Lyk to go lay down on his bed near the fire.

"Most husbands give jewels or silks, but yours, a wild beast!"

"He thought Lyk would be a fierce companion – that he would protect me in his absence."

"Ah yes, in the absence of his domestic responsibility. How silly of me to have not thought of getting my own wife a wolf. I'm sure she'd also find it a suitable substitution for a husband away on business. Maybe while I'm in the region I should trap her a bear?"

"You can jest all you want, but contrary to your belief, Lyk has proven to be a handsome guardian."

"I must disagree," George said, relaxing his foot.

"Why so?" I felt my own defenses perk up.

"He allows another man in your bedchamber. A proper guard would have killed me upon entry.

"He did not because he senses my approval."

"Ah, but if a husband was present, I would not be, therefore, proving my case that Lyk is a sorry substitute."

I turned away. "He keeps me company at night," I said.

I felt George's arms tighten around my waist. I let him kiss the nape of my neck. Lyk growled from his bed near the hearth letting me know of his disapproval.

"Tell me you don't want me and I will return to my chambers," George whispered.

I knew I should resist, but I could not pass another night in silence with only pillows to provide comfort. The isolation was unbearable. Draco's letters offered little assurance of his return. I did not know when I would see him again. I invited George not because I truly thought his influence remarkable, but because I knew he would come, and here he was standing in my bedchamber, his real, warm breath caressing my skin, his arms clutching my waist, his body wanting mine. I did not have the will of the faithful nor the care. My heart I feared had grown cold and indifferent with each fleeting day I spent within the walls of the fortress Cachtice. "I will not utter the request," I replied. "I will not tell you to go."

George kissed me. "Mistress of my heart," he said. "Forever my mistress."

I hated the title, but I was no longer a foolish girl. I was a grown woman too aware. I knew George and I would never be anything more than this moment. What we shared was a crease in time where we snatched any opportunity to experience passion. Tonight, our love was concealed behind reinforced walls and witnessed only by those who could not speak. I did not know if there was a tomorrow, nor did I care. I had to seize what little I could and I was tired of feeling sorry for loving that which I could never have.

***

Ficzko was standing even with my bedside and holding my robe. I slipped from the bed and into my dress while he eyed George sleeping, his hair tasseled against the feathered pillow and lying on his side with the covers draped over his body exposing the bare, smooth skin of his chest.

"What are you looking at?" I hissed.

"He is not like other men, he does not possess a single blemish," Ficzko said.

"He has many, they're just invisible. His are on the inside," I said, annoyed. I twisted my hair into a bun.

Ficzko edged around the bed to gain a better look. He lifted the edge of the covers. "On the inside?"

I slapped his hand. "Stop it, you'll wake him."

"Who knows he is here?" Ficzko asked.

"No one and it better stay that way. That means you must keep your tiny mouth shut. If you don't, I'll personally stuff you in that barbaric cage you like to play with so much."

Ficzko grumbled something beneath his breath as I finished dressing for the funeral procession. When all was in order we quietly departed leaving George sleeping alone in my bedchamber.

"You're grumpy this morning," he noted, closing the door behind him. "Perhaps a nice funeral might cheer you up."

I quickened my pace knowing my long strides would be difficult for Ficzko's short legs to match.

He trotted down the hall, his voice wavering as he breathed. "I've enlisted the services of Andreas Berthoni; he is a local Lutheran pastor. I believe when he sees how kind the countess is, by giving her servants Christian burials, the rumors of her practices will cease. No one will believe a witch would commit such a decent act."

I stopped cold in our path. "That is ridiculous! What if Berthoni questions the cause of death?"

"They are servants. He won't care how they died, only that the countess is concerned about their souls."

I threw up my hands. "This is your plan to redeem the peasants faith in Elizabeth?"

Ficzko shrugged. He ran ahead to open the door for me to pass through. On the other side waited Anna and Elizabeth. We exchanged greetings before proceeding across the grounds and down the incline toward the monastery. The occasion was forcing an awkward formality within our intimate circle. Up ahead I could see the morning sun playing in the stained glass windows of the cathedral. The gardens were well tended and an adequate patch of land was lying dormant in the winter frost. In the months to come it would be plowed and seeded for the harvest crop. The heels of our boots scratched along the hard limestone path, each stone underfoot grinding against the stubborn Earth. I found the sound comforting. It was a reminder actual life existed in the crags, and that breathing bodies moved about taking in the air waiting for something to happen.

Ficzko pounded on the weathered door. Dangling above our heads was a lantern, which had already been snuffed out. A man shrouded in a plain brown robe appeared, the vastness of his hood swallowed his face and muffled his voice. Inside the cathedral seated in a pew was the pastor Berthoni. He rose as we approached, his hand outstretched and eager to accept Elizabeth's. "Good morning, Countess," he said.

She rejected the gesture by keeping her hands tucked inside her ermine muffler. "Is everything prepared?"

Berthoni said all was in order.

"Very well. Let's get to it then," Elizabeth said.

"This is most kind and generous," Berthoni said, letting his rejected hand fall.

"They were most helpful in my time of convalescing," Elizabeth lied.

Berthoni closed his eyes, nodding as if in reflective thought. "Yes, caring for the sick is a noble occupation."

We waited for him to say more, but he did not. He only grinned, still nodding as if we clearly understood what this meant. "Shall we go?" he finally asked. The hooded man of God led us to the cemetery. Headstones jutted from the ground in varying shapes and sizes depending on the importance of the deceased. The superior grave markers leaned under the weight of their ornamentation while the lesser, plainer stones stood rigid in place. I tried to read a name on one as we passed, but black mold disfigured the etched epitaph.

"Because the ground is still frozen, my men had some trouble. I'm afraid the graves are shallower than we'd like," Berthoni apologized.

"Will this be a problem?" Elizabeth asked.

"I think the animals will leave it alone, but if we get severe rains they might float to the surface."

Berthoni held open an iron gate leading us from the cemetery. "If it happens, we will take care of it."

"Where are we going?" I asked.

"This ground is sacred to the monastery," Berthoni explained. "Please follow me. The site of the burial is by an old oak near the meadow."

Just beyond the cemetery was another fenced plot of land where heaps of dirt stood beside shallow holes. As we approached I saw two flimsy pine boxes at the foot of the holes both tied with knotted ropes. Upon Berthoni's orders the gravediggers began to untie the ropes.

"What are you doing?" Elizabeth snapped.

"It is customary to bless the dead," Berthoni said.

"Can't you do it without opening the box?"

Berthoni was puzzled.

"I'm only thinking of my daughter," Elizabeth said.

Anna moved to my side. "Why are there two boxes?" she whispered.

"But, it is customary," Berthoni repeated.

The men continued to untie the knots. The ropes fell to the side of the boxes. We stood quietly as the first lid was lifted. Anna's question was answered. Inside the casket lay the corpse of the drawing room maid, the young girl who cut her wrist while cleaning the smashed Russian egg from the floor. At the time, I hardly thought the wound fatal. Holding onto my arm, Anna leaned in to get a better look. The corpse remained dressed in a nightshift with her naked arms prone by her sides. I recognized the deep cut along her wrist but as I originally thought the wound was not fatal. No, it was the other slashes across her arms slicing through the drained veins, which killed her. I determined by the lack of scarring from healing she died rather quickly leaving behind gaping grotesque purplish wounds.

Berthoni opened the Bible and moved closer to the box. He began to mutter words, but hesitated when his eyes settled on the inflictions. He stopped reciting the blessing. "How did this girl die?" he asked.

"Why does it matter?" Elizabeth asked. She was clenching her jaw in a forced sympathetic smile.

"In most cases it does not, unless she took her own life. The cuts to the wrists…"

"An accident while cleaning up a broken dish," Elizabeth interjected.

"All of them?"

"Of course not!" Elizabeth snapped as she stepped forward. "Just that one, the others were from bleeding her – there was an infection. She begged for the arm to be amputated, but I could not approve the method." Elizabeth was agitated. I touched her arm hoping to calm her. She relaxed and allowed a practiced somber expression to fall across her face. She blinked slowly and deliberately to control her concentrated gaze. "I could never order a maid's hands cut off. Perhaps I should have. It might have saved her life."

Berthoni responded as any good man of God would, with an agreeable frown. "It was good of you to seek any treatment for the poor girl."

Satisfied, Elizabeth took a step back.

Berthoni continued with his blessing and then moved on to the second casket. The lid was lifted and inside was the tortured, mutilated corpse of the escaped servant girl. The wounds invited decay and the smell of rotting flesh assaulted our senses causing Anna to retreat with a handkerchief over her nose.

Berthoni cleared his throat. "Bless thee, what fate reigned down on this dear girl?" He was clearly shocked by what he saw in the box.

"Troubled young thing, she grew homesick and in the midst of night tried to find her way to the village. My men found her like this dead in the woods. I can only imagine the beast she encountered. I shudder to think what horrible creature took her life. The guards believe it was a vicious pack of wolves. I'm informed they hunt the area during the sparse months tracking any carcass for food. I have on good authority this innocent fell prey to hungry animals."

"You say she was seeking her family?" Berthoni asked.

The question caught Elizabeth off guard. Her explanation for the injury was not as well thought out as she imagined. However, where a less clever person might falter, Elizabeth was quick to recover. "A sick mother, but she has recently passed. I believe this was the true reason for the young girl's disobedience. She must have received word of her mother's failing health and was desperate to see her mama one last time. It is a sad story. You can see why my daughter insisted we give this poor creature a proper burial," Elizabeth explained.

I fought the urge to applaud. It was a superb performance, the delivery, and the hush at just the precise moment and then the recovery timed perfectly with a heart felt gesture of the palm to the chest. It was beautifully executed and if I had not known the truth, I would have believed Elizabeth whole heartily. The supporting cast completed the scene, Ficzko removed his felt cap and Anna dabbed a pretend tear from her eye with the handkerchief. I rolled my lip pulling it tight between my teeth. I was relieved the formality of the occasion was broken by mischief. After all, it was all a sham arranged to pacify Anna.

Accepting the explanation, Berthoni ordered the boxes nailed shut. The ropes were again tied and used to lower the corpses into the hallowed ground. He said a final blessing before the gravediggers began tossing the dirt in the holes. Within moments the boxes disappeared and the mess was finished. Or so I thought.

***

Regrettably, the lawn around the oak tree did not remain abandoned for long. There were more servants who perished by unusual and sometimes what seemed unexplained circumstances. Their bodies cut and bruised, blackened and bloated and tossed into flimsy pine boxes. Pastor Berthoni continued to preside over the burials at Anna's urging. Each time his inquiries about the condition of the bodies were put off or, after some pressing, a tidy explanation offered. Finally, when he could no longer turn a blind eye, he decided to write his superiors. He asked that an investigation take place. Of course, this letter never reached the council. Elizabeth's guards received word of the betrayal and intercepted the courier carrying the request.

In the letter, Berthoni stated he no longer could perform his duties with a pure conscience because he felt those delivered to him by the countess had died by, 'unknown and under mysterious circumstances.'

In truth, we knew exactly how the servants died. There was nothing mysterious about it. When a servant was thought to be stealing from Elizabeth she heated coins and placed them in their hands branding the image of the crime permanently in the skin. When the wash was not done to her liking an iron was set in the fire. Elizabeth paced back and forth watching patiently as the metal turned from a steely gray to amber red. When satisfied it was plenty hot, she ordered the servant to strip free of clothing and with great care thrust the hot iron against their exposed naked body scalding the flesh and singeing it to the bone.

Once, when a chambermaid was sloppy with her sewing chores Elizabeth pulled so violently on the girl's mouth that it ripped apart splitting the corners and tearing into her thick cheeks. To teach the subordinate a lesson, Elizabeth used the maid's own needle and thread to sew the wounds shut. The girl looked like a gypsy puppet properly stitched together and decorated for festival. Elizabeth said the girl's reflection should be a reminder to improve her skills. With no recourse, those punished labored on with open sores often consumed by wicked infections. Many tried to cut the spoiled flesh from their own bodies and by doing so, ended up bleeding to death or making the infection worse.

Some might think Elizabeth cruel, but in her defense she truly believed she was keeping order. After all, these were different times. Servants were property of the master and rarely lived to see old age. When death occurred they were disposed of in the same fashion as slaughtered livestock. It was the damn burials that made them human. At least the ceremonies played a part in tricking the pious Berthoni's delusional mind. I supposed it would have been wise for Elizabeth to explain to Berthoni the true purpose for the funerals. To tell him all efforts were merely a means to appease a sensitive child, but Berthoni was also a servant of Cachtice and of God. He was to serve—not question those superior in position and power. It goes without saying that Elizabeth was furious when she read the letter Berthoni intended to send to the council. However, before she could share her displeasure, he fled. We found his crude chamber empty and a horse missing from the monastery stables.

Somebody had got to him first; someone had warned him Elizabeth was coming.

The Night, He is a Vampire

The doors of Elizabeth's private chamber flew open. Francis stumbled in clutching his overweight belly. He looked awful. His black hair soaked and matted. The whites of his eyes blotched with reddish streaks and sweat beaded on his forehead. I'd never seen him so distressed. He swayed uneasy, the buckles of his boots clanking as the heels hit hard against the floor. Spittle freckled his beard. His tongue, swollen and purple, thrashed around with each curse between breathy groans.

I could not hide my horror. He was a disgusting sight. I dug my nails into the cushion to prevent fleeing the room. Elizabeth was unfazed. She managed to stay perfectly erect and phlegmatic beside me. I did not understand how she maintained composure because it was taking every bit of my strength not to scream.

"What is the matter?" she asked, her voice unnaturally steady given the scene.

Before he could answer, Francis wretched a stomach full of vomit upon the floor, the splatter missing our slippers by only a few feet. The smell was obscene and I gagged on the stench. The chambermaid ran to attend to the mess by quickly tossing a cloth over the offense. Francis weaved about, his knees caving under his own weight. The guards raced forward to catch him by the arms just in time. A second more, and he would have collapsed on the floor and cracked his skull.

"Call a doctor," Elizabeth ordered. She clapped her hands encouraging them to carry out her demand.

The guards labored beneath Francis's unconscious mass. The heels of his heavy boots scraped across the floorboards as they dragged him from the room. A spot of sloppy vomit trickled down the front of his velvet doublet soiling the honored emblem of the Black Quintet. I resisted using my handkerchief to clean the offense from his clothing. I did not know what contaminated his body, and since it was still a mystery, I did not wish to chance a contagion.

Elizabeth was more bothered than panicked. "Come. Let us wait in the drawing room for the doctor."

Dorothea and I obeyed following Elizabeth through the castle and sweeping into the small parlor used to greet less distinguished guests. The room was cold, the lighting harsh and unwelcoming. Maids donned in nightshifts dressed up with aprons hurried to prepare for a midnight visitor. In contrast, Elizabeth was just the opposite. She paced methodically across the room. Her hair was neat and pulled tight in a bun, but the rouge on her cheeks was faded. She paused by the window catching her reflection in the pane. She straightened her dress, glanced at the veins on the back of her thin hands and sighed. She was more concerned with her own appearance rather than the state of her husband.

As I sat in the cold room I thought about how much time had passed. It was difficult to believe more than a year had lapsed since King Rudolph condemned Elizabeth to illness. After much waiting, Draco finally returned to Pressburg and gained the opportunity to meet privately with Francis. Although I was never privy to the conversation, I imagined Draco expressed my concerns regarding our situation at Cachtice because, within a month, Francis left the court and made the long journey home to visit his recovering wife.

Fortunately, George had also taken leave from Cachtice and the two gentleman's paths never crossed. Needless to say, I was saddened to see George go, but since he was secretly visiting I could not expect he would stay away from his commitments for too long. As it was, his absence was raising alarm and he thought it best to depart before those of any importance noticed his withdrawal from society. I said my farewell with a heavy heart, but knew neither of us had a choice in the matter. I knew our brief time together was about to expire and I would once again have to let him go.

In parting, George hastily begged me to leave Cachtice with him. In desperation he clutched my cloak, a gesture that might be misconstrued as violent, but I knew otherwise. He said we could escape from this life neither of us ever wanted. His speech was full of romantic notions involving the two of us fleeing to a foreign country where we'd live along a coastal beach in a small villa. I pictured a villa like the one Elizabeth and I had visited while in Venice. It sounded lovely and for a moment he had me convinced, but then I looked into his nervous eyes, those delicate orbs trying so intensely to be valiant, but not capable of hiding shame. I winced wondering how far we would get before money ran sparse and George's drinking tainted his bravery. I kissed his lips to calm his mad ranting and whispered a promise we'd dance again in better times. We'd have our stolen moments in the privacy of courtly chambers where perfumed rooms and satin dress was part of the next scene. After all, it was just another act and this was our intended fate. Reluctantly, but with little resistance, he released his hold and regained his sanity. He then returned my kiss and mounted his horse. His mouth was dry and his face showed a tired defeat. I suspected he was beyond recovery from his dependence.

I'd seen this countenance before on older gentlemen of the court. I recalled how they sat complacent in high back chairs stuffed to the gills with ruffles, their light colored eyes milky and distorted. It was a beneficial malady affecting the wealthy—a kind of blindness enabling them to ignore indiscretion. Contrary to Draco's sharp intuitive stare, these gentlemen rarely fixed on any particular backdrop. They were condemned to live out their days in comfortable confinement.

I could see it now. George suffered like those men. I believe this is the reason he never questioned the secrecy surrounding Elizabeth's movements through Cachtice. Not once did he probe for an explanation regarding the burial ceremonies or inquire about the whispering servants who we encountered around every corner. Once, during a stroll about the grounds we happened upon two men carrying a pine box toward the monastery. Caught off guard, I hesitated. However, George continued walking with his hands securely behind his back, never breaking stride or conversation for that matter. He simply diverted his gaze and, with decided care, guided our party in a different direction. I remember thinking I should ask him to keep what he'd seen or possibly overheard during his reprieve a secret, but then I determined this was unnecessary. He had not witnessed anything unusual, not because it did not happen, but because it was impossible for him to do so. He was conditioned by years of social occupation and through careful breeding. He taught me clarity for the elite was only beneficial when self-serving. It was then that I realized George could never utter a word even if he wanted to. In doing so, he'd compromise himself and be forced to explain why he was at Cachtice in the first place. Although not officially circulated, it was understood the countess, during her time of convalescence, was not to receive visitors. To visit us was to directly disobey the king's order. Despite his recent bravado I knew George would never find a noose a very becoming necktie. It was all too risky. I could count on him taking the coward's way out and ignoring everything.

***

The light flashing through the paned window followed by the grinding of carriage wheels drew me away from my private thoughts and back into the small parlor I occupied with Elizabeth and Dorothea.

"The doctor has arrived," Elizabeth announced. She did not bother to face me when she spoke. "We will receive him properly. Tell him nothing specific, is that understood?"

"Of course," I answered. I was annoyed by her instructions. Her words lingered in my head. I bounced them around arranging them in a different order, or was I recreating them all together? *Do not betray me.* This is what I heard. I thought this was always understood or was Elizabeth beginning to distrust me? Was she questioning my loyalty? The unexpected visit of George and now Francis must have caused her distress. She knew it was my doing. I had made no effort to hide my correspondence. I fought back a yawn. This was not the time or place, but I could not stop the words from coming out.

"Why did you not intercept my letters?" I asked.

"Should I have?"

I did not answer straight away. I was distracted by the muddled exchange of conversation taking place down the hall. It sounded as if the doctor was interviewing the servant who was taking his coat. Unable to discern any of his words I decided to abandon my effort at eavesdropping.

"What I did was out of loyalty to you, Elizabeth. I was only trying…" I began to explain when the parlor door suddenly popped opened interrupting my plea.

There stood the doctor with an eyeglass set between thick brow and cheek. The hair on his head had migrated south covering his ears and chin and I noticed the toes of his shoes curled at the ends. They did not fit properly and I surmised it was because the shoes were not his own. Maybe they'd been given to him as payment for services.

"Thank you, Doctor, for coming," Elizabeth said. She offered a frigid hand for his taking.

"I've already been told Count Nadasdy is unconscious and resting in bed. Since he is unable to speak, you must tell me what happened."

"I don't really know," Elizabeth answered. She crossed her arms and moved away from the doctor and toward the fire where the wood smoked.

The doctor removed his eyepiece and began polishing it with the soft lining of his undercoat. "When did he fall ill?"

"I can not be certain," Elizabeth answered.

The doctor replaced his eyepiece to the proper position on his face and glanced at me. "Perhaps someone else was with the count when he became sick?" the doctor asked.

"Not to my knowledge," Elizabeth said. She turned away from the fire. Noticing the doctor's interest in me, Elizabeth replied, "Lady Amara was in *my* company this evening."

"Are there any other *ladies* in the residence?" he asked.

"All were in my company at the time," Elizabeth clarified.

"Very well." With out invitation, he took a seat beside me on the sofa. "Perhaps Lady Amara can be more forthcoming?"

"Pardon Doctor, but should you not go and examine the count?" I asked. His presence was making me very uncomfortable. I noticed his glass piece magnified a portion of his face accentuating the folds of fleshy wrinkles. These were not the kind caused by hard work in the burning sun, but from years of worry.

"Yes, but before I do I must make certain it is not the plague."

"The plague?" I said aloud. I did not even want to imagine such a disease had breeched the castle walls.

"The count has traveled aboard recently and I've received word from my colleagues about a deadly and extremely contagious sickness. It strikes swiftly and is, at this time, incurable. Has anyone else in the count's traveling party fallen ill?"

"No, I do not believe so," Elizabeth answered.

"How about in the household? Any deaths? Servants gone missing or complaining of illness?"

"What are you suggesting doctor?"

The doctor cleared his throat. "May I have a drink? I believe some dust from the road is caught in my windpipe."

"Certainly," Elizabeth said. She did not enjoy his line of questioning.

"If by chance a plague is present we must quarantine the castle. No one must enter or leave. It is the only way to prevent the spread. I must know if anyone else has fallen ill."

"Are you insinuating Francis carries this nasty disease?"

The doctor was unmoved by the implication. "I don't mean to insult the count," he said dryly. "I suspect the contagion does not originate with him, but perhaps a servant from the village carried it and unknowingly infected the count."

Elizabeth took a seat while the maid offered the doctor a drink. "You know the symptoms of this plague?" she asked.

"Communications between my colleagues and I have been very specific. Now if you can, please describe what you saw."

"It was very late and it all happened very suddenly. We were taken quite by surprise," Elizabeth started.

The doctor nodded adding a, "ah-hum," for emphasis.

"He was sweating and moaning and I think gripping at his throat like this," Elizabeth said, demonstrating the event by grasping at her own throat. "Maybe it wasn't his throat, perhaps he was clutching his stomach," she corrected, changing her mind.

"Ah-hum," the doctor said.

"Then he vomited on the floor of my chamber." She removed her handkerchief and held it to her lips.

"Ah-hum, I'm sure that was very unpleasant. Was his tongue swollen or black in appearance?" the doctor asked.

"I don't know? It was late and he lost consciousness. That's when I sent for you."

"Thank you, Countess." The doctor opened his bag and pulled out a mask. It was ivory with two holes cut where the eyes go and a long, molded nose shaped like a bird's beak. He tied it around his head before standing. "This will protect me from any contagions," he said, his voice muffled by the apparatus.

Elizabeth called for a maid to show the doctor to Francis's chambers. After he was gone and I was sure no one was looking, I let another yawn escape.

"How did you know about the symptoms of the plague?" I asked.

Dorothea's smirk fingered her as the mastermind.

"We will be quarantined," I said.

"Only a few weeks, a month at the most," Dorothea said, obviously proud of herself. "It really is a perfect plan. The poison I concocted mimics the plague. The doctor logically assumes a servant infected Francis. This will help explain all the recent deaths and divert any misgiving away from the countess and Cachtice."

"I can't believe you've poisoned the count. Do you really think you can fool the doctor?" I whispered.

"If Francis dies no one will be the wiser and we will be free in a month at the most," Dorothea repeated, her face glowing with excitement.

I was irritated that I'd been excluded from the scheme. Again, I wondered if Elizabeth distrusted me. I squirmed in my seat. Was Dorothea as Elizabeth's intimate companion finally replacing me in the order of importance? "Why was I not told?" I asked, my temper flaring contrasting sharply with the gleeful expression of the other two women.

Elizabeth hugged me. "Oh my dear Amara, don't be cross with us. It is true, we used you in a way but it was necessary. I wanted you to write to Draco. The letter, it needed to sound sincere. Your urging delivered Francis to us."

I now had my answer as to why she had not bothered to intercept my letters.

"Of course George was an unexpected arrival, but his presence was harmless," Elizabeth said. She released her motherly hold on me. "I am not angry with you – I know you better than you know yourself. Dorothea had doubts, but I told her you'd write sooner or later. I can see how you hate being locked up here. Eventually you'd do something to gain reprieve from this place."

"So I was a pawn?" I asked.

"Oh Amara, you know you are more than that. You're a very important player," she said. "Without you we couldn't have managed."

I envisioned my head on the chopping block. "So I lured Francis to his death?" I asked.

"If you must be so crass," Elizabeth said.

"If he dies it is on me."

"Do I need to recant the long list of offenses he's committed against us?" Elizabeth asked.

I looked at Dorothea and wondered what offense she'd suffered. She edged uneasily beneath my probing glare.

"Your imprisonment is his doing or have you forgotten?"

Had I forgotten? Had I some how become resigned to my fate and accepted this life of solitude? Was I allowing another to dictate how I should live? It was clear Elizabeth had not. My skin prickled.

"If not of yourself, please think of Anna and Katelin. Think of how they are trapped, denied a life which they are rightfully entitled."

Both Dorothea and Elizabeth were staring at me, both waiting my reaction to Elizabeth's speech. Her twist was brilliant and her claim that she knew me better than I myself was painfully true. She was also correct to assume I cared more for the children, and although I never spoke outright in their defense, it was apparent I would do anything for them.

"What do you think will become of Anna?" Elizabeth asked.

I raised my hand indicting there was no need to continue. My imagination was forming a dreadful picture quite nicely all on its own. Any further prompting was unnecessary. "What do you want me to do?" I asked.

"Nothing, the plan has been executed. We simply must wait and play this out. It should come naturally. We've rehearsed the burial procession many times," Elizabeth said.

We'd been rehearsing for almost a year now. Elizabeth had not just been behaving strangely. In fact, she was practicing for a very important role, the role of widow. I should have known better. It all suddenly made perfect sense; the experimenting with torture techniques and making use of devices, the tainting of food and lately, the burial ceremonies – all rehearsals for a grander scheme.

"Of course, you may have to improvise a bit, but that should be easy. Just follow my lead," she said.

I was capable of doing what Elizabeth asked. I'd been doing it my entire life. However, somewhere I had lost sight. I let pity blind me to my true occupation. I was, after all, a loyal servant of a Hungarian countess who, since her early start, was horribly mistreated. Suddenly I felt renewed. My purpose was clear.

***

Unfortunately, before Elizabeth's tragedy could run its course it was plagued by a slough of uninvited dilemmas. The first being Francis did not die. Death was knocking but the tough bastard fought diligently and finally won the battle and beat the ordeal. The doctor was stunned. He had never heard of anyone surviving a plague, especially one this severe. He contributed the victory to Francis's superior inherited prowess. After receiving the news, Dorothea cowered. Her radiant glow banished to a tarnished hue of yellow. For failing Elizabeth she expected a thorough lashing, but instead got an earful of cursed words. The timidity of Elizabeth's wrath was unnerving, but subdued by the idea this was a temporary remission. Dorothea was to brew another poison, and Elizabeth was to ensure it be administered swiftly and discretely. Francis, in a weakened state was certain to perish quickly. She rationalized this was merely a setback and was easily redeemed. Well, it might have been if it was not for the second hindrance.

In the days to come, not a single person crossed the threshold of Cachtice during the daylight hours. We were under strict quarantine until the doctor was certain all risk to health had passed. I was just about to extinguish the flame of my lantern for the night when I heard a commotion in the passageway. I slide the secret panel on my door open just in time to see the passing of soldiers escorting a dark figure. I barely caught sight of a black cape as it swept by my room. I sucked in a deep breath; the Quintet had arrived and with them came Draco. I slammed shut the secret panel. My pulse quickened. I did not know what to do first: run to Elizabeth or prepare my chambers for the return of my husband. He'd come back, he'd returned to me after all. I hurried to my bedchamber to dress. I was in the midst of twisting my hair atop my head when it hit me. Draco had not come for me. He had marched by my chamber door and gone directly to Francis's side. He was here for his commander. It was not the pages of my letters, but a scribbling of words penned on a scrap of parchment, which compelled him to ride through the night. I threw my brush against the wall. It broke to pieces, its delicacy no match for the unforgiving stone.

Instead of prettying myself, I raced to Elizabeth's chamber and roused her from sleep. "The Quintet has come," I said shaking her shoulder. "I saw them pass by my chamber door. Draco is with Francis now."

Elizabeth rubbed her eyes. "The Quintet?"

"They received word and no doubt have been riding straight through," I said.

Elizabeth threw on a robe and went to Dorothea who, despite the commotion, remained sound asleep. "Wake up!" she snapped, shaking Dorothea violently.

Dorothea sat up in bed. She looked ridiculous with her nightcap slipping cockeyed atop her head. "What is it?" she asked.

"Is the poison ready?" Elizabeth tried to whisper, but excitement heightened her voice.

"Not yet, Countess. Maybe in a day or two."

"That won't do. We need it now!"

"I can't be sure of its effect," Dorothea said, her sight working to adjust to the dimness.

"Get up!" Elizabeth yelled pulling Dorothea by the arm.

"Ouch, you're hurting me," she whined.

"Go at once and retrieve the poison. I will spike his morning tea. He will be dead by luncheon."

"Elizabeth, do not be rash. It is too late. I'm afraid we've missed our chance. We mustn't try now that Draco has arrived. He is not easily thwarted. He will detect foul play – he will turn this castle upside down until he discovers the culprit or worse, your secret," I said.

"You think him too clever," Elizabeth said.

I grabbed Elizabeth hand. "I warn you, do not underestimate Draco Lorant. He is not like other men."

Elizabeth screamed in frustration. I leapt to stifle her cry before the guards heard.

Dorothea was so frightened she began to cry.

"Stop your blubbering!" I ordered. "If you had gotten it right in the first place this would never be happening."

Dorothea tugged the bed linen up around her sulking shoulders. "I don't know what went wrong?" she muttered.

"It doesn't matter now. The plot is a bust, and all is lost. We must play it out if we are to not be found out," I instructed.

Elizabeth began tearing at her hair. I slapped her face, but she refused to stop.

"What is wrong with her," Dorothea cried.

"Help me. She's worked into a fit," I snapped. I was no match for Elizabeth's strength.

"Make her stop," Dorothea said.

"Fetch me that pitcher of water."

Dorothea grabbed the pitcher from the dressing table and thrust it toward me. I splashed Elizabeth, drenching her face and chest. She gasped, wiping the water from her face.

"How dare you!" she growled.

Dorothea stepped away, but I stood my ground.

"That's enough," I said. "Get yourself dry and into bed. They will call for you in the morning to be questioned. Draco suspects something is amiss or he would not have come."

"His commander is gravely ill," Dorothea said. "It is understandable that he comes."

I rounded on the witch. "Gravely ill with the plague? How stupid do you think Draco is? No one else got sick. Did it ever occur to you that perhaps infecting another member of his party might be wise? It would work to confirm the doctor's diagnosis?"

Dorothea's mouth moved, but nothing came out. She was struck dumb by my tongue-lashing.

"The count has a contagious disease that no one else appears to have contracted!" I said.

"Several servants died," Dorothea pointed out.

"Incompetent fool!" I cursed. "They died before he even arrived!"

Elizabeth removed her nightshift and used it to towel her damp hair. "What do you propose we do?"

I had to think. I must think fast and come up with a plan. "We blame the doctor. We claim he made a frightful error in diagnosing Francis. Of course the doctor will balk at the accusation, but don't worry. I will convince Draco to discredit this man's expertise. However, I will need your help Elizabeth."

"Anything. Just tell me what to do."

"You will be a dutiful mother and wife. You will attend to the household and perform all chores expected of a woman in your position. You mustn't do anything or act out of the ordinary." I was not certain she understood, since hardly anything she did was considered ordinary. "I will tell Draco this is the doctor who also diagnosed your illness. When he sees with his own eyes that you are clearly not infected he will assume this man is inept. He will need proof and you will be our proof."

"What if he interviews others?" Dorothea asked.

"I'm positive he will, but most of the others are too scared to talk. Most likely they will say nothing to prove or disprove our situation. We will use Ficzko to eavesdrop and inform us if there is any betrayal."

"We are cornered," Elizabeth said. I knew her fear because I felt it as well. As long as Francis lived, we remained trapped. However, I was not ready to gnaw off my own arm to be free. I was cunning. I'd use my experience and clever mind to compose a misdirection and by doing so, hopefully distract from the truth.

"We may be cornered, but we're not dead," I said.

Elizabeth bit her lower lip causing it to curl to one side. She looked almost vulnerable sitting on the edge of the bed.

After getting both women to agree, I took my leave. My pulse was still racing as I navigated the passage to my bedchamber. Come morning I would place Draco in a terrible predicament. I truly did not think I could deceive a seasoned commander. It would be difficult to convince Draco that Francis fell ill on his own. He was at Cachtice because he suspected foul play. It was clear he already believed Francis was poisoned and that there was an assassination attempt on his life. It would come down to a choice: to apprise his commander of his suspicion and serve his majesty, or spare my life.

When I arrived I discovered my chamber just as I had left it, pitch black. As I stumbled toward the table where a snuffed lantern awaited, I noticed a peculiar dark void near the hearth.

"Where have you been?" I heard a voice ask.

"Who's there?" I moved across the room with my hands outstretched as I felt my way blindly toward the voice.

"You do not recognize your husband?"

"Draco? Is that you? Why are you standing in the dark?" I felt my way back to the table. I fumbled to light a candle.

"I did not wish to wake you," he answered.

The flame flickered, illuminating the area where I now stood.

"Ah, there is my beautiful wife." His tone flat and there was an absence of emotion on his face.

"I'm so happy to see you," I said, kissing his check.

At first he remained rigid causing our reunion to be awkward, but after some urging he gave in to my affections and eased his hand to the small of my back.

"It's been so long. Why did you not write you were coming?"

"The visit was not planned. I came immediately when I heard of Francis's illness."

"You received my letter then?" I asked. It was a lie. I had not sent a letter.

"I got word through another source."

"But you came to me first," I said.

Draco looked away. "I confess, I went to Francis before coming to your room."

"Good. Then you found him recovered."

"In a weakened state, but sleeping sound."

I worked the fastens on Draco's cape. "You must be exhausted," I said. The fastens were worn from exposure to poor conditions and difficult to undo.

Draco slipped his arms from his undercoat and pulled the tie loose on his shirt.

"Yes, I'm near collapse," he said. He plunked down in a chair and began working his tired feet from his boots. "If you don't mind, I'd like to go straight to bed. We can get reacquainted in the morning."

I did not protest. Instead I gave him another kiss and let him go to bed. It was always the same when Draco returned home. He was weary and cold. It was like meeting a stranger for the first time. Eventually, the distanced between us closed and the uncomfortable formality fell to the wayside, but I'd have to wait until that happened for us to feel at ease in each other's presence again. When it did, it was heaven. It was this brief interlude in time I loved the most, but it never lasted. It was always interruption by Draco's restlessness. At first he'd be content with the mundane, but then boredom, a domestic side effect crept in and began to decay at our acquaintance. Instead of wanting to spend every moment with me laughing and telling stories, Draco would begin wandering the grounds. I'd find him grooming his horse in the stables or walking alone across a high ridge. I'd tease he was patrolling the area and surveying the landscape for weakness. The thing was, Draco never could hide his discontent behind a smile or a brush of the hand. He did not possess the character necessary to deceive his wife. It was just a matter of time before he'd mention a letter requesting his return to duty and then all would be lost. He'd be gone again.

I did not immediately follow him to bed. Instead, I sat staring into the night while Draco's snores echoed from the bedroom. I knew my husband no better than the first year of our marriage. His nomadic soul was a mystery and I feared it would never be settled. After a while I snuffed the candles illuminating the room and took my place by his side. How different his form felt beside me compared to the slight gentlemanly frame of George. I longed to feel joy, but I was painfully aware that the weight next to me was a temporary fixture. I turned on my side pulling the covers up over my shoulders. I closed my eyes. I did not know what a worse fate was; being incessantly in the company of a man one did not love, or always apart from the man one did. Even with Draco so near, I felt as if he was a thousand miles away. I was jealous that his mind was wrought with worry for his commander and not filled with romantic dreams of his wife. I heard the familiar creaking of the door and tapping of Lyk's nails on the floor. I could barely see the outline of his nose probing the air sniffing the fresh smell of a foreign man. He gave a low growl as he edged near the bed.

"Shhh, your father is home," I whispered patting the side of the bed.

Lyk obediently came to my side. I petted the soft spot behind his ears before snapping my fingers indicating I wished for him to lie down. He circled three times before flopping to the floor half landing on his feathered bed. After a few moments Draco's snores were matched by Lyk's soft wheezes. Silence was at bay, but still I could not rejoice. I did not trust the eeriness of nothingness would stay away. I began to drift to sleep. My body felt strangely light before everything in my rational world disappeared and gave in to my dreams.

When I awoke, Draco was gone. I dressed quickly and went to the antechamber. Still, I did not find him. The dirty dishes on the table proved he broke fast without me and took leave on an early morning errand. I questioned the maid, but she did not know where Sir Lorant was off to, only that he seemed in a hurry and intent on not waking me. A basket of rolls was uncovered for my choosing. I took one, dipped the edge in some tea and quit the room. I roamed the halls. The castle was quiet in the morning hours. I questioned each servant I happened upon to Draco's whereabouts, but none had seen him. It appeared my husband moved like a ghostly specter. Even though he had managed to elude the staff, I knew of one person who he'd be unlikely to outwit.

I climbed the spiral staircase to Ficzko's cramped chamber. At first came no answer, but I was persistent. Finally, the door cracked open and there stood Ficzko groggy and annoyed.

"What do you want?" he asked.

"My husband has gone missing. He rose early and no one has seen him since," I informed.

"Why should I care? He is your dog to leash," he snapped.

"What my husband is up to may turn out to be your concern! Especially if he is snooping around passage ways." With a good hard shove I pushed past the door and invited myself into the room. "If Draco should find anything I assure you Elizabeth will not be blamed. It will be the witch and the monstrous little dwarf." I lifted the lid from a wooden box. Inside was a dried twist of sage and a partially melted black soap candle. "Needing protection from something?" I asked.

Ficzko slammed the lid shut nearly pinching my fingers in the process. "Stay out of my things!"

I moved to the window. The view was breathtaking from this vantage. "You can see most of the grounds from up here." A misty steam released from the earth. Crows landed on the fence post, their heads twitching about looking for a morsel of food. "Get dressed," I ordered.

Ficzko began to protest, but a stern look quieted his appeals. Reluctantly, he obeyed my command. "I do this for her, not because you order me," he said, his small fingers working the ties on his shirt. He tugged on a hat and opened the chamber door. "After you, milady."

We parted ways at the bottom of the stairs after agreeing we'd meet up in the parlor. I took the usual route through the corridor while Ficzko disappeared through a secret panel hidden behind a grand portrait. I waited all morning, fidgeting about in the parlor. It seemed the only person readily out in the open was myself. Around noon Anna and the children passed by on their way to the stables for a ride. I offered to accompany them, but was assured Anna was quit capable of attending to her siblings. I could not help but smile at Katelin who looked adorable in her riding cap and snug boots. Once they passed, the room was again irritatingly still. That is until I was startled by the sound of a panel sliding behind me. I rounded to find Ficzko closing the wall through which he entered.

"What have you learned?" I whispered going to him at once.

"Count Nadasdy must trust Sir Lorant for he informed him of a secret passage to his private chamber. It is a maze and even more difficult to fit through. I discovered the pair meeting in the closet," he informed.

"What were they discussing?" I asked.

"Francis also suspects poison."

My worst fear was realized. "Did he mention who he believed was trying to murder him?"

"Not directly, but he expressed after demanding sworn secrecy from Sir Lorant, that he thought it might be his wife."

I was queasy. "Francis admitted this?"

"He said she terrifies him."

"Terrifies? Strong words from a renowned warrior." I paced about the room, my mind working around the words. "Did he say why?"

"No, although Sir Lorant did ask what made him say such things."

I put my hand on my hip. "So, he did not actually accuse Elizabeth of the offense."

"Not in so many words."

"Then it is our duty to do so. Gather a list of people who have both motive and opportunity to commit the crime," I said.

Ficzko nodded and left me alone to contemplate my next move.

The day passed with everyone milling about in different areas. None of us were in the presence of another until that evening during dinner. A grand meal was prepared in celebration of the return of Sir Lorant and the health of Count Nadasdy. Elizabeth took great care over her appearance and arrived wearing a peach and blue dress donned with tiny pearls. The tight hold in which she normally wore her hair was loosened. The soft appeal complimented her high cheekbones and elongated neck. The respects to her beauty by the gentlemen were well received and only enhanced her already vibrant complexion.

Francis sniffed at his food before asking a guard to taste the cuisine. The guard's hand trembled as he lifted the spoon to his lips. I did not see how this benefited Francis since any result would take time to reveal.

"Are you worried about the quality of your dinner?" Elizabeth asked Francis.

"I am a high officer. I've learned to take precaution."

"This is your home. You are safe here." Elizabeth sipped her soup. "I assure you we all sup from the same pot."

I drew up my spoon. Francis would not partake until every member of our dining party tasted the dish.

"There dear, you see we are all fine," Elizabeth said. She patted the corner of her mouth.

"Tell me, Draco. Is my husband always this paranoid?"

"He has reason to be cautious."

"His life is threatened?" she asked.

Draco set down his spoon. "Perhaps you can answer that question for me."

"I? How should I know?"

Francis cleared his throat. "Now don't go upsetting the countess."

Draco's inquisitive eyes met mine. He held firm waiting for me to drop my gaze first, but I refused. "Forgive me, Countess. I didn't mean to imply," he said.

"Tonight I will not take offense. I am too happy to have your company. It has been too long since we all joined together. Let's make a merry time of it, shall we?" Elizabeth said.

The rest of the dinner was unexceptional and was followed by a lovely concert performed by Anna and her sister. Francis relaxed in the company of his children and took every opportunity to shower compliments on the young ladies. Paul was allowed to join us for a time before being excused to the nursery and put to bed. Francis boasted how the tot already possessed a stoic build, which he attributed to the Nadasdy hereditary. He predicted young Paul would follow in his footsteps and be a smash at court and gain the admiration of many young ladies. I did not see what Francis saw. I thought Paul was undersized and anemic. I worried whether the poor youth would grow to adulthood. He did not display a thirst for learning or courage for adventure like his elder sisters. He withdrew easily and preferred to remain in private titling with blocks or staring out the window. Even when in the garden he did not rumble and tumble like most boys. Often he'd complain about dirt speckling his shoes or grains soiling his hands. I believed the boy would never stand for a callous defiling his fingers or mud dulling his riding boots.

After Anna and Katelin were dismissed, Elizabeth turned the conversation away from the Nadasdy heir and back on the girls. She asked Francis if he believed it was time to send Anna to court. She was coming of age and now was an appropriate time to arrange suitors.

Francis replied with a chuckle. "I find it amusing you of all people, my dear wife, wish to arrange a marriage. I recall how much you detested your own mother and father for yours!"

"I am older now and understand what needs to be done to secure my daughter's future. However, I shall like to go about it a little differently than my own parents."

"How so?" Francis asked.

"I would like permission to go with Anna to court so I may see for myself the eligible men. I will give her some say in the matter. She may choose from the lot and, with our permission, marry the man she most desires. I think this is a suitable compromise."

Francis threw back his head and boosted a loud laugh. 'How modern. A wife arranging a marriage!"

Elizabeth did not flinch. "I think a woman is best suited for the chore."

Francis folded his hands in his lap. "Marriage is a matter of economy, a matter that a woman knows nothing about."

"The men attending court all come from good families. I beg you, please allow Anna to at least choose from the assembly," Elizabeth asked.

"Some attend in name alone! They have little to offer in forming an alliance. Let me remind you, dear wife, a daughter's duty is to serve her family's interest. Anna will do as I say and marry whom I choose. I will not give half my fortune to just anyone!"

"Francis, please!" Elizabeth begged.

"I see no reason why either you or Anna should attend court. It will only confuse the young girl. I am capable of arranging a marriage for her and when I see fit. She will arrive on her wedding day and then be off."

Elizabeth did not say anything.

"I see how the court corrupts young women – how the games they play inspire romantic dreams and impossible ambitions. I will not subject my daughter or her future husband to such things. No, Anna and Katelin will remain here until I say differently," Francis ordered.

Although Elizabeth's eyes remained dry, my own began to well. I resented Draco's complacency. Not once did he protest or try to sway Francis in the matter. He was a man, after all, and could have at any time influenced the decision, but he chose to remain quiet. After we returned to our chamber and were alone, I expressed my disapproval.

"Why did you not say anything?" I asked.

"It is not my concern."

"You only speak on matters which concern you?"

"Generally, and I suggest you do the same."

"Well I think that very cowardly," I said. I flung my gloves on the table.

"And what would you have me say?"

"I'd have you take my side."

"Your side? I thought this was between Francis and Elizabeth?"

"A woman can not speak her mind. She needs a man's voice to express her wishes."

"You seem to voice yours just fine."

"Voice them, perhaps, but have them heard? Well, that is another matter," I said.

"Why do you care?" he asked.

"Because it is unfair!"

"It is the way it is."

"She is only asking for a small say in choosing whom Anna marries," I said. I flopped down on the sofa. Draco joined me.

"A small say is asking a lot," he reminded.

"I know, but Francis has the power to grant his wife's wish."

"And he clearly gave his reason for rejecting the request."

"Just because he gave one, doesn't mean it is superior."

Draco shrugged. "It is the circumstance of her birthright, whether I think it is fair or not." He nudged my chin. "Sweet Amara, I must agree with Francis. This is a problem of economy, which a lady does not comprehend. It is much more complicated than you give it credit. Men have been doing it this way for years because it works – it protects the crown and the class."

Repulsed by his words, I pulled away.

"Amara, don't be unreasonable. Anna is lucky her father is in a position to make a good match. He is in a position to choose a man with title and money. How is that so bad?"

I was despondent. "You do not understand." I did not have any fight in my voice.

Draco attempted to comfort me, but I refused his advance.

"Have it your way." His sudden coldness stunned me. He stormed off into the bedchamber leaving me to suffer alone. I hated him for it. My dejection fueled into anger. The walls squeezed in on me while terrible thoughts twisted in my head. His snoring slumber mocked my unsettled state and I knew I must escape before I did something unforgivable.

I stormed the halls of the castle. I was filled with a rage I'd never known before. My feet carried me up the winding staircase to Ficzko's tiny chamber. I banged so hard on his door that the flesh split across my knuckles.

"Who's there!" Ficzko shouted. He was indeed startled by my aggression.

"Open up!" I yelled.

The door swung wide and in the shadows was the outline of a frightened little man.

"Meet me in the workshop and bring an offering," I ordered.

He tried to ask for whom, but I did not leave time to answer. I retreated just as quickly as I had come, down the stairs and through the castle until I reached the kitchen. I paused only to grab a torch from the wall. Without further hesitation, I descended down the narrow staircase leading to the passage below. I despised this place, but with each step I felt more empowered. For once I was in control of something. I moved swiftly in the direction of the secret room. The part of my mind that bound my being in restraint was abandoning me for the moment. I was giving in to the foulness coursing through my body. I did not fight the rage; instead I let it consume me allowing it to take me completely over.

The room was dimly lit and cold. In anticipation I paced around as I waited for Ficzko to arrive. The rattling of chains in the next cell interrupted the eerie stillness of the workshop. My pulse quickened. The rush was elating and my body tingled with excitement. By now I thought my anger would subside, but the waiting only enhanced my desire. The delay gave me time to think of all the injustice I'd suffered. I fed on the thoughts and by the time

Ficzko waved me into the room I was ready for release. There, trapped in iron cuffs dangled a stripped man from the ceiling. I was impressed at how quickly he was acquired for my use. His half-starved body readied for my taking. I found the filth covered rack of bones set before me to be almost inhuman, the very sight was repulsive and I could not wait to unleash my frustration. I moved to the table where the instruments were hidden beneath a thick burgundy velvet cover. Ficzko kindly removed the cloth unveiling a variety of devices. I touched several before wrapping my delicate fingers around the handle of the whip given to Elizabeth by Francis. It was the first of her collection and befitting of the occasion. I chose it for my inauguration. I knew she'd approve of the choice and I was always hungry for her approval.

I faced the offering. He hung moaning in his captive state.

"Why isn't he begging?" I asked, my grip tightening on the whip.

"Sorry, milady. He is still under the influence of the drug. It is the only way to get them here."

Ficzko had a point. He was certainly no match for a fully-grown man, even one so pathetic as this creature. I moved closer clutching the whip. I raised it poised to attack. Then I did something I thought myself incapable of. I snapped it, licking the flesh of his side. The whip cracked back nearly striking my arm. I was overwhelmed by a surge of something, a heat coursing just beneath the surface of my flesh. It urged me to continue. I had to do it again. I struck a second time. The man moaned. He made a feeble attempt to pull away. I hit a third, then a fourth, each time it got easier and more inviting. With each attack of the whip I pictured another face. The first vision that came to mind was Count Thurzo, then the disgusting Turk who tried to rape me, and at the height of my rage I saw Francis laughing. Now, I was completely enraptured. Seized by unseen fury, I was incapable of stopping the abuse. After delivering several more lashings, I was aroused from my trance by Ficzko gripping tightly to my arm. His little hands clung as his heels skidded across the floor.

"Stop!" he yelled. "There is nothing left."

I wiped the sweat from my forehead and face. I thought it was sweat, but as I regained focus I saw it was blood and bits of brain matter. I was covered in it. My clothes, hair and skin sprayed in cast off from the mutilated corpse barely discernable in front of me. What I had done was brutal and inconceivable. I had lashed his flesh clean off from the bone.

Ficzko led me to a water basin across the room. He wrung out the cloth and began to clean the blood and pieces of fat from my face. I suppose it was natural to feel remorse at a time like this, but for some unexplainable reason, I did not. Instead, all I felt was release. I was overwhelmed by a strange, but surprisingly pleasant sense of euphoria.

"I assume by how you go about your business, things such as this are commonplace?" I asked.

"I have witnessed many things, but nothing like this."

I untied my hair. I touched the strands sticky with blood. "Surely Elizabeth has done this many times." I knew of her cruelty and could not imagine I'd done worse.

Ficzko labored at removing the goop from my hair. He was trying to keep quiet but was having difficulty in doing so.

"What is it? You can tell me," I prodded.

"Do not take offense, milady, but you and Elizabeth's practices are very different."

How was this so? She used the devices in a similar manner.

"The countess takes pleasure in experimenting. She tries many things and is aware of her offerings responses. Death is not the object. Pleasure is. You, milady, came not only to inflict pain, but also to kill. You chose a single weapon and within a manner of minutes made a man into mincemeat."

"You are mistaken. I assure you, I achieved much pleasure from the experience," I said. This was the truth. Sick as it was, it was the truth.

Ficzko wrung the bloody rag out in the pot. "I'm not judging. I'm simply saying that it is quit different."

My pulse remained heightened and my breathing still rapid. "Is there more?" I asked pointing to another chamber concealed behind an ill hung curtain.

"I sent Nicholas on an errand. Wait here while I check to see if he's returned with anyone. You must understand this is all very sudden and completing the task at this hour may be troublesome."

Ficzko disappeared behind the curtain. I stood in awe of the remains hanging in the middle of the room. It seemed impossible that a woman of my size could inflict such wounds. The man no longer possessed a face or much of a head. He looked more like a side of beef hooked from the rafters of a smoke house than a man.

It did not take long for Ficzko to return. He waved his pudgy hand for me to come hither. I ducked beneath the curtain and entered the dressing room. Several candles burned on the dresser where light danced upon the crystal cuts of perfume bottles. The interior was in direct contrast from the room with which it shared a wall. I sat in front of the mirror admiring my reflection as Ficzko tamed my hair before loosened my bodice.

"I must tell you, we had difficulty," he said.

"You found a man?" I asked.

"Yes, but he may not be what you wish."

I stood clutching the loosened bloodstained bodice against my chest. "Is he lowly?"

"Just familiar."

"We are acquainted?" I asked.

"I fear so, but when I asked whether he was sure he wanted to do this, he assured me he did, and promised absolute secrecy," Ficzko said.

I wondered what familiar man would risk his life to have an affair while my husband snored in the chamber above. The door to the innermost chamber was ajar and through it streamed an ominous glow. I thought about the interior workings of the castle, how many doors lead to passages and to other interlocking rooms, a maze snaking above and burrowing beneath. Ficzko had my curiosity peaked. The rush I experienced from torturing the anonymous servant had not yet abandoned me. I could feel the venom still burning in my chest and down my legs. It was comforting and gave me courage to see who stood on the other side. I placed my palms against the wood. "You may go," I said to Ficzko.

My heart quickened with anticipation. The smell of incense overwhelmed the air and drowned the unpleasant scent of rotting earth common to the underbelly of Cachtice. There, waiting for an audience stood a tall figure dressed in high boots and a dolman. Upon hearing the approach of my footsteps, he turned to face me. He did not smile, but stood waiting for my reaction to his offering. He mistook the flushing in my cheeks as embarrassment; not realizing it was from an unaccustomed exertion.

"Please Milady, do not be uncomfortable. I shall go at once if you insist and never will speak of this to anyone," he said. The lighting of the room enhanced the ginger coloring of his hair.

"What are you doing here?" I asked.

"Please do not be cross, but when I heard it was you who made the request," he said moving closer, "I knew it'd be difficult to find anyone suitable at this hour. I could not stand sending just anyone. After all, it is you, Milady, and you deserve…"

"Deserve what?" I asked.

"Better," he said softly. He was now standing before me.

How had I not seen? How had I failed to notice the man who stood before me, familiar, but not so for his appearance was changed? A flash of recollections crossed my mind. It was he who was always there in times of trouble stepping forward when I was in need. Was it not he who rode with Elizabeth and me to rescue Draco from the camp? It was his hand that snatched me from the cellar door when the Turks penetrated Cachtice. It seemed whenever I was in peril, it was Nicholas who manifested to give service and here he was now offering himself once again. I stood before him embracing my bloodied clothing, unclean with traces of a dead man stuck in my tresses. Was he here to rescue me this time from myself?

"Do you know what I've done?" I asked.

"Yes," he whispered closing the space between us. "And I do not blame you."

"It does not repulse you?"

"On the contrary," he said, his eyes roamed over my soiled dress. "Tell me, did you enjoy it?"

I wanted to lie, to say the act that I committed was a horrible mistake and that I shall never again do such a wicked thing again.

But, lying to Nicholas would be an insult and I owed him more than that. "It was exhilarating," I confessed. "I feel alive, renewed somehow."

"Yes, yes" he said, as if he knew exactly what I meant. "It is a powerful feeling."

I let him touch my bare shoulder. "You should know I did not ask for you," I said.

"But, it is I who you want."

I did not know how to answer. What did I want?

"You should know why I make this offer." He removed his dolman and then poured a glass of wine. "I've been watching you. Even if you do not know, I do know what you want, Amara." He gave me the wine. "In the beginning you were nothing more than a lady placed in my charge, but then, after awhile, you became more to me. Ever since Venice…"

I held the glass, but did not drink.

He removed his boots and placed them side-by-side at the end of the bed. Draco had the same tendency; carefully placing boots was a soldier's habit.

"Perhaps it is not wine you thirst for?" he continued.

The more he spoke, the more I felt myself drawn to him. His words were soothing and seductively foreign in the manner of delivery. They played on my ears and like sweet kisses on a warm afternoon. My body urged to be close, my breathing slowed, relaxing with each word issued from his lips. Every movement seemed precise and destined to beckon me to come closer. My head began to swoon. The glass of wine slipped from my hand and smashed against the floor. I steadied myself against the chair. I focused on the outline of his body beneath the shearing of his undershirt.

"I confess I've laid in wait, patiently bidding for the moment when I could take you. I've wanted you for so very long." He wetted his lips as he moved toward me. "I'm starving," he said.

"Starving for me?" The words did not come from an experienced lover, but sounded as if spoken by a chaste maiden, innocent and naïve. I expected him to laugh at my lack of seduction, but he did not. He outstretched his arm reaching for mine to take. It was the only aggressive gesture he'd make. From then onward he

266

would not initiate intimacy. It was up to me to do what I pleased, and to my delight, I managed to please myself repeatedly. Renewed domination was intoxicating. Uninhibited by convention I achieved sensations I never knew existed. Nicholas was a willing partner and did not suffer in the presence of my own eager appetite. To my astonishment I discovered his pleasure heightened at the reversal of roles. I also uncovered something else, something I'm afraid very sinister. In the throws of passion I bit Nicholas. I bit him hard in the delicate area at the curve of his neck and sucked at the flesh before sinking my teeth again into the skin. I expected him to reject my violation and shove me from him, but he moaned and curled his head to the side surrendering to my ravenous attack. Shocked by my primal advance, I withdrew. I covered my exposed breasts with my arms and began apologizing. Nicholas hushed my stammering by placing a single finger over my trembling lips. With his other hand he felt around beneath the pillow and pulled out a knife. What had I done? I did not recognize myself or understand what was happening to me. I backed away from the weapon in bed with us.

"A soldier's habit, I always lie with a blade just in case," he said. "Don't be startled, I mean no harm."

I'm not sure why, but I believed him. "What are you going to do?" I asked, still sitting straddled atop his body.

He placed the sheathed knife by his side. "Kiss me again."

I bent down and kissed Nicholas softly at first, and then more aggressively as I grew aroused. The way he was responding coupled with the manner and places he touched me peaked delight to the point of frenzy. As my desire heightened so did the urge to bite my obedient lover. I heard the snap of the sheath and felt the sudden movement of Nicholas hand. I pulled away just in time to witness Nicholas cut a shallow mark above his collarbone. He dropped the knife and turned his head. I sat frozen for a moment as the blood seeped from the infliction. He did not say a word, but lay very still with his eyes closed. I bent down and sealed my lips over his wound. He exhaled, his whole body giving over for my taking. The salty copper taste filled my mouth and mixed with saliva, which I swallowed willingly. I licked his neck and sucked at his flesh until it turned purple from abuse. The intimacy exchanged between us was beyond comprehension. He was not offering merely pleasure but literally his flesh and blood. He did not expect anything in return and for that I decided to reward him. I took the knife and as I had watched him do, I cut a mark, but mine was along my wrist. I held out my arm for him to suckle. He closed his lips around the tender wound and took my blood into his body. The fever in which he drank caused the injury to grow sore. When I could take no more I pried his mouth from my wrist and guided it to join mine. With this kiss, our sensual union was consummated.

When all was exhausted and I could take no more I laid folded in his arms. Although I could not tell by the darkness in the room, I knew much time had passed and morning would be breaking soon. I rose from the bed and rummaged through the drawers. Folded inside was a robe Elizabeth had discarded from a previous rendezvous. I decided to leave my own soiled gown on the floor with explicit instructions it be burned. Nicholas also dressed and followed me to the antechamber where I had abandoned the mutilated body of the unknown man. Thankfully, he was no longer there. Someone had made sure to dispose of the corpse while I was entertaining in the adjoining room. I went to the door assuming Nicholas still followed, but realized he was moving to the other side of the room.

"Where are you going?" I asked.

"Through which I came," Nicholas said pointing to what appeared to be part of the wall.

I was not certain what to say at the moment. A declaration of love was out of the question, yet I felt more alive and fulfilled than ever before. Was this what Elizabeth experienced? Was this the true secret hidden between these walls? Nicholas noticed my awkward pause. "What are you waiting for?" he asked.

"I'm not sure. I suppose this is goodbye then?"

Nicholas crossed the room and came to my side. "Milady, this is not goodbye, only goodnight, or if we don't hurry, good morning. Remember I ask nothing of you; however, you may ask anything of me." He turned my hand over exposing my tender palm. He kissed it. He let his lips linger just enough that the softness tickled my skin sending a shiver up my arm.

"For a soldier, you are well practiced in the art of pleasure."

Nicholas touched my cheek. "Please do not make me wait too long. I shall suffer if you do."

I left through the door through which I came carrying with me a single torch for a companion and attired in Elizabeth's robe. As I made my way toward the cellar stairs I thought about the demons I exorcised by killing that man. Had I not been possessed? The purging of anger had led to a most and unexpected delicious feast. Through death I was reborn and through Nicholas's blood I was replenished. Why was I not frightened by this revelation? Instead, I was unnaturally calm and quite at peace. I crossed the kitchen and climbed the staircase. I did not return to my chambers, but decided it was best to go to Elizabeth's where I could bath. My appearance was in a terrible state. I was sticky with blood and reeking of infidelity.

Elizabeth's chambermaid was troubled by my sudden intrusion. She was put out by my request for a hot bath and fresh dressings. Morning was breaking. The sun was rising and a rooster was crowing in the distance. She fumbled with her overcoat and boots before taking up a large pail to heat water in. In the meantime, I poured a cup of tea and watched the fog roll over the hillside. It was a supernatural awakening. I sensed everything around me, the breathing of Elizabeth in the adjoining room, the water dripping from the eaves and the smells of household chores underway, including the hearths being stoked and the bread kneaded for baking.

The maid's boots clunked along as she heaved the heavy pails of hot water down the hall and into the room. I fixated on the steam cloud surrounding her head as she poured the water into the tub. Once it was half full, I tested it with my toe and climbed in. It took my breath away but soon I was acclimated and able to relax. I closed my eyes letting the lavender scent of melting oils rinse over me. I cleansed the blood from my hair and Nicholas's sweat from my skin.

As I soaked, I thought about the dead man. The image took hold along with the changing faces I envisioned during my rage. I'd seen them all, every last one of them who brought pain to my life. They manifested at the height of my fit and I was convinced whatever evil came through me also used this man as a portal through which to escape. I put my hand to my chest. How long had such malice been locked inside my own vessel? Then there was the question of Nicholas. I wondered if our union was a chance happening arranged by the strange circumstances surrounding that precise moment in time. I wanted it to happen again. Now that I had tasted enchantment, I craved it like an addict. I wanted more. I wanted to feel it all again.

I remained in the tub until the water was intolerably cool. Afterwards, I dressed in another borrowed gown from Elizabeth's wardrobe and returned to my chamber. To my surprise, Draco was sitting by the fire reading a novel picked from my private collection. He asked if I rose early and I lied that I had. I told him I had trouble sleeping and spent most of the night walking around Cachtice. He was pleased to hear the walk settled my restless nerves and was also relieved that I did not take up the previous night's issue that had led to our terrible argument. I explained I was perfectly over the topic and, after much deliberation, concluded marriage was a manner of economy and should not be confused with passion. Pleased, he patted my knee.

"Leave passion to the young," he said.

I reminded Draco that he was twelve years my senior and although I was not considered youthful in most circles, I was neither dismissed as a gray mare. To this he laughed, agreeing he had forgotten our age difference. Marriage, he claimed, bridged all gaps.

However, unlike Draco I was not ready to toss passion aside. I had not gotten my fair lot in youth and was damned to collect my share. When I agreed to marry Draco it was for many reasons, the most important was his ardor for life. However, the conviction through which he now lived was smoldering and the modest reserve that remained was rationed for the crown. I admired my stoic knight reading intently with a wrap around his legs by the fire. Old scars marked years of service and mapped the path of tired, aging bones.

"I understand Francis no longer rides out but commands from the palace," I said.

Draco did not take his eyes from the pages of the book. "Um hum."

"Have you given any thought to retiring your post and taking up a ministry of arms at court?"

"I, a paper pusher? A map reader? No, I am not one to sit idle in closed meeting rooms seated behind a desk advising from a safe perch."

"You have served your years. Perhaps it is time to move aside and let another take command. As you said, leave passion to the young."

Draco turned the novel over resting it on the arm of the chair. "Are you saying I'm too old?"

"All I'm saying is, I worry about you, Draco."

"My experience is invaluable. As long as I can mount a horse and God willing, wield a sword, I will command from the field."

"Then you will die on the field," I said.

"I pray not in the near future, but if you must know, it is how I wish to go," he said.

I bent over and kissed his cheek. He did not return my affection; instead he resumed reading his novel. The last spark popped and fizzled out leaving behind a pile of comfortable ash to be sweep neatly into a pile. I felt what hundreds of other wives must have felt at a time like this, this was it. This was all I had to look forward to; a settled comfort and occasional exchange of words. Some women tried to convince themselves this station in life was achieved by ascending to a deeper, more committed love. I did continue to love Draco very much but never did I feel truly close to him. Rather, it was more like he was fading from me, evaporating like the mist over the hillside of Cachtice.

***

In the beginning I said I loved two men. I must now confess that was a lie. At the time I could not speak of my third love because it was a secret. Nicholas was my most precious secret. Whereas George and Draco were years my senior, Nicholas matched both my age and intensity. Long ago when we first met, he was merely a boy taking up his first post. Now he was a grown man and chief of arms. His private quarter rested on the outskirt of the barracks and was obtainable under the guard of night through the corner door leading from Elizabeth's workshop.

I'd wait for sunset and, for the first time in years, I'd welcome the night. As usual, I supped with Draco and kissed him before bed. He always fell asleep before I did, leaving me alone in the chamber. It was then, in that void of time that I found myself drawn to the balcony. I looked out over the grounds and listened to the fading noise of working men. I was passing time, laying in wait for something to say it was right for me to freely roam about the castle. I was anxious to go to Nicholas, but feared my impulsiveness might be unwise. I had the sensation I was being watched and when I turned around, there was no one in the chamber. The sensation grew more intense and I realized the impression was not coming from within the room, but from somewhere out there, just beyond the courtyard bend.

Lanterns were being lit in the barracks and in the cast off I spotted a figure. His dark cape blended with the wall he leaned against, but the warmth of his breath meeting the cool night air gave him away. I pretended I did not see him. After a while I quit the balcony and turned down the lights. I wondered if my admirer was furious by my disregard for his pursuit. I was certain I had played it beautifully and gave nothing of his discovery away with my movements. I thought about how our separation was torturing him, how Nicholas must be imaging me bedding down with my husband while he lingered out in the cold. I got a sick amusement from his yearning and decided it best to allow some time to pass before ending his suffering.

For several nights I spied Nicholas lurking in the shadows from the vantage of my balcony. Down below, his breath against the bitter night revealed his phantom presence. Admittedly, the severance of our souls toyed with my mind as well and I began to think my eyes played terrible tricks. Was the ghostly outline imagined, the breath merely smoke drifting from a nearby chimney? Rational thought begged me to investigate, it urged me to seek out the person I believed waited, but my heart feared what it might discover. I stood consumed by seeping doubt in my outlook. I wondered if Nicholas and I would ever share another night of intimacy. Had our affair belonged to chance and was doomed never to repeat?

Meanwhile, during the days Draco remained weary and aloof. He reserved all strength for Francis with whom he spent the greater portion of his time locked in private meetings and catering to the progress of his health. I confess I was less than sympathetic. In truth, I was downright resentful of the attention Francis was receiving from my husband.

One morning after Draco abandoned our chambers to tend to Francis, I decided to go for a stroll about the grounds. I did not know if it was my anger or the craving gnawing in the pit of my stomach that drove me toward the barracks. There, I hoped to find Nicholas and put an end to my concern once and for all. My desire to speak with him was unbearable. It was I who now yearned for an audience. I deviated from my customary path and wandered through the muddy walks around the camp. Soldiers quit their chores out of respect for my passing. It was odd for a lady to inspect the area, but then again nothing about Cachtice was routine. The men allowed me to pass with a slight raise of eyebrow, but no true alarm. To my dismay, Nicholas was nowhere to be found. Discouraged, I returned to the main house and before taking tea decided to visit my favorite garden to waste more time.

The weather was brisk and the sun shone as if it were on the other side of the world. Its thin rays reached through the overcast to brighten my remote existence for a mere few hours. The warming clashed with the dampness hanging between the trees creating a backdrop upon which I could see all the impurity in the air. My skirt stirred pollen from the nestled centers of withering blooms. The stale fragrances tickled my nose as I went by and a butterfly, unremarkable in color and variety, flirted with the petals of a nearby flower. I'd been told the brilliant colors of its species belonged to the males. I thought this a defect in creation until it was explained the advantage was for survival. What I viewed as ornamental vanity was really camouflaged armor. I watched the female butterfly flutter about touching petals, then zipping to the next before settling on the leaf of a bush, her dull color in sharp contrast to the deep fleshy greens and vibrant pinks of the blooms. How vulnerable she looked resting in Eden. This was no place for the likes of her. This was a place for the advantaged. She belonged in the gray areas of the world where she'd be safe from preying beaks wishing to devour her. With a wave of my hand I sent her flying upward and over the hedge.

I reveled in my rescue. I bent down to sniff the scent of a rose bush. The edges of the blooms were brackish and the heads drooping as if in prayer. A hint of perfume remained but was tainted by the overpowering smell of decay. How short the vibrant life! It was then, as I was trying to pluck the last beauty of the red roses that something hidden near the path distracted me. My skin tingled with the eerie sensation I was being stalked. I glanced upward at the windows to see if I was being watched from above, but they stood empty and draped. I released my grasp on the flower and took a turn scrutinizing the scenery. I moved subtly giving nothing away in order to protect my susceptible position amidst the garden. I resisted the urge to call out. Instead, I assessed the distance from where I stood to the garden doors. It was at the very least a hundred footsteps, if not more. I took another turn, this time looking beyond the immediate to discover in the recesses a glint of bronze. As I moved, so did my pursuer. The rustling of leaves matched the crunching of stone beneath my slippers. He had the advantage of cover, but I was clever. I was drawing him towards a weak spot where early frost damaged the foliage. Just a few more steps and I'd snare him, but to my dismay the rustling stopped short. True to my kind I pursued the danger and went straight to where I thought he'd quit. As I neared, I saw him. The glint was the reflection of brass fastens caught in the sunlight. I was impressed at how his ginger hair blended with the turning leaves and the embroidery of his uniform patterned with the natural landscape. He did not retreat upon discovery; instead, he once again matched my movements mirroring them along the pathway.

"Nicholas, why do you not come out? I see you there, beyond the brush."

Nicholas did not speak but pointed upward toward the veiled windows.

"No one goes there," I said.

"Do not look as the crow flies," Nicholas whispered.

I took a turn at the end of the path and retraced my steps. Nicholas followed my lead by also changing direction and continuing along the familiar path over which he just crossed.

"A waltz is better suited for the ballroom," I said.

"Settle on the bench so I may speak with you."

"Why not join me? It is not a crime to stroll in the garden," I said.

"Gentlemen stroll at leisure. I am no gentle man."

I did as Nicholas asked and took a seat on the bench. I waited, but he did not speak. "What are you doing?" I whispered.

"I wanted to see you in the light. You look lovely this afternoon."

A flush of heat colored my cheeks. I had not dressed for admiration. A noise opposite of Nicholas caused me to jump to my feet.

"Someone goes there," I said, loudly.

Silence followed and nothing presented. I folded my hands in front of my skirt and again, made as if I was admiring the dying roses. In the cast of day Nicholas remained.

"I do not understand what has happened," I said. "I only know I desire it again."

Nicholas approached leaving the only obstacle between us the thorny rose bush. I reached for him. The sleeve of my coat knocked some flower heads from their browning stems. They drifted to the ground settling around my feet.

"Can it be?" I asked. I leaned in, a branch poked in my rib.

"I dreamt of you," he said.

"Was it a dream?" I asked.

Nicholas snapped the neck of the last living red rose. I eagerly took the gift. It was flawed with imperfections. The fragrance an imposter to the original form and the edges of the delicate face withered and trimmed in black.

"If it was, may we sleep forever?"

I became dizzy and stumbled. The thorny branch poking my side tore a tiny rip in my bodice. Nicholas leapt forward crushing the branches of the rose bush. The prickling fingers snagged at his uniform tearing small holes as he caught my arm.

"How do you fair, milady?" he asked, his grip firm on my forearm. I detected a slight panic in his expression.

"Well," I answered. I was embarrassed by my fragileness.

Nicholas's hand was badly scratched and streaks of blood rushed from the afflicted skin. He raised the injury to his mouth and licked it clean. Aware of his position, he retreated trying to work the material of his uniform free from the grasp of the clinging bush as he went. In haste I grabbed at his coat sleeve. I did not want him to go.

"I must not be seen," he said shying away from my embrace.

I took his hand and kissed the shallow reddening cuts. The taste of salty copper delighted my lips and played on my tongue. Nicholas let out a moaning sigh as he felt my lips kiss his injury a second time. Regretfully, he withdrew disappearing in the cover of the shadows.

"What is this that seduces me?" I whispered to him. I heard someone calling my name. It was a maid sent by Elizabeth to find me.

"I must go," Nicholas said.

"Before you do, you must tell me Nicholas, how did you come to practice such magic?" I begged, for it had to be magic casting a spell.

He retreated further as the maid drew closer.

"Yes, yes, I hear you. I'm in the garden," I shouted to the maid.

Nicholas was slipping away.

"Nicholas, please," I pleaded.

The rustling ceased for a moment. "Venice," he replied.

"Venice?"

And Nicholas was gone...

"Venice? The countess said nothing about Venice. She requested you join her for luncheon," said the maid. She was standing in the garden.

"Tell her I will be up shortly," I said, irritated.

I fingered the rip in my bodice. The rose bush was a sorry mess. It stood partially crippled on one side. A cascade of petals scattered the ground leaving behind naked stalks brittle and battered. A good pruning and a long sleep would remedy the abuse. Come spring all would be renewed. At least I thought it would be, but it wasn't.

***

The rose bush that stood between Nicholas and I never did recover. The gardener replaced the wasted brown twig with a novel variety he acquired from his brother, the gardener to the Duke of Austria. The rare garden beauty was drained of color. The buds were an ideal white designed to match the tasteless fancy of the empirical elite. The gardener explained because the white rose was scentless it was the perfect compliment. It would not clash with other alluring perfume blooms. I complained the flowers reminded me of poor health. I disliked the bluish pale petals saying they resembled sickly bodies bobbing in water. Elizabeth disagreed arguing the white rose, which she favored, was a pure clean canvas free from contamination.

"Color is character, it defines uniqueness," I said. I longed for the red, traditional bud that once decorated the path.

"Color imposes," Elizabeth answered.

Soon thereafter my favorite garden, where the red rose once ruled, transformed from a brilliant, sensual paradise to a monochromatic maze of pucker face corpses. For me, the absence of color did not give the impression of either pureness or cleanliness like Elizabeth believed. Instead, it enhanced the dullness of our surroundings and unmasked the smell of dirt and rot.

Wicked as the Wind

It was the heart of winter and the year 1603 was about to become history. Today was a bitter cold December morning and Francis had recovered from his illness and was preparing to leave Cachtice. Elizabeth and I met in the courtyard beneath frosted trees, their branches were sparkling in the early light like jeweled wares poised for a party. We were obligated to wish the men a safe journey and hopes of prosperity, along with victory. Although we did not express it, we both secretly desired that on this occasion that we'd be pardoned and granted permission to once again travel. A few precious words, if spoken, gave us freedom from the fortress we no longer benefited from calling home, but regarded as a prison. Regretfully, a blessing from our guardian was not offered. Not even a nod was tossed our way. We were trapped and completely at the mercy of the men who still held power over us.

As the procession commenced, I searched for Draco. I was desperately afraid our situation would go unchecked. Panic rose when at first I did not see him, but then there he was emerging from the stable and leading his horse. He hooked his foot in the stirrup and flung a leg over the horse. I made no attempt to conceal my distress. My expression was a plea, it said, *Do something! For God's sake do not abandon me here again, in this dreadful place!*

"We've been summoned to Bucharest. The Voivode Radu Serban is requesting a meeting," Draco called out as he neared the place where I stood.

Radu Serban was the appointed governor in charge of rebuilding Bucharest. It had been nearly ten years since the city witnessed the terrible day of violence when the man the people called, Michael the Brave, revolted against the Ottomans. The mission was to murder the Ottoman creditors who controlled Wallachia's resources. Sinan Pasha, the Ottoman leader retaliated against Michael the Brave's uprising. He ordered a counter attack and in the wake almost completely destroyed the center of cosmopolitan life. When the dust cleared, Bucharest lay in ruins.

Draco leaned from atop his horse and took hold of my hand. "I shall do what I can," he promised. I should have felt relief that he interpreted my silent plea correctly, but the words brought little assurance. This was his scripted answer to my distress call. I followed his glance toward the head of the procession where Francis awaited. Draco had been promising assistance for years. *I'll do what I can.* These were powerless words that troubled my heart. I was disappointed and realized I had little to cling too. I do not know if Draco believed what he said to be a lie, but I believed the utterance to be precisely that – a lie. I studied my husband's face locked behind the armored mask, his impenetrable eyes glassy from the nipping wind. The portrait of my hero was muddying, slipping from my imagined golden frame and ripping at the seams as my hand released his. My immortal knight reduced to a mere man, a servant of the kingdom. As he fell in line and took his place in the march of the Quintet my heart sank under the burden of truth. Draco would not rescue me.

After the last horse had pass beneath the arch, I heard the chains begin to churn through the pulleys as the iron gate lowered. It was closing us in. I learned to dread that sound—that horrid echo of the handle being thrust downward met by the eerie quiet that always followed. Oh, the finality of it all! When nothing else could be done, Elizabeth withdrew from the vacant space we shared in the yard.

Framed in the shadow of the castle, the trail of her ermine coat moved toward the open recess. What an odd picture she painted. A royal accompanied by a gypsy dwarf and the far-sighted witch, Dorothea, who huddled beneath a bearskin shawl.

I am not sure what compelled me to do so, but I dropped to my knees. Small flakes of snow began to fall and were wetting my hair and cheeks. I blinked clearing the snow from my lashes. I begged for a miracle. I dared something to intervene and release us from this life. I cursed God and all that was holy for my suffering. From my teachings I knew this was unwise, but my anger was such that I did not care. I had been good, and I had been bad. I doubted either course was punishable or rewarded by God, rather I had the nagging suspicion fate was determined by man. Yet, I prayed.

While I was antagonizing what I could not see, nor had evidence existed, a gust of wind whipped through the courtyard. It was so fierce that it nearly knocked me to the ground. When I regained my balance I saw walking toward me a hooded figure. As the person drew closer I recognized the pale face and the thicket of reddish hair curling from beneath the fur cloak. Quickly, I got to my feet. I brushed the dirt from my skirt.

"I'm afraid your curses have angered the Gods," Nicholas said looking north at the storm clouds moving across the sky.

"It is impolite to eavesdrop," I said.

"I was concerned," he answered. The wind was blowing steady, causing the sleet to move sideways across the yard.

I nodded. I was not surprised. I had sensed I was being watched. This would have disturbed me if I thought it anyone else but Nicholas, but I found a strange comfort knowing he was there, in the shadows. It meant I was not alone. Another gust blew pressing against our bodies trying to push us off our feet.

"The weather is worsening. Take my arm. I will escort you to the castle," Nicholas said. I tugged up my hood to guard my face against the beads of ice. "No, I refuse to go there," I said, sharply.

"If not there, then where?" Nicholas asked.

"You have plenty of wood for your hearth?"

"Of course, but my quarters are not fit for a lady."

"Take me Nicholas, take me there now." The wind caught my words and whisked them away giving the impression they came from somewhere else in the yard.

Nicholas wrapped his arm around me and together we hurried down the path leading to the towers where the guards bunked. The sudden onset of the storm sent everyone scrambling for cover leaving the compound abandoned. Nicholas wrestled a key from his pocket and turned the lock. A rush of wind pushed the heavy door open flinging it against the wall and sending a stack of papers and maps sailing from his desk. He hurried me inside and used all his strength to force the door closed and sealed it with the twist of the latch. "We're in for a nasty fight tonight." He went directly to the hearth and began stoking the grate with dried wood and brittle twigs. I lit a candle and poured water into a pot to place over the fire. Nicholas cursed at the down draft, which sent a puff of smoke into the room. I coughed choking on the thick air.

"I told you this was no place for a lady," he said, fanning the room.

"I am not a lady. I am an orphan," I said dully. He had no reason to feel embarrassed at the crudeness of the room on my account.

There was hardly any furniture in the quaint place so I chose to sit on the bed pushed against the far wall. Nicholas worked a spark into a glowing flame. The wind rustled the shutters and whistled through the minor cracks in the frame.

"Here, wrap this around you to keep the draft away," Nicholas said handing me a fur skin.

It smelled of burnt pine and rabbit stew. When all was settled Nicholas joined me on the bed. Together we sat, neither of us speaking a word. Instead, we watched the flames dance along the logs while listening to the angry wrath outside. Given the size of the room, it warmed quickly, and soon the temperature was pleasant enough that I no longer needed the fur. The morning's events left me tired and weak. I decided to remove my boots and lay my head on the feather pillow. I closed my eyes fully aware that Nicholas was watching. I felt his hand smooth the hair from my forehead.

"Such a wicked woman you are to conjure up this malevolent storm," he teased.

I was flattered he thought I had the power to do such a thing. "You think this my doing?"

"Who else could infuriate God so?"

I laughed. "I did no such thing."

"Why, yes! I heard with my own ears. You dared God to intervene."

"Did I? Did I really dare God?"

"Am I mistaken, or is that not a challenge?" Nicholas said, more serious this time.

I cocked my head. "You're serious. You believe I have the power to be heard?"

Nicholas lowered himself over me. "Can you not feel it? Something stirs in you, something unsettled. Too much passion, such restlessness in a woman, they say it is dangerous." Nicholas shook his head. "I believe you upset the natural balance of things making it, well, quite unnatural." His eyes widened as if suddenly hit by an idea. "An upheaval of cosmic forces." He let out a sinister laugh. He pressed his nose to the nape of my neck. "Wicked, very wicked indeed," he whispered.

Should I have been offended or flattered? I did not believe I was a force to be reckoned with, rather, I felt small and insignificant, like an ant in a massive forest.

**

I could tell Nicholas was uncomfortable by the rudimentary interior of his quarters. The more time I spent at his place, the greater effort he put into trying to make improvements on my behalf, which I politely rejected stating I quite liked the simplicity of the room. It was Nicholas who I desired, not an extravagant chair or a silver tea tray, but I had trouble making him understand this. I explained I had an entire room in the castle filled with heartless objects that no longer held my fancy, but still he tried to reform his surroundings.

I passed a fortnight between the castle and Nicholas's quarters. I thought myself very clever for keeping our tryst secret.

However, my delusion burst when a rap fell upon the chamber door. It was still dark when the visitor arrived. I hide beneath the covers of the bed while Nicholas cracked the door.

"Who goes there?" he asked.

I could not identify the whispering voice. I poked my head out from under the covers when I heard the door shut. To my surprise the unexpected guest had not gone, but now stood in the middle of the room. I shifted to the side of the mattress bumped up against the wall. My hand groped for my dress that had been passionately tossed aside and now lay in a ball at the foot of the bed. I snatched the corner and shimmied it up my legs and over my rear. I jammed each arm in a hole while Nicholas fumbled on the other side of the room trying to light a candle.

"What is it? What message do you bring?" Nicholas asked finally getting the candle lit.

Elizabeth dropped her hood and pulled a letter from her pocket. "You need to return to your room," she said to me.

"How did you know where to find me?" I asked.

Elizabeth rolled her eyes. "You can't be serious."

"I don't want to! I don't want to return to my room. I want to stay here with Nicholas." I sounded like a spoiled child.

"You must!" she snapped.

Nicholas was reading the letter. "Elizabeth is right, you should go."

"Then you will come with me," I said to Nicholas. I was determined to get my way.

"Milady, that is not possible."

"Nothing in that letter is going to change my mind."

Elizabeth ripped it from Nicholas's fingers and tossed it on the bed. "Read it for yourself."

The letter was addressed to Elizabeth and was written in an unfamiliar pen:

Dear Countess Bathory,

I wish this message brought joyful tidings, but I regret I have the unpleasant task of informing you that during his visit to Bucharest and on the fourth of January 1604, a servant to the honorable Governor Serban discovered your husband, Count Francis Nadasdy, in terrible distress. A doctor was immediately summoned and after proper examination confirmed Count Nadasdy suffered multiple knife wounds from which he regretfully never recovered. It is the governor's wish that you come at once to bare witness to the unjust injury and oversee the funeral arrangements. May God be with you during your journey.

"Can this be? Is he truly dead?" The message slipped from my hand.

"We must hurry. I will give orders at daybreak to prepare for the journey. As soon as everything is ready we will leave this place," Elizabeth said.

I jumped up and hugged Elizabeth. I could not contain my excitement. I whirled her around dancing in circles shouting: "He is dead! He is dead!"

Elizabeth laughed as we danced about the room. "It is glorious news!"

I released Elizabeth and wrapped my arms around Nicholas. I kissed both cheeks. "The count is dead, isn't that wonderful!"

Nicholas agreed but his face did not shine with the same delight as Elizabeth's and mine. "Yes, Milady, the count is dead. He has been murdered."

I stopped jumping. Murdered? The word rattled around in my mind. I'd been so pleased to hear of Francis's death that I had not given a second thought to how he actually met his fate. Someone had finally got to Francis and it was not Elizabeth. We had a new chore, to find out who benefited from his death, and to ensure we remain safe from harm. I turned to Nicholas. "Protect Paul, he is heir and you, Elizabeth are regent."

Nicholas nodded. "I'm certain all precautions are being taken."

"If they can get to Francis, they can get to us," I said.

I was spot on. Francis was heavily guard. It would not be easy to murder such an important figure and renowned swordsman. Whoever was responsible was certainly more than capable of exterminating us as well.

Charlie Courtland

What Is Done, Can Not Be Undone

W e tried to hide our impatience. After all, we were expected to be distraught over Count Nadasdy's untimely death. Much attention was given to our disposition. It was the general opinion that women were predisposed to fragility. They were prone to fainting spells and contracting fatal illnesses, especially in times of great despair. Despite my inward objection to this opinion, I did see how the belief could be useful. An unchecked giggle viewed as uncivilized might now be explained as hysteria brought on by stress. The desire to exercise at an odd hour could be presented as evidence of denial – denial to acknowledge loss. It was common for physicians to warn a widow might suddenly begin to wander about when being without a man to serve. It seemed any determined inappropriate behavior was easily justified by blaming the inherit feebleness of the female psyche. Restraint and proper guidance was recommended. This meant living out remaining days as a burden to male relatives or, in the case of a young fertile wealthy widow, arranging marriage again. In our case, it was encouraged we'd immediately be placed in the company of family.

In spite of the leniency granted for peculiar behavior, I checked my mood for Elizabeth's sake. Still, it was difficult to achieve a somber mood with the expectation of travel looming over the castle. While packing my belongings, I counted to ten in my head before taking up a new chore. It was an irksome ploy, necessary not to raise alarm. My worst fear was the doctor would change his recommendation and send word Elizabeth was not suited for travel.

When all was stowed in its proper place, I aided Elizabeth with the laces of her mourning dress. She made it very clear she had no intention of draping some drab garment across her body. She insisted the customary gown be fashioned from fine silk and layered in folds of dyed black Spanish lace. She was also adamant about wearing her beloved onyx necklace. Traditionally, grieving widows maintained an understated appearance. Even though the necklace was a gift from her late husband, the rare jewel hardly fit protocol. I considered raising this point with Elizabeth, but decided my complaint would be met by a rebellious argument. Besides, the adornment was quite befitting of the ensemble. I could not remember ever seeing a widow's dressing flatter as Elizabeth's did now. She looked absolutely stunning in her gown. Perhaps it was the occasion for which she wore the garment that brought a youthful rosy glow to her cheeks. Seeing her radiate with renewed life caused warmth to stir in my own tired flesh. I fought to repress a grin but failed in preventing my lips from curling upward. My timing could not have been more ill planned, for a guard appeared in the doorway. He announced the last of the trunks were loaded and it was nearly time to depart.

"I know it is improper to state, and my expression is most unbecoming, but I cannot help admire the beauty of the countess. Is she not at this very moment the most beautiful spectacle of poise and grace?" I asked the guard. It was a shameful attempt to relieve my blunder.

However, it worked. Upon hearing my words his furrowed brow righted itself. He cleared his throat before answering, "God has been very generous with his gifts." He presented a formal bow while Elizabeth thanked him for the fine compliment.

I noticed as we left our chamber Elizabeth took one last glance at her reflection in the mirror. I too, could not resist vanity. I snuck a peek at my own image. Today, I was cautious. I chose a simple black frock and matching gloves complimented by a pair of pearl earrings and a dainty choker. For a split second in the reflection of the mirror I thought I saw a young girl smiling. The captured memory of my former self took me by surprise and just as quickly as it appeared, the mirage disappeared. I shook my head trying to regain my senses. Despite the passing of forty years, it seemed my imagination was still very active. I did not curse, but rather chuckled. I found it strangely comforting. Perhaps it was a sign *ingénue* had not entirely abandoned me. Was this a message all was not tarnished?

A busied scene of servants and horses dressed in royal colors and feathered plumes crowded the courtyard. How regal the horses chosen to draw the carriage looked as they stood proudly with heads cocked. The other geldings assigned with the chore of transporting passengers on saddled back pawed restlessly at the dirt while snorting puffs of hot air from flared nostrils. It had been some time since such a spectacle was made for our benefit and I admitted I was enjoying every ceremonial second of it. I acknowledged Nicholas who was waiting at the door of our carriage. I gladly accepted his offered hand and was delighted when he too boarded.

"I hope you do not object, Countess, but I thought it best that I accompany you during the journey. I've been assured a safe passage, but still I do not completely trust the informant. You do understand?" Nicholas asked.

"As you wish," Elizabeth replied. She adjusted her skirt taking special care of the long train tucked and pinned underneath. "And the children?"

"They are following in a second carriage supervised by Dorothea. I've taken the liberty of posting four guards, two flanking each side," Nicholas answered.

Elizabeth pulled back the curtain and tied it in place with a neat bow. She pressed her face close to the window. "Yes, I see. Very good."

Waiting for the procession to commence was unnerving. As my anticipation grew, so did the heat rising in my face. I could hardly believe I was about to embark on a journey to a foreign land accompanied by none other than my secret, Nicholas. I thought days such as this were long past. I shifted in my seat. I put a glove to my mouth concealing a smirk. Only in my life could a funeral bring bliss. *Ah, Death is not the end, but a door through which life renews!* I thought.

"What is taking so long?" I asked. It was torture being so close to Nicholas without touching. I focused on the grim view of the stone wall hoping the dullness would drain the heat from my face. The passing of Fickzo's hat beneath the window interrupted my efforts. The carriage leaned to the side as he climbed the small steps to the roost taking a seat beside the driver. A horn sounded from the tower and the clanking of chains announced the freeing of the iron gate. This time the noise of metal grinding through the pulleys was welcoming. A fluttering danced in my stomach. It was a glorious tickle. Without thinking I reached across the small space separating Nicholas and me and grabbed his hand. As I did, the carriage lurched forward and began rolling toward the vast wildness beyond the walls. I squeezed tight before letting go. Elizabeth did not take notice. She was too consumed by the scenery. It blurred by the window at an increased speed. The inclement season had left gouged grooves in the road. Normally, I would find the rocking unbearable, but today I did not mind the jostling.

As we neared the village Elizabeth's beloved subjects abandoned their cooking pots. They were eager to get a glimpse of the allusive countess and her party, on this occasion, shrouded by mourning black. It had been quite some time since anyone had caught sight of Elizabeth and many wondered if she lived at all. We received on good authority that rumors were stirring. Talking, so much talking and conjecture was taking place. Of course it was merely absurd folklore to offer an explanation for her disappearance.

Two particular favorites were brewing. The first rumor spreading said she died a most tragic death and her spirit was now earth bound and compelled to haunt the grounds of Cachtice. Those who thought this strange obviously never spent a winter eve at the castle. I could see how ghastly the castle looked from below and when the fog set, it was sheer terror.

The second rumor was more elaborate and told quite a different tale. People spoke that the countess was not dead at all, and this was the truly bizarre part, but that she was also neither alive. The tale began by claiming Elizabeth was a sorceress. On one extraordinarily dark night while working magic in a secret chamber beneath the castle something went wrong. Some think perhaps a divine power intervened. It was said at first the countess believed the spell she'd cast had worked, but soon she realized she was trapped for all eternity in her human form. The curse was that her beauty would neither improve, nor change. She'd forever look just as she did at the very moment she spoke the last lines of her sinister spell. To some this may sound wonderful, but like in any good moral tale, the price for vanity was costly. The countess was no longer truly alive, nor was she dead. She was something caught in between. Some argued it was not a bad fate, but others said it was most awful. It was rumored Elizabeth would never age or die. Her reflection would remain the same from now until the end of time. Imagine! The story went on to tell that when the count got news of his wife's evil practices he vowed never to visit again. These were the rumors, the tales being told about Elizabeth, and if I hadn't seen the truth with my own eyes, perhaps I too might have believed them.

I suppose this was the most bearable explanation for our abandonment. I wondered what tales were forming in their simple minds as they now looked upon her carriage rolling through the village. What tales would be told tonight around the dinner table to explain the scene set before them? What explanation would be confirmed?

I glanced at Elizabeth's profile. I imagined if looking from a distance one could say she appeared unchanged. However, at intimate inspection it was apparent youth was very much fleeting. Fine lines blemished her once perfect skin. I often found Elizabeth studying the flaws of age in her hand mirror. She'd touch the delicate areas around her eyes and lips as she turned her face just so in the afternoon light. Dorothea tried to relieve Elizabeth's anxiety by concocting several creams made from pumiced flower and rare herbs, but the results did not satisfy. Elizabeth applied the cream for many days and when she saw little result she'd fly into one of her triads. The conversation always turned to the same subject - the elixir Dorothea bragged Queen Katherine possessed. Now more than ever I feared Elizabeth would insist the potion be acquired. Her beauty was her greatest weapon and, with Francis dead, Elizabeth would need to cling to it if she had any hope of manipulating her position in the Empire.

As we continued to ride through the village Elizabeth remained poised in her seat. She resisted all temptation to lean forward exposing her face to the darting eyes of her curious subjects. However, I was inclined. I hooked a finger on the edge of the curtain drawing it back just enough to gain a better perspective of the townspeople. Neither the village nor the people were as I remembered. The serfs were shadows of their former selves. Skin covering bone draped in ragged soiled clothes. Their shacks were falling to ruin from neglect and damaged by the harsh weather elements. Rotted planks leaned against each other and no smoke billowed from the chimneys.

A man pointed when catching sight of my face. The crowd shrank away as if I were medusa befitted with the power to turn them all to stone. A woman shielded her small child's eyes before turning him around and sending the babe back inside the house.

How strange to think we once dined among the people. How we had been welcome and honored in the villages attached to the castle. Confinement changed everything. The mystery of our disappearance allowed suspicious minds to conjure monsters. Little did they know our allusiveness was an involuntary act. To them the privileged led an unfettered life. They could not envision women of our station were nothing more than chattels of those they also served. I closed the curtain. It was no matter. One thing was certain; Fate had intervened. Today, a murderer set us free.

The carriage rolled onward driving us toward the city of Bucharest where the corpse of Count Nadasdy rested in the *Curtea Veche*. During our journey the three of us did not humor each other by filling the empty span of time with idle chatter. Instead, like so often before, we rode in silence. Each submerged in private daydreams; mine filled with inventions of the city I was about to visit. Would it look like Aunt Klara's palace? A place where billows of colorful silk drapes hung and bowls were heaped with exotic fruit? Would the servants dress in turbans with their brown faces hidden behind coarse beards? My lids felt heavy and I could no longer fight to keep them open. I must have dozed because I was startled awake by the ringing out of our driver's gruff voice announcing we were nearing Bucharest.

I tied back the curtain and pressed my face to the window. It was difficult to see through the dusty film coating the pane. However, I could tell this place was nothing like the miserable village at the base of Cachtice. I was relieved the entire world had not fallen to ruin while I was confined to the castle. I felt the beating in my chest quicken. I was not met by gaunt faces clothed in tattered rags, but by rows of thriving crops and fenced livestock framed by a thicket of forest edged along a river. In the distance, the river flowed toward a bend forming a protective moat around the city. As the carriage turned I saw rooftops peeking above a stone wall. The drawbridge rested open creating a giant portal through which merchants drove carts filled with wares to market. This did not look like a city concerned with invasion and plagued by warfare. I was curious as to why Draco neglected to relay any of this wonderment in the letter he'd sent. Was he afraid I'd want to come at once to see the metropolis for myself?

Instead of conveying the bright points of the city, he'd described Bucharest as it was on the night Francis died. He said it was unusually cold and a snow fell. A bitter northerly wind turned the moist air to ice sealing the roads in a treacherous casing making it impossible for a doctor to arrive in a timely manner. Draco included he was told the delay made no difference since the inflicted wounds were deadly, but I could tell by the manner in which he wrote he was less than convinced. I knew he was not a man to dwell on nature, but in the letter he continually referred to the odd character of the weather and the role it played in Francis's death. The more I read, the more I wondered if Draco had completely lost sight of the tangible wounds. I thought perhaps it was guilt that made his tone accusing and diverted his attention from the obvious to the supernatural. Draco had failed to protect his commanding chief. Francis had been murdered under his watch, and this was a misfortune he would live with forever.

I wrung my hands. The torment he must be going through. I knew Draco would never rest until he brought Francis's murderer to justice, a quest that very well might take the remainder of his life. Again, I let the curtain fall. It seemed I was the only person interested in observing the world outside.

"Who do you think murdered Francis?" I asked, breaking the long silence.

Elizabeth tugged on her gloves pulling them up to prevent against a draft. "I'm afraid we may never know."

The idea sickened me, not only for Draco's sake, but also for our own. "Surely his men have a suspect?" I said.

"It is quite possible they don't. The count was a man of great power with many enemies," Nicholas said. He leaned across the seat to tie back the curtain I had just let close. I took the opportunity to breath in his scent. A hint of smoky hearth nestled in the woolen threads of his jacket. It reminded me of his quarters and the time we spent together. The snow blanketing the ground reflected back a harsh iridescent light. The cast made Nicholas's face appear bluish which would be quite unflattering if it were not for the warming influence of his copper hair. "You were told the count was stabbed?" Nicholas asked. His hand swept the top of mine as he returned to the comfort of his seat.

"Yes, that is what was written in the letter," Elizabeth answered. "Do you have reason to believe it is untrue?"

"No, just the opposite. I'm afraid the cause of death is hauntingly familiar," he said.

"Familiar, how can it be familiar?" I asked.

"You are aware of Mircea's court and its reputation for disposing of enemies?"

I looked to Elizabeth. I was not aware of Mircea or his habits.

"It was during the reign of Mircea Ciobanul. He was a man of remarkable achievement and a man of merciless violence. Once, he received word from his advisor that certain officials were plotting against him. Despite much effort, the precise persons could not be fingered. So Mircea devised a rather ruthless plan. He decided to throw a grand dinner party to which all officials were invited. Over two hundred guests arrived to take part in the auspicious celebration. Mircea carefully watched his guests but still he could not be sure who amongst them were traitors. He concluded there was only one way of ensuring the plot foiled. He ordered all the officials be stabbed to death. The entire lot was slain within the palace walls. From then on, a dinner invitation was considered a death sentence."

"You think Governor Serban continues the tradition?"

Nicholas shrugged. "I can't say for certain. All I'm saying is it would not be the first time a guest was stabbed at Curtea Veche."

"Maybe if we knew why Francis was invited in the first place, we'd know what business he had with the governor and if such business put his life at risk."

Nicholas shook his head. "I do not know. I imagine King Rudolph is proposing the same question to his men." Nicholas brushed horsehair from his coat. "Perhaps your husband will shed some light on the subject."

The mention of my husband pricked. Being abandoned at Cachtice made it easy to justify the affair, but now both men would be in close proximity of each other. I had not given this much thought, until now. Of course I had been in this situation before with George, or had I? George was a gentleman of the court. I never worried when it came to George. He played by the rules. His public display of bored indifference was a practiced courtly behavior. Could Nicholas provide the same convincing service? I lightly touched Elizabeth's arm. "I will find out what Draco knows once we are settled in our rooms." I wished to reassure her I wanted to be of help.

"It makes no difference to me. Francis is dead, that is all I need to know."

Her coolness stung. "I think it does matter," I said sharply. "We need to understand who sent the order and why. They may come after you, or worse, the children."

Elizabeth continued to stare out the window.

"I agree, Countess. We should know if your own life is in jeopardy," Nicholas said.

I nodded. Two out numbered one.

"You worry for nothing. What consequence am I?" she asked.

"It is reasonable to assume you are now regent to the Nadasdy heir."

Elizabeth raised a brow. "I suppose this is true." Elizabeth paused. "However, I believe I have more to fear from a plot of marriage than I do of an assassination scheme."

The carriage rounded a corner. The driver maneuvered through the narrowed streets dodging the pull carts and pedestrians darting about as we made our way to the center of the city. There was no mistaking the Curtea Veche. The reconstruction after Sinan Pasha's attempts to completely destroy the symbols of the city had taken time and it appeared no expense was spared in restoring grandeur. However, Nicholas explained, princely authority and a decline of state resources were sacrificed as a result of rebuilding. The royal family could not fund the project and had no other avenue but to beg the council for allocation of monies. In return, officials proposed liberties to be granted to certain members. With a swipe of the pen certain privileges were no longer a privilege of blood, but of state. Despite the dispense of power, Mircea continued to rebuild and as a warning to those who might be eager to forget, he resurrected a statue of Vlad Tepes at the gate of Curtea Veche. This was a symbol of caution. He wanted to remind the ambitious that all words could be rewritten, but blood was divine.

I could not take my eyes from the chiseled statue of Vlad, the gaunt cheeks and pointed beard exquisitely rendered. The soulless likeness captured in the marbled sockets drew goose bumps to my arms. Although in good conscience I knew this was not a man but a mere chunk of stone, the image shot alarm through my flesh. How could I fear something that was not alive?

The carriage came to a halt. Coming down the walk to meet our party was Governor Serban. Although he and his heads of state now occupied the Curtea Veche and with it, inherited much power, I found him to be quite a benign figure and questioned how he managed to maintain his hold over the growing cosmopolitan city. Nothing about him was imposing, and I doubted he alone was capable of conspiring murder.

"He seems rather harmless," I said to Nicholas, taking his hand and descending the carriage stairs.

Nicholas drew me close. "Take caution, milady. Like all men, he has only his best interest in mind. It is wise to remind one's self he is a man of power and influence. We do not know yet if he is an ally or enemy."

"I intend to make him an ally," I said.

"What if he is not one to make?" Nicholas asked.

I did not have time to answer. The governor and his party were upon us. After pleasantries were exchanged we were shown to our chambers and informed other members of the family were arriving shortly. A small reception was to take place in the formal drawing room later that evening.

Dorothea aided Anna and Katelin with their belongings while we refreshed, taking tea and eating a light dinner set in the antechamber. While dining I received two messages: the first from Nicholas telling me where he resided and the second from Draco announcing his pleasure at our arrival and apologizing for not being present to greet our party. However, he did not offer an excuse, and I determined I would make sure to inquiry when I later saw him.

Several hours passed before we received a note that said members of the family were gathering in the reception hall.

"Do you know who awaits downstairs?" I asked Elizabeth.

"No, only a letter from King Stephen sending his deepest sympathies, but he made no mention of making the trip."

"What family then?" I asked. I found it strange the King of Poland was not making the trip. He was the most decorated and certainly the family would want him to represent properly.

Before Elizabeth answered, a guard entered the chamber. He announced he would escort us to the reception. I fixed a jeweled necklace around my neck and checked my hair one last time in the mirror. Beyond the door, standing in the hall, was Nicholas. He was dressed in official attire and following the formal procedures of Elizabeth's chief guard. He was no longer our companion, and any concern I had about conduct vanished. Exchanges between Nicholas and me would be in secret and suspect to probing eyes. It caused me great pain to brush coolly by him ignoring his presence in our party. I prayed he'd understand and not take offense by my behavior. I determined if given the slightest opportunity I'd ensure him of my feelings. Until then, I could only hope he would not lose sight of duty.

I took in a deep breath and descended the grand stairs. I expected to see Draco waiting at the bottom, but discovered he was not. Standing outside of the reception hall was one of Draco's men. I paused to ask if my husband would be joining us. The man replied Draco apologized for the delay but could not avoid being detained. I, in turn, asked if the detainment had anything to do with investigating the count's murder. The man gave a slight bow and returned to his post saying that he did not know.

The doors pulled open and, with it, revealed a vast room. At the end squared by a woven Turkish rug and an enormous stone hearth gathered a small group of gentlemen. From my vantage I did not readily recognize the occupants, but as we drew closer a particular form seated in a high back chair with one leg crossed over the other struck me dead in my tracks. As Elizabeth approached, all the men rose from their chairs except for one. He was someone I prayed never to rest eyes on again. He remained as he was with crossed leg and swirling an amber liquid in a crystal goblet.

"What is *he* doing here?" Elizabeth snapped. She was going to make no effort to hide her feelings.

"He is family," Governor Serban replied.

"Whom my husband sent to exile."

"I might say the same about you," Count Thurzo said, his throat raspy from age.

Elizabeth's eyes darted around the room. She was searching for someone familiar, an ally who would jump to aid, but all the men stared indifferently back at her.

"These men are not family," she pointed out.

Count Thurzo leaned forward placing his drink on the side table. "Don't mind them. They are appointed representatives of the family's interests," he said with a wave.

"I shall write straight away to the King of Poland and employ his assistance," Elizabeth threatened. "Surely he will do something about this as soon as he gets word."

"By all means," Count Thurzo said. "I shall warn you it will do no good. He has agreed to the arrangement. But if you must, write away."

I felt the prickling of cool sweat trickling down my back. I did not feel like a grown woman seasoned and experienced, but rather a small child. I cleared my throat.

"You mean to tell me King Stephan does not wish to honor my dead husband's wishes?" she asked.

A few of the men returned to their seats. Another rummaged through a sack from which he pulled a scroll.

"Much has changed since you became ill," Count Thurzo replied.

Elizabeth set her attention firmly on the governor. "I want this man seized and taken from my sight immediately!"

The governor took a step forward, "Please calm yourself, Countess. That which you request can not be done."

"Can not be done!"

"No, Countess. I think you gravely misunderstand."

"You misunderstand! I want this man taken from sight," she snapped. Her voice echoed through the chamber.

"I have no authority to seize a Palantine Prince of Transylvania," said the governor.

Count Thurzo found the scene amusing. "Come now, Elizabeth. You've entertained us with your tantrums long enough. All you've done is validate my concerns to everyone in this room. I'm sure you're aware since your husband's death you will be named regent to the heir. However, for several years we've received numerous letters concerning, how shall I put this, crude practices and disturbing behaviors. The family clan has gathered on several occasions and often discussed issues concerning the care and management of you. Francis assured us all he was capable of handling your needs. I must say you were very fortunate to have such a loving and sympathetic husband." Count Thurzo sighed. "But, the time has come for someone else to take up the burden of

297

your care, and this chore has been placed on me, again. It seems we've come full circle."

"I can take care of myself as well as my children!"

"Manage your own accounts?" he asked, with a condescending laugh.

"I see no person better fit for the task."

This was absurd. I could not believe what I was hearing; to be placed in the care of Count Thurzo again was terrifying.

"Perhaps, Governor, this is a good time to present my records to the countess."

"What is this?" Elizabeth asked, looking at the unrolled scroll.

"It is customary for Hungarian nobles to finance their knights. This has been common practice for as long as records have been kept. The crown very rarely funds the army. I'm afraid this burden falls squarely on the shoulders of the elite. Your husband was the most elite of all. He generously loaned a great deal of his personal funds to the king."

"Then the crown shall be asked to make good on the king's debt and pay it back at once!" Elizabeth demanded.

"A woman makes demands of the king?" Count Thurzo laughed, and all the men in the room laughed with him. "This is a matter between men, a matter which takes a great deal of diplomacy. I assure you the king does not wish to distress you, Countess, but he is also not willing to deal with you either. He has given word to the family that he will pay back his debt in stipend as long as I am overseeing the accounts."

"He does not trust me to handle my own money; monies which rightfully belong to the heir and regent?" she asked.

"Do not take offense, Countess. It is not personal, but law. No woman shall possess full custody over property or finance. It is the way it has always been."

"Well I do not wish it to be you! I want another appointed to the estate at once!"

"I'm afraid you have little say in the matter."

"Why not King Stephen or Gabriel, Andrew, any of the others for that matter. Anyone would be more suitable than you."

"King Stephen does not want scandal entering his house and Gabriel has political ambitions. Any tie to you could greatly tarnish his plan. Frankly, Andrew is a man of the cloth. He is neither knowledgeable nor willing to take on the task. I fear, dear Elizabeth, you are the one who remains exiled. I suggest you embrace the one family member you still have and fall on bended knee to give thanks that I, too, have not turned my back."

Elizabeth snatched the papers and read them over. "I do not understand what this means," she stammered. She was scanning the scrawling across the page. The grid was littered with tiny ticks of ink placed in columns and rows.

"My point precisely," Count Thurzo said. I could tell by his tone he was losing patience.

The clicking of shoes on the floor drew attention to Elizabeth's daughters entering the room to join their mother. The men rose from their seats again. I noticed one of them stepped forward taking a place to the right of Count Thurzo. They exchanged approving looks as the man gripped the lapel of his jacket and puffed out his chest. The girls curtsied before taking their place behind their mother.

"Ah, how beautiful your daughters have become," Count Thurzo boosted. He was taking stock in their worth.

"Never mind my daughters," Elizabeth replied.

The governor waved for the men to again take their seats. However, Count Thurzo and the gentleman to his right remained standing.

"Shall we continue to the next order of business?" Count Thurzo addressed the governor.

"May I present Lord Zrinsky. He is a friend from the Gorski Kotar region of Croatia."

"What business does Lord Zrinsky have in these proceedings? He is not family." Elizabeth said. She was exasperated and losing hold on her nerves.

My hands trembled. I knew if this went on much longer we'd be in for a frightful scene. It was not Elizabeth's nature to flee when sensing danger, but rather to stay and fight – and fight to the death she would.

"Ah, but he will be soon. Come, come Elizabeth this visit does not have to be all dread and dismay. I propose a marriage in the future which shall brighten everyone's spirits!"

As if on cue, a unified sigh was released from the men's chests and several clapped their hands applauding the announcement. I caught my breath. This was inappropriate. I knew nothing good could come from such an arrangement. Francis was not even in the ground and these vultures were already planning another wedding.

"Marriage? I will hear nothing of a marriage!" Elizabeth snapped, clapping her own hands demanding silence. "Pray, do tell who is to marry?" she asked after the room quieted.

Count Thurzo walked over to Anna and presented his hand for her to take. She obliged accepting the escort to Lord Zrinsky.

"May I present Countess Anna Nadasdy to Lord Zrinsky," Count Thurzo announced.

Anna curtsied, bowing to the elder gentleman twice her age.

"I'm sorry my son Nikola was unable to make the introduction. However, he will be attending the king's court in a month's time and is looking forward to meeting you."

Despite my shock, I admitted I was relieved it was Nikola Anna was to marry and not the older Lord Zrinsky.

"I have not agreed for my daughter to marry your son!" Elizabeth said. She again clapped her hands demanding silence. "Stop this nonsense at once!"

Another man stepped forward and presented a piece of paper. Elizabeth snatched it from his hand. "What is this?"

"A marriage contract signed by Count Nadasdy," Count Thurzo said, annoyed.

Elizabeth read it quickly. "He is dead, the contract is void," she said, tossing it to the floor.

"I'm afraid not," Count Thurzo replied.

"It is fine, Mother. I will do as Father wished," Anna interjected.

"*No, Anna,*" I whispered, but no one heard over the fuss being made.

"He is a lord and she a countess," Elizabeth argued. "Surely, Francis would never agree to such an arrangement. He is beneath her in every way."

"Lord Zrinsky holds land of value. In exchange for use of a trade route the king has agreed to the late Count Nadasdy's request to grant title of *Count* to Lord Zrinsky's eldest son, Nikola. In addition, the newly named Count Zrinsky will ask for Countess Anna's hand in marriage, thus ensuring the agreement not be broken. Countess Anna is doing a great service for her country by honoring her father's wishes. She is strengthening the allied relations with the Croats and expanding trade transport and economic commence."

Everyone except Elizabeth applauded her sacrifice.

Anna curtsied again.

"She is not for barter." Elizabeth rounded on the crowd. "She is not an animal up for auction."

Count Thurzo clicked his tongue. "Nonsense."

"I intend for Anna to choose her own match," Elizabeth said waving her hand.

A few men coughed. Others shifted in their seats.

Anna walked over to her mother and took her hands in hers. "Mother, I do not mind the arrangement. It is my duty to do what my father asks and if it benefits the people of my beloved country, how can I refuse?" She lowered her voice, "I must do what I can to protect the family." Anna released her mother's hands and turned back toward Lord Zrinsky. "It will be an honor to meet your son in a month's time. I look forward to taking my place at court as his wife."

I would have admired Anna if I had not known the truth and the ultimate misery such sacrifice brought to young ladies.

Lord Zrinsky cheered, "Ah, then it is settled. I will write to my son immediately with the good news."

Elizabeth stood guarding her remaining daughter. "Nothing is settled," Elizabeth snapped. She could say what she wanted, but in the end she was powerless to do anything.

Lord Zrinsky looked to Count Thurzo who reassured him all was indeed well.

"Let the record and account show that I determine after attending the funeral at Varrano, Countess Bathory will return immediately to Cachtice. There she will remain for the mourning period of two years. Of course, I will grant permission for her to attend her daughter's wedding. However, the visit shall be short. She is to arrive directly prior to the wedding and take leave immediately thereafter," Count Thurzo dictated to his secretary.

The men rolled up their papers and tucked them into satchels and left the room, leaving Elizabeth to stew. As soon as the doors closed, Elizabeth came undone. She ranted that she was no chore that could be swept neatly aside into a manageable pile. If Count Thurzo insisted on calling her one, then she'd make sure he'd be sweeping up after her all across the country and perhaps even the sea. Oh, she'd give him something to manage all right!

At first I did not understand why Anna did not protest, why she agreed to the arranged marriage, but after hearing Count Thurzo's orders and seeing Elizabeth's state, I realized Anna was smarter and more mature than I originally gave her credit. She had not been consumed by the romantic notion of freedom nor blind to duty. I believe she was mindful of her father's intentions and knew not even death would allow her to escape Fate. Yes, she was more aware than her mother that arms reached from the grave. Besides, in the case of Anna, marriage provided benefit, a change of scenery. Existence at Cachtice was difficult and solitary. If she could not be the custodian of her own future, she'd settle for a crumb of happiness. A fine dress, a grand party, a chamber of ladies for company and, if Fortune blessed, a tolerable husband. After all, this was the very best our sex could do. It was an accomplishment and prized above all else. I thought of the prostitutes working the Turkish soldier tents. They were mere objects of pleasure to be used on whim or whipped. Then there was the servant girl strung up in a cage for attempting escape. Her crime was trading information for promise of bread and a few coins. All this scraping, clawing and plotting was good for what—a glimpse of a better life? What did the risk get you, but a few moments of security until the next threat entered the scene? Not even a queen was safe. If she did not produce a male heir or if a younger woman took her place in the marriage bed she'd be exiled, or worse, lose her head. Women were a disposal bag of flesh and bones – hallow wombs placed on Earth to serve a purpose, and when all was done, it was undone.

I listened to Elizabeth complain. Her hair was slipping from the pins holding the twisted braid in place upon her head. Her eyes narrowed, her lips moved sucking in air to form each word exhaled. She swung her arms around in circles as she paced across the floor. It was as if she were trying to tread water to keep from drowning, but her layers of dress dotted with jewels and strung with lace were boggy sacks yanking her down. Still, she fought gasping for each breath and cursing those whose hands pressed upon her trying to shove her under. Perhaps it would be a better course if Elizabeth simply turned on her back and chose to float, but she kicked and thrashed making it all worse and exhausting herself in the process. Still, her instinct was to fight to survive and that was what she'd do. Despite all our adventure, nothing had changed. I had no choice but to swim beside her and hope for rescue.

***

After the funeral we returned to Cachtice. Katelin rode without the companionship of her eldest sister in a separate carriage. Count Thurzo did not allow Dorothea to continue her service to Anna. I believe he feared Dorothea's influence and loyalty to Elizabeth. Instead, Dorothea was placed in the charge of Katelin. It was a tearful goodbye, but Anna assured us all she'd get on quite well in the King's court and was looking forward to her new life. I gripped tightly to her sleeve finding it difficult to let go. I dreaded the long journey up the winding mountainside leading to Cachtice and the nothingness that waited. I too, wanted to attend the court. I hungered for conversation, music and the whisper of scandalous gossip. I released Anna from my affectionate hug. I lifted the hem of my newly fashioned gown and climbed into the carriage taking my place across from Nicholas.

"You look radiant in your new gown," Nicholas complimented.

"What good is a new gown if there is no one to admire it?" I asked.

"I admire it," he said.

"I did not mean…of course I'm grateful," I began.

Nicholas shook his head. "Do not apologize."

"It's only…it's only," I stammered fighting back the tears. I wiped the salty dribble from my cheek with the back of my glove.

Nicholas pulled a handkerchief from his pocket and gave it to me. Elizabeth climbed the stairs of the carriage. I tucked the handkerchief in my lap hoping she would not notice I'd begun to weep. She was calm. She looked at me with the same motherly gaze she'd just bestowed on Anna.

"Do not waste tears on this goodbye, Amara," she said.

"It's not the goodbye, but the return I sorrow for," I said.

"You do not wish to return to Cachtice?" she asked.

"He said two years, Elizabeth. I do not think I can bare two more years," I said, tears welling up again.

The carriage lurched forward. Elizabeth patted my leg. "It won't be that long, dear. I just need a bit of time to get things in order—devise a plan."

I should have begged Elizabeth to play by the rules of man, but my own selfishness prevented me from doing so. I knew nothing good could come from any scheme we plotted, but I did not care. I tasted, albeit briefly, the delight of freedom and the possibility it brought. Then in a flash Count Thurzo extinguished the flame rendering us once again helpless dependents. Each day was determined by the mercy of someone else and the manner in which we moved begged permission.

I rested my head on Elizabeth's shoulder. I closed my eyes. My mind wandered, picturing Draco. He'd aged since our last visit. The lines on his face deepened and the spread of gray peppered his hair. We had barely spoken during the funeral proceedings. His determination to discover the culprit of Francis's murder consumed his every wakening minute. In passing, I mentioned Count Thurzo's plan to send us to Cachtice and expressed my displeasure, but Draco only grunted, mumbling it was best for now. When I argued it was certainly not in my best interest he scolded me, saying I knew little of political unrest and diplomacy. He spoke of rumors concerning a rebellion by the Protestants. Eternal fighting would leave the kingdom vulnerable and the Turks surely would not hesitate to take advantage. Cachtice was remote. I was told it was the safest place for us to be. I asked if the King's court were also safe. Draco knew I was concerned about Anna. He assured me the intimate party would be well protected. Of course, I seized the opportunity, inquiring if Elizabeth and I might also be allowed to remain at court.

"Anna is Count Zrinsky's concern. If there is trouble, he will be responsible," he said. When I pressed further Draco grew irritated. "I will hear no more, Amara. On this subject I am in agreement with Count Thurzo. You will return to Cachtice with Elizabeth."

Draco was always an impassive, tough man, but there had been times when he softened to my persuasion. Those days appeared lost. I barely recognized the man I married. Years of separation and honored duty gutted the heart and soul of my husband. He was iron, cold and rusting.

"Will you not come home – retire to the country?" I asked.

"You would have me die in a rocking chair?" he snarled.

"I wish for you not to meet with a sword," I said. After all, he was my husband and I was not ready to be a widow.

"That is an honorable death. A soldier cannot wish for better."

I began to wonder if this was all that kept Draco away. "Is there someone else?" I asked.

He walked over to the window. The moonlight cast an enormous shadow against the wall. "My mistress is the crown I vow to serve."

"No, I believe I am the mistress and country your wife," I whispered, knowing this was the painful truth.

Nothing more was said. No affection exchanged. It was left at that and no more.

The carriage hit a rut causing my head to bounce against Elizabeth's shoulder. I sat up rubbing my temple. Nicholas was reading.

"How long have we've been traveling?" I asked.

"Several hours."

I sat quietly for a few moments waiting for the effects of waking abruptly to wear off. "Are you not miserable?" I asked.

"No, should I be?" Nicholas said, glancing up from his book.

I sighed. "Cachtice is a dreary place. The very essence pollutes the brain. Wouldn't you prefer a different assignment? Do you not long to utilize your skill as a soldier?"

"I only wish to be where you are."

"That is enough?" I asked. I did not trust it was for I knew a soldier was a wanderer by nature and remaining too long in one place was deadening to their soul.

Nicholas sensed what I was thinking. He knew I was questioning his love. "It is enough. You are enough." He drew the curtain shutting out the world. "I desire nothing else."

I was not certain I felt the same for I wanted more of the world in my life. If given the chance, I would run, run far away from the cold mountains and damp walls leaving the rot and decay of the region far behind. Still, I was drawn to Nicholas, needing him in a manner that was empowering rather than disabling. My dependence on him gave me strength and I knew as long as we remained together I'd get through the worst. I folded my hands in my lap. "It is enough for me as well," I said.

A Soul's End

A month lapsed. Elizabeth decided this was long enough. She'd mourned the loss of her husband and was ready to begin a new life. Despite Count Thurzo's orders, we were definitely moving our household to the Nadasdy townhouse in Vienna. She gave instructions to close up Cachtice and requested only a few servants remain to look after the place while the rest of the servants were sent packing. They were to return to the dreadful shacks leaning in the village. Elizabeth sent word to the Bathory family that traveling to Vienna was necessary to prepare Anna for her upcoming wedding. After all, she was the mother of the bride and was expected to be present at several formal occasions as well as be available for fittings and planning. Consideration was given and conditional terms were sent in response. Although she was granted approval, it was duly noted all preparations were to be supervised by Count Thurzo and to take place in the privacy of the mansion. Elizabeth read the conditions delivered by messenger and to my astonishment gave word she'd obey. When I asked whether she intended to comply with the terms placed on us Elizabeth replied, "How can I be expected to keep my word when I'm obviously not of sound mind? An insane person can not be held accountable for their actions."

By law, this was true. It was a loophole the family readily created when they deemed her an unstable invalid plagued by grief and prone to delusions and fits. At the time it had been a convenient excuse to impose exile and dependency. As was her nature, Elizabeth cleverly turned the tide using the same unfair diagnosis to breech agreements and excuse future behavior. To condemn her, was to also condemn themselves. Count Thurzo could not publicly accuse the countess without incriminating himself and other members of the Bathory clan. There would be questions. Someone would feel compelled to make an inquiry.

Nicholas once again offered his hand to aid me into the carriage. "This is becoming a habit," he teased.

"We're going to Vienna," I said, gleefully.

"Yes, milady. Vienna."

I choose not to fret over the restrictions. I was accustomed to struggle and knew a great deal of our time in the city would be spent sparring for control over our freedom. It was worth a fight, and I was prepared for all the twist and turns Count Thurzo would spin our way. For the past twenty-eight days I'd been pacing the empty corridors of Cachtice. The mindless task inspired defiance and I was ready to take on a new scheme. During our journey I braced myself for confrontation and renewed my faith in Elizabeth's sharp mind. This was no time to possess rigid morality. Rather, it was an occasion demanding action. I justified that any display of improper behavior was warranted in order to serve the greater good, meaning our survival. This was not simply living by definition—air expelled through the lungs and the beating of the heart. No, it meant something quite different. It was gaining control, having a voice, about being the gatekeeper of destiny. Rebellion was coming. I felt it in the very essences of my being. At our last meeting Draco had felt it too, and warned me accordingly. He feared a rebellion was about to be laid at the king's feet. The wind reeked of rumors and despite the glossy exterior of excess the stench of unrest spoiled palace parties.

I took a deep breath. Indeed, it reeked terribly sweet. The smell of fortune changing piqued my senses sending them tingling with delight. The wicked current pushed at the rear of the carriage encouraging our small travel party onward to Vienna. Let Draco worry about Protestant rebels. It was better for us if he remained occupied with duty rather than domesticity. For once I was pleased to hear of conflict; in this case, a religious conflict provided a timely distraction. It gave a cloak for us to brew a much more sinister uprising – the Blood Countess, as Elizabeth would later become known, was about to descend on the city.

Years of confinement and bitter treatment had not broken her will. Rather, such abuse caused mutation in her soul giving birth to the infamous woman I forever called my mistress and my dearest friend. If she were a monster as many say she was, then it was man who created it, not God or the Devil. It was man who would have to live with this fact and prevent history from ever repeating the sequence of events that once set in motion could not be derailed from this fateful course.

It was dusk and in the ominous twilight I saw the first hint of night in the form of stars. I stared out the window at the twinkling dots appearing in the sky. Patterns emerged connecting one to another as they winked at the Earth below. The king's astrologer discovered a new star in the sea of gems that he called a *nova*. I wondered if I could see it, or had it already faded to blend in with the others; its fire so bright it burned itself out. I heard the astrologer even wrote a book explaining his discovery and the scientific method employed to document his findings. The star was said to be more radiant and, because it was so, determined to be a universal sign of what was to come. For some it was believed to be a warning that the dominant reign of the Roman Catholic Church was coming to an end. To others, such as the rebel reformers such as the party's leader Prince Bocskay, the star was a symbol of hope and encouragement that he was set upon the right path. I did not understand how tiny sparkles millions of miles away predicted the course of mankind. Why should the universe concern itself with the trivial trials of humans? I had many thoughts along the way, but I will not dwell on the details of our journey, for it was mostly uneventful. The interesting part of the tale continues when we rolled into Vienna.

***

I rubbed the top of my legs. My bum was sore and my limbs restless with anticipation as our carriage navigated the streets of the city. In the evening light I could still recognize the gardens where ladies of leisure strolled and, in the distance, viewed the peaks of the palace as we traveled toward Lobkowitz Square. Just ahead was the Nadasdy townhouse. It was securely snuggled in the shadow of St. Augustine's Cathedral. What a magnificent sight the city was with its colors and scents swirling together like mixed oil paints creating a beautiful scene. I straightened my back, stretching my spine as we came to a halt. Nothing was going to prevent me from enjoying this moment, not even the sour face of Count Thurzo could dampen my mood.

Waiting on the front stoop was Greta Hanover, the housekeeper. As we approached she tucked a piece of white linen into her apron and wiped her hands on the back of her skirt. She was older, but her breasts remained, to my dismay, perky and busting over the low cut of her work dress. Ficzko called to the houseboy to unload our trunks while Greta greeted us nervously.

"Welcome, Countess. I was not expecting so many trunks. I will tell the boy to fetch help quickly."

Elizabeth lingered on the street allowing all those spying through lace curtains a good look. "Very well," she said tugging off her gloves.

"Count Thurzo indicated you wouldn't be staying long in Vienna," Greta said, her eyes widening at the cargo being unloaded.

Elizabeth said nothing. After all, she did not owe a servant an explanation. She was mistress of the house. She'd stay as long as it pleased her and I was hoping it would please her to do so for some time.

The Harlot Stain

1628: Present Day Vienna

My visit with Kate was over. Any trace that she'd spent time in my home was swept clean and everything returned to its proper place including removing the Turkish rug from the floor of my writing room. I twisted in my seat, tapping the tip of my pointed slipper on the floorboard. There, as it had been for some time, were the remnants of a faded burgundy stain. It unnerved everyone in my household, so why did I insist it remain exposed when I possessed a perfectly suitable rug to conceal the blemish beneath? I adjusted my things upon the desk. I suppose because the stain meant more to me than anyone would ever know, well, until now. I dipped my pen in the inkwell. I'd share this tale with Count Drugeth or John, as I had begun to refer to him, because the bloodstain was real evidence. It was a piece of actual history that still existed. If he were so inclined to investigate, he'd discover the gruesome treasure. It hadn't been destroyed or altered to appear as something else and because of this, for me it represented the truth about Elizabeth and our life together.

I always believed nothing in this world was so simple as good or bad, or even evil for that matter. No, in fact, I'd learned most things were quite the contrary. People were complex and I hoped in time John would learn this too, and in his own way manage to make sense of it and understand, even forgive if he could.

While I was lost in my thoughts the ink on my quill dried. I picked at the flakes before again dipping it in the ink and resting my hand on a blank page. The worn tip scrapped the paper as I wrote, each letter bleeding into the next as I worked the sentences across the linen. Tiny veins broke from the fat strokes as the ink absorbed, permanently imprinting my thoughts into the fibers. With every pause, a tiny blot formed revealing my hesitation, but I did not let my lack of fluidity distract from my task. If I focused too much on the appearance of my work, rather than the detail, I would kill the rawness and with it might feel compelled to censor my writing for the mere sake of sparing my reader any unease. I ignored the flaws and continued scratching out the account of our arrival in Vienna.

***

For the most part, Elizabeth behaved and followed the rules set forth by Count Thurzo. She attended all necessary occasions regarding preparations for Anna's wedding, as well as all that demanded making an appearance at court. Although King Rudolph cringed at the sight of Elizabeth, he was bound by custom and knew even he could not deny her company.

The wedding was beautiful. Anna appeared happily married and very eager to get on with her future. Nikola, and the newly titled Count Zrinsky, seemed like a fine gentleman and a proper husband. I was certain Anna would enjoy his home and the freedom distance from her mother provided. Although she was now bound to Count Zrinsky, she'd at least be given opportunities requiring social interaction. We all hungered for such things. I was relieved to learn she was finally getting her wish to escape, albeit to a new cage.

During our stint at the royal court we mingled with King Rudolph, a man of science who also had an appetite for the bizarre including a collection of dwarfs and an army of giants. He preferred occult-oriented subjects and surrounded himself with astrologers, codes and art pertaining to the extraordinary. Considering their similarities in taste, I did not readily understand his blatant dislike for Elizabeth. I suppose it had something to do with her being a stubborn-minded woman, but I am not certain. I was inclined to think he'd find her fascinating rather than brazen. Nevertheless, he recoiled at the very sight of her and, as time passed, his dislike for us intensified.

His disdain did not immediately deter Elizabeth. She continued with social obligations and befriended anyone with like interests, including employing Darvulia, a woman with a reputation for alchemy. Along with Dorothea, Ficzko, Darvulia and the added addition of a washerwoman named Kata, our strange party was a much-discussed spectacle. We turned heads and drew unwanted gossip. There was no reason to believe we were any different from the other nobles at court, but Elizabeth provoked this kind of reaction wherever she went. She was a magnetic vessel of curiosity and the more she ignored the whispers and gawking, the more she radiated mystery. I knew if things continued, we'd have to leave Vienna to avoid further scandal.

One afternoon while strolling through the park I overheard a woman say while sneering at Darvulia, 'That woman is a witch from the forest.' I shivered knowing all too well what an accusation such as being called a witch could entail. It was a death sentence, a horrible painful death with little hope of mercy or pardon. I relayed my concerns to Elizabeth, but she dismissed it as harmless gossip. After all, what proof did the woman in the park have? What proof indeed!

I did not press the issue because I selfishly wanted to remain in the city. I should have known ignoring signs was blasphemy, but I wanted to believe things were different, better for that matter. They just had to be! The city was too beautiful, too alive with shades of pink and basking in bronze glow in late afternoons to bring dread and mayhem. I allowed myself to be fooled, mesmerized by the glory of civility and progress. However, not far away Prince Bocskay and his Ottoman allies were organizing a revolt. They were muddying the scene and amassing their troops in reaction to the imposed sanction of Catholicism. The Ottoman army was sensing turmoil and moved to capitalize on vulnerabilities in the territory. They were circling into place, strategically assimilating to attack, to rebel against the turbulent reign and demand religious tolerance. Trouble was not lurking in some far off territory, or just outside the city walls. Trouble, I'd soon find, was much closer and poised to knock upon our door.

The bell gonged, alarming the maid to a visitor. She sighed while pushing her tired bones from the chair in the hall. She was obviously irritated by the intrusion and wondered who was bothering the household at this hour. We were preoccupied and gave little attention to the commotion downstairs. It was probably just a late messenger who had been delayed by the weather. I was certain there was no need to worry. That was, until Greta appeared in the doorway.

"Sorry to bother you, Countess, but there is a woman downstairs who demands to speak with you. I tried to send her away, but she insists she have an audience this very moment. By the looks of things, it seems she's traveled a ways to find you and I don't think she will go easily."

"What is her name?" Elizabeth asked.

"She refused to give me a name, Countess. She told me to tell you she is a friend of Count Nadasdy and that you'd be interested in meeting her."

"A *friend?*"

"No friend of Francis would intrude so rudely unannounced," I said.

"Does she know he is dead?"

"She did not say," Greta replied.

Elizabeth glanced at me.

"If I might add, Countess, the woman does not appear to be *noble*. She is, if I were to presume, a *friend* of another kind."

No further explanation was necessary. It was probably best this woman came alone and at night. I assumed she wanted money to remain quiet or, better yet, so she could disappear.

Elizabeth checked the time. "It is late. Invite her to stay and show her to the room at the end of the hall."

Greta did as she was asked and in minutes we heard footsteps passing outside the door. The woman had accepted Elizabeth's invitation and was settling into the guest room. I imagined she came prepared with a speech and a list of demands. It would be easy enough. A simple discussion, an exchange of monies and she'd be gone after breakfast. No one would be the wiser.

Elizabeth made a move toward the door.

"Where are you going?" I asked.

"Wait here. I'm going to see what this is all about."

I too wanted to know, but Elizabeth raised a hand indicating I was to stay. The severity of the gesture told me this was an order, and not a friendly request. So I obeyed. I paced about the room fussing over the smallest things and contemplating whether or not I should rearrange the books on the shelf. I was looking for anything to occupy my time while I waited for Elizabeth to return. I crossed my arms griping my sides as I continued to circle the rug. It had already been a while and with each tick of the clock I grew more anxious. Who was this woman and what did she want? Would the situation easily be remedied or was there more trouble to come? I jumped when the door opened.

"Come with me," Elizabeth said.

I eagerly followed her down the hall. Inside the guest room sprawled on the floor was the body of the woman. She was younger than I expected, barely more than a child and obviously inexperienced in the art of extortion. A burgundy pool fanned out around her flesh and oozed toward the walls. The room was disheveled and the girl's gloves dangled over an open drawer as if she were interrupted while putting them away. I grabbed a blanket and tossed it on the puddle inching closer to the bedpost. The wool quickly soaked up the fluid turning the gray threads a rusty brown. Elizabeth unfolded the blanket and began rolling the body on top.

"Help me move her," she said, grunting.

The dead weight took all my effort to roll on the soiled blanket. Never in my life did I think I'd have to take up this kind of task, twice. First, there was the soldier in the camp, and now this girl – both enemies, but of very different types. I did not have to ask if she was dead. I'd seen enough corpses and witnessed plenty of blood to know she was done for and would not, to my horror, be awakening anytime soon. Elizabeth nudged the door ajar with her foot while she pulled on the bundle. The heavy mass slide across the floor, snagging on small wood splinters as we dragged the body into the hall.

"Who was she?" I asked, huffing as I secured the feet at the top of the stairs. I used the word *was* because the thing I saw on the floor did not resemble the person who entered the house. The lump in the blanket was disfigured, her tan features like clay putty covered in mashed berries.

Elizabeth let her end drop. I heard a crack as the head thumped against the stair. She put her hands on her hips as she tried to catch her breath. "She was a harlot from Bucharest. She wanted money, but I wasn't about to give her any. She said she was owed, but not by me."

"Francis?" I asked.

"Yes," she nodded.

Elizabeth picked up her end, and together we dragged the corpse down the steps. Ficzko and Darvulia who must have been aroused by the commotion, met us at the bottom of the landing. Elizabeth let go of her end and I released the feet. I was out of breath and beginning to break a sweat.

Ficzko volunteered to take up the unpleasant chore. "What do you want us to do with her?" he asked, wrapping his infant arms around the wad of blanket.

"Take her to the cellar for now. No one knows she is here, so it should be safe. You can dump the body tomorrow night. I don't care where. Just get it out of here."

The blanket was completely soaked with blood and so was the front of my nightdress. I wiped my hands on the rear of my skirt.

"Do you think she has tasted the pleasure of love?" Darvulia asked curiously.

"I'm certain she was not a virgin," Elizabeth answered.

"Pity. I can do so much with virgin blood. I suppose this will all go to waste," she said tugging on the mass.

I didn't want to know exactly what she meant and I didn't much care. I wanted them to leave so Elizabeth and I could talk freely about what aspired in the guest room. When we returned upstairs Kata was already scrubbing the blood trail from the hallway floorboards. She worked like it was an ordinary stain at an ordinary time of day or, in this case, night. I stepped by her, tiptoeing around the soapy pink scum sloshing from the rag.

"This is not good. This is not Cachtice," I said, pulling my soiled nightdress over my head and tossing it on the floor. I cleaned my hands in the basin and dried them before putting on a fresh dress. "It won't be so easy to dispose of a body in the city."

"She's a whore. No one cares about her," Elizabeth said. She changed out of her clothes. "Nobody even knows who she is. Besides, Ficzko will make sure I'm not compromised and the rest of the household is certain to keep their mouths shut."

I shook my head. "This is bad, this is very bad."

"Don't be so melodramatic Amara. I had to do what I had to do."

The rush was subsiding and I was able to get a hold on myself. "Okay, then please tell me why it was necessary to gut the girl in the guest room? It is so messy and I'm positive that Kata will never be able to scour the stain from the floorboards."

"I'll buy a rug," Elizabeth said.

I gave her a perturbed look.

"It wasn't the ideal way to be done with her, but I didn't have time to brew a potion or cause an accident. I improvised. Trust me, it was just."

Again, I shook my head in disbelief. Honestly, I was not upset because of a dead girl. Why should I be? I didn't even know the woman. I was worried about our safety. If this woman could somehow be linked to us, it would be disastrous! "Wait a minute. It was *just*?" I asked. It certainly would not matter in the eyes of the law. They frowned upon civilians issuing punishments; however, the *just* reason for the maiming might settle any dilemma I was creating in my own head. If risking our safety were to ensure our safety, well then, it was just.

Elizabeth poked her head out the door to see if Kata was still working in the hall. She had moved on to the guest room.

"That woman was Francis' mistress. She claimed he owed her money and she came to collect. I asked her why she didn't ask

Francis herself and she laughed. She knew he was dead. She knew because she killed him," Elizabeth said in a low voice.

"She murdered Francis?" I whispered. I wondered why we were whispering. I was sure no one was listening, but the occasion and conversation seemed to demand we take such a tone.

"She insists it was an accident. When he refused to pay her more money after she gave birth to a son, she stabbed him, repeatedly. She confessed she hadn't meant to kill him, only hurt him so he would pay. She admitted that she'd become so enraged when he told her she was merely a whore and he would not be blackmailed into acknowledging the bastard." Elizabeth paused. "Ha! Once she started cutting, she just couldn't stop. It does take nerve and I do envy that. It's a shame. In another world we might be friendly."

"Why didn't you give her some money and turn her away? It would have been easier."

"She knows about Paul and she threatened to harm my son if I even thought about accusing her. If he died, then the law would have to recognize her son and compensate him accordingly. That whore came here to *scare* me! She thought she had the perfect scheme." Elizabeth clicked her tongue. "She didn't know who she was threatening."

"Oh!" I was beginning to understand.

There was a long silence before Elizabeth spoke again. "This woman killed my husband and threatened to also dispose of my only son. She left me no choice but to avenge Francis' death and protect the family. You see now, I had to do what I had to do, even if she did me a favor by killing Francis."

"The chief commander murdered by a harlot. No, that will never do – it can never be known," I said. "No one can know what truly happened or that this baby exists. It is best she is done away with for your sake and the children," I said, giving her a hug.

Elizabeth was not a cold-blooded killer. If that woman hadn't thought herself so clever, she'd still be alive. I mulled Elizabeth's explanation over in my head. I had to agree. She had to do what she must to survive. After all, power was money and she held all the chips while remaining regent to the Nadasdy heir, Paul.

As long as he was healthy and well cared for, we all remained protected.

In a morbid sense, Francis's death was poetic. His life ended by the enemy he never saw coming; a woman scorned, and a lowly born insignificant fragile woman to boot! After all the battles he headed and powerful enemies he conquered, he was taken by surprise and ambushed in his own bedroom. Oh, the dishonor!

The moonlight streaming through the window illuminated Elizabeth's face turning it a bluish white. She looked more like a statue than a breathing, living person as she stood still staring at nothingness. She'd avenged her husband, but not out of love. It was out of duty to her family and country. If I squinted I could see the resemblance she shared with her ancient ancestors and realized how the blood, which fueled their reign, also flowed through her. Her instincts were not learned, they were inherited, much like an animal in nature born with spots to blend in or venom to protect against predators. It was a gift, an advantage for survival so the species would not die out.

"Tomorrow we will buy a rug," I said.

***

And, that is exactly what we did. The next day we went to market and purchased an imported rug. It was large and thick with woven details of birds of paradise and exotic garden flowers. As I suspected, Kata was unable to dissolve the traces of blood from the porous wood. An outline forever soiled the guest room floor. Together we moved the furniture and arranged the rug. With a mere flip of the corner the nightmare disappeared and everything went back to normal. The beautiful carpet we acquired covered the imperfection perfectly.

I stood atop the rug and clapped my hands. "There, all is well," I said.

Elizabeth surveyed the room. While we were gone all the belongings tossed in the struggle were returned to their proper place. The curtains were half drawn and a little light broke through the far window. Was it really that easy? She brushed her hands against her skirt.

"Things look proper and fit," she said. She studied the room one last time making sure nothing was out of place.

Folded atop the bureau were the harlot's gloves. I held them up. "Should we burn these?"

Elizabeth tapped a finger to her chin while she thought. "No, I think I will hold onto them just in case I need proof."

She was tucking away little bits of evidence in every household just in case she needed to throw an ace in her defense. I replaced the gloves on the table and walked out of the room. The church bells were ringing but not to announce the time. Someone was pulling the rope repeatedly sending a loud echoing call throughout the city. It was a warning. Something was threatening the area and all the civilized citizens residing within the walls. By the time I got downstairs the servants were already scurrying through the halls shouting orders and packing items into crates.

I grabbed Dorothea's arm as she rushed by. The force of my restraint flung her around. "What is going on?"

"The people are revolting. Count Thurzo demands we return to Cachtice at once. Please, pack quickly before they quarter off the city."

I went to the drawing room and looked out the window. In the street was chaos. People scattered like rats from water. Just this morning we'd been to market. Everything was as it always was; sweet and sunny. The air had been filled with scents of baking and mingled pleasantly with the bustling sounds of commerce. How had it turned so suddenly? I watched as a man pushed another man down as he ran by. I was mesmerized by how instantly polite people turned into barbarians. Two carriages thundered to a halt outside the townhouse. Someone tried to grab onto the door and the driver hit him over the head with a cane beating the man back leaving him bloody and cursing as he stumbled further down the street.

I did not have time to stare in awe or grieve the loss of my contentment. I rushed upstairs and threw open a case. I stuffed what I could inside and immediately threw on a coat and hat. Ficzko was dragging cargo down the stairs and piling it by the door while Elizabeth shouted orders to Greta. She'd remain behind to close up the house before returning to her parent's farm outside the city. The shouting hurt my head and the disruption of my routine threw me for a whirl. I was not prepared to leave Vienna, not yet, not so soon! I felt a sting at my elbow. Someone had grabbed it tightly and was pushing me down the steps to the carriage waiting outside.

"Get in!" Nicholas shouted, shoving my rump through the door.

I tumbled onto the seat, my hat sliding to the side as the fastener of my cloak twisted, choking my neck.

"Christ on a cross!" I cursed. I straightened my attire.

Elizabeth was right behind me with the rest of her entourage in tow. Once they were securely in the carriage, Nicholas slammed the door. He fought off a fellow who was begging for a spot in our travel party. He was offering money, but Nicholas refused. There was no room and it was time to go. He gripped the side of the carriage and swung himself up alongside the driver. He pounded three times and the reins snapped sending the horses forward and racing toward the exit of the city.

Vienna had turned into an ugly smear as pandemonium erupted in the streets. Fires burned and glass broke as people fought to escape. It did not matter whether they were Catholic or Protestant. No one wanted to be trapped in the middle of a revolt. When the dust settled and resolve returned, so would the normalcy of daily life, but until then a riot raged against tyranny rule. The carriage was speeding around corners and avoiding blockades. The motion was making me sick and I didn't know how much more I could take, but I knew we had to keep moving to get ahead of the Imperial Army.

I held onto the seat. "Why didn't Count Thurzo order us to the palace? We'd be protected there with the rest of the court."

"I can think of a few reasons," Elizabeth shouted over the noise of the turning wheels.

"After all, your husband funded most of the king's army. I'd think now would be a good time to reap the rewards of the investment," I replied. My voice sounded distant in my own ears among the rattle of the carriage.

"The king hates me. If I'm dead, there is no debt. My death would bode well for Count Thurzo, too. I suppose if we are slaughtered in the confusion while fleeing no one will investigate any wrong doings. Besides, Prince Bocskay is related through marriage," she reminded me. "That makes me even more unpopular to the king."

"Everyone is related through marriage," I said.

"True, but most aren't committing treason by leading a revolt against the ruling king."

She had a point. However, our lack of invitation to the palace probably had more to do with advantage than diplomacy. Many would benefit if Elizabeth unfortunately died in route to Cachtice, but the biggest benefactor was Count Thurzo. I wouldn't put it past that filthy scoundrel to orchestrate an assassination. After we were dead, he'd raid the coffers and seize properties. Oh no! The properties, I thought. That meant the townhouse. The gruesome images of the previous night flashed before my eyes. In all the mess, I'd almost forgotten what was stashed in the cellar.

"What if they stumble upon the harlot?" I asked. I knew there had not been time during the scrutiny of daylight to dispose of the body rolled in the soiled blanket.

"Count Thurzo isn't the only person taking advantage of this little skirmish. I had Ficzko and Nicholas toss her in the alley. Authorities will assume she was killed in the riots."

It was convenient and virtually untraceable. The streets would be littered with maimed bodies. Another corpse rotting in the back street would hardly raise a brow. At last, there was no need to worry, well, not about the dead girl anyway. No, my mind was shifting to other concerns, namely our survival during the journey to Cachtice. I knew Nicholas was a step ahead and would take precautions with the priceless cargo he was guarding. He'd ensure nothing happened to Elizabeth and me while under his watch, still, I could not help be anxious. Our departure was hasty and our outlook uncertain.

It took longer to return to Cachtice than expected because we had to alter our route several times, but eventually the familiar jagged crags and enormous stone fortress came into view. Although I should have been ecstatic to be alive, I found I was overcome with dread as our party eased up the winding mountainside. My mind struggled with dark thoughts and for a moment I wished I were dead instead of facing another day breathing in the gloomy air. I never understood why Elizabeth didn't share my displeasure for the place, but she seemed pleased to be home and eager to resume her duties as mistress of the castle. She was better suited for the isolation, and besides she had her workshop, which provided a private place for her to dabble without intrusion.

The carriage jerked to an abrupt halt causing me to whip forward. I clenched my stomach. I'd been ill the entire way home and felt like I was going to toss my lunch. I waited patiently for everyone to exit before I slide over to the door. I steadied myself against the arch. My knees were weak and my face hot. Nicholas took hold of my waist and lifted me down. The cool air was comforting and so was the concerned look upon his face. At least I had Nicholas. Cachtice wouldn't be so terrible if he were here with me. He stroked my cheek and raised my chin. His lips were chapped from exposure, but I did not mind when he kissed me. The nausea was replaced by pleasant flutters in my stomach. I took a deep breath and surveyed the courtyard. Yes, we were home and together we'd survive whatever fate threw our way. I took hold of Nicholas's hand and allowed him to escort me into the castle. The servants had returned and were busy tending to rooms and cooking in the kitchen. It was strange not to have Anna in our company but I was pleased she was happy. More importantly, she was far away where her life was unthreatened and her future blissfully optimistic.

***

More than a year passed before we got word King Rudolph's brother Matthias subdued the rebels by issuing the 'Peace of Vienna' which guaranteed religious freedom. Bocskay's troops remained in the surrounding area near Pressburg, but the violence receded and hope for a new way of life was crossing everyone's lips. Barely a person spoke without discussing the treaty. As soon as Elizabeth received the message, she issued one of her own. Her scouts reported Ottoman rebels were intruding on Transylvania territory. She ordered up the guards and gave word to deliver a stern warning to their commander. If they did not turn coat and leave the territory she would make sure none of them ever saw their beloved country or families again. Just in case they did not take her threat seriously, she boxed up some bones and a metal badge from the remains of one of the Turk's she'd castrated years ago. We had no idea what the badge represented, but believed it carried meaning and the commander would recognize the token. The contents of the box were evidence that Elizabeth was capable of enforcing the law on her land.

I grimaced at the tarnished piece of metal resting among the bones, stripped clean of flesh and identity. Honor and disgrace sealed timelessly together. The presence of the items held meaning; they were a warning to anyone who tried to violate the remote territory. I played with a tiny bone wondering if it belonged to a finger. I clenched my thighs together remembering the probing hands of the dirty Turk soldier who tried to rape me by the river. My skin crawled and I shuddered. I slammed the lid of the box shut and secured the lock. I did not want them coming any closer. I turned to Elizabeth who was watching my expression carefully.

"Will this work?"

She knew I was scared. I imagine she was also remembering our last encounter with the raiders.

"They will think twice," she answered. "This will buy us some time."

"We should send word to Draco. He will deploy his men to the area." Draco had been occupied in battle with the rebels. It was a different enemy he faced and flushing them out was harder than anyone initially imaged.

"I will handle this, Amara. If I weaken now, they will think I cannot protect myself or command my guards. It will prove I'm vulnerable."

I felt a sting of guilt. I doubted whether we could survive on our own. The moment things got tense I immediately wished for men to save us. They were strong, trained, and best of all, heroically fearless. If blood spilled, I preferred it be theirs and not mine. It was selfish and cowardly. How could I insist on equality when I was unwilling to do what life demanded to be equal? I admired Elizabeth. She remained true by showing no sign of being the weaker sex;

however, I could not make the same claim. I was ashamed by the betrayal of my natural instinct to want to be shielded from danger.

Lyk nudged the side of my leg. He lifted his snout and sniffed the air and then the side of the box. His lip pulled back and he snarled; the shackles on his neck prickled in defense. I patted his head, trying to calm him. He resisted, he was on guard and sensed something was amiss. Although he was not as spry as he once was, he did his best to impose fear. After all, he'd grown into a large wolf with piercing eyes and a fierce growl which, when unleashed, caused the most seasoned soldier to twitch. I secured a leash around his collar and gently pulled him back so the men could lift the box and load it onto the cart waiting in the courtyard. It was a dangerous mission, delivering Elizabeth's message, but it was their duty and the men went about it with amazing courage.

Nicholas was by my side. He petted Lyk who continued to grumble as the men secured the cargo.

"He senses unrest," Nicholas said.

"He's just being protective."

Nicholas stroked Lyk's back. "Good boy," he soothed. He then put his arm around me. "We'll keep you safe."

I flinched at his words. They should have made me feel better, but instead I felt inferior. I pulled away and returned to the castle. The stone corridors and iron candelabras mocked my delicate frame as I stormed toward my room. The sound of my skirts whooshing against my legs as I rounded the corners annoyed me even more. I wanted to tear off my silly dress and cut my hair. I wanted to feel my bow and arrow strapped to my back as I rode hard out along the ridge. This was my home, this was my land and I should be willing to defend it at all cost. Lyk tugged on the hem of my skirt as if he were trying to hold me back.

"Stop it!" I yelled, snatching my dress from his mouth.

I threw open the door to my room and marched inside. I looked around trying to spot anything I could wield as a weapon. A vase of flowers sat beautifully upon the table. A lantern, a porcelain basin and embroidered towel, a silver tray of tea and biscuits; it was all dainty and feminine, proper things for a lady to possess and utterly disgusting in this light.

The booming sound of Nicholas's boots hitting the floor echoed in the hall. He was nearing, coming to my aid to comfort me in this time of trouble. I turned and put up a hand causing him to stop short in the doorway.

"Please, I want to be alone."

He said nothing while he blinked helplessly at me. It was obvious by his distressed expression he had no idea what to do in this situation. How was he to make things better? I didn't want him to fix it. I just wanted him to leave me alone with my thoughts.

"Please, Nicholas. Go!"

My words wounded, but he did as I asked. He left me alone in my pretty room with velvet curtains and stuffed pillows, bottled scents and an ivory handled hairbrush. Lyk circled three times before settling on his cedar bed near the hearth. He huffed before resting his head on his folded paws. It was unfair. He should be racing through the woods at the head of his pack instead of lazily baking in the warmth of my fire. He looked as out of place as I suddenly felt. I took my hair down, letting my wavy locks drape over my shoulders. It was wild and untamed and the sight of my reflection in the mirror was startling. Where had that girl gone? I touched my face tracing the tiny lines inevitably formed by time. My pounding heart began to relax and I sighed letting the anger recede. This time I'd be ready for the Turks if they came. I'd never allow them to take me by surprise again. I wouldn't give them the satisfaction.

I went to my trunk and took out a set of men's clothing. I dressed quickly. I retrieved my bow and arrow and headed outside to the field for some target practice. I'd train, I'd be ready to defend my home. Along with Dorothea and Darvulia masters of potions and Elizabeth schooled in weaponry, we were not helpless bits of bait waiting to be devoured. We wouldn't go without a fight. We would not surrender or be owned by the enemy. I'd slit my own throat before I'd let them take me. Like Vlad's wife, I'd jump from a tower window to my death before I'd give myself to the enemy.

As I stretched my bow, aligning the arrow and taking aim at the target, I felt a presence watching from across the field. I released the string sending the arrow whizzing through the air and pinging into the target. Nicholas lurked in the shade of a tree, carefully keeping watch while I sharpened my skills. I suppose it was impossible to expect he'd truly leave me alone. At least he respected my wishes enough to keep a distance. I'd make amends tonight. I'd give him a kiss earning immediate forgiveness for my vile behavior.

I reloaded and pulled the string tight. I closed one eye. Patiently, I waited letting the breeze die before releasing the string. Again, the ping and sweet whizzing sound of the feathers cutting through the air as it raced toward the target. The arrow stuck, the shaft vibrating at the force of impact. I took several steps backward. Tomorrow I'd practice with knives. I'd hone my talents and devise a strategy. I'd chart the best advantage points and survey the grounds. I was taking back control. I was in charge and it felt incredible, empowering in fact, and I finally realized what I'd lost in all the frills and lace during my stay in the city.

A light fog blanketed the treetops sending a dewy mist falling to the ground. The gray cover did not seem so dreadful. I eyed the contrast thinking it was beautiful after all and for the first time I believe I saw what Elizabeth had always seen in this place. I took a breath, held it and exhaled, clearing almost all the air from my lungs. It was wet and clean. It tasted like rain and pine, pure and cleansing without a hint of smoke or sewage. I steadied my hand, waiting for the precise moment when the wind was most calm. I calculated the effects of the dew weighing on the arrow, the current of airflow and slope of the ground. I released the string and hit my target for the third time.

***

My hand ached from writing. I set down my quill and stretched my back. I looked over my shoulder at the old stain on the wood floor. I didn't want to cover it up. I wanted it to remind me of Elizabeth and what she stood for, her bravery and determination and yes, even her insanity. I felt alive again, inspired and raw. The stain was like the forest mist cleansing my senses and conjuring courage the city often squelched. In this room I did not feel old and vulnerable, feminine or frail. The bells of the cathedral chimed loudly reminding me it was time for tea. The maid delivered a polished silver tray right on cue just like she did every day. I smirked at her effort to avoid the mark on the floor. It repelled her, causing her to retreat and tiptoe around taking a detour instead of the quickest route, a straight line to my side table.

"Do you need anything else?" she asked, setting down the tray.

"I think I'd like to get some fresh air. Please tell my driver I'd like to take a ride to the park, the one on the far side of town this time." It was the closest I was going to get to the country. At least I'd smell the trees and hear the birds for a few hours. I gathered my papers, carefully stacking them in a neat pile before replacing the stopper in the inkwell. I poured a cup of tea and gazed out the window. It was all so civilized, I thought, taking a sip of warm water.

Folded on the bureau was a pair of woman's gloves. They were out of fashion and discolored. They were sad little things. Forgotten by someone; carelessly misplaced and left behind. I knew they'd never be claimed, but still I could not bring myself to toss them out. They were just as much a part of this room as the desk and the bed, the bloodstain and me, for that matter. Everything was connected, tied together and impossible to escape. Even if I boxed the gloves, their memory would haunt the room. I'd know they'd been here whether anyone could actually see them or not. Just like the stain on the floor, nothing was going away, so what was the point of covering it up?

Blood, My Salvation

October 27, 1607

A servant girl screamed and slumped to her knees. She frantically waved signs of the cross over her heart as she muttered a superstitious verse. I recognized the phrase. I'd heard it before from the mouth of our cook. Unfortunately, this happened every time we employed a new servant. It was always an encounter with the portrait of Vlad Tepes that inspired the reaction, and usually the first shriek was the worst. The picture hung above the hearth in Elizabeth's chamber and despite my numerous pleas for it to be removed, the dark face of her ancestor remained. It was apparent the eerie rendering of the infamous prince was again haunting the household and disturbing my peace.

I did my best to ignore the outburst and the loud talking of Darvulia and Elizabeth in the adjoining room.

"Amara!" Elizabeth called.

Her voice had more of a shrill to it than a singsong ring. I was comfortable and didn't want to be bothered, nor did I wish to budge from my chair, but I decided it was best to get it over with. I knew she'd keep calling my name until I came.

"Is something wrong?" I asked joining them on the balcony.

Darvulia had a star gazing instrument propped against the railing and aimed at the sky.

"You've got to see this, Amara. It is amazing!" Elizabeth cried. It had been a while since I'd seen her so giddy about anything.

I did not need an instrument to view the bright streak of fire crossing the night sky. It was a blazing ball of light from which a long tail trailed dimming as it stretched. It was not like any star I'd ever seen and it did not resemble lightening before a storm. It was mysterious, wondrous, and altogether frightening in the most exhilarating way.

Even though I knew it had to be very far away, I still wondered if it would crash into the Earth and set it ablaze. Maybe it'd land in the ocean and be squelched.

"What is it?"

"I think it is a nova, like the one Tycho discovered," Elizabeth said.

Tycho was an astrologer who wrote books about such universal things. He saw what others did not, and gave further explanation where many had failed.

"It looks like sparks from a bonfire," I said.

"I think it looks like a mythical dragon flying across the sky," Elizabeth added. She was leaning on the railing.

In the distance a glow twinkled in the tower of the monastery.

"The monks are star gazing too," I noted.

Usually the place was dark, but tonight even the monks were curious about the fire in the sky.

"They probably think it is a sign of doom," Darvulia snorted. Her mangy hair hung unkempt down her back. The ashy dullness blended with the plain black of her dress. She was weathered, aged beyond her years and, like Elizabeth, prone to fits.

Monks, fire in the sky, doom, I thought. This was sounding familiar, but why?

Elizabeth held out her arms as she pressed her belly against the railing. "Spread your wings and fly!" she shouted into the night. Her high-pitched cry echoed against the stone walls. The resonating warning bounced back louder than I thought was possible, assaulting my ears.

I stumbled backwards catching my heel on an uneven stone. I tumbled to the floor landing hard on my bum and facing the disapproving glare of Vlad Tepes' painted face warming above the hearth. I scrambled to my feet.

"I know why this is so familiar!" I shouted, grabbing Elizabeth by the arm. "Come on, I'll show you." I didn't allow them another second to question the errand we were running. I was hurrying as fast as my legs would carry me through the castle, winding down the stairs and along the passage leading to the kitchen.

Elizabeth and Darvulia were breathing hard as they tried to keep up.

"Where are we going?" Elizabeth panted, as I unlatched the cellar door.

"To the tomb," I said, giving her an impatient nudge down the steps. I lit a torch and handed it to Darvulia.

Even though her eyesight was failing, Darvulia knew the way to the workshop better than I did, but we weren't going there. Instead, I was taking them deeper beneath the castle, through the dank tunnels and into the bowels below the monastery.

In the center of the room stood the podium. The Holy Bible rested beside the remains of a tiny skull. Nothing had been touched since my last visit and I was certain I'd find what I was looking for locked inside. I pried the lid off and slipped my arm into the body of the stand. My fingers felt around in the void searching for the dried pieces of vellum. Darvulia raised the lantern throwing light in my direction.

"Do you have it?" she asked.

"Almost," I said, my fingers pinching the pages together. I carefully pulled them out.

Together we sat on the floor with the papers spread all around us.

"These look like old maps," Elizabeth said.

By my feet I spotted the piece I was looking for. It was faded and worn, but the message was undeniable. "Here!" I announced.

Elizabeth eyed the words and then as if reciting a chant, read them aloud:

It spreads its wings across the sky, stretching the length our eyes can see, two tails, one reaching west, and the other east. Its majestic awe, colors of gola riding on a rippling flame. God sends a warning, branding the sky for us to heed. We shall obey, or suffer. Suffer catastrophic events by his hand. Beware his wrath comes in many forms.

"Ah! The nova *is* a sign," Darvulia whispered, her milky eyes opaque in the firelight.

I tapped the symbol drawn in the corner. "The Dragon."

Elizabeth looked at the date. "1456," she said. "It makes sense."

"I know it means something, but I can't make any meaning of it," I said. I collected the maps and placed them in a neat pile.

"Legend states that monks foresaw the future. It came in the form of a giant dragon branded in the sky. Vlad Tepes is called the 'son of the dragon.'"

"Uh-huh." I wasn't making the connection.

"Vlad was not a villain in everyone's eyes. To some he was a hero. He murdered many, but by doing so he spared thousands."

"It's not murder if it is war," I corrected.

Elizabeth shrugged. She knew it was what it was and, although war made killing just, some still refused to call Vlad Tepes anything but pure evil.

"Like in most royal palaces, especially during times of war, there was scandal. One of Vlad's advisors convinced him that his enemies were conspiring with a witch. He had on good authority that they paid the woman to cast a hex. Soon tragedy struck and many terrible things happened. Of course, this validated the advisor's claim and, despite his reluctance, Vlad worried he was cursed. However, he was a strong prince and he was determined to survive. The people believed this angered the witch and made her even more resolved on destroying him. She tried many times to kill him, but he would not die. The legend goes that she was left with no other choice but to do the next best thing. She cast a spell, and by doing so she trapped his soul in a portrait for all eternity. He is not dead, but rather sealed away," Elizabeth explained.

"The painting! This is where I found it," I said, pointing to the podium. "But why hide it in there?"

"There's more to the tale," Elizabeth continued, a bit impatient. "All curses can be broken, unlocked if you will, if a person can find the right key."

"Silly tales," I huffed.

"Just listen!"

I rolled my eyes at Darvulia. Her annoyed glare was burning an imaginary hole through my skin. She believed in curses and legends. After all, she was a proclaimed witch empowered with abilities to heal or poison as she wished.

"I don't know how it became known, but it is said that the prince would rise again when the dragon returned, branding the sky."

"That's it?"

"Well, also when drops of blood from his kin are spilled on his portrait. The blood, along with the sight of the dragon in the sky is the key. He will come again to avenge his death and bring peace to his people."

"Let's say this legend is true. This would be good right?"

Darvulia puffed out her cheeks. "There are always consequences. There are laws to the universe. He will not return as he was. It is against nature to resurrect."

"But, he is not dead, not really," I said. I was thinking that this knowledge was a kind of mystical loophole.

Darvulia's eyes widened. "It's worse! He will rise from the *undead.*"

"Undead?" I asked.

"It's much worse, very unpredictable," she said.

"Probably why the monks hid the portrait and the prophecy."

She nodded. "Vlad's enemies accused him of thirsting for blood and if he ever returned he'd be driven by hunger. He'd feed on the living, drain them of their life source. He is a damned soul." She tapped her finger on the prophecy. "His first taste will be the blood of his kin."

"Are you believing this?" I asked Elizabeth.

She was deep in thought. She blinked coming back to the present to answer my question. "There is only one way to find out." She stood and brushed the dust from her skirt and gathered up the maps and the prophecy. She returned them to the podium and set the lid in place along with the Holy Bible and skull. She patted the skull as if it were a silly child. "What do you think this is all about?"

Darvulia gave a dismissive wave. "More superstition."

"I think it is a warning. God's wrath brings death, that sort of thing," I added.

"Man's wrath brings death," Elizabeth corrected. She was always testing the unseen. But, one thing she did know was man caused pain and destruction. It was his nature to do so. God, she was not certain about and therefore, was quick to dismiss any warning as pure myth.

Together we quitted the tomb and made our way through the long passages leading by the workshop and towards the stairs to the kitchen door. As we walked, I thought about the tale and wondered if there were any truths to the legend. Obviously, the peasants in the village and the monks in the monastery believed the stories. That is why so many reacted to the portrait of Vlad Tepes the way they did. How'd they know it was *that* portrait? Maybe there was another painting hidden away or buried in a vault.

The castle was quiet as we climbed the winding stairs to Elizabeth's chambers. The air was much warmer and I was pleased to be rid of the damp chill. Looming above the hearth was the portrait of the prince. There he rested for all eternity, locked beneath a red silk hat laced in pearls, his black waves of hair touching his neck. His pale skin emphasizing his penetrating green eyes and his broad brows tipped at the ends seemed to freeze him in a constant state of disapproval. His lips were too red set below his thin, perfectly twisted moustache. He was not smiling or frowning. He was eerily still, which I found intimidating. Was this how he appeared in life? Was there any warmth to his presence or was Vlad always so cold and distance?

Elizabeth pushed over a stool. She rose on tiptoe taking hold of the gold frame and lifting it from the hook.

"You really do not think this will work?" I asked. My eyes darted from Darvulia to Elizabeth.

We gathered, forming a circle around the portrait.

"I need something sharp," Elizabeth said.

Darvulia snatched a knife from the serving tray. We'd used it early to cut bread.

Elizabeth winced as she carefully pressed the knife into the palm of her hand. The crease split filling with blood. She made a fist and held it over the lips of her ancestor. Slowly, tiny droplets rolled down her hand and dripped, one by one, onto the painting.

"How much is needed?" I asked, looking to Darvulia.

She was dazed, her eyes wide with anticipation.

My own heart thumped rapidly in my chest.

"A few more," she said. "Just to make sure."

Elizabeth gave another squeeze before pulling her hand away. The cut was shallow and was already drying up. Mindlessly, she wiped her hand on her skirt smearing a red streak across her hip.

"Now what?" I asked. This wasn't a very well thought out plan. We had no idea what we were doing or if it would even work. What if the legends were true and Dracula was unleashed to avenge all the wrongs executed against him? Or worse, what if Darvulia was right and he returned as something much more sinister? Would we be safe because we resurrected him, freeing him from eternal damnation and that picture or would we be fair game, just more victims set in his path? I made the sign of the cross.

"Not you too!" Elizabeth hissed.

I blushed. The gesture was stupid, but I didn't know what else to do. So, I waited.

***

For eighteen clear nights the fiery dragon was visible in the sky with branding tails stretching west and to the east while the portrait of Vlad Tepes lay on the floor of the chamber with dried blood spotting the canvas. With each passing day Elizabeth grew more impatient. She so badly wanted something to happen. She desperately desired proof that her blood was powerful, that it contained some special essences. She was obsessed with the idea of resurrection and shut herself in her chambers. As long as the nova burned, anything was achievable, and this meant she might be all-powerful.

I visited her room often making sure she had food and drink. I didn't know how long this would go on, but I was concerned if something didn't happen soon, Elizabeth would go mad. Unfortunately, Elizabeth's health was not my only concern. Darvulia's fits were getting worse and with each spasm her eyesight faded.

She stumbled around the room moving from one piece of furniture to the next until she settled upon the sofa. She was more unkempt than usual and the haze in her eyes was severe. They looked like the inside of raw bird eggs, swirls of purplish blue goo, slimy and searching. I despised the hag, hated the crippled dependent constantly at Elizabeth's side. What did Elizabeth find so appealing about the woman? I secretly wished she'd just die already. It was a horrible thing to think but, nevertheless, I thought it.

Darvulia reached for something on the table, but missed. She knocked a pillow to the floor. She tried to retrieve it and hit her forehead.

"Aw!" she howled.

It should have been pathetic if the scene hadn't been so comical. She was always doing that, missing her target and bruising herself in the process.

The noise annoyed Elizabeth who was already more agitated than normal today. I moved carefully about the room trying to avoid her wrath while the daylight faded over the horizon. I fingered the bottles and jars on her dressing table. There were new crystal vials of creams and cakes of cosmetics strewn among her feminine things. Before I realized it, Elizabeth was at my side.

"Beauty in a bottle?" I said lightheartedly.

"I don't want to end up like her," Elizabeth hissed in a low voice. She glanced at Darvulia who was staring at nothing particular. "She's hideous, poor creature."

I scoffed. "You're not even close."

"Matter of time," she said, picking up an amethyst bottle.

We were not young maidens, but we were certainly not *old*, especially not Elizabeth. Hardly anyone would guess her age. She appeared much younger than she actually was. She was fortunate, an exceptional beauty with long tresses of glossy hair set off by the marble white complexion of her skin. Her eyes were almond-shaped and the color of honey sap dripped over mossy bark. Her figure even after having children remained voluptuously youthful. Sure, she had some fine lines if you looked closely, but that was to be expected, given the weather.

She bent over pressing her face close to the mirror. She fingered the skin around her eyes and lips.

"There is no change," she said. She rubbed some cream on her cheeks and then powdered her face in a cloud of cosmetics.

She was obsessing over her appearance, fretting over the ever-spreading wrinkles plaguing her face. Wrinkles I could barely notice, even if I concentrated really hard. I dabbed some cream under my eyes and rubbed it in. I pulled a face. What did it matter how we looked? We seldom had visitors, but I had to admit, even I understood vanity. After all, I was a woman. I too was guilty of not wanting to end up looking like Darvulia, the haggard witch with brown spots and glassy stare.

I was startled by a loud crash on the opposite side of the room. Something metallic spun before coming to a halt on the floor. My head whipped around to spot Darvulia convulsing on the floor, the tea tray and all its contents scattered a few feet away.

"Oh no!" I gasped. I rushed to her side and fell to my knees.

She was thrashing about like a child shaking a rag doll. I tried to hold down her legs, but the muscles jerked violently sending me tumbling backwards.

"Leave her be," Elizabeth said, watching from across the room.

"We've got to help her!" I yelled.

"It will be over soon. She's just having another fit. They happen more often now."

Spit foamed from Darvulia's mouth, bubbling out over her lips. Slowly, she convulsed less, the jerks growing further apart.

"See, she's almost finished," Elizabeth said turning away.

Eventually the fit ceased and Darvulia groaned back to consciousness. I helped her to the sofa and propped her head up with a pillow. She had more bruises than I could count and I realized it was probably from the fits rather than caused by clumsiness.

I remembered how Elizabeth use to pitch fits when she was younger, but it had been quite some time since she lost control and it was never as severe as Darvulia. However, I knew Elizabeth was aware of the condition and I realized she was terrified. I wrinkled my nose. Darvulia was a sight lying on the sofa, dull hair tangled around her blotchy face, spit crusted on her dry lips, an aged dependent trapped in pending darkness.

I eyed Elizabeth seated at her dressing table. I understood why she couldn't hate Darvulia, why she couldn't allow herself to be repulsed by the woman. The witch reflected her worst nightmare. She reminded Elizabeth of herself and what might happen. Of course, nothing was guaranteed, but I knew from experience leaving the future to chance was dangerous. If Elizabeth could avoid the same horrible demise, then she would do everything she could within her natural power to ensure she didn't turn into a monster.

After the servant girl was finished cleaning the mess made on the floor by Darvulia's fit, she tended to Elizabeth. She began gently brushing her hair preparing the countess for bed. Although she wouldn't sleep for hours, the ritual was lengthy and if done properly was better than tossing slop to the pigs or wringing laundry. The servant must have been preoccupied in thought because she carelessly snagged a snarl in Elizabeth's hair.

"Ouch! You stupid fool!" Elizabeth screamed. She was rubbing the back of her head. "Look what you've done!"

The servant stood dumbstruck with the ivory handle of the brush griped tightly in her calloused hand. A wad of Elizabeth's ebony hair clumped in the bristles.

Before the servant could beg for forgiveness, Elizabeth reacted, assaulting the girl across the face with an infuriated slap. The force of her hand meeting the girl's cheek sent her whirling. Blood spurted from her nose splattering Elizabeth's face and speckling the mirror. The girl hit the floor, her arm cracking as her wrist bent in an awkward manner.

I shut my eyes tight and slapped a hand over my mouth to conceal a shriek. I waited for a scream, but all I heard was a whimper as the servant crawled across the floor towards the door. Elizabeth paid no attention; she was too busy wiping the blood from her cheek. Through the dots of blood on the mirror Elizabeth tried to assess the damage done to her hair. Then she paused. She leaned forward, the tips of her fingers tickling her skin.

Darvulia rose from the sofa, one arm stretched out towards Elizabeth as she waved it hopelessly around in the air.

"What is it, Countess?" she asked. She sensed the quiet and was concerned.

Elizabeth was speechless. She just kept touching her skin. Finally she spoke. "The lines, they have vanished," she said, stunned.

"Vanished?" Darvulia asked. "My creams are working?" Excitement rose in her voice.

"It's a miracle," Elizabeth cried.

I hurried to Elizabeth's side. To me she looked as she always did; beautiful, flawless and...

"It's not the cream," Elizabeth said.

Darvulia had found her way to the dressing table and was clutching at Elizabeth arm. "Tell me, what happened?"

"I wiped the blood from my cheek...the lines are no longer visible," she stuttered, amazed by the reflection in the mirror.

"Yes, yes, I see," Darvulia agreed.

I rolled my eyes, as if she could *see* anything! But, I was not going to be the person to disagree with Elizabeth, especially on this subject.

I hadn't noticed in all the hubbub, but the servant girl had crept from the room.

"Youth, I can regain my youth," Elizabeth said. She was exhilarated by the discovery. She was absolutely thrilled by the possibility, so much so that she'd completely forgot about the nova and the discarded portrait of Vlad Tepes by the hearth.

Darvulia shook as if she were having a spiritual revelation.

"Is it another fit?" I asked, taking a step back from the twitching witch.

She held her hands up as if praying to God. "The secret to eternal beauty is the life source. It's what is missing from my potion."

Elizabeth grabbed the jar of crème. "I had just rubbed this on my skin before…before I slapped the girl."

To me it was a coincidence, but to them it was the answer. Mystery solved.

Elizabeth gathered up the various jars on her dressing table and with her arms full of magic crèmes and oils she headed for the door. She stopped short, "Where'd she go?" she asked, looking for the servant girl.

I shrugged. What did it matter?

"Never mind, she couldn't have gotten far. I'll have Ficzko fetch her."

"For what?" I asked. I was bored.

"We need more blood," Darvulia answered.

"Oh," I said, wondering how much blood.

Together Elizabeth and Darvulia set out to the workshop. They'd toil through the night if they had to in order to perfect the formula. This was Elizabeth's redemption. It was the insurance she longed for, the preservative needed to prolong her survival and lessen the threat against her existence. She'd stay beautiful and independent, and most importantly, influential and in control.

The room was quiet and the doors to the balcony shut. Outside the nova burned in the sky, the star gazing instrument leaned abandoned against the railing while the light in the tower of the monastery shone in the distance. Inside, the dressing table was speckled with blood. Small voids revealed where the bottles of crèmes once were, and the mirror was smeared with a streak of iron red. On the floor basking in the glow of the evening fire was the forgotten portrait of Vlad Tepes. Drips of Elizabeth's life source drizzled across his firmly pressed lips. I fixated on his soulless eyes while pondering the seduction, the mesmerizing obsession humans had for blood. It was all-powerful, all determining and the most significant ingredient to life and all its infinite possibilities. Or was it? I picked at the dried dots stuck to the canvas.

Outside the body, blood was nothing more than an excretion soiling everything it touched. I leaned close trying to see the mystery in the substance. It was worth killing for, marrying, birthing children, and even scheming after when necessary. It was the *key* to the world. It was the rise and fall of kingdoms, wealth and immunity. It also destroyed, crippled, and riddled others by polluting them with disease.

I poured myself a glass of wine. I swirled it around, breathing in the woody scent and admiring the impurities of age. I took a long drink. *Drink the blood of Christ*, I thought. A warm tingle rushed through my belly. Consume the blood of Christ. Drink in his life source and you'll find salvation. I wasn't religious, but I did remember a lesson or two. I held the glass in the firelight. It was only wine, but what if it were the blood of Christ? Would it make a difference?

An Unexpected Blow

"Ha!" Elizabeth hooted, holding up a letter.

"Good news?" I asked, threading my sewing needle.

"My cousin Gabriel has been named Prince of Transylvania over Francis's kin, Count Thurzo. He must be infuriated!"

Hearing of any injustice to Count Thurzo brought me joy. He was so sure he'd be named prince, so certain he'd done everything right to climb the social ladder and claim the title.

"The Bathory's tipped the scale once again," Elizabeth said, obviously pleased by the news.

"Is there to be a party?" I asked. I was praying the paper she held included an invitation, a means for an escape from Cachtice. I was restless. Even though I spent most of my time with Nicholas, I was ready for a change of scenery.

Elizabeth continued to amuse herself by playing with ingredients to perfect her beauty potion. Most of her days were spent in the hidden confines of her workshop, but I could tell by her reaction to the letter she was eager for an adventure too.

Elizabeth spread the word that we were traveling to Pressburg at once. The household was bustling with activity as everyone hurried to pack their belongings and make arrangements for the ensuing journey. Once Elizabeth made up her mind, action was immediate. She did not consult with an advisor or seek the escort of a relative. She didn't follow traditional protocol, but rather sprung spontaneously. It was exhilarating and the rush exploding in my sedentary veins was addicting. I would not protest or caution her to consider danger and decorum. What did I care? It was a party, a time of celebration and certainly everyone was in a forgiving mood. Well almost everyone! Count Thurzo was very sour to say the least!

The line of carriages assembling in the courtyard was becoming a grand spectacle and symbolic of the growing entourage accompanying the countess. With Anna married and Paul with his tutor at Varanno, that left only Katelin who was old enough to ride in her own carriage along with her attending servants. Meanwhile, Darvulia the witch, the burly sorceress Dorothea, Ficzko the dwarf, and I, the dutiful lady in waiting, joined our mistress. We were servants of privilege and, although we were a peculiar clan, we were fiercely loyal.

Nicholas led the guard along the snaking trail leading from the castle toward the dilapidated peasant villages. I wondered what the procession looked like to the people below and if they still thought Elizabeth was infected. As was customary, she rode with the curtains drawn, which only added to the mystery of her existence.

"The dragon in the sky was a good omen," Darvulia said, confidently. She was reveling in her prediction.

The nova had disappeared, or moved on, or simply burned out. I wasn't sure which, but it seemed the only thing resurrected by the star was our luck. As soon as the night sky became an ominous black, the portrait of Vlad Tepes was returned to the hook above the hearth. His soul was not freed and he did not feed on the blood of the living. The painting was just a painting, and the wives tale – just a tale. With the room set to rights, the legend of the famous prince drifted from our memories like a fading ghost story. It had been frightening, but with the passing of time, it lost its mystique and was forgotten.

***

When we arrived in Pressburg we found all the usual players shuffling into the palace and the main hall buzzing with celebratory energy. I was drunk from excitement and could not wait to make an entrance into the grand ballroom. The puckered face and rigid posture of Count Thurzo brought us pure pleasure. Knowing he was unhappy was very satisfying and I was going to savor his misery for as long as possible.

Draco came early in the day and now stood across the room. He did not wait to escort me to the party because he was in charge of escorting someone else. He was promoted to private guard of security for Prince Bathory. It was a prestigious assignment and I was pleased he was finally away from the field of battle. He had survived all these years and it was time for him to ease into retirement. I knew he would be disappointed, but it was for the best. It was selfish of me to hope he'd die from old age rather than a fatal wound. I knew he'd rather have it the other way. Like Elizabeth, Draco had his own fear of growing old and disabled.

He did not seem to notice my presences when I entered beneath the tall arch. I dangled from Nicholas's arm like a jeweled accessory as we melted in with the other distinguished guests. My skin prickled, alerting me to the obvious distance between Draco and me. So much time had passed and with it, the passion we shared fizzled into nothing more than mutual respect and endearing friendship.

He was on patrol, scanning the crowd, stoically protecting the ruling prince and his small private party. I was acutely aware that, for him, this evening's festivities involved managing the crowds, not dancing with his wife. He was foremost a soldier, not a courtier, nor a husband.

"Shall I take you to greet your husband?" Nicholas whispered in my ear. His warm breath was seductive and sweet as it swept across my neck. He was always good at making me aware that I wasn't alone in the world. He was by my side and the feel of his arm tucked around my waist was comforting.

"He's preoccupied. I do not want to be a bother," I said.

I was not ready to accept that Draco and I were no longer drawn to each other with the same intensity. Somewhere along the path of our shared life he'd became a stranger. I did not want to admit I no longer knew him, and confronting that reality was more frightening than avoiding him. So, I chose to admire Draco from afar. I'd remember *my* Sir Lorant and choose to ignore the cold, statuesque man impenetrable to fear and bound by a lifetime of servitude. Although I knew it was time to admit the line between soldier and man had permanently welded together, I was stubborn to the idea. I was afraid not even love could severe who he'd become. I felt the zing of pity. Was his armor so thick, he could not sense the loss like I did?

Nicholas reacted to my sudden discomfort. "Love, this is a party."

The even tone of his sultry voice instantly put me at ease. I glanced around the room. "A rather grand one at that!"

Elizabeth was enjoying herself and was gloating at Count Thurzo who slumped in a chair shoved against the wall. He was sullen and nothing was going to improve his mood, especially not Elizabeth. This should have been his party, his moment in the shining light, but instead he was passed over for a Bathory. After everything he had done, all his plotting and scheming, he went unrewarded.

I took a turn about the room greeting couples and complimenting the women. So many pretty dresses and sparkling jewels! Anna was there with her husband and accompanied by his family. She fit in by his side as if she were born to be the missing piece of a larger puzzle. Katelin was mingling with the other unmarried girls who were being ogled by a flock of eligible bachelors. One by one, the girls were asked to dance. They paired up for a song or two before parting and coupling with someone new. The courtship of youth was pleasant to witness as a member of the audience, rather than from the vantage of the stage. It was more enjoyable watching the drama unfold. I was detached from the ache of young love and disappointment of betrayal. I smiled thinking about how much wisdom and advice I could pass along to these unsuspecting girls. Really, what good would it do? I knew they needed to learn the lessons for themselves. A warning would fall on deaf ears anyways. They'd have to get burned, experience elation and satisfaction as well as the terror of abandonment. This is what would make them strong. This is what would turn them into survivors, mothers and decent wives. Or in the end, kill them. Either way, my telling would not change any of the suffering or ensure great reward. I squeezed Nicholas's arm. Despite it all, I felt at this moment satisfied and strangely fortunate. I knew love, had known it more than once in my life. I had suffered. That was undeniable, but I had also known love. How many women could confess to that? I looked around the room. Husbands and wives laughed and chatted, each engaged in proper behavior and postured accordingly. Sure they had contentment and comfort, but passionate love?

Nicholas guided me to the balcony. The air was crisp, but refreshing. He pulled me close, scandalously close. After all, I was a married woman.

"You look like you swallowed a canary," he teased.

I pressed my palms against his chest and gently eased away. "Mind your manners."

"No one is watching," he said, tossing a glance over his shoulder.

"Just the same."

He took a step back. "This better?"

I nodded, even though I hated him drawing away.

"What were you thinking back there?" he asked. He gestured to the ballroom.

"I was thinking about passionate love." I didn't feel the need to confess my other thoughts, mainly those pertaining to Draco.

"Ah. Passion." Nicholas approved. "It is everlasting."

I weaved my fingers with his. "Everlasting love is not the same as passion."

His brow furrowed. For a man I realized it might be one in the same, but for a woman, the defining differences were apparent.

"Which is best?" he asked.

"Everlasting love endures over time, but passionate love burns deep and is the most exhilarating aphrodisiac. Every part of your body is alive and the pleasure is heavenly. Nothing in the world can compare."

"Sounds delicious," Nicholas smirked.

"There is a drawback. There is a price one must pay." I thought about Draco. Although he was under the same roof, he felt like he was on the other side of the world. "Because it is on fire, it can only burn itself out. It turns to ash and blows away."

"Like a comet," Nicholas said, staring up at the sky. "Majestically beautiful, awe inspiring, but never lasting. You have to pause and savior, but if you hold on too tight you'll smother it."

"It is true you must savor it, but it will fade whether you hold tight or not. Because it burns, it will eventually go out. Such is the nature of passion. This cannot be changed," I said.

"Then our love is everlasting," Nicholas said, decidedly.

I forced a smile.

He suddenly looked upset. "You do not agree?"

I thought about our nights together in his quarters at Cachtice. We shared a physical hunger, a lust that never was satisfied. No matter how hard I tried, I could never be close enough to Nicholas. I was a fiend and he was my prey. Even as we stood dressed in a gown and adorned in livery, I wanted to devour him. It was taking every ounce of self-control to keep my attraction in check and even though I tried immensely, I knew I was failing with each passing hour we spent in the company of the other guests.

I inched closer. "I dare you. Tell me you don't feel it?"

The energy between our bodies pulled like opposites attracting one to the other.

Nicholas wanted to resist, to prove his case, but his will was not strong enough. He caved, snatching me in his arms and stealing a kiss. He nibbled at my lip.

I gasped. "Nicholas, no!"

"I don't care what your theory is. If our passion dies out I swear on my life I will go against nature and relight it," he said with conviction.

I knew he meant it. I so badly wanted it to be true, for it to be possible in the end, but I was wiser. I wasn't like the young girls mooning over the boys on the dance floor. I knew better.

I kissed Nicholas on his cheek, letting my lips linger before I spoke. "Cherish the passion," I said, my voice light. "So few have the chance."

I shivered. The night air was blowing through the fabric of my gown. Nicholas wrapped his arm snugly around my shoulder and pressed me against his warm body. Together we returned to the dance, neither of us speaking. We were content to silently observe the glorious scene. Nicholas tapped his toe in rhythm with the music while I allowed my eyes to wander. My permanently planted grin dropped the moment my gaze locked on a man trying to blend in with a small gathering loitering across the room. I don't know why it hadn't occurred to me earlier. I should have realized he'd be invited.

His deep-set eyes so cunning in concealing what they were observing. He was careful to never stare or give anything away. He was the perfect gentleman dressed impeccably and engaged dutifully beside his wife.

My palms went wet and my knees weak. I was not as skilled at hiding my emotion and although I didn't want to give him the satisfaction of knowing he had startled me, I wondered if it was too late. I was overcome with a wave of nausea. I regretted snacking earlier in the evening and decided roasted goose had not been a brilliant choice. I was in a bit of a panic and considered bolting from the room before he noticed me. I could not tell if he had, well, not until his hand nervously smoothed back his hair. It was his tell tale habit, a dead give away that he suddenly felt nervous. I couldn't bring myself to look away, and just when I thought I might be able to, his eyes met mine.

There he was, my everlasting love. My feelings for George spanned the test of time, never fading or burning out. The dull ache in my chest reminded me of the hole that remained.

"Feeling all right?" Nicholas asked, concerned.

My face was hot and I had the urge to flee, run from the room as quick as my legs would carry me.

I shook my head. I was certain if I opened my mouth to speak I would vomit, splattering my dinner, which balled in the middle of my throat, onto Nicholas' shoes. I darted from his side and headed for the nearest exit, but crowds of people forced me this way and that way. Each time I saw an escape, my path was cut off by a strolling, giggling group of partygoers. It seemed instead of getting farther from George, I was somehow being herded toward him. If I weren't careful I'd end up in an unwanted confrontation. I could not make small talk, I knew I was incapable of being pleasant, at least until I collected my nerves. I spotted my opening and, as I hurried towards it, a large man smoking a pipe bumped into me sending me bouncing in the opposite direction. He grumbled an apology and continued on, but the collision was disastrous. I was tossed into a crowd of people. I smacked against someone's shoulder whirling off into yet another direction altogether. A man caught me by the waist and steadied me before I tripped over the hem of my skirt. My stealthy escape was causing quite the scene and drawing attention. George was only a few feet away. I gasped and tried to scurry the other way. I felt something brush my hand and as I turned I saw George reaching out almost catching my arm before the crowd closed sealing off the space between us. I picked up my skirt and raced from the room. I was breathing heavy and the lump in my throat was pressing hard, threatening to embarrass me further. I fanned my face trying to get air flowing and cooling off my hot cheeks. I was mortified. I could not have been less graceful.

As soon as I was in the hall the scene settled and less people were gawking at me as I searched for an empty bench. Before I could sit down a set of bony fingers pinched my arm and spun me around.

"Ow!" I snapped.

"There you are," Elizabeth said, letting go.

I just wanted to be left alone. However, I was relieved it was Elizabeth and not Nicholas or George.

I plopped down on the bench. Without an invitation, she joined me.

"Guess what I just heard," she said. By her tone I knew it was probably nothing good.

"Hum?" I was distracted. I kept looking towards the ballroom, half expecting George to appear through the tall arch.

"As a consolation to being passed over, the king announced he is appointing Count Thurzo to *viovode*! He is to become the Palatine Governor of Transylvania."

"Really?" I asked. I barely heard what Elizabeth said. My head was throbbing and my stomach flopped. That roast goose was getting the better of me. I had my own problems at the moment, but she hadn't noticed. She was worried about the scales tipping back in favor of Count Thurzo.

She was prattling on about the ordeal and what it meant for the country when Katelin came bounding up.

"Mother! I've meant the most amazing man!" she cooed.

I felt like I was being ambushed from all sides. All I wanted was a moment of peace, just a little time to gather my thoughts and make sense of the strange feeling racing through my body. I had to think. I had to quickly figure out my next move. Now, their crisis and drama was cluttering my mind, clouding it entirely, and I was growing more annoyed with each word they spoke.

"Amara, did you hear what I said?" Elizabeth voice was piercing in my ear.

"Appointed governor, it's terrible," I repeated.

"Mother! Are you listening to me?" Katelin whined; her round eyes bright with excitement.

"Excuse me," I said, trying to slip away. If I could just get free of all the noise I could sort my world and put it back together again. How could a single glance from George shatter my perfect picture of my sufferable life?

"Oh no you don't!" Katelin cried, pressing my shoulder so I couldn't stand up.

"What's this about a man?" Elizabeth asked her daughter.

"He's asked if I can join him for a walk tomorrow afternoon. Of course, I will insist upon an escort, but I so very much want to go. Can I? *Please!*" she begged.

"That depends. Who is this gentleman?"

I leaned to the side trying to see around a group of women chatting in the doorway. I wondered why George had not followed me. I couldn't seem to make up my mind. Had I wanted him to?

"His name is George. He is the son of the Count of Humenne. He is so adorable and such a gentleman. He's already introduced me to his parents. They seem very nice."

Hearing the name cross Katelin's lips startled me. I was not expecting it and by Elizabeth's reaction, neither was she.

Elizabeth was stunned. "The son of Count George Drugeth? How old is he?"

"Old enough," Katelin said. She let out a squeal. "Can I *please*? Can I go meet him tomorrow?"

"What do you even know about this young man?" Elizabeth asked. Her posture immediately stiffened and turned to guard me.

I knew plenty about the Drugeth family. I had been mesmerized by their charms. If Katelin were indeed enchanted, it would be impossible to persuade her from seeking the young man out.

Katelin crossed her arms definitely. "Well he comes from a wealthy family," she began. "Powerful land owners, just like Papa."

I bit my lower lip. Her father was a poor artist, but the truth didn't matter.

"George says they hold an important trade route connecting Hungry with Poland. Nothing can pass without their permission."

I had been set aside for such a trade route. It was a wedding present and now it appeared it was George's son's inheritance. The trade route was about to claim another victim of my adopted family.

"George will take a seat in Parliament. He is an officer of royal customs."

Elizabeth scrunched up her face. "He is a man of business."

"That doesn't change the fact he is also titled," Katelin added.

"You can do much better," Elizabeth said. The discussion was over.

It was ironic that Elizabeth would mettle in her daughter's affairs. After all, she wanted her girls to have the choice. If Katelin wanted George, I was certain Elizabeth would never stand in her way. I was missing something. Was Elizabeth protecting her daughter or me?

"If you get to know him, maybe you will see what I see," Katelin pleaded.

"I do *know* him, well enough."

"His mother approves," Katelin said. This was a mistake.

"His mother! Ha! Of course she does, Katelin. Aligning with our family through marriage is an advantage. Did you forget who you're related to or is your head swooning so much that you forgot we're on the rise?"

Katelin scoffed. "Is it so terrible to imagine maybe George actual likes me and not just because I'm related to Prince Gabriel or the King of Poland?"

"Oh dear," Elizabeth said, patting Katelin's hand.

She was wounded by the notion and I thought it cruel to burst the girl's joy so harshly, but Elizabeth was right. Even though Katelin was beautiful and charismatic, it was likely it was her position and dowry that young George's mother, Fruzsina Drugeth, found most charming. Naturally, she'd approve of the alliance.

Maybe this was not as awful as it seemed. Perhaps young George really did love Katelin. If they could both get what they wanted, how could it be wrong? It wasn't like Katelin was being forced to do anything she didn't want to do. This was a welcomed courtship by both parties.

"Maybe you should consider there could be a happy ending for everyone," I suggested to Elizabeth.

Katelin perked up.

"You of all people, Amara! You of all people know what they're like, what that family is capable of doing—the charade. It's all bells and bonnets now, but wait until they get their claws in her."

"What charade?" Katelin asked. Her eyes filled with tears, in another second she'd be sobbing.

The hole in my chest tore. I hated seeing her in pain. When I looked up I found he was standing a few feet away. He immediately recognized the tension in my expression and knew something was amiss.

Elizabeth was fierce. Instinctively, she put herself between George and us. "You tell your wife I do not care for her scheme." She snatched Katelin by the arm and tugged her away.

Katelin was fighting her mother as tears streamed down her cheeks. Before I had a chance to intervene, they were gone.

"I'll tell her, but it won't make much difference," *my* George mumbled. He sat down beside me on the bench. "Enjoying the party?"

"Immensely," I said, rolling my eyes. I was still nauseous and the pain in my head had turned from a throb into a screaming boom.

"It's *supposed* to be fun." He chuckled.

"It's supposed to be *entertaining*," I corrected.

"Ah, yes. Very clever."

"Things are never what they seem, are they? It is all a charade."

I felt another pair of eyes on me. Leaning against a column was Nicholas. His arms crossed against his chest and his face dark with jealously. He wouldn't make a scene, but he also wouldn't spare me the displeasure of watching him stew.

George remained relaxed as if he didn't notice Nicholas vying for attention. He was a courtier schooled in the art of calm indifference.

"Sometimes things are *exactly* what they seem." I knew he was referring to Nicholas. We hadn't hidden our relationship very well and it was easy for someone like George to pick up on it.

"He wants me to leave," he said.

"He wants you dead," I teased.

"Can't say I blame him." He leaned closer. "He's not the only one. Draco wants me dead, too. Of course, he probably also wants *him* dead," he said, referring to Nicholas. "I want him dead, he wants me dead, your husband wants us both dead…" he waved it off like the scenario was a boring ordeal.

"No one is killing anyone," I scolded.

"Precisely my point."

"Can you get away later tonight?" he asked.

I was not sure I wanted to. It hurt too much to be with George, but before I could answer Nicholas made a move.

"There you are, milady," Nicholas interrupted. "Please excuse us. The lady is not feeling well. I've agreed to escort her to her room. I apologize for making you wait. I am here now," Nicholas said, offering me his arm.

The intrusion answered George's question. Nicholas was not going to let me out of his sight.

George did not protest, but I didn't expect him to. He bowed and said good evening. He loved a good parlor game and he had plenty of time to make a counter move of his own. He wouldn't act hastily and, if everything went according to plan, the tiny seed he planted in my mind would grow and I'd willing come to him.

***

I was not the only female to fall victim to the seductive pulse of a Drugeth. Katelin was determined to defy her mother and took ever opportunity to sneak off with young George. She was falling deeper into his snare and it was just a matter of time before she was hopelessly in love. Of course, Fruzsina did all she could to make it exciting for the young couple. Amazingly, she was always one step ahead of Elizabeth, which was difficult to achieve. I had to give it to her, she was clever and very talented at courtly pursuit. There was no question she was capable of getting what she wanted. After all, she had once secured the king with her irresistible virtue. For years, she had been King Rudolph's mistress until increasing age forced her aside for a younger, more fertile favorite. But, it did not matter because by then she had gained the benefit, children, jewels, and the security of a proper marriage. She had done well for herself and was driven to do the same for her children.

The following day I took advantage of Nicholas' absence to seek an assignation with George. Nicholas and Draco had gone on a hunt for the afternoon and it would be hours before they'd return with Prince Gabriel's party. I assumed George would make up an excuse to stay behind. He'd find a way to speak to me in private. I knew him well enough to know he'd also take advantage of the situation. When I didn't find him in his room, I looked for him in the gardens.

"Ah, there you are, smelling the roses," I said.

He was sniffing a plain red rose. His effeminate, manicured hand carefully cradled the bud.

"Unescorted today?" he asked.

It was disturbing how well we knew each other, even after all the years that passed between us.

"I'd like to ask a favor," I said.

"Um-hum?" He took a deep drag of the floral scents.

"Call off your wife. Convince her to leave Katelin alone. Tell her she is not right for your son. Tell her anything..." I begged.

"Even if I did, it wouldn't do any good. She doesn't listen to me." He moved on to the French daisies. "Are these weeds?" he asked, flicking the petals.

"Elizabeth is about to tear your whole family apart," I snapped. A brief hint of panic cracked as I spoke the words. He wasn't really listening to what I was saying.

"Don't be dramatic."

"I'm not! You don't know her like I do. Katelin is her favorite and she will never let you have her."

"Let me? *I* don't want her," he said. "It is my son who wants her." He chuckled. "My *son*."

I knew as well as he did young George was really King Rudolph's bastard. It was because of this known truth George did not concern himself with his family's well being. Maybe he was hoping Elizabeth would tear them all apart. The Drugeth clan probably deserved it.

"She'll never consent to the marriage," I said.

"She does not have to. Count Thurzo along with Prince Gabriel has already expressed approval for the match. It won't be hard for Fruzsina to get the king's blessing. It is as good as done."

Even if Fruzsina had not been the king's mistress, he still would give his blessing just to spite Elizabeth. My shoulders slumped. George put his arm around me, drawing me into his chest.

"There, there," he hushed.

"I can't believe this is happening. I can't believe this is happening to Katelin!" My thoughts raced. After the isolation, all the scheming and protecting, we were still helpless in stopping the course of things. I took a deep breath. I had to think of something. "What if Fruzsina were to find out Katelin was not of Nadasdy blood, but was instead the bastard of a poor repulsive Italian artist? She'd be forced to void the contract. It would be scandalous to proceed given the knowledge," I said. It was not my finest idea, but it was a start.

"It'd ruin Katelin. You can't do that to her. Besides, it would bring all the Nadasdy children into question including the heir, Paul. Not only would the children suffer, but also Elizabeth would lose everything. It's too risky."

He was right. It was too risky. "You're better at this. Can't you think of anything?"

He took my hand and led me further down the path along the backside of the garden. "If it's any consolation, Amara, I believe young George really thinks he is in love with Katelin."

"Everlasting love or passionate?" I asked.

The sun was lowering in the sky and I knew the hunting party would be returning soon.

"It's too early to tell." He stopped. He lifted my hand and kissed the top of my glove. "Shall *Peter Funk* send a note requesting an audience?" he asked. He gave a wink.

The sudden change in conversation was disruptive and it took a second for me to process the words he spoke. I had forgotten about our little scheme. Peter Funk was just a name Elizabeth and I had made up; a lascivious proposal to lure Francis to continue his affair with the Lavender Lady. It was a strange arrangement, but it had bought Elizabeth time and allowed her to avoid the company of her husband. George had been privy to the scheme and was proposing we continue with the amusing game, this time securing the services of the imaginary Peter Funk for ourselves. Of course in my case we'd have to create a feminine name for the purpose of appearances and false appointments. Since there was such a large party attending the festivities, hardly anyone would question my newly formed friendship with the allusive *P. Funk*.

For a moment I considered receiving a note. It was tempting and I was weak in the presence of George. I wished to give in to him, but something stung deep in my chest. I was thinking of Nicholas and how the lie would hurt him. What was I thinking? I was already having an affair and now I was scheming to trick my lover so I could rendezvous with my former lover? This was getting ridiculous. Still, it was George and my heart had belonged to him first. I was trying to rationalize the irrational.

I silently chided myself. I should be thinking about hurting my husband, but instead I considered Nicholas. He had been so uneasy about leaving me behind today. I had seen it in his eyes. He must have sensed my plan to meet with George and the idea was driving him crazy. He'd be impossible tonight. He'd never willingly let me out of his sight. His grip was tightening and his passion was burning him up. If I didn't calm him down, he'd turn to ash. It wasn't fair to do to him. Nicholas had been so good to me and when we were together he was all I wanted. But, when he was gone I found myself drawn to George. I had my answer. I knew what I had to do. I must fight the urge and resist the pull George had over me, for Nicholas's sake, and for my own.

"No, not tonight," I said, letting my hand drop.

"Very well," George muttered.

I was suspicious. His acceptance of my rejection was too complacent. He hadn't tried to convince me to change my mind by lamenting on about lasting love or soul mates. Instead, he accepted my answer and with it, gave a polite bow while uttering a good day.

Before I knew what happened, I found myself standing alone in the garden. The scent of flowers mingled in the late afternoon breeze. Lavender and rose, a hint of mint and orange spice lingered above the earthy smell of well-manicured dirt.

***

All the ladies were warming in the afternoon sun. It was a pleasant day and the prince suggested we dine on the terrace. The young girls were playing a game in the yard while the boys teased from the sidelines. Katelin was completely enthralled with young George and I knew the impending occasion of their marriage greatly disturbed Elizabeth. She had always wanted a different life for Katelin because she saw the free spirit of her father beneath the frills and manners. She worried in time Katelin would become restless and wither under restraint.

"I should send her away, perhaps, to Venice to study art," Elizabeth said. Tiny distress lines creased her forehead.

"Oh heavens no," said the lady sitting across from us. "Venice is not a proper place for a lady of seventeen. Besides there will not be time for her to study drawing and prepare for a wedding."

Elizabeth tensed at the mention of nuptials.

As George predicted, King Rudolph sent his blessing and the marriage contract was drawn. Elizabeth could do nothing but express her disdain. The worst she could deliver was an arsenal of dirty looks and litany of unpleasant comments, neither of which were very useful in preventing marriage.

The lady sitting at our table continued, "You should be very proud. Katelin is such a wonderful girl. Everyone just adores her. Where did you send her to be taught?"

Elizabeth did not make eye contact. "She stayed with me at Cachtice."

"Interesting! You did a fabulous job with your girls. Everyone says so," the lady said. "I suppose your home will seem empty now that all your children are leaving the nest."

Elizabeth winced.

"I'm sure your halls will echo with the pattering of little feet soon," the lady added, bestowing a wistful glance in Katelin's direction. "Grandchildren will be such a blessing." She sighed, amused with the idea.

"First there must be a wedding," Elizabeth growled.

"Oh yes, of course!"

"You know, there are several young ladies looking to be placed in a respectable home and you've done such a superb job with your girls and you certainly have the room. Maybe you could start a school. Start small of course," the lady suggested.

Elizabeth ignored the woman. "Who's the young lady Katelin is playing with?" she asked me.

I shaded my eyes from the sun and squinted trying to focus. "I don't know."

The lady copied my gestured and shaded her eyes as well. "Oh, that is Lady Ursula. She is a delightful girl. She and Katelin have become quite inseparable during the celebration. I'm surprised you haven't been introduced."

I wasn't surprised. Katelin was doing her best to avoid her mother. She'd had enough of Elizabeth's protests and was filling her time in the company of others by mostly occupying the attention of young George or spending afternoons with Lady Ursula.

"I'm not familiar with the girl. Where is her family?" Elizabeth asked, eyeing the probing faces of the chaperones.

The lady leaned over the table and put the side of her hand to her mouth as if shielding her confession from prying ears. "Her father is dead. Died in battle, I think," she whispered.

I did not understand why there was the need for secrecy. Many fathers died in battle and it was nothing to be ashamed of, so why the dramatics?

She glanced around checking if anyone were listening before she continued. "It was his dying wish that his daughter be granted title and allotted a significant dowry."

So some man had recognized his bastard on his deathbed. How poetic, I thought. Also, how very fortunate for both the girl and her mother. Very few men would do such a thing; especially if they thought it might bring disgrace to their rightful family.

"Whom was the father?" I asked. I could not resist the temptation.

"A small circle of men know, including the king, but they are sworn to secrecy. All I've been able to find out is whoever this man was, he was very important, highly ranked and most honorable," the lady said.

"Honorable, indeed!" I scoffed.

It was fitting the girls were drawn to each other. They had more in common than they even realized; two weeds blossoming in the garden of cherished rarities, mixed blood firmly taking root in the field of advantage. It was deliciously scandalous and I could not help but feel pleasure in the blatant betrayal of class and privilege. The girls seemed so sweetly innocent as they laughed, adorned in silk and frill, but beneath it all they were pollutants spoiling the balance of tradition. I got a certain satisfaction knowing one of the pollutants was going to taint the Drugeth lineage. A king's bastard was a badge of honor compared to the bastard of a Venetian artist. Even Lady Ursula ranked above Katelin in the pecking order. Of course, splitting hairs did not matter much when it came to rights and inheritance, but still, a family could present the argument if necessary. But, no one would because the truth would never be known and if it were, it would be ignored.

The lady shifted in her seat. She was doing her best to discreetly examine the party. "Ah! There is Ursula's mother. She is sitting over by the fountain."

At the same time, Elizabeth and I turned to get a better look. There was a rather large party gathered around the water works.

"Which woman are you referring?" Elizabeth asked.

From this distance it was difficult to readily recognize any of them.

The lady waved her hands around her head as if she were miming in a game of charades. "Um, she is the woman with the hat."

By her grand gesture I got that the woman she was talking about was wearing the rather large hat that hid a great potion of her features beneath a vast rim.

"Do you see her? She is wearing the lavender gown."

Elizabeth's mouth twisted. She stiffened. Her fingers tensed as she gripped the edge of the table. I thought she might just crush it into dust.

"Are you ill, Countess?" the lady asked.

"Please excuse me." Elizabeth rose from her chair, the iron legs abruptly scraping against the stone leaving thin, white chalk marks. "Amara, if you will…"

I quickly followed, excusing myself as I hurriedly trailed behind Elizabeth's hem. When she was sure we were in private she stalled. The creases running across her forehead were scrunched into deep folds. She was obviously distraught. Something on the veranda had spooked her a great deal.

"Do you know the woman?" I asked. It had been too far for me to see any discerning features.

"It's her. It's the Lavender Lady," Elizabeth hissed.

I felt my jaw go slack.

"Her daughter is Ursula," Elizabeth included.

I tried to wrap my head around what she was saying. "Ursula is a fairly common name and many woman wear lavender."

Elizabeth took hold of my arm. "It's her. She has returned."

I could think of several reasons why Elizabeth should be mortified by the discovery, but I chose to point out the positive. "She does not seem to want to embarrass you or the family. She's had the opportunity." I supposed the Lavender Lady was much smarter than the harlot from Bucharest.

Elizabeth was pacing. "Francis confessed on his deathbed. He acknowledged the girl was of his blood." She stopped and turned to face me. "Why? Why would he do that?"

I could only think of one reason, but I was hesitant to suggest perhaps Francis was more aware than we thought. He must have suspected he was not the true father of the Nadasdy children. Of course, he had a legal claim. It was the law that the husband claimed any child birthed by a wife whether it belonged to him or not. But, the law did not rule the heart and, no matter what it stated, a father always longed for the connection made through blood. Not being able to have children of my own, I thought the idea ridiculous. I'd do anything for a child, whether it was of my blood or not, but in the end it all came down to inheritance. That's why there was a law in the first place. The law did not care about the heart, but rather concerned itself with the proper passing of property, title and money. If none of these things existed queens would still have their heads and barren wives would never be set aside. Giving a man an heir was a woman's sole obligation and it had everything to do with material goods and claiming advantage. Only the poor and destitute bore children out of love.

My feelings toward the Lavender Lady should have been pity, but at that moment I was envious. She had faced the worst. She had been cast out and sentenced to a penniless, unfamiliar life of struggle. She confronted the world with only her babe cradled in her arms and had survived. Not only survived, but risen and come full circle. The Lavender Lady had done something neither Elizabeth nor I ever had the courage to do. Even though I hated our life, the isolation, the rules and the restraint, I admittedly was not willing to give it all up. Despite the drawbacks, there was a certain amount of security in our existence. We were warm, fed and dry. We did not scrounge for food or want for warmth and accommodations. My head lay every night on a soft pillow and my wine was served on a silver tray. If I were genuinely brave, I would have turned my back on it all and took the first step out into the cold, unknown world. If I were a man it might be easier, but that was no excuse. I felt my cheeks flush, not from anger, but from embarrassment. Oh how I had ranted, scoffed and sulked, but what had I done? Nothing. I risked nothing to free myself.

By the expression on Elizabeth's face I assumed she was slowly coming to the same conclusion. Francis had known the truth about the children after all.

"How did he know? Who could have told him?" she asked.

"Lord Buckley?" I suggested. "Maybe he blackmailed him to keep it a secret."

"Francis would never humiliate himself and pay a bribe. He'd just as easily have killed Lord Buckley."

This was likely. Lord Buckley was insignificant and offing him would have been simple for a man in Francis' position.

"It had to be someone close, someone Francis trusted. A person he would rather believe than kill."

That narrowed the list. In fact, it dwindled it down to just one possibility.

The name popped into my mind before it crossed Elizabeth's lips.

"Draco," she whispered. The betrayal in her voice sent a shiver down my arms.

"No! He wouldn't," I protested, even though I believed she was right.

"You know as well as I where Draco's loyalty rests."

I was his wife and anything shared in our marriage bed was sacred. It was understood what we exchanged was secret. At least that is what I thought, that is until now. I was speechless. My mouth tried to form words, but nothing coherent came out. I stuttered about in an effort to defend my husband. Frustrated and in disbelief, all I could manage were tears.

I wanted to hate him, but then I thought what I would do in his position. If Elizabeth were dying would I confess? Only if it made a difference. But had it? What had changed? Nothing for

Elizabeth, but for the Lavender Lady and Ursula, everything was much different. The course of the young girl's life drastically took a turn in another direction.

We were silent for some time, both lost in private thought. I waited for a scheme, a master plan of retaliation to pour forth in brilliant fluidity that would inspire justice. Elizabeth would never let this go. She'd never let it rest. I waited some more, but to my astonishment she just stared. Was this surrender? I could hardly believe my eyes. Was she resigning to defeat? The Lavender Lady was victorious. She had risked it all and in return won the spoils.

I edged closer. Elizabeth looked statuesque, the creases in her face disappearing as the muscles relaxed.

"I don't think she is much of a threat," I said. My voice squeaked from my dry throat.

Elizabeth nodded.

"You won't seek revenge?" I asked. It was stupid of me to even suggest it. It was like poking a hive with a stick.

"No."

Oddly I was relieved. However, my curiosity got the better of me and I could not keep from asking why she did not scheme against the woman.

She shrugged. "It is strange, but I find I respect her. Besides, she did not ask for this," she said. "Francis willed it to her all on his own."

I hadn't given it much thought. The Lavender Lady had not sought Francis, schemed or plotted blackmail. She stayed faithful to her agreement and by doing so spared her life once again.

The sound of heavy footsteps storming down the corridor caused me to pause. They were nearing quickly and a rush of concern pulsed through my body. Every prickle tingling my skin told me something was wrong. I was instantly alert and on edge.

Nicholas rounded the corner, his brows turned inward and his lips pressed tightly together.

"What is it?" I asked, hurrying to his side.

"Countess, you must come. Something terrible has happened. I'm afraid I am the messenger of bad news," Nicholas informed. He was out of breath. He must have been looking for us everywhere.

"Is it Katelin?" Elizabeth asked. Her first thought went to her daughter.

I gasped. It couldn't be Katelin. It just couldn't be.

Nicholas relaxed just the slightest but the intensity drawn upon his face was distressing. "No, Katelin is fine. It is Darvulia." He hesitated taking a moment to catch his air before speaking again. "I found her on the floor of your chamber. She has not recovered. I'm sorry, but Darvulia is dead."

A strangled noise leapt from Elizabeth's throat. It was more like a shriek than a cry. She picked up her hem and hurried toward the staircase leading to the chamber. I took hold of Nicholas's arm and followed.

Lying on the floor was the contorted body of Darvulia. Her lips bluish purple and coated in a film of spit. Her milky eyes fixed upward at the ceiling as if she had been frightened to death. I could not look away. I locked on her eyes, the round, haunting marbles empty and dead. She didn't look human anymore. The life was gone from her flesh and her body was turning rigid. I took a step closer. She died having a fit, alone in Elizabeth's room. I pictured her flopping about as her body seized and sputtered trying to recover. This time it could not manage. The disease had finally claimed her.

Elizabeth dropped on her knees by Darvulia's side. "We can't leave her like this," she said.

"Nicholas, get help," I said, shooing him toward the door. I wanted the monstrosity taken care of as soon as possible. The ugly corpse was a horrible reminder of our own mortality. I clasped my hands over my mouth as I tried to compose my nerves. I selfishly wished I would not die in the same manner. The thought of being found looking so horrid with my body twisted and mouth gaping was petrifying.

Elizabeth reached out and tenderly closed Darvulia's eyelids. That was better. She seemed more at peace with her eyes shut. Tears ran down Elizabeth's face as she held the cold hand of her friend. I knew she regretted not being with her in the end. Of course, she could have done nothing to prevent what happened.

Darvulia was riddled with disease and we both knew her days were numbered, but still, the knowledge did not seem to prepare us for the shock of reality.

The clanking of boots hurrying down the corridor broke the quiet softness of Elizabeth's sobs. Nicholas had retrieved a group of men to aid in removing Darvulia's body from the countess' chambers. Reluctantly, she allowed a blanket to be draped and wrapped around Darvulia. The men lifted the stiff corpse and carried it away.

"I will make sure she is prepared for burial," Nicholas said.

Elizabeth nodded, but before Nicholas could leave she stopped him. "Wait! Make certain to spare no expense. She served me well and it is the least I can do for her." Her sincerity was touching. A hint of vulnerability cast over her face as she rocked back on her heels, still kneeling on the floor. She looked tired with her shoulders slightly slumping forward and a strand of hair dangling loose from her braided twist. Anyone who witnessed the scene could never think her cruel. The invisible iron clasp shell that usually protected her from the outside world crumbled and was letting all emotion in. I knew it was a brief window and it would slam suddenly, but it was in these moments that I truly saw Elizabeth. It was in this state that made me love her.

"Does she have family?" I asked softly.

Elizabeth shook her head indicating there was none.

"Do you know where she wished to be put to rest?" I had not given much thought to my own wishes nor had I ever expressed them. If I were to die tomorrow, what would become of my body? Where would I spend eternity?

Elizabeth looked puzzled. Obviously, she had never asked. She rubbed her temple. "We will return to Cachtice. I will bury Darvulia there. I think she would want to remain close to us."

I shuddered. I hoped Elizabeth would never assume the same of me. It would be a nightmare to be buried in the cold hills of Cachtice in the thicket of trees and beneath a layer of limestone and snow. How morbid and unfeeling it seemed, but I did not argue. Elizabeth was probably right, Darvulia would want to be near the castle she loved and toiled in. Like Elizabeth, she did not see the ugliness I saw and never felt the heavy dread hanging over the place. The garden was not so bad, but it was a small beacon of light in a shroud of remoteness.

That evening we prepared for the long journey home. Our things were packed and arrangements made on our behalf. Elizabeth sat in front of her mirror brushing her black tresses before removing the lid from several of her crème jars. She examined her skin looking at all the barely visible fine lines defining her face. She dotted the lotion beneath her eyes and above her brow. Gently making small circles, she rubbed the beauty potion into her delicate skin.

The sliding of paper beneath the door distracted me from my trance. I went over and picked up the folded note. It was addressed to me. I glanced around the room to see if anyone was paying attention before I opened the letter.

I've heard a rumor you are leaving. Please tell me this is not true. I must see you, please.

Sincerely,
P. Funk

I crumpled up the note and tossed it in the fire. The sparking flames devoured it immediately singeing the edges and curling it to ash. I could not do this now. I would not allow myself to rip open an old wound and feel the bleeding of my heart the entire way home. I didn't have the strength for it anymore. I had agreed to steal moments with George, but even they were no longer enough. The memories of our time together were too painful and with each encounter the separation that followed hurt more than the one before. I could not bring myself to endure the torture for his sake. I sat on the edge of the bed. Would I regret not saying goodbye?

Elizabeth tugged back the covers and I felt her body move beside me. I promised I'd stay with her tonight, but now I wished I could retreat to Nicholas. I'd feel safe in his arms and his comfort would affirm my decision. He'd make me strong again.

I crawled into bed and waited for Elizabeth's breathing to settle into the rhythmic draw of slumber before I crept from the bed and quietly slipped on my robe. I slide through the door and tiptoed down the corridor. The palace was chilly and the dim lights cast shadows along the decorative walls. When I got to the door I found it locked. I rapped lightly hoping my stirring would wake only the occupant inside. I heard approaching footsteps and the fumbling of the latch.

Nicholas rubbed his eyes. His cooper hair ruffled from the impression of his pillow. He had been asleep for a while and was having a difficult time adjusting to the light in the hall.

"What is wrong?" he grumbled. He was not fully awake.

I threw my arms around his neck and kissed his cheek. I held tightly pressing my body against his. He gently eased my arms from his neck and held them by his side. He stared into my eyes searching intensely as if he were reading my mind. He did not ask another question. Instead he took me by the hand and led me to bed. I curled my limbs around his warm body and nuzzled my face in the crook of his neck. I felt safe, connected to something real and alive. I burned for his touch and protective strength of his arms. He kissed me tenderly at first, but as our passion grew, his kiss became more forceful. This is what I needed. This is what I craved. I playfully bit his lip and when he groaned I nibbled harder until I tasted the salty iron substance on my tongue. The intimacy was exhilarating and I felt joined with his soul. I realized we were one in the same; two pieces fit perfectly together. I did not think of Elizabeth or Darvulia or even George for that matter. I was in the moment and this time I was certain it would last. I would hold on to it as long as I could.

The Foul Unearthing of Pandora's Box

With ropes knotted, the witch's coffin was lowered into the ground. The men grunted and cursed as the heavy box swung before thudding six feet under. Grains of dirt scattered and rolled, soiling the lid of Darvulia's box. The finality of the ceremony was abrupt, like the first boom of cannon fire; but then again, all final goodbyes are shocking. I don't think anyone is ever prepared when that last string of a living bond is severed and all that remains are the memories. All there is…is the past. There is no future, no tomorrow or until another day.

The pitter-pattering sound of dirt balls hitting the wood dulled as more earth was heaved into the hole, burying what was left of Darvulia for all eternity. The men groaned with each shovel full, until at last a mound spilled over the rooted grass. The fresh grave was marked with a headstone and cut flowers withered on the turned earth. I wanted to picture Darvulia in a state of peace, but the stark expression of her filmy eyes and twisted mouth frozen in that horrid pose in which she died kept flashing in my mind. I silently prayed for her soul, although I did not know whether I'd be heard or even if it mattered. I consoled myself by thinking at the very least she was no longer in pain. The disease that riddled her body could not harm her anymore. It had done its worst, taken her life in the end, but it would not possess her soul once it fled the cage of her body.

And then that was it. It was done, and there was nothing else to say. She was gone for good. The birds chirped and the men cleared. Time ticked away as the sun began to set. I hesitated for a moment, not certain what to do next. I was afraid to turn my back on the grave, but as the small party retreated, I too resigned to make the quiet walk back to the castle.

Darvulia's death and the arrival of Katelin's wedding announcement greatly influenced Elizabeth both mentally and physically. Despite the nightly ritual of applying creams and oils to her face, she was convinced she was aging. I assured her this was a natural process and, although no woman enjoyed it, it was inevitable. She refused to accept what was happening and in desperation tried to improve upon Darvulia's original recipe. I think her obsession grew because it was all that remained of her friend, the witch. It was the loss and the memories that got to her. The desertion of her daughter for a life she did not approve of, and for her trusted friend who was broken down until she was too weak to resist. Both endings were unbearable for Elizabeth and, to cope, she fixated on a chore. She justified her principles by reasoning it was in the name of science and for Darvulia. She owed it to her to finish what they so eagerly started. Success would give the time she spent in this world meaning. Together they'd leave a tiny blot in the history books. Elizabeth was determined she'd not be forgotten.

She mixed several ingredients trying more or less of certain herbs before determining it was the secret ingredient that held the key to eternal youth. Instead of a few drops of blood from the pinprick of a servant girl's finger, she drained a bit more from a deeper wound. When I questioned whether she worried about rumors, she told me any foreseen breech was dealt with immediately. I figured it best not to press and, at the present time, it was best to plead ignorance. If what she was doing was questionable, then it was beneficial to know the least possible. I was not as self-confident that accusations could be dealt with so easily. It took only one person to report the conditions at the castle for there to be an inquiry. Of course, the source needed proof to be taken seriously, and a servant's claim of abuse by presenting a pinprick or a small scrape seemed rather harmless. After all, small cuts could be reasonably explained by any number of legitimate chores.

When a potion failed to meet Elizabeth's expectations she'd violently hurl the bowl across the room sending the pot clanking and spilling the contents all over the floor. The servants were terrified of the brews and unsure how to clean up the mess. So, they carried buckets of cinder ash and covered the liquid causing it to congeal into a clumpy paste. In a few hours the soiled goo looked like dirty adipose gutted from a beast, and after several days it reeked of decay. I wondered how a thing so vile could be the answer to lasting beauty.

One day when I visited the workshop, I found Elizabeth humped over a wooden stool with her face in her hands. Her defeated posture was out of character and I approached cautiously. The stink of rotten herbs and God knows what clung in the aged air of the cellar. How could she stand being locked in this place? I took special care to avoid the lumps of cinder spotting the floor and made my way across the room.

"Nothing works," she mumbled.

I didn't want to anger Elizabeth by agreeing. I had never personally witnessed any change in her appearance except for that she was paler and the circles beneath her eyes were more prominent. Common sense told me this had more to do with her sleepless isolation in dark corners than from failed crèmes and oils.

"When Darvulia died, so did the cure," she sighed.

She was convinced that the success of the potion was somehow magically linked to Darvulia. I thought this was silly, but I was no expert and didn't dare contradict her conclusion. I made the only suggestion I could think of. I asked if we should seek the services of another alchemist.

She raised her chin, her back arching in defiance. I tensed, expecting her to scream some obscenity in protest but, just as quickly as her expression sharpened, it softened as she gave my suggestion some serious thought. I braced myself for her answer. Pride was clouding her judgment and I could see failure was killing her slowly.

"I could send Ficzko to inquire on your behalf," I continued.

She turned her back to me and said nothing. I lingered, but the silence looming between us was making me very uncomfortable. I could not read her and, with my ability hindered, I feared I was doing more harm than good. I decided it was best if I said nothing and turned to leave. I was practically out the door when I heard her speak.

"I'll agree. Send Ficzko to find a replacement."

I shuddered. I hadn't thought of a new alchemist as a *replacement*, but rather an addition. I suppose, however, that is exactly how Elizabeth perceived my suggestion.

***

It did not take Ficzko long to procure the services of an underground alchemist. The rumor was Erzsi was a powerful sorceress capable of conjuring anything a master or mistress desired. She was an attractive woman with corn silk hair and sea colored eyes. Her movements were deliberate and graceful and I imagined she had little difficulty convincing men of her gifts. They were probably more often swayed by their desire rather than from real evidence. Her beauty was bewitching and the innocence echoing from her delicately accented voice was charming. She appeared as harmless as a fawn grazing in a meadow. Any child would readily take her hand and any man would leap into a burning barn or head long into battle to protect the dear girl. She was the kind of woman who could rely on chivalry to save her whenever her abilities were questioned, but would she be so fortunate in the company of women?

In the morning I slipped from Nicholas's quarters to join the ladies for a late breakfast. Elizabeth was gradually warming to the newcomer and, as each day passed, she seemed more at ease with the addition to our household. I found on this morning she was actually smiling at Erzsi as she took her place at the dining table. Seeing Elizabeth grin was uplifting and, for the first time in a while, I had hope she would recover. Perhaps, the mourning period had endured long enough and it was time for her to begin living life again in the company of her friends.

Elizabeth offered Erzsi a piece of fruit before taking a chunk of bread and cheese. This was pleasant and civilized. Not a hint of

371

rot or stink stained her dress and her hair was clean and neatly braided. I, on the other hand, still smelled of smoky wood from Nicholas's damp hearth and my mouth was thick with a coat of stale ale and iron. We had drunk heavily and, after hours of sleep, the spirits fermented leaving a hideous taste of citrus that I was desperate to wash away. I gulped down a glass of water resisting the urge to swish it around in my mouth.

"You are perky this morning," I said to Elizabeth, hoping my breath didn't offend her.

She glanced at Erzsi. "I believe we've had a break through in our experimentation."

"Really?" I swallowed hard to choke down the glob of dough lodged in my throat.

"We've determined the answer is collecting small amounts of virginal blood from the noble born."

"Noble blood? But, Dar…" I caught myself before letting the entirety of the dead woman's name slip. "But, I thought it was vital to use only peasant blood because the collection proved to have very little recourse?" How was she going to get noble born virgins to cooperate? It would not be easy to get aristocratic girls to willingly let the countess prick their fingers and, if she tricked them, they would tell.

"I was thinking of opening court and starting my own academy for privileged ladies."

"Given the burden and expense of sending girls from the local gentry abroad, I think opening court is an excellent idea," Erzsi added.

"My generosity and hospitality will restore my reputation with the people."

Or *destroy* it, I thought. I was not as eager to warm to this idea as the other two were. It seemed preposterous, but then again we'd never done anything customary.

Erzsi tossed her silky locks over her shoulder. "I'll go as an ambassador to the houses of the lower gentry and convince them that living alongside the highly-ranked and richly-connected countess will bring their daughters immense rewards. They'll be packing their bags in no time, no time at all!"

I sifted through the onslaught of thoughts rattling through my head. I could make an argument for how this could all go wrong, but I was not brave enough to say it aloud. So instead I asked, "What happens when there is no reward?"

Elizabeth frowned. "Are you saying being connected to me will bring little advantage?"

I did not wish to bruise her sense of self, but I was acutely aware of her reputation in polite society. They tolerated her because decorum insisted so, but a reference penned by Elizabeth hardly knocked down doors. In fact, it might just raise suspicion.

"I think an association would be invaluable," Erzsi answered. Her bright smile calmed Elizabeth's mood.

As long as Erzsi pleasantly agreed, she'd win Elizabeth's admiration. She did not know her well enough to present a challenge. I could hardly blame the woman. Elizabeth's wrath was legendary among the servants and I was certain someone had cautioned Erzsi to toe lightly.

"And what does this academy offer?" I asked, taking another bite of bread.

"Well, the usual…music, language, manners and etiquette."

I tried not to gag. I could not picture Elizabeth having the patience to teach any of the recommended subjects.

"What? It might be fun, besides you need a chore to occupy your time. I'll assign a subject for you to teach, maybe history or poetry," she said.

"Ah… I see. I am to be an accomplice in this scheme of yours?"

"Do you have something better to do?" she asked. I didn't appreciate the tone of her voice. She was implying I did nothing useful. Looking after her was a full-time job and now I was expected to advise a household of young girls.

"But, it won't just be the usual subjects we'll be teaching," Erzsi added.

Here it comes, I thought.

Elizabeth grinned her *I'm so clever* grin. "We'll teach them the art of alchemy. Once they're hooked and interest piqued, we will ask them to donate to the experimentation process."

"You think you can just ask, and you shall receive?" I said.

"It's a small price to pay. I'd wager a fortune on the notion that every young girl would be willing to endure a minor cut and offer up a smidgen of blood in hopes of discovering the potion for eternal beauty. What noble girl wouldn't do so little, for so much?"

"What if they tell?" I reiterated. Apparently, I was the only person giving this complication any consideration. I was always playing the role of the Devil's advocate.

"We'll take on a few girls at a time. Besides, they cannot tell because by doing so they'll incriminate themselves by admitting to practicing witchcraft." Erzsi wiped her mouth with the back of her hand. "Even those who refuse will keep the secret to protect their families."

"It seems you have it all figured out," I said. I hoped they detected the sarcasm in my voice, but if they did neither of them paid much attention.

Perhaps I should have said more. A morally righteous person would be appalled by the conversation, seen the monstrosity in the proposition, and the truly good would have done everything within their power to prevent it from ever happening. I should have thrown myself in Elizabeth's path and begged her to reconsider, but I didn't. Instead, like all her servants, I was guilty of amusing my mistress and partaking in all her crazy schemes. I suppose it had more to do with self-preservation, but if I had foresight I would have seen that my protest would have saved us all.

Nevertheless, Elizabeth and Erzsi were excited about the venture and believed the ruse would work to everyone's benefit. After all, they'd convinced themselves that giving a tiny vial of blood was hardly much of a sacrifice and the rewards would be great. If they could master the formula and trap the essences of beauty, they would achieve power, importance and, most notably, become immediately revered as scientists. The discovery would demand respect. The snickers behind the back would cease and the comments regarding Elizabeth's sanity would stop. She'd make everyone see she was clever, brilliant and, in fact, extraordinary. The idea set her aflame and her ambition made her susceptible. Any hint ruling against proceeding enraged her already unstable temperament.

Night after night I listened to her plan and in time I began to question whether she was of sound mind or indeed truly gifted. Much of what she said made perfect sense and the hideous idea even began to seem plausible. What if she was successful? What if she invented a potion that could slow aging? I too was becoming swept up in the possibilities; riches and fame promised to follow if the pair accomplished the task.

Those closest to Elizabeth were loyal to the scheme and willing to aid her under the guise and in the name of science. It really was not so bad: get a few girls and acquire small samples of blood and in return. They would advance their position. It seemed simple enough. Besides, everyone knew throughout history girls of nobility were often asked to sacrifice much more to aid in their family's station. In the end, I had to admit we were all convinced what we were doing was scholarly. We were pioneers of the scientific community and, like the others that came before us, we were obligated to challenge the parameters that hindered progress.

Over the next several months Erzsi and Ficzko set out to seek eligible noble girls from nearby villages. It was not as straightforward as they anticipated. It appeared word had spread about the strange practices taking place at Cachtice. Few legitimate, well-bred girls were swayed to take the bait. Erzsi was not discouraged. She knew she could never return empty handed. Out of desperation, she and Ficzko were forced to journey further away to find young women willing to attend Elizabeth's academy. The expense of procuring noble born girls was double what they thought, but they justified the extravagance as necessary. I fretted about the cost, but Elizabeth assured me she was living well within her means.

The deception was painfully excruciating to suffer. It took a great deal of my energy to teach the bright-eyed girls a number of subjects. The laziness with which they learned was inexcusable and at least two in the bunch I determined were completely hopeless. However, Elizabeth insisted we continue even when I begged to abandon the school, and after months of tending to the academy I was finally relieved of my tedious duties.

Upon Erzsi's recommendation Elizabeth vigilantly and most subliminally made suggestions. Like willing whores, the girls were manipulated step-by-step until they found themselves facing a blade. There was no escaping, and all of them offered up the valuable life source flowing through their delicate veins. Elizabeth was delighted her plan succeeded and foolishly ignored the horrid expressions on the girls' faces. She thought she had them all convinced, but I could see through the veil shading their true horror.

Within days, the girls had made their move and together fled the castle. Thankfully, Erzsi had been right about one thing, none of the girls confessed the real reason for their abrupt departure. However, their silence only instigated more rumors to swirl. This was tragic. We had enough unpleasant stories pinned to our dainty tails. We were already the lead actors in several moral legends. Not the happy ones with joyful endings, but the kind used to give children nightmares and scare them into walking a straight path.

There was much talk about bizarre happenings and secret tunnels running below Cachtice and without confirmation to the contrary people were quickly becoming suspicious. Despite my careful urgings to wait, Elizabeth ordered Ficzko to find replacements. He was saddled with a bag of gold and ventured further to explore remote areas. He tried to entice young ladies with promises of fortune and snagging desirable suitors. Despite the money he offered, he was refused. Doors slammed in his face and curses hurled upon his head. He kept the difficulty of the errand to himself for fear of upsetting Elizabeth, but when he turned up empty, he was obliged to admit his failure to Erzsi. The cunning woman who was desperate to spare her neck devised a scheme of her own. She revised her thought and abandoned using the blood of noble born woman as part of the plan.

At Erzsi's underhanded request, a small group of Elizabeth's loyal inner circle was instructed to acquire peasant girls. Erzsi made sure to emphasis they had no choice; they had to play along or risk the fury of a displeased mistress. There was not a brave soul in the lot and all agreed to Erzsi's detour from the original plan. They preyed on the foolhardy and the desperately poor. Once they arrived at the castle, the girls were washed and scoured. Their hair stylishly coiffed in modern fashion and then dressed in reasonably fine garments. It was frightful how effortlessly the transformation was performed and with such convincing manner. Once the alteration took place, the girls were ushered into the dining hall where they took their seats in accordance with Erzsi's stern instructions. She told them they must speak in low voices while they awaited the main event, the entrance of their gracious hostess and sponsor, the grandest royal countess in all the land. Her boastful speech was motivating and even I could not help but clap loudly when Elizabeth appeared.

All anxious eyes widened as the mysterious woman they heard so much about entered through the tall arch. Her hesitation in the doorway was purposely theatrical. It was her trademark and the pause never failed to cause a stir. Elizabeth dressed in a luxurious scarlet gown embellished with lavish pearls, gracefully floated across the floor and took her place at the head of the table. Her choice of attire contrasted starkly with her pale skin and ebony hair. It was dramatic and harsh, but befitting of her character. If I had not known differently, I would swear everyone seated at the table was superior. Only an extremely trained eye could make the imposters. Elizabeth was smart enough, but pride would never allow her to see the cast beneath the costumes assembled for her entertainment. I smirked as I thought of all the young girls dressed similarly and shoved before princes and kings. Those noblemen had been unwilling to see imposters too. The result of the trickery was always unlucky. I felt my smirk relax into a frown. I winced. I was sick of tragedy. It was a performance I did not wish to replay.

***

Elizabeth announced during our next private meeting that she would not waste months on schooling the girls. She was impatient and had learned from her previous mistake. She ordered guards to patrol the grounds and requested the girls adhere to a regimented routine. I thought she was being hasty, but my opinion met resistance. Within a matter of days the girls were led to the cellar and presented with the madness of our intentions. Having no recourse, the forged noble girls went along with Elizabeth's request. They followed dutifully and feared breaking the rules or attempting any escape. Ficzko was rewarded handsomely for his part in providing obedient students and praised for his foresight in securing the castle.

When the sham became too bothersome, I retreated to Nicholas's quarters. The reprieve was temporary, but it gave me time to collect my thoughts and recommit to the plan. He was indifferent to the scheme and I made sure not to repeat my own mistakes by confessing too much while lingering in his bed. Although I doubted he'd give any of it much care, I was not willing to provide details that might later place us in jeopardy.

The effort with which the layers of threads were woven together to construct the farce was astonishingly genius. I awed at the complexity and wondered if Elizabeth was wise to the fraud committed by her adorning subjects, namely Erzsi. Had she become so consumed by her own dream that she honestly believed the parade of girls eagerly offering their wrists for her taking were noble virgins?

Unfortunately, as is often the case and consequence of experimentation, some of Elizabeth's subjects did not fair well. Despite the appearance of washed skin and beneath the shroud of fine silk, some of the lowly born girls were diseased and vulnerable to infection. Their wounds refused to heal properly and festered with pus. They became weak and the flesh surrounding their cuts blackened and sloughed away from the thin fatty layer clinging to frail bone. The dark patterns littering their bodies gave the impression the dying had been brutally tortured, but in truth it was the result of an invading and invisible parasite. We could not see the culprit with our naked, human eyes, but we witnessed its handy work as it fed on the skin of the unfortunate girls.

By the time the pestilence had run its course it claimed five lives. When they first fell ill Elizabeth ordered that the girls be quarantine from the healthy ones. She feared any awareness would hinder her scientific research. The healthy girls would be less willing to donate blood if they believed they could die from contamination. To maintain appearances, Elizabeth insisted food be brought daily to the private quarters of the ailing women even after their death so everyone in the household would believe they were still alive. It was a temporary solution. It would buy her time until she could decide a better course of action and acquire replacements.

"We could say you determined they were not suitable," Erzsi suggested. "We'll say you sent them home."

Elizabeth considered Erzsi's explanation. It was acceptable. She could invite and reject whomever she wished for whatever ridiculous reason.

"How do we dispose of the bodies?" I asked. I thought this was the more pressing issue. "I'm told three more girls have fallen ill and are not likely to recover."

The smell of something rotten was wafting through the corridors. Sickness was tainting the air we breathed and all efforts to cover it up were failing. Soon, we'd be unable to disguise the unpleasantness of our doing.

"We've stripped the linens and sprinkled the bodies with lime and stowed them beneath the beds for a time. It is helping with the smell, but the affect on the corpses is disconcerting," Erzsi said. "We will have to remove them soon."

"I think we should give them a decent burial," I said. After all, as far as Elizabeth knew they were supposed to be gentry.

"This may be problematic," Erzsi replied.

Elizabeth raised a curious brow.

"The lime is eradicating all discernable features. Along with the progress of the disease I'm afraid identification at this point is impossible. I no longer can tell who is who, besides if we have a ceremony we will be held accountable or at the very least we will draw unwanted attention."

Erzsi played her role perfectly even her choice of words managed to provide a scientific overtone. Too bad her lovely appearance blurred the picture. If only she were a bit more homely, she might have passed for intelligent.

"Don't forget I am virtually unassailable," Elizabeth reminded; the cool confidence in her voice hauntingly defiant. She was drunk on her rising position in society acquired through her kin and also self-absorbed by her independence. All this blinded her to the flaws of humanity. I did not see clearly myself, but at least I never lost complete sight of the possibility or stopped imagining the capability of our enemies. I would not overestimate my influence by underestimating that of another.

When had she bought into the idea she was above reproach? It was not so long ago she sat powerless upon her bridal stool sobbing with grief for the loss of innocence and seething with hatred for those who denied free will. I had no doubt she still seethed with hatred, but part of her was embracing the control her bloodline bestowed. It was an invisible armor moving in unison with each step she took whether it was down a heavenly path or not. The metamorphosis was heartbreaking and I worried her error in judgment would be fatal.

***

Barely a week passed before several more girls met Death. The bodies were beginning to pile up around Cachtice. One by one the corpses were hauled from the castle and loaded on the rear of a horse-drawn cart. In the middle of the night they were taken into the woods and tossed like rubbish among the sticks and leaves. It was unholy but crucial and I hoped God (if there was one) was forgiving. As for the lumps of cinder-covered refuge soiling the cellar floor, it was scooped into buckets and discarded in the vegetable garden outside the kitchen door. Surprisingly, Elizabeth's aborted concoctions were good for something. It seemed the fatty clumps made for a useful fertilizer because the potatoes and rhubarb flourished. The bed was full of healthy greens and hearty spuds. However, Elizabeth was not satisfied with this discovery and despite my meager objection she'd continued with her original pursuit.

Erzsi cleaned and dressed new recruits of peasant girls and passed them off to Elizabeth as noble bred virgins eager to bask in the glory of the countess. The herbs mingled and the blood mixed. And like before, each disastrous blend ended up coated in cinder ash and eventually tossed in the vegetable garden. More girls fell ill and were subjected to the same horrible fate as their predecessors. It was becoming more difficult to convince those remaining that the missing girls had been sent home. None had said goodbye, not even those who bonded during their stay. I could not come up with a rational explanation as to why they were never heard from again. In attempt to ease the healthy girls racked nerves, Erzsi and I penned several letters and signed them with the dead girls names. It was a pitiful attempt but, to my pleasure, the messages were very convincing. Most accepted the reasons and returned stupidly to their worthless studies. Oh if everything could have been so plainly manipulated!

To our misfortune, we did experience a bit of a conundrum when a mother knocked upon our door wishing to visit her daughter. Of course, her child had unfortunately been infected and died, so granting a visit was impossible. Elizabeth made excuses but the woman was most persistent and eventually Elizabeth had to blatantly refuse her request. The mother became angry and ranted that the rumors about the countess must be true. The woman was realizing the full terror of the possible situation and in her grief spoke hastily. She was dragged from Cachtice by Elizabeth's guards and threatened accordingly and paid handsomely to secure further silence.

It was a snag in her grand scheme, but Elizabeth believed the matter had been rectified. I had to agree, since I knew the dead girl was nothing more than a poor peasant decorated in fancy attire. The mother had been a fool to even risk a confrontation. She was lucky to leave with her life let alone a purse full of guldens. My main concern was that other riff raff would come seeking the same reward. I knew Elizabeth would not be so generous with the next person who tried to exploit her private practices.

We soon learned we should not bother worrying about mothers. Our troubles still festered with the loathsome woman who first knocked upon our door. It appeared both Elizabeth and I shamefully underestimated the love of a humble mother for her child. Neither threats nor money prevented the woman from solving the mystery of her daughter's disappearance. I'd never understood the parental relationship, so naturally I stumbled when it came to dealing with the unfamiliar bond. My only example of motherhood was Elizabeth, and although she was fiercely protective, she managed to rationalize the value of a female whether she was privileged or scanty. This woman was breaking all the rules, putting her life in peril and managing to cross borders never believed capable of crossing by a woman of her station. She'd marched right up to our royal doors and demanded an answer, which she was vehemently denied. It was incredible her head had not been lobbed off to silence her inquiries.

Instead of pocketing her guldens and returning peacefully to her ratty homestead, she sought sanctuary in the nearby monastery.

A new pastor, the Reverend Janos had accepted lodgings in the neighboring tower. I'd met him on a few random occasions while I was strolling the grounds around Cachtice. He seemed pleasant enough for a man of the cloth. He was quiet and reserved. He averted his eyes and politely removed his hat when spoken to, and for the most part minded his business. Surely he'd heard the rumors of his sponsor, but like most seeking a commission he was obliged to ignore the folklore of common villagers. The life of a pastor was a solitary existence and nothing was more remote than the worshipping stone halls of Cachtice's adjoining monastery. Here he could reside in the mountains for decades, alone and undisturbed. Temptation was minimal and therefore, made following the laws of the church more tolerable.

Since I myself was not privy to the conversation that took place between the peasant woman and the Reverend Janos, I can only speculate that her plea was most convincing. Whatever she said sparked the reverend's curiosity. He promised he'd look into the disappearance of the daughter and encouraged the woman to return to her village for safekeeping. I can only presume he must have had his own qualms in order to make such a promise. Likely, it was the churning of wagon wheels rolling past his window in the middle of the night. Surely, he must question what errand was essential at that hour. Once was excusable, even explainable, but after several occurrences he must have become uneasy. He'd taken an oath to never lie or deceive, so when he told the woman he would investigate on her behalf he had no other recourse but to follow through. Such honesty was respectable, but I believed unwise.

The reverend unschooled in the art of espionage took a direct course of inquiry. He made an excuse to visit the countess at her home. His amateur strategy consisted of spying about the rooms hoping to get a glimpse of the young ladies attending the academy. I'm certain his intentions were well thought-out, but his lack of discretion alerted Elizabeth's protectors. Ficzko snuck about peering through peek holes and listening behind hollowed wooden panels collecting information to be passed to Elizabeth. The reverend never wholly mentioned the missing girl, but took it upon himself to ask about the habits and activities of the students in general. It was obvious he was making a mental note of who remained at the academy.

"Do you serve many young ladies?" he asked the serving maid.

"Oh yes, sir. Several at a time."

"Have they been here long?" he asked.

"Some, sir."

"And the others?"

The maid poured a hot cup of tea and handed it to the reverend. "You know how young girls are, they get homesick and some are just not fit for learning." The maid twisted her mouth realizing her mistake. The reverend had no familiarity with young ladies so this explanation was most foreign.

"I have little experience, but I can imagine," he assured the maid, noticing her discomfort.

She anxiously curtsied and darted from the room.

Ficzko, who was eavesdropping behind a crack in the wall heard the entire conversation, and within minutes was scurrying through the secret passageways leading to Elizabeth's private chamber. I was use to the scraping sound the secretive panel made when it opened. The noise no longer startled me nor did the sudden appearance of his tot-like figure. Upon entry he made his mission clear. He was there to warn Elizabeth of the reverend's intent so she could properly prepare her answers. There was no doubt the reverend came under false pretense, the problem being we did not know who had sent him. Ficzko was terribly nervous because he believed he'd been so careful, but now his thoughts were racing and he relived every moment in his head. Who had seen? What had they seen? His imagination was creating the worse possible scenario. His hands trembled as he relayed the conversation to Elizabeth.

"He's asking questions about the students?" she asked.

"Yes, Countess. He wants to know details."

"Interesting," she said. "Then I will be certain to give him what he seeks."

"Yes, Countess."

"In the meantime, be a good little mole and keep an eye on the reverend. I'd like to know from whom he gets his orders."

Ficzko bowed and slipped from the room. He disappeared just as swiftly as he had entered.

"You're not bothered?" I asked.

"It is most unsettling, but I am not going to panic just yet. He may be merely making conversation. What else does the man have to talk about? The only change that's occurred at Cachtice in the last decade is the addition of my academy. It is not unreasonable to believe he is just asking questions to be polite. After all, we have nothing else in common. Besides, it is probably his pathetic way of beating around the bush to get what he really wants, which is more funds for the monastery. I'll amuse him by being impressed he takes an interest in my schooling, and then I'll give him half of the monies he's requesting."

I knew a mistress never wanted to give a dependent exactly what they asked for, otherwise they'd ask for even more the next time. There was no reason to go bankrupt for God or any other frivolous pursuit for that matter.

That day when the reverend did not acquire the answers he sought from Elizabeth, he formed a new approach and resigned to trying an even sneakier means of investigation. Instead of entering Cachtice through the front door, which was getting him nowhere, he decided to explore the underground passages connecting the monastery to the castle. The boarded up tunnels were difficult to maneuver and it took many weeks of tenacious pursuit before the reverend mapped out the surest route.

Having no access, Ficzko could only report that the reverend was spending his nights in the tombs beneath the monastery.

"What is he doing down there?" Elizabeth asked.

"I'm not certain, Countess."

"That's not good enough!" she snapped. The curtness of her scolding made Ficzko flinch. Despite his crude exterior, he was severely sensitive when it came to disappointing his mistress. He loved her a great deal and it pained him to be the sole cause of her unhappiness.

"What does it matter if the reverend is toiling in the tomb?" I asked. "We should be pleased he is so far off course. If he was roaming the woods we'd have reason to be concerned."

Ficzko nodded in agreement.

The reverend was not pursuing the trail of the phantom wagon, but instead was exploring the subterranean rooms below his modest home. It was a harmless past time. I too, had once found myself rummaging around the dank corridors tunneling beneath Cachtice; the labyrinth halls widening and narrowing as I plunged deeper crossing through the rusty thresholds and finding myself among the crumbling bones resting in a circular tomb. The stacked pine crates and debris of worthless trinkets sprung to mind. I vividly recalled the podium with the skull and Bible protecting the hidden contents nestled in the base. The scrolls of vellum maps remained, but the portrait of Vlad Tepes was now propped against the wall behind Elizabeth's chamber door. The fading mystique of the painting lay forgotten as she dabbled with another fantastic myth: that of finding eternal youth. She no longer tinkered with the whim of raising the undead, but rather wished to prolong life or at least the outward appearance.

I leaned over the arm of my chair to catch a glimpse of the gold frame tucked behind the door. Even with my best effort all I could see was half the portrait, the muddied background and part of the hat and a deep-set eye, which seemed to stare at me. The curl of the moustache and a portion of the fleshy lower lip dotted with flecks of dried blood remained motionless as if scorning my presumptions. I recoiled. I still did not care for the peculiar painting and I was pleased it no longer hung above the hearth.

Even though I had looked away I couldn't shake the scene of the hidden tomb or its contents from my mind. It was as if I was immediately sucked back in time; the images I recalled rushed forth from memory. I was flying through the corridor, down the staircase and into the kitchen. I saw the cellar door burst open and pictured myself descending the narrow stairs. The smell of fresh earth hurried past my nostrils as the tunnels twisted and turned. I gasped. "Beneath the monastery!" I blurted out.

Elizabeth was stunned. "Have you been paying attention?" she asked.

I bolted from the chair and to the door. I was waving for them to follow as I struggled to form a coherent sentence. "The pine crates…the soldiers," I stammered.

"Slow down Amara." Elizabeth guided me back to the chair. "Tell me what is going on."

"We think the reverend is looking for the missing girls and he very well might be."

"Yes, yes we know that," Elizabeth said impatiently.

"He's on the wrong trail, but not free of discovery. He won't find the girls, but that doesn't mean he won't find bodies! If he makes his way through the connecting tunnels he will eventually stumble upon the remains of the Turkish soldiers."

Ficzko's eyes twitched back and forth.

I could tell by the sudden panic in his expression there was more to the story than I even knew. It was the *need to know* part, and it was time I knew.

"Don't tell me there are more than just the soldiers down there?" I asked, the dread apparent in my voice.

Elizabeth shrugged trying to dismiss my concern.

"Elizabeth? What have you done?"

"That servant girl who perished in the cage and then a few others who deserved to be punished or were shamefully weak might have been toted off and stored below."

"Elizabeth!" I screeched.

"Well, you can't honestly believe Ficzko has the strength to haul every bloated corpse from the castle. I wasn't sure who I could trust and often there wasn't time."

"It's much easier to dispose of bones," Ficzko added. "They can be bagged and thrown from a carriage window. Even if they're found, they'd be impossible to identify."

"How many remain?" I asked.

Elizabeth looked at Ficzko. "I'm not sure, I've been preoccupied."

"Ugh," I moaned. "Perhaps it's not too late. We should journey below and see if anything has been disturbed. If we're lucky there will be time for Ficzko to clean up the mess. We'll have to do our best to distract the reverend."

To our horror we were too late. The reverend had made the discovery and our shameful secret lay exposed in the light of my lantern. Nine pine crates containing mutilated remains sat open. I glanced in the boxes taking note of the bodies in various stages of decomposition. It was impossible to tell if they were men or women but I knew the relevance was minuscule at this point. Dead bodies were dead bodies and the illumination of the slain victims was enough to get us all hanged.

"You didn't even bother to nail the lids shut!" I chided Ficzko.

"I didn't think it was important."

Elizabeth admired the pieces as she passed by the boxes with their lids slide askew. "He doesn't know I did this."

"Oh, and who do you think he will assume is responsible!" I said, my comment flirting with catastrophe. I should have taken more care to disguise my disdain.

"He has no reason to believe it is me," she answered.

Was she in complete denial? "If he believed you were innocent he'd never have bothered with this escapade in the first place." I went too far. I hit a chord.

Elizabeth pursed her lips. She was frustrated and adamantly wanted to deny what I said was true, but given the situation it was difficult to protest. Admitting I was right, which meant she'd been wrong, was a confession she did not readily make. Everyone in the room took a step backward as her eyes darted about looking for someone to blame. It was like a game of tag and we held our breath waiting to see who was it. My body felt heavy and my feet stuck in place glued by panic to the floor.

"He won't confront me by himself," she said. Her eyes settled on Ficzko.

I exhaled in relief.

"He'll send a letter to report his findings and request advisement in the matter."

"We need to intercept that letter," I interjected.

"Make yourself useful and get word to my most loyal guards. They must dispatch at once and stop anyone riding out. My orders are to search and take into custody," she said to Ficzko.

"What do we do?" I asked, feeling helpless.

"What you always do. Go about your business as usual."

"And, what do we do about these?" I asked, gesturing to the bodies.

"Nothing can be done until night fall. By then the guards will have returned and we will know more."

Ficzko was already running his errand. His tiny feet were pattering through the tunnels leading to the guard quarters. A brigade of Elizabeth's henchmen (a name given to the soldiers by the townspeople) would assemble and ride out scourging the woods for the traitor. I hated not knowing if a letter even existed, but if it did, it must be found. I grimaced thinking of what dreadful things the reverend had written. How would he describe what he discovered in the boxes in the tomb? The evidence Elizabeth was keeping to prove she slaughtered the Turks was nothing more than parts tangled in rags and bones. The king's examiner could conclude anything from the remains and depending on advantage would determine what was favorable. In the given state of decomposition he could say anything – he could report the deceased were women, men, nobles or servants. Who was to contradict his findings? The mere storage of the corpses screamed foul play. Any sensible person would deduce the hidden, unmarked boxes implied intent to conceal.

I took a step forward. "Regardless, we must get rid of the bodies," I said. Dump them anywhere, bury them if you must, but for the sake of warding off the Devil, get them away from here."

By nightfall the traitor was shackled in the castle dungeon and the letter delivered to Elizabeth's waiting hand. It was addressed to Reverend Janos's superior, Reverend Elias and, as I feared, contained incriminating details of the discovery as well as the accusations of the missing girl's meddling mother. Coupled together, there was warrant for investigation. However, our men had been successful and the correspondence intercepted.

Elizabeth read thoroughly over every painstaking detail before crumpling the paper and tossing it in the hearth.

"He warns I may be the 'worst killer under the sun.'" She scratched the side of her head. "I don't know if this is a compliment or an insult. Does he mean by *worst* that I am incompetent or do you think he means accomplished?"

I tried to see the upside of my answer. If I implied it was meant as an insult then she was seen as inexperienced and possibly defendable. However, this would not please her. If I said the comment meant accomplished, then she was skilled and calculated. It was admitting she was capable and guilty of cold-blooded murder. Which was it, innocent or guilty? Was there a third choice?

"He doesn't know you," I said avoiding answering the question altogether.

There was no excuse for a woman to rightfully or willingly murder a man. Perhaps if given the knowledge the men were Turks a court would pardon the deed, but this tidbit of information was absent from the reverend's letter. As I thought, he could not discern anything remarkable about the bodies in the boxes.

"I've got the messenger, I have the letter, now all I need is the reverend," Elizabeth listed off on three of her fingers.

"And the informant," I said wiggling a fourth.

"That might be difficult. There could be more than one," she noted.

This was true. By the contents of the letter we knew the missing girl's mother had complained to the reverend. However, someone clued him in on the underground tunnels. It was safe to assume it was a servant who was guilty of guiding him in that direction. Perhaps, to divert him from the woods or, more likely, to accomplish what actually happened. It was feasible to consider the aim was indeed for the reverend to find the bodies in the pine crates. The suspect knew the discovery would vindicate his suspicions and force the reverend to alert authorities to the crimes of the castle. Only a servant had anything to gain by getting Elizabeth in trouble. The most obvious suspect was the person with the least to lose if the mistress was taken away. The trouble was detecting the person before they realized they'd been exposed.

A guard entered. He was breathing heavy as if he'd run the entire length of the castle. "We searched the monastery," he panted. "The reverend was tipped off. There is evidence he's fled."

"He can't have gotten far," Elizabeth said.

"I have men looking, but the reports are grim. The trail is growing cold."

"Be diligent. I want him returned."

"Of course, Countess." The guard gave a sharp bow before turning on his heels.

"Well that answers our question. There is another traitor in our service," I said.

***

We were experiencing a bad case of déjà vu. Like his predecessor Pastor Berthoni, the Reverend Janos had fled the monastery. Elizabeth was seemingly scaring off every religious man who came to serve at Cachtice. Certainly, another man of the cloth fleeing in terror was going to raise further suspicions. The soldiers did as Elizabeth asked and they diligently continued to search the woods and nearby villages, but the slippery reverend was never found. He had escaped and was depending on the generosity of Elizabeth's subjects to aid in his underground journey to safety. The notion of her people's betrayal was maddening and sent Elizabeth on a crusade like no other.

Each day we inspected the servant's by counting heads. The guilty party surely would be absent for fear of being found out. But, each day everyone was accounted for and the drain of unearthing the traitor was taking a toll on our clan. The stalled query ignited Elizabeth's paranoia. She was feeling outwitted and she saw nothing but contempt and mockery on the peasants' gaunt faces. Their appearance was disgusting and their silent obedience humiliating. When she looked at them she did not see labored citizens dolling along with their daily tasks, but painted fools smiling and laughing at her expense. They were like the gypsies entertaining her father's guests and she was the jest. Everywhere she turned hideous characters cackled and sneered. They whispered and pointed; passing notes and conspiring against her. Of course in truth, they were

390

harvesting potatoes and washing floors, making lists for the market and sorting the daily post. They whispered because they feared upsetting the mistress and moved about the castle as silently as mice at midnight.

Quarters were ransacked and guards repeatedly harassed anyone seeming out of place during the daytime hours. One-by-one Elizabeth ordered servants to the dungeon where they were beaten and tortured. She wanted answers and had sunk to the lowest means of getting what she wanted. Impressively, not a single peasant confessed to being the accomplice or to any wrongdoings, but under duress some turned on their fellow mates and hinted to possible involvement citing the most mundane behavior as evidence. Eventually, they were released and sent back to work. However, not all of them recovered from injury. Infection and disease crept in to bruised wounds and open sores, nearly half of our staff perished as a direct consequence of Elizabeth's vengeful persistence.

There was no denying the life of a Transylvanian peasant was trying and their masters often treated them harshly, but servants were considered chattels and had no real rights or recourse. They were rounded up and forced to work for the ruling landlord. Suffering bodily punishment was a way of life, but brutality leading to death was over the top. It was too much. I warned that if Elizabeth continued in this vein, we might find ourselves victims of a peasant revolt.

As was becoming all too common in our home, the dead were hauled away and more servants were given notice and forced to serve at the castle. The turn over in help was creating a problem because our intimate group did not recognize many of the servants now tending to our needs. We did not trust those preparing our food or washing the clothes. Elizabeth saw them all as spies and stalked about the grounds like she was running from an angry mob. Her behavior was bizarre and her movements encouraged gossip. She'd slip from one room to another unnoticed, appearing and disappearing so quickly that the servants' thought it was by magic. I knew it was through the use of Fickzo's secret panels and passages, but her whereabouts scared the simple-minded. They did not understand how she got from one place to another and, because of this, the staff was constantly on edge.

To make matters worse, a letter arrived from Count Thurzo scolding Elizabeth for her excessive spending. The ledger presented for our review questioned household expenses and threatened further inquiry. Elizabeth had been padding the detailed sheet in order to fund her academy and scientific research. In midst of the chaos, Elizabeth reacted the only way befitting of her temperament, violently. She raged through the castle tearing everything standing in her way. Velvet curtains ripped and vases crashed as she stormed the corridors. I fluttered in the wake of destruction skipping over shards of porcelain and dented gold. The gothic fortress was in ruins and the mundane routine of our dull existence in tatters.

I was spinning in circles running this way and that way as I tried to make sense of what was going on around me, and of Elizabeth. I turned to the one person who seemed to still have his wits about him. Nicholas was the keystone of my world and, as long as he remained stable, I could withstand what may come. Experience told me that if I just endured and weathered the storm like I'd done so many times before, all would return to normal. Well, as normal as our lives ever got. In time, some new scandal would occupy Count Thurzo's concern and Elizabeth would eventually grow impatient and unlock her chamber door. There was comfort in routine, even in a routine as unusual as ours. If repeated enough, sooner or later, even the strangest of tasks appeared a manner of common course. I presumed Elizabeth would eventually return to her modus operandi and the entire hodgepodge of nonsense piling up around us would fade.

Charlie Courtland

A Cursive Plague, Cometh!

Summer 1610

A stifling heat suffocated the land. Days passed without a hint of breeze and the thicket of greens withered in the drought. Worst of all was the sickness spreading through the villages. It crept from house to house infecting the most vulnerable and killing them quickly. Every living person was terrified of the invisible mist capable of squeezing through cracks and crevasses. Doctors did not know how the plague began or how to prevent its reach. We heard it came in many forms and invaded prominent towns in times of extreme heat, but the disease was easy to ignore because it was always far from home. Those who could afford to leave packed their belongings and fled. I urged Elizabeth to consider leaving the area, but she believed the remote location of her castle in proximity to the afflicted towns was sufficient. It never occurred to her that her own servants were carriers. It did not take long for signs of the sickness to appear on our doorstep. It began with a cough and a wheeze before consuming its victims in bubbling pockets of sores and filling the lungs with fluid.

Within days the entire kitchen staff fell ill and was shuttled to makeshift beds set in a row along a rear corridor. At Elizabeth's request, a doctor was placed on retainer. He worked with his assistants around the clock desperately trying to save the servants lives, and when that failed he made every attempt to contain the contagion. The beds were stripped, linens burned and the bodies tossed in a communal grave near the woods. One-by-one they were stacked on top of each other until the pit was full and then covered in dirt. There were so many and they died so suddenly that there was not time to give a proper burial. Besides, we still had not found a suitable replacement for Reverend Janos at the nearby monastery.

The doctor demanded the bodies be disposed immediately to dampen the further spread of the disease. He believed it best to bury them together to lessen the risk of contaminating the wells or crops. We had no idea how the vapors spread and hysteria was ruling over common sense. Out of fear or ignorance, no one questioned the doctor's recommendations. We followed his advice even when a treatment seemed absurd.

Every effort unfortunately had a fatal result and the sickness continued to consume. It seeped through the passages of the castle snaking its way up until it found the supple lungs of the countess. I froze in panic when the first rattle of a cough escaped from Elizabeth's throat. I clutched a handkerchief over my mouth and without thinking I backed away. It had found its way to this very room and now there was no escaping, no safe place to run.

I'll never forget the horrified look on the doctor's face when he heard of the countess's illness. He knew he had failed her and by doing so, put her in grave danger. There was nothing else he could do, but insist she leave as soon as possible. He instructed the driver to take us to a health retreat in Piestany. The healing waters were rumored to cure the plague and restore the health of the worthy. God willing, the countess would survive. Given the current state of the household many of Elizabeth's forged noble ladies were not fit for travel, so naturally they'd be left behind.

To prevent further spreading, the doctor devised a drastic treatment which included denying the girls' food or drink while the countess was away. For eight days they were to fast. The lack of nourishment would starve the pestilence from their bodies, and with nothing left to feed on, the disease would lose strength and give up. Also, as part of their cure the girls were to bath in cool water at night and while draped in damp nightshifts take in air in the courtyard. The lack of heat would hinder the disease from festering and reduce any fever. It sounded perfectly logical. At this stage we were all willing to try anything to survive the outbreak. During Elizabeth's absence from Cachtice, Dorothea was placed in charge. She was responsible for making sure the girls adhered to the doctor's orders and oversee the general duties of the household.

Before we climbed into the carriage, Elizabeth had one last parting word with the doctor. "You must do everything to keep them alive. They are gentry and my responsibility. I will have to answer to their parents if something unfortunate should fall upon them."

The doctor's hands trembled nervously. "I will do my best, Countess, but this strain is strong. I do not know how many will survive. Perhaps, you should send word to their parents regarding the direness of the situation."

In her weakened state I worried Elizabeth might agree with the man. Our deceitful plan was in peril of being revealed. If this went any further I'd be forced to confess Erzsi's scheme along with my own involvement and risk the wrath of Elizabeth's anger. I stepped forward. "Sir, I've already taken the liberty."

Elizabeth was surprised.

"Well then, I shall wait for word. I'm certain Dorothea will let me know if accommodations for the young ladies should be arranged."

I nodded, averting my eyes from Elizabeth's quizzical glare.

"I cannot lose my girls," Elizabeth said, once we were settled inside the carriage. She covered her mouth while she coughed; the closeness of our intimacy made me nervous. I still had not shown any symptoms of being infected.

For a moment I was moved by her concern for the welfare of the girls in her academy. That was, until she said, "Everyone is dying. Finding replacements will be most difficult and I am so close to discovery. I just need a bit more time." She hacked in rapid succession. "Damned plague upon my house," she grumbled.

We were to stop in the town of Domolk to fetch an aristocratic girl who was to be a companion to Elizabeth during her stay at Piestany. The girl's family agreed to the arrangement because they feared their daughter might also be infected. They were desperate to find a cure and jumped at the offer to secure a ride to the spa. In return, the girl would keep Elizabeth's company and, upon recovery, continue her education at the academy. The opportunity was too good to be true, and of course, it was. If only the parents of the noble girl knew her real intentions they would never have agreed, but they were eager for hope and in haste flung their daughter into the waiting arms of Elizabeth. She received the girl with sugary encouragement and promised to return their precious child in restored health and pedigree.

"The new student is promising," I whispered. I did not want to wake the sleeping child.

"Her blood is tainted. I can only hope the waters will purify. She is no good to me in her current state."

"If the waters heal, then there is hope for more noble born women," I said, cheerily.

"Bah! Can you imagine the expense?"

Actually, I had not given it much thought. "Is it costly?" I asked.

Elizabeth rolled her eyes. "It's obscene. The medical authorities that run the place are no better than raiders. They should be tried and quartered for what they charge to treat the sick and feeble. It is no wonder so many die."

"Surely, the burden is minimal for you," I said, hoping Count Thurzo's concerns for Elizabeth's frivolous spending were nothing more than miserly greed.

"I'd have nothing to be concerned about if the king would repay what I'm rightfully owed. I've learned my darling deceased husband lent the crown over 17,000 guldens to finance his majesty's knights. I told Count Thurzo that he better convince the king to make good on his debt or else I will be forced to sell some of my properties."

"Sell your estates!" I said, shocked.

"Oh don't worry. Count Thurzo and the family will never allow such a thing to take place. My threat is merely a ploy to put pressure on the crown to repay the debt."

"I don't know if pressing the king is a wise idea."

"It is a matter of politics. If I have to, I will submit a formal complaint appealing to Parliament to take action. There are laws regarding debt even the royal crown must obey."

"What is Count Thurzo's response?" I asked.

"He says I am tarnishing my late husband's good name by making the demand. Francis lent the money in good faith and set no time line for payment. I think that is all too convenient. I have myself and our children to consider." Elizabeth was accosted by another bout of coughs. "If it were my choice, I'd have given not a single hair for their stupid war. I've no desire to fund a bunch of barbarians thirsty for blood. If they want to slay each other, they can do it with their own guldens, not mine."

"But it is to protect Hungry and the principle territories from the Ottoman," I said.

"They can do without all the ceremony and livery. I say, tighten up the belt and make do with less provisions."

She had a point. The king's army was well supplied and more comfortable than the people they swore to protect, but this was how things were, this was how it'd always been. The gentry spent a hideous amount of money while the country's subjects wallowed in squalor.

At our next stop I shook the girl from Domolk, but she was impossible to rouse. Given our long conversation I hardly noticed that the girl had not moved a muscle. Her body felt rigid beneath my grip and the hardness of her skin was familiar. He lips were blue and dry.

"Wake up miss," I shouted, giving her a good shake.

"What's wrong with her?" Elizabeth asked, poking her head through the doorway.

"The worst. I think she's dead," I hissed, trying to keep my voice low.

"Dead?" Elizabeth looked puzzled. "She didn't even seem that ill."

"I know. What should we do?" I shoved the girl upright so she appeared to be sitting peacefully inside the carriage.

Elizabeth peered around the side of the carriage to see if anyone was coming then ducked back inside. She stifled a cough. "I'll tell the driver the girl is too ill and is resting."

"Then what? I don't want to ride with a corpse all the way to Piestany." I tried to hold my breath just in case the girl expelled a toxin in the cabin.

Elizabeth took hold of my hand and dragged me from the carriage. "Just act normal. I'll think of something."

She was becoming gravely ill and in her weakened state was hardly capable of devising a plausible scheme, but I wanted the dead girl out of my space. I'd no attachment to her, why should I? I'd known her no more than a day, most of which she'd spent sleeping. My skin crawled at the very thought of having to ride with the decay in the carriage. I'd seen enough death in the last month and I was tired of being afraid for my health. My sleep was erratic and I grew anxious with every tickle at the back of my throat. I determined I was going to drink the waters at Piestany just as a precaution. Certainly, it could not hurt.

Our delay was cut short by Elizabeth's insistence we move onward. The carriage rocked and lurched as we raced along the busy road. The girl from Domolk's head banged against the carriage wall each time we hit a bump. The thumping noise was haunting and I could not take another second breathing in the same air as the stiff corpse.

"Get rid of her already," I complained, holding a handkerchief over my nose. "I'm going to be sick if I have to stare at her a moment longer."

Elizabeth pulled back the curtain. "The road is heavily traveled. I don't think we can risk stopping. Someone will think there is a problem and offer help."

I was cranky and did not care for possibilities. All I knew was I wanted that body dumped.

"We should wait until night fall," Elizabeth said, dropping the curtain.

"Night fall! I can't wait that long. Besides, how do you suggest we get her out of the carriage?"

"The two of us will do it," Elizabeth said. Her hand trembled as she coughed. The fluid building in her lungs rattled as she worked the spew up her throat and discarded it in her handkerchief.

I gagged on my disgust. "You're too weak to lift the body, and even if we did get her out of the carriage we'd never be able to drag and bury her."

"Your pessimism is not helping," she snapped. The purplish circles beneath her eyes were becoming more prominent and whether she'd admit it or not, she was losing strength.

I yanked back the curtain. The passing of carriages along the road were unpredictable. If I could spot a big enough gap, I could shove the girl from the carriage before anyone noticed. When I thought all was clear, I unlatched the door.

"What are you doing?" she asked.

I steadied myself as I maneuvered the girl from the seat. She was heavy and cumbersome. The force with which she flopped against my shoulder caused me to lose my footing and I stumbled landing hard on the opposite seat. The girl toppled on me, her skirt nearly burying me beneath her stiff weight. I grunted, shoving the girl to the side and rolling her over. I secured my arms under her armpits and hauled her up and over to the door. The rocking made the task exhausting and after several attempts I finally inched her to the edge. I peeked from behind the curtain to see if it were still clear. My view was obstructed, but I was fairly certain we were out of sight. I flung open the door. The wind rushed in whipping my hair from my loosely tucked bun. With one hand braced against the interior, I hurled the dead girl from the moving carriage. She tumbled head over heels as her body flipped through the air before smacking the ground and rolling down a storm bank. I stuck my head out the door to get one last glimpse of the girl who was laying face first in a puddle of stagnant water dribbling through the gully of weeds.

I latched the door and sunk into my seat. I wiped my hands on my skirt. They felt dirty and sore. I wanted to scrub them clean with fresh lavender soap and coat them in crème. I pulled off my gloves and tossed them on the bench beside me. Those would have to be burned when I got the chance. In the struggle, my ring had dug into my finger leaving a pink mark in my pale flesh, a branded reminder of my marriage and what good it had done me. I was alone still taking care of Elizabeth and myself for that matter. I rubbed the mark as I readjusted my ring so it would not continue to irritate.

"She'll be found soon," Elizabeth scolded. "Someone will report the finding. She's dressed too well to be disposable. Once they track her back to her parents they will connect the girl with me. I will face questioning." She crossed her arms over her chest. "Lucky for you my station in this country makes me virtually untouchable before the law, otherwise I might be facing trial."

"The girl was ill. We didn't kill her. She died just like a thousand others have recently."

"Yes, but you tossed her from the carriage and left her body to rot in a drain."

I relaxed my head against the back of the seat. "Well, we have lots of time to get our story straight. We'll say the girl gave us the slip at our last stop. She must have risked accepting a ride with a stranger. We searched and searched, but never found her."

"And why would she do that?" Elizabeth asked.

"I don't know. Why do young girls usually run away?"

Elizabeth shook her head disapprovingly. "I don't know. It doesn't sound believable."

The noise of wheels grinding on the gravel road filled the silence in the cabin while I thought of a better excuse. "We could say she was kidnapped and held for ransom," I purposed.

"Aha, that is more like it. I think that story just might work. I'll pen a letter at our next stop and post it immediately."

"Do you have the strength to sound desperately convincing?" I asked.

Elizabeth did not dignify my question with an answer. Of course she did. It was second nature.

When my nerves settled and my breathing returned to a normal rhythm, I was struck by a ping of guilt. I wrestled with the feeling before I finally asked, "Do you think it is terrible to let her parents believe she was murdered by raiders? The image is horrifying."

Elizabeth rolled her eyes. "She was going to die no matter what. Either way it was going to be unpleasant. At least she passed in her sleep. Really, she did not suffer too much."

"I did toss her from the carriage," I added.

"She didn't feel it," Elizabeth said.

"Still, it is humiliating."

She chuckled. "Yes, it is. We could turn around and pick her up to ease your guilt."

I scowled. I did not want that, but still, I did feel remorseful for my impulsive action. I was overcome with disgust and in my panic reacted naturally to the situation, but now it seemed disgraceful. It *was* disgraceful because I was happy the polluted girl was gone and I was rid of the threat to my person. I no longer felt a tickle in the back of my throat, in fact, I felt strangely cleansed as if the bad air had been purged from the carriage. I think Elizabeth felt it too because she closed her eyes and rested peaceful against the pillow propped beneath her head. The bouts of coughs subsided, and at last she slept.

***

Elizabeth's eldest daughter, Anna, joined us in Piestany. She received news of her mother's illness and insisted she visit immediately. The spa was delightful despite all the ailing residents and the company was energizing. We spent our lazy days lounging beachside while drinking waters and eating properly. It was a relief to be free of the heavy heat of summer and I willingly embraced the moist air and cool breeze licking at my sun-soaked skin. Even the abrasive grains of sand pinching between my toes were invigorating.

As luck would have it, Elizabeth had not contracted the dreaded plague. She was ill, but with an aggressive ague that, although it was bothersome, was not life threatening. Anyone with a weaker constitution might perish, but not Elizabeth. It'd take a lot more than a shivering fit to put her six feet under. However, we were not keen to share the good news. We were enjoying our little reunion with Anna and were quite determined to remain on holiday

401

as long as possible. The expense was excessive, but as long as the family thought it necessary they would approve the funds.

After a few weeks, and when Count Thurzo did not receive word of Elizabeth's untimely death, he had no choice but to assume the opposite occurred; that she was on the mend. Reluctantly, Anna penned a brief note stating that her mother was indeed in better health, but not yet ready for travel. We figured the news best come from her if we wanted it to be believable. Just as we suspected, Count Thurzo responded. In his letter he mentioned the unfortunate incident with the Domolk girl and how he regretted hearing of her demise. He reported the body was found stripped of all valuables and left disheveled on the side of the road. An investigation pursued, but the men suspected of being responsible were never captured and brought to justice. It seemed the assailants would go unpunished.

"It is all neatly tied up and topped with a pretty bow," I said, after listening to Elizabeth read the letter aloud.

"It was a good story," she said with a wink. The dark bags beneath her eyes had disappeared and the luster returned to her hair. The fish oils and kelp wrap had worked miracles and even my cynical eye could not deny the difference in her appearance. "Ah, but there is a snafu," she said.

Count Thurzo never disappointed. He always managed to conclude a letter with an irritant that lingered. His letter closed with the latest refusal of Elizabeth's request that she be reimbursed by the king for the loan made by her husband. The funds were not readily available for there was no excess of guldens in the coffers due to the expense of defending against revolt. Surely, Elizabeth would understand and make no further demands regarding the matter.

"Understand indeed!" she scoffed. "I understand they are willing to take my money, but not repay it."

"There may be some truth to what he writes," I said. "We've been warring for years and Parliament continues to complain of the expense. Draco has spoken of the deficit on the crown."

Elizabeth spent the entire afternoon composing a vile response. She did not share the contents of her letter to Count Thurzo with me, but based on what came next, I can imagine the phrasing was most uncouth.

Soon thereafter, Count Thurzo determined Elizabeth was fit to travel and requested she depart from the spa. To insult her further, a large bill was delivered to our room. Apparently, the family refused payment and the owner was insistent that Elizabeth pay up before she departed. He did not wish to get caught in the middle of a family dispute and told her if she rejected the notion, then she'd have to take it up personally with her family. It was terribly embarrassing and the amount owed was frightfully enormous. I had no idea how we managed to rack up such a bill, but after careful review, it appeared all charges were valid.

"This is how I'm treated on my death bed!" she yelled, stalking about the room. She tossed her things into a case.

Anna tried to calm her mother, but her pleas fell on closed ears.

"Oh, I will take the matter up with my family. This is not over. They will hear from me," she said.

Exactly the approach that got her into this mess in the first place, I thought.

"Mother, please…you'll make yourself ill again," Anna begged.

Elizabeth rummaged through a black travel pouch. She took out a necklace and fastened it around her neck. She drew the string tight cinching the velvet bag.

"Make sure you deliver these to your brother Paul at Sarvar." She stuffed the bag in Anna's hands.

"They're your jewels," Anna said, trying to give them back.

"The family is cutting me off. I want to make sure your brother gets as much as he rightfully deserves. Tell him I will send more when I get the chance. I plan to move all valuables from my court."

"Surely, the family will come around," Anna said. "There is no need to get hysterical. I will speak with Count Thurzo if you wish. I'll have my husband intervene on your behalf. He is very smart and will know just what to say to the men in the family. He can be convincing when it comes to matters of money."

I had no doubt Count Zrinsky was well schooled in finance. He had secured Anna's hand in marriage and with it inherited a great deal of wealth.

"He does have a controlling interest, doesn't he," Elizabeth answered.

"That's not what I meant to imply..." Anna said.

I motioned for her to stop speaking. There was no reasoning with Elizabeth when she was in an agitated state. It was best to let the tantrum roll.

The bill was paid and our bags packed. I was sad to leave the retreat. I kept the curtains drawn as we drove along the road. The calming cries of the gulls disappeared and the dusty air of impoverished villages replaced the sweet smell of seawater. Soon our diet of fresh fish chowders and tonic water would turn to fatty mutton and wine. My only consolation was the awaiting comfort of Nicholas's cozy quarters. His absence restored my passion and I was anticipating a joyful reunion. The separation had done us good and I knew he'd be just as excited by my return, as I would be by his.

***

The situation was worse than even I could imagine. The plague swept through the villages and devastated the castle. All that was left was the beating hearts of our small clan. This included my beloved Nicholas who was now standing in the courtyard awaiting my arrival. His mouth hung slack. Much like me, he stood in awe as he viewed the overgrown grounds and the emptiness of the windows glaring down at us. So many died and those who remained eventually fled out of fear. Those who had the strength had managed to dump the dead at the edge of the woods, but as death mounted so did the bodies. When there was no one left to drag them out, they remained were they dropped.

I clutched a handkerchief over my nose as we stepped inside. In the corridor lay the rotting corpse of a maid. Maggots had eaten most of her flesh and flies buzzed about the ceiling. The scene was repeated throughout the castle; a chamber girl found dead in her bed, a stable boy slumped in a stack of hay in the barn. The horror was everywhere and the stink was beyond anything I thought was physically possible.

Dorothea and Erzsi returned along with Ficzko and Kata, the washerwoman. Elizabeth embraced her trusted circle of friends and graciously praised God for sparing their lives. They had deserted the castle in time and, despite the rapid onset of illness, managed to escape its wrath. The six of us stood dumbstruck in the dusty, dreary shadow of the drawing room. The doctor was gone along with his assistants and the charges of forged noble girls enrolled in Elizabeth's academy. They were all dead…dead, dead, dead.

"We cannot stay here," I said, when I finally found my voice.

Elizabeth ran a finger over the top of her favorite table. White powder clung to the tip of her glove. The trace of her effort was left in a long streak across the surface.

"It will take some work, but it can be cleansed."

I pointed toward the window. "They're all dead! D-E-A-D!" I spelled out. "Who is going to restore this place?" I paced across the room taking a position beside Nicholas. "Why must we stay? We can close up court like you said and move to another residence." I looked to Nicholas for encouragement. I was frightened and wanted someone else in the room to side with me.

He stepped forward. "I must agree with Lady Lorant. I think taking a temporary reprieve from Cachtice would be the wisest move." Nicholas cleared his throat. "There is something you should know." He hesitated. "The people blame you for the plague. They say you brought this on."

"I? How did I bring this on?" Elizabeth asked. She whirled around to face Nicholas.

"There is talk you drove the reverend from the monastery. Coupled with the rumors about mysterious practices, well, the people are whispering you are a sinister killer, and that you might be a witch."

"They think I unleashed this upon my own house?"

"Not intentionally. However, some believe God is punishing you for your actions."

"Then why am I not dead?"

Nicholas shrugged. "I am only conveying what I've heard, Countess. I thought it proper you know what is being said."

"Elizabeth, please. We cannot stay here," I repeated. I figured if I spoke the words loud enough, she'd have to listen. I didn't think I could be more repulsed by this place, but to my astonishment, I could. The ivy crawling up the stone was eating the walls and blocking out what little sun shone through the windows. The overgrown shrubs drowned out the daylight and the torches in the halls went unlit. The hearth sat in sooty blackness while the past coated every piece of furniture and trinket in a grimy film. The abandoned castle bared a resemblance to a condemned crypt described in an epic novel. It was grotesque and inhabitable. Surely, Elizabeth could see that! She just had too.

She raised her chin in defiance. I knew what was coming next. "They will not drive me from my home. Not yet."

"This is not a home!" I cried.

"It is *my* home and I will determine when I leave." She turned her back on me. "I won't be run out. I rule the land. I will decide what happens."

"You have other homes," I insisted, my voice calmer. If I just could make her see the sense in what I was saying.

"I've sold the Theben Castle and pawned my home in Beckov."

"What?" I asked, shocked by her confession.

Elizabeth waved off my shock as if she were swatting a fly. "I sold Theben to the crown. The place was a worthless frontier fort. What was I going to do with it?"

"Beckov?" I asked.

"Worthless as well. I only got 2,000 gulden for the place."

"But why? Why did you resort to selling?"

"Obviously for money," she hissed. "I still own Sarvar, Keresztur, and the townhouse in Vienna. And, the property near Venice," she reminded. Slowly, she turned around, "And Cachtice."

"Sarvar. We could join Paul in Sarvar!" I said, hopeful she'd agree.

"I'm not infringing on my son. Besides, my work here is not finished."

I bowed my head and rubbed my eye with the heel of my palm. This was not happening. This was not logical. Was I the sole person willing to see the insanity? I appealed to Erzsi for support.

"We are close. If we could remain for a few more months I'm certain the countess and I will discover a solution," Erzsi said, referring to the potion. That stupid potion was all she could think about.

"In the meantime, I will ship the valuables and arrange for more suitable accommodations," Dorothea added.

"It won't appear the countess is on the run; rather that she has chosen to relocate her academy," Ficzko chimed in.

The words they spoke pleased Elizabeth. She was relieved her loyal servants stood by her task. It was the assurance she needed and she ate it up like cake.

I was in disbelief at the twisted faces of her devoted clan; the dwarf with bulbous eyes, the deceptive witch with corn-silk hair and petite figure, and Kata, the stout washerwoman with calloused hands and ruddy cheeks. This was her royal court and Dorothea the governess was promoted to royal advisor in Anna's absence. When Anna married, Dorothea should have moved on and been referred to another household to chase children, but instead she remained in Elizabeth's service and was now speaking quite out of turn.

My head was spinning and I began to sweat. I tore at my hair and shook uncontrollably. "I will not listen to this. I will not!" I screamed. I ran from the drawing room. My feet carrying me through the claustrophobic halls and past the diseased remains lying on the floor. The buzz of flies swarmed in my ears and I pushed open the front door and stumbled into the courtyard. The toe of my slipper caught the hem of my skirt and I tumbled to the ground scraping my knees on the jagged stones. A searing pain stung my skin and I knew the wounds on my legs were bleeding. I crumbled in a ball and wept. I sobbed until my guts wrenched. I heaved dryly choking on the air driven from my empty stomach. If only I had something to toss, I thought. The tears wetting my lips were salty and the snot running down my face was clear. I wiped the foulness from my chin with the edge of my sleeve.

"There, there," Nicholas cooed. He knelt beside me and began rubbing my back.

I flinched. I was in no mood to be touched.

"I hate it here. I want to leave this place forever. Why must we stay? Why must she keep on with this business?" I cried.

He wrapped an arm around my shoulder and pulled me close. "I will take you away if that is truly what you want. I will go right now. I swear I will. All you have to do is ask, Amara, and we will go."

I gave in and allowed the weight of my body to press against his chest. I sobbed some more until every last ounce of grief was expelled. Oh how I wanted to say yes, say that I wished to leave this instant. Nicholas and I could ride far away and settle in a small home in a pleasant place, perhaps near a beach where the air was moist and the smell of fresh fish whispered through the trees. I squeezed my eyes shut. I wanted to see it, so desperately desired to picture our future, but I could not. All I saw was the darkness lining the back of my eyelids. I opened my eyes and all was the same. I was soiled in dirt and staring at the crumbling remains of the fortress walls locking me inside Cachtice.

"I can't leave," I whimpered.

"We can leave," Nicholas urged.

"I can't abandon her. I promised I'd never leave her alone," I said. I sighed as the last sob left my throat.

"You've served long enough. Perhaps it is time to go your own way."

I thought of Elizabeth and the loyal servants gathered around her in the dim drawing room; the dwarf, the witch, the washerwoman and the advisor. They had no one else but Elizabeth and in honor of her kindness they swore an oath of servitude. They were willing to do as she wished to please her even if it meant the worst. I rocked back on my heels. I wiped my cheeks. I thought of the years we passed together; remembered all the adventures as well as the disappointments. We made it through because we had each other. We survived because we were bound for better or for worse. I realized it was not so much a choice, but a connection much like an umbilical cord. If I cut it, one of us might very well die.

"I think I am the only string that binds her to this world. If I leave she will be lost and so will I."

"You will have me," Nicholas said. There was an unsettled desperation in his voice.

"Who will she have?" I asked, pointing in the direction of the castle.

"She has...she has them," Nicholas said with antipathy.

"You know as well as I do that she needs me. I keep her grounded. I am what joins her with this world. I am her reason, her compass and..." I paused.

"You are not her life source," Nicholas said.

I would not protest. I was not her source of life in the traditional sense, but nevertheless, our energy was mingled and if severed the consequences might be fatal. Even though I despised this place and wanted desperately to escape, I knew I would not make it beyond the wall without Elizabeth by my side. No, if we were to go, it would be together. I'd made her that promise and I knew now I had every intention of keeping it.

I rose from my position and brushed the dirt from my dress. Nicholas held me by the elbow and tenderly guided me towards the castle. I stiffened, resisting our progress in that direction. "I will remain, but I will not return to my chamber in that cursive heap of rock."

"Very well," Nicholas said, turning me toward the arch leading to his quarters. "I'll have one of the men retrieve your things."

I expected Elizabeth to dispute my demands. To my surprise, she did not argue. She granted me the small consolation and saw to it that all my precious belongings were neatly arranged in Nicholas's cabin and Lyk's dog bed was nudged in the corner closest to the hearth. It was cramped, but comforting and I felt more at ease in his presence than in the vast void of my prior chamber.

In time, I appeared on several occasions to break fast in the dining hall. Although our staff was scant, the active areas of the castle were cleaned and, for the most part, made livable. Elizabeth assured me our stint at Cachtice was temporary. We'd close up the house as soon as she had time to ensure proper accommodations at one of her other properties. I knew this meant moving her workshop and all its contents. Of course it would be difficult, seeing how there were fewer servants and even less who were willing to enter the remote parts of the castle and haul mysterious crates from the chambers of Cachtice. The unmarked crates were secured on every available cart and stored under cover in the stables. The move was going to be a grand chore and the procession troublesome given the lack of able-bodied workers. Those who had survived the outbreak were reluctant to serve at the castle. However, they had little say in the matter and, with some urging, they returned crouching like beaten animals to serve the mistress.

Exorcizing the Demon Woman

By now word of Elizabeth's disobedience and underhanded selling of her properties had reached the family. To their displeasure, they were becoming very familiar with her tendencies and, at Count Thurzo's urging, the clan gathered for a meeting. Of course, the person in question was never privy to the conversation and therefore, Elizabeth was not present to defend her actions. However, later we learned of the secret meeting when Anna's husband sheepishly confessed every last slanderous detail the family confided.

In his all-important manner, the newly appoint Governor, Count Thurzo twitched his moustache and diverted his accusing eyes when he recommended Elizabeth be ordered to leave Cachtice and be sojourned to Varanno where she'd temporarily remain. After answering for her behavior, she'd be spirited off to a convent until the end of her days. Her evil ways would be exorcized and her soul saved. It was determined she was too old to marry, and her reputation too despicable to be restored. In the end, the majority ruled and, when put to a vote, the family determined a convent was the only plausible solution. Count Thurzo was excessively pleased with the result and, without further ado, scribbled a letter announcing his future visit. Since the decision was a delicate matter he did not wish to deliver it via messenger. Rather, he resolved it was best to make the family's position known in person. A face-to-face victory was always preferable and he did not want to be denied the ceremony.

However, several days before Count Thurzo's scheme was put in motion, he received word that the Impre Megyert had registered a formal complaint against Elizabeth before the Hungarian Parliament. Her disgrace was no longer a family matter. It was made public that for three days Parliament would hear numerous witness testimonies and accusations against the Blood Countess. The ordeal was most scandalous and stirred a great deal of concern among the nobility.

During the era of tumultuously rule, the power of the government was changing, and not in Elizabeth's noble-ranked favor. The lawlessness through which the gentry ruled the land was coming to an end as the righteous Holy Roman Emperor, the Archduke Matthias II, was gaining determination and further support to distribute power and extinguish mayhem. To his pleasure, the archduke was ecstatic to hear the proceedings surrounding the countess and approved monies to start his own investigation against the corruptive practices of certain nobles. More specifically, Matthias sought any opportunity to discredit the Bathory family since he was at odds with Elizabeth's cousin, Gabriel. The Transylvania prince wanted to expand his territory and was gathering support to absorb some of the empire's land for his personal gain. So it was in Matthias' interest to destroy any person of position within the Bathory clan, especially Elizabeth. By doing so, her property would be seized and, most importantly, her claims to the debt that the crown owed her late husband would be voided. Elizabeth was about to find herself in the middle of a political crossfire and to her unfortunate circumstance she was to suffer the consequence. It was complicated, calculated and ensnaring to say the least.

Everyone was making their move and jostling for an advantageous position. Some were merely spectators, while others were players in battle. I found myself cast in the unique role of both. However, I did not have a lead so my involvement went unnoted. In truth, much of what sincerely occurred was poorly documented and showed a lack of investigation. The neglect of any real evidence illuminated just how many key decisions were placed in the greedy hands of a tightly woven political circle. Despite the publicity, the persons in charge were a mere few who came to the party armed with only the almighty pen. These were the lawmakers, judgment enforcers and court recorders. All of whom, in my opinion, were nothing more than scavengers pecking at the carnage tossed at their feet. They filled their bellies on the spoils of others and did little to earn an honest living. At this time, there was no such thing as a fair trial. Especially, when so many others were at fault for committing similarly heinous acts and avoiding punishment.

Count Thurzo called an emergency meeting to covey the learned rumor before the family. The members were in shock when they heard the turn in events. They feared Elizabeth would be found guilty of the charges made against her and in turn, she would lose all property rights. A negative verdict warranted confiscation of the estates. To prevent this from happening, the family uniformly agreed to cooperate in her capture and subsequent trial, if it should come to that, but of course they all hoped it would not. It was a messy business and no one wanted to take part in the betrayal.

From March to July of 1610 the testimonies of thirty-four witnesses were sparsely recorded. These included dramatic accusations of satanic rituals, bloodletting in the form of vampirism and practices of witchcraft. All were presented through false evidence and repeatedly supported by the local lore. However, a few nobles who would benefit from Elizabeth's demise validated the ridiculous claims and bared witness to the documents submitted to the court. I was astonished such outrageous accounts were taken seriously. Common sense should have alerted any sane man that what was being said was rubbish. Well, most was rubbish and that which held the teeniest of truth was well within the established law.

Also during this time, an inopportune adversary resurfaced. Reverend Janos had managed to get his report to Count Thurzo. As suspected, it included his disturbing findings concealed beneath Cachtice. The position of governor that had been bestowed on Thurzo gave him the full authority to act in the absence of the king. As much as he relished in the details enclosed in the reverend's letter, the information placed Count Thurzo in a very delicate position. Since he was a direct relation to the accused and would be greatly affected by the seizing of property, he was far from eager to bring the information to light. Thurzo's own properties were adjacent to those of Elizabeth's and he had a huge interest in procuring the land for himself and little ambition to hand it over to the crown.

Being a cunning man, Count Thurzo considered the one loophole in the law that he could use to his benefit. As the widow of a leading lord of the noble realm, the law protected Elizabeth from being arrested. It would take a special act of Parliament to incite her on any charges – even the outlandish accusations being flung around the court. The worst punishment that she could endure was exile and a small allowance.

But, pressure was mounting from the Hungarian Catholic nobles and Parliament was summoned to Bratislava. It was here, that the political heads of state again listened to the complaints. They were largely annoyed that Elizabeth had indulged in barbaric acts. The standard was imperfect and unfair. What was barbaric for a woman was well within the common habit of men. There were sympathizers; those who did not fault Elizabeth for her behavior. They placed blame upon the absence of a husband. If the countess had been influenced to remarry in a timely manner, then there would be a man to keep any unwanted tendencies in check. It was believed a man would have kept Elizabeth in proper line.

Count Thurzo was in a quandary. In the midst of his attempts to find some face-saving angle and preserve Elizabeth's properties for his own profit, he requested an audience with an emissary of Matthias. He requested a royal grant of permission to travel to Cachtice to collect the facts and punish the guilty. In other words, he'd find a scapegoat for the misdoings if he had to and return empty handed stating the rumors were propagated in an effort to discredit the countess and procure her wealth. Thurzo was determined to handle the situation under the strict instruction that any action taken would be to the family's advantage. To guarantee he'd have the upper hand in the matter, he planned his visit to Cachtice over the Christmas holiday when Parliament was not in session. He knew by doing so, proceedings would stall, giving him time to solidify a strategy.

Let Them Eat Cake

Many of the rooms at Cachtice were shut and unused. They remained draped in darkness and covered in dust. The place was a skeleton of its former shell and the holiday garland that once colored the halls hung sadly to the hooks in the main entry and across the mantle of the drawing room hearth. The drifts of snow and iced crusted banks hid empty doorways and swallowed abandoned stable yards. With the anticipation of Count Thurzo's arrival, Elizabeth withdrew further into the belly of the castle. She was retreating to a secure place where the hurtful words of the people and accusations of Parliament could not reach her. No matter how far she tunneled, she could not escape the inevitable visit of our most unwanted guest. It could not be prevented. Thurzo was coming.

I knelt beside the small tree Nicholas had cut and placed in the corner of his tiny room. Beneath the rich, luscious needles rested a package tied with a fancy ribbon. The grandeur was miniscule but the picture was pleasing and despite being reduced to living in a pauper's dwelling, I was shockingly content. In this room, I felt worlds away from the misery moving like a biblical storm over the main house. The tightly constructed walls provided a strange comfort and I began to identify more intimately with Elizabeth. Although, I did not completely comprehend her method of diversion, I imagined the appeal of the remote workshop tucked beneath the earth and how she felt the enclosed space safely enveloping her from the tedious decorum of noble life. It brought her the same consolation Nicholas's quarters provided me. A place to where I could disappear and forget all that was terribly wrong and wrongfully done.

A brisk gust cut through the room as Nicholas entered. He shook the snow from his overcoat and stomped his boots. "Bitterly cold out there," he said with a shudder.

I took his gloves and hung them on the rope tied above the fire to dry.

He paused, eyeing the festive decorations adorning the tree. He was always considerate that way, taking the briefest moment to appreciate my efforts. "It's beautiful," he said, grinning. "And what is this?" He gestured to the box beneath the tree.

"Just a little something," I said. I could not help smiling. For a soldier he possessed an innate warmth and kindness. Perhaps, it was the cooper tint of his hair or the broadness of his grin that gave the impression.

He overturned his hands, "I come baring nothing."

"You brought me the tree," I reminded.

"That I did, that I did, but a lady deserves much more."

"I have everything I could ask for." And I did. Perhaps, not everything I desired, but I did have everything I was allowed to ask for and for that, I was grateful.

Lyk nudged at Nicholas's leg. He mindlessly patted the dog's head before shooing him back to his bed. He removed his boots and propped his feet on a stool beside the hearth. "Word has it Elizabeth is aware the vultures are circling. She is taking steps against her plotters."

"Uh-hum. And, what is the mistress brewing?"

"I was hoping you could tell me," he said.

I raised a brow. "Me? How shall I know what Elizabeth is plotting?"

Nicholas rolled his eyes. "Is there any truth to it?" he asked.

"I don't have the slightest idea what you are talking about." I put my arms around his shoulders and rested my chin on top of his head. It was nice cuddling with him by the fire.

He patted my hand. "If you say so."

It was true. I had intentionally stayed away from the castle. I really did not know what Elizabeth was up to, but Nicholas piqued my curiosity and I was certain I'd get to the bottom of things by tomorrow. Whether I'd report my findings to him was another story, but I'd relieve my anxiety by paying Elizabeth a visit.

The next morning before I set out on my errand to the main house, I was delayed by the delivery of a letter. I recognized the handwriting of my husband and determined it was another regret for his neglect. I tore open the envelope and quickly read the short note scribbled upon the page. As I suspected, Draco begged my pardon for his delay and assured me he'd arrive for the season as soon as the weather permitted. I crumpled up the note and tossed it in the diminishing fire. I was unmoved by disappointment and no longer felt the great pains his words inflicted. I'd grown to expect nothing more than avoidance and duty from Draco and once my mind resolved this internal conflict, I was numbingly at ease with his long absence. The days we spent together and the Draco I loved were gone, dead to me forever and replaced by a harden shell of a man who'd spent too many years in battle. The fierceness in which he had shielded himself from the horrors of war had inevitability won and seized what was left of his heart. I was finished shedding tears and mourning the sorrowful loss of our love.

I unlatched the door and tightened my hood to protect my face from the razor bite of the winter's snarl. Trudging through the newly fallen snow, I cut a path toward the main house. Trailing behind was a weaving pattern of footprints distorted by the dragging lengths of my overcoat. I stopped in the walkway debating whether to enter through the front doors or make my way around to the kitchen. The gnawing in my stomach answered the question and I decided the smell of fresh baked bread rising through the smoke in the stove was persuasive.

My appearance caused quite a stir as I pushed my way through the kitchen door. I was met by a bustle of curtsies and good mornings before being offered a sweet roll. I picked through the warming basket before choosing a golden buttery bread folded around a dollop of jam. The flaky bits melted in my mouth as the sweet preserve tickled my tongue. I closed my eyes savoring the delicious cake for just a moment before giving my compliments to the cook. Without giving it much thought, I turned toward the door leading to the narrow stairwell.

"Forgive me, Milady, but the countess is not toiling below this morning," the maid said.

I pulled a face. "She is not?"

"No Milady, the Countess is bathing in her chambers."

"Very well." I removed my overcoat and handed it to the maid. With my hunger satisfied, I climbed the winding grand staircase leading to the upper floor of the castle. Small droplets of melted snow from my boots dampened the stairs and wetted the corridor as I strolled toward Elizabeth's chamber.

"Good morning," I announced cheerfully as I entered her room.

Soaking in a steaming tub of water was Elizabeth. "Come to spy? Do you want to know what I am up to?" she asked.

I gawked playfully at the accusation. "Why, I'm offended by such a suggestion." I placed my hand over my heart. "I only came to pay my dear friend a visit."

Elizabeth folded her arms on the edge of the tub and set her chin firmly upon them. "Damned spy! Pray do tell who has sent you?"

Erzsi ignored our banter. She was preoccupied with stirring the contents of a bowl.

I scooted a chair near the tub. "The maids, they are talking," I ruefully whispered. "They say you are bathing and it is most suspicious." I burst out laughing.

Elizabeth laughed as well. "Are you certain it is the maids and no one else who has urged you on this errand?" She could barely steady the delivery of the sentence.

I put my hands on my hips. "Well it certainly was not Count Thurzo if that is what you mean!" I tried to sound serious, but I could not hold in my giggle.

She splashed me with a handful of water. "Don't remind me!"

Erzsi ladled a scoop of Elizabeth's bath water and mixed it with the dry ingredients in the bowl.

I wrinkled my nose. "What are you doing?"

"We're making cake!" Elizabeth exclaimed, excitedly.

"Making cake, with dirty bath water? It is not a cake I wish to eat!" I said, disgusted.

"Well, I should think not!" Elizabeth relaxed into the tub letting the water submerge her shoulders. All that poked out was her head and the tops of her knees. "It's a special cake for Count Thurzo and his majesty."

Erzsi vigorously beat the ingredients into a batter.

I peeked into the bowl. "How many cakes do you plan on making?"

"We have to test them first, but once we are certain of the result we plan on making two." She glanced at Erzsi, "Two should do it, right?"

Erzsi nodded while she continued to work.

"What is the desired result?" I asked.

"Death by poison, of course," she said. She rose from the tub and dried herself off before slipping into a dressing robe. "I will serve a cake to Count Thurzo as well as have a cake sent to his majesty." She ran a brush through her hair. "He is a glutton. Everyone knows he can't resist sweets."

***

Erzsi baked a batch of her special seed cake and served it to a few of Elizabeth's retainers as a reward for a hard day of labor. Like she had done years ago, Elizabeth waited for the desired result. Nothing immediately happened, but after a while the retainers began to complain of terrible stomachaches. They gripped at their squeezing ribs and moaned as the potion invaded their weakened bodies. One by one, they were escorted to their beds and observed from afar.

"It's taking too long," Elizabeth hissed. "All this damn moaning and thrashing is unacceptable."

The splattering of vomit hitting a basin echoed from the room. More wrenching and moaning and cursing erupted as the stomach cramps strengthened.

"They've eaten something spoiled," a maid informed. She emerged from the room carrying a pot of soured water.

"Will they recover?" Elizabeth asked.

"We'll know more in the morning when it has run its course."

Noticing the smell was offending the mistress, the maid hurried away to discard the sickness.

"Morning, we'll know by morning!" Elizabeth sneered.

Erzsi cowered, her back pressed against the stone wall. "I can make it stronger," she said.

"I hardly think any of my retainers will be so eager to eat the next batch of your seed cake since the first one made them violently ill."

"I can put it in something else then."

"This potion is too unstable. If I can not be certain of the outcome I will be forced to abandon the idea." Elizabeth paced. "Oh why can't I just run them both through with a sword!" The more she paced, the greater her temper grew. She hated failure and in times of threat and desperation her patience wore thin.

Our harmonious fun was over and I knew it was time to return to Nicholas's room. I listened to another bout of vomit hitting a freshly emptied pot. "It is getting late," I said, taking my overcoat from the maid. I gave Elizabeth a hesitant hug. "Things will appear better in the morning," I encouraged.

She grunted, returning my sign of affection with a half-hearted pat on the back.

As I plodded through the deepening snow I considered what I'd tell Nicholas. Since the potion was an utter failure, I surmised it best to let the whole incident be forgotten. There was no reason to alert him to Elizabeth's escapades. After all, she'd have several more schemes prepared before Count Thurzo arrived and who knew which one of them would be successful.

My boot sunk in the path. I felt the sting of wet snow tumbling over the top of my tightly laced rim. I cursed, yanking my leg free of the drift. I brushed the snowballs from the edge and rubbed my calf. The damp stocking pinched at my skin. I quickened my pace along the walk leading to the soldier quarters. I was still cursing when I entered Nicholas's house. He was lounging at the wooden table, his shoulders rounded as he slumped eating the last bits of rabbit stew. I unlaced my boot and tossed it aside and without consideration stripped off my wet stocking.

"Sink into another drift?" he asked.

I scowled.

"How many times do I have to tell you, you need to be mindful of where you're walking? You're going to get frost bite."

I wrapped my legs in a blanket and inched my chair close to the fire. "I wouldn't have to be mindful if I lived in a reasonable place," I mumbled. Being cold made me irritable and it seemed it was always cold these days.

Nicholas waited for the tension to lift before he continued the conversation. He knew better than to directly ask what I'd been up to, but nevertheless, he was curious. "Besides the snow, did you have an enjoyable day?"

"It was uneventful," I lied.

He smirked. "Really?" His half-cocked grin told me he did not believe me in the least.

"Elizabeth is anxious about the arrival of Count Thurzo."

Nicholas broke the heel of the bread from the loaf and began gnawing on it. "I'm told there is another plague sweeping through the house. It came on suddenly and has only affected a few."

"A plague?"

Nicholas shrugged. "Another illness of sorts."

"Oh that, that is not a plague, but rather an isolated incident. They ate something spoiled and it made their stomachs turn. The maid said it should run its course by morning."

He sniffed at his stew. "Wasn't the rabbit, was it?"

"No, I think it was a spoiled seed cake."

Thankfully, before I could further explain, our evening was interrupted by a pounding knock upon the door.

"What is it?" Nicholas demanded as he opened the door. He invited a shivering guard inside.

"Sorry to bother you sir, but we have a situation which has inspired concern."

"Concern with whom?"

The guard glanced over Nicholas's shoulder at me sitting in the chair. I would have given them privacy if there were anywhere else to go, but we were stuck in the room and I was not about to move. I suppose if he really did not wish me to hear he would insist they step outside.

"The staff sir," he said, lowering his voice. "They think they've found blood."

"Probably just a fresh kill," Nicholas answered.

"The men do not believe so sir."

Nicholas dressed quickly, throwing on several layers of fur before pulling on his tall boots. "I'll return soon," he said before slamming the door shut.

As soon as I heard the door latch I threw aside my blanket and tugged on a dry stocking. I laced up my boots and fastened my overcoat. The night air was still and I was pleased the wind had finally died down. It was easy to determine the direction the men took by the set of footprints in the snow. I followed them around the main house taking care to stay inconspicuously in the shadows. Few torches burned and the path was difficult to see, but I knew the grounds well and easily tracked the small investigative party to the rear of the main house.

I stopped short when I heard the mingling of male voices. I was breathing heavy and big puffs of air rolled in a cloud from my nose. I edged closer to the corner, the palms of my gloves pressed against the uneven wall. I couldn't make out what they were saying. It was irritating to be so near, but still in the dark. I slyly poked my head around the edge so just the side of my face and one eye was visible. Standing in a half circle was a group of guards with Nicholas kneeling in the middle, his hand touching a dark spot in the snow. The men were grumbling amongst themselves while Nicholas animatedly talked with the highest-ranking guard. It seemed they were in a hot debate and from my vantage I could not tell if what he was saying was being well received. I squinted attempting to get my eyes to focus, but my effort was no use. Frustrated, I spied for a better hiding place but any movement on my part would draw attention so I determined it best to remain. It felt like an eternity. I wished they'd hurry it up before I froze to death with my body pressed against the icy wall, motionless and silent.

Finally, the men finished their inquiry. The increasing sound of crunching snow alerted me that they were coming. I ducked in the cover of a nearby doorway. Crouched in a ball I held my breath while the group of men passed by. I couldn't feel my feet even though I knew they were steadily beneath me. I had to get moving, had to get the blood flowing through my limbs. My legs were heavy as I willfully pushed them through the snow towards the stain beyond the exterior wall.

When I arrived at the spot, I knelt beside the dark splattered mess just like Nicholas had done moments ago. There were no traces of fur or bone, but one thing was certain, there was a brownish liquid spreading like spilled wine soaking into the snow floor. It was blood, that was for sure, but as the men suspected it was not from a fresh kill. I sniffed the air. A familiar sour odor assaulted my senses. I poked around at the edge of the splatter. I was not an expert of detection, but I presumed that the mysterious stain was the discarded stomach contents of Elizabeth's retainers. The pungent bile mixed with spoiled seed cake. Although altered in its current state, the dessert was not difficult to recognize. Not wanting to venture far in the cold, the maid must have hastily tossed the bucket from the back door. I stood up. The painful bite of the growing numbness in my feet urged me to return to Nicholas's room.

I winced with each step I took. The walk seemed to take twice as long on the return journey. The sight of the blood was disturbing. I deduced the poison had burned the soft lining of the stomach and when the victim vomited, the push of expelling the rancid seed cake tore and cut causing their insides to bleed. What I witnessed was not mere traces of pink, but hot thick blood congealing in the snow. I doubted the poisoned patients ailing upstairs would make it to morning. They were bleeding profusely from wounds no one could see and therefore, could not be mended. They'd bleed out by morning and rumors of misdeeds or another plague would spread quicker than fire on dried hay.

I did not expect Nicholas to be at home when I arrived. I assumed he'd still be meeting with the other men discussing the possible explanations for what was in the snow. To my shock, he was sitting in his favorite chair at the table. His disapproving eyes glared at me as I removed my boots. I felt like a child caught misbehaving. Embarrassed, I avoided a confrontation.

"Out for a night walk?" he asked.

Who was I fooling? He knew exactly what I was doing. My actions implied I knew something about the mysterious stain in the snow. I'd have to tell him what Elizabeth and Erzsi did. It was the only way to make any sense of what he'd seen. Defeated and uncomfortable by the thawing of my numb feet, I flopped in a chair. I rubbed the life back into my toes as the burning log on the fire crackled and snapped sending sparks into the chimney.

"The guard was correct when he surmised the blood was not from a fresh kill," I said matter-of-factly.

"And what do you know of this?"

I gave a big stretch as I stared at the ceiling. "It's the remains of the vomited seed cake. The lazy maid tossed the buckets outside the door. She should have taken better care of discarding the sickness."

"But there is so much blood," Nicholas pointed out.

I sat straight. Why couldn't he just drop it? I knew he'd never let it rest so finally I admitted the entire story. "The seed cake wasn't spoiled, rather more like poisoned. It was an experiment that went wrong."

"Poisoned? Why would Elizabeth wish to poison her own retainers?"

"They were test subjects and not the intended target, but the poison is ineffective. It made them sick. As you saw for yourself, it caused great internal distress, but it did not work quickly and therefore is too risky."

"May I ask who is the intended target?"

I threw up my hands. "Count Thurzo, of course!"

"Ah! I see." Nicholas rubbed the stubble on his chin. "I can't very well offer this explanation. It reveals a plot to kill the governor."

"He deserves it," I muttered.

"Even so, I can't report the facts."

"You can give a half truth. The spoiled seed cake made the retainers violently ill causing them to spew their own blood. You'll just have to omit the intentional part of the story."

"Once again you've placed me in a difficult situation."

"Me! I didn't come up with this crazy scheme. Oh no! This was all Erzsi and Elizabeth and I won't be dragged into it." I tightened my lip. I'd already said too much. "If anyone is to blame, it is the lazy maid," I mumbled.

Nicholas undressed and crawled into bed. He patted the space beside him. With a blanket wrapped around my shoulders I curled up next to him. For a few moments I peacefully listened to the crackling fire and the slowing lumber of his breathing.

"They think she bathed in blood," he said.

I propped myself up on my elbow. "What? That's absurd."

"They think the discarded buckets were dirty, bloody bathwater."

"No, no, no…" I sighed. "Elizabeth was taking a bath while Erzsi mixed the batter." I paused. "Well, she did use a scoop of bathwater in the recipe, but there was no blood in it."

"Bathwater?"

"It was an ingredient for the poison." This was becoming complicated.

I laid my head on Nicholas's chest. "Elizabeth was taking a bath while Erzsi mixed the poison. Part of the ingredients was bathwater…the mixture was combined with the batter of a seed cake and cooked. The retainers ate the cake and got very sick which made them vomit blood. Bathwater and blood, they are connected but not directly," I recanted, as if it all made perfectly logical sense.

"The explanation is not helpful," Nicholas said.

"I don't see why you just can't explain that the seed cake made the retainers vomit blood. It is plausible and I'm certain can be confirmed by a doctor. It is, after all, for the most part, the truth."

Nicholas sighed and gave me a kiss atop my head. "I imagine no one will ever dare eat cake again."

"Not I! That is for certain," I said. I closed my eyes thinking that would be the end of it, but I was mistaken.

Even though Nicholas provided the explanation to the investigating guards, rumors of bathing in blood still circulated among the household and eventually made their way on the wagging tongues of the peasants into the villages below. I thought in time the silly story would lose its fascination, but again I misjudged the longevity of superstition. Admittedly, Elizabeth had done very little to dispel the rumors and her attempt at piousness was feeble and pathetic. Simply attending church on occasion was not enough to persuade the common folk of reform and penitence. Her presence had the opposite affect. Many thought her appearance was the Devil's mockery. She was a vessel through which he could enter their world. Instead of embracing the occasion, many shrieked and cowered from Elizabeth. They pulled away or retreated altogether from the church when she arrived. I urged her to repair the situation, but she dismissed the scene saying it would resolve itself in time. However, time was passing too quickly.

The Bells of Boredom

Present Day: 1628 Vienna

The relentless bells of St. Augustine rang. The singsong secession of the noise bouncing off the stone made my jaw clench. I did not want to be reminded of the time or of how long my aching body laid in bed. The tugging of the cathedral ropes was a menial task and, in my opinion, was a waste of perfectly vital energy. It was an alarm sounding over the city telling everyone to change their position, to move from one place to another and keep in step with the daily routine and demands of everyday life, but I couldn't. I was stuck in this room. I was incapable of participating even in the most mundane duties I dreaded. I was unable to conform or rebel spontaneously and denied the joy of laughing at my daringness to reject form. What would happen to the liveliness of the city if I, its sole sprite, lingered in my sick bed?

When the ringing ceased I tried to sigh, but my breath caught in my tightening chest. I expelled a gripping cough, which seized my entire body making it shake uncontrollably. Through the curtains broke what was left of the day, another reminder of time, the rising and setting sun.

The maid set a warm pot of herbal tea beside my bed.

"I don't want any tea," I scowled, my gravelly voice making my illness sound worse than it was.

"Please, Milady, the doctor insists you drink the fluids." She poured the clear liquid in a teacup and waited for me to sit up.

I took it from her calloused hand and held it beneath my nose. "It smells like cut weeds after a rainstorm." I frowned.

"Shall I squeeze some lemon?" she asked.

"I don't see how it will make any difference." I took a gulp. The water burned my raw throat. I coughed, choking on the liquid.

She handed me a handkerchief so I could wipe the spittle from my chin. "The post has arrived," she said.

"I'm in no condition to attend a party or compose a letter." I was sorry I was bedridden and quite unable of doing anything useful.

"Lady Draska sends a note wishing you wellness. Your friends are very concerned about your health," the maid said, thumbing through the stack of letters.

"Lady Draska is just fishing for something interesting to discuss in her garden group. It would be wonderful if I contracted some rare disease that required a miracle cure." I coughed again. "Her and Lady Manning will be so disappointed to hear I'm merely suffering from a common ague."

However, the ague I suffered was hardly common. In truth, it was reoccurring. My lungs would clear, but after some time I'd wake congested and fevered. I dismissed it as a bothersome effect of aging, but the doctor seemed to think my misery was more serious.

I coughed harder and in rapid succession. A trace of pink smeared my white lace handkerchief.

The maid grimaced. "You need to drink the tea," she said, eyeing the streak on the linen.

"Why don't *you* drink the tea," I muttered.

"Because I'm not sick you grouchy old coot." She pulled a letter from the middle of the pile.

"I heard that," I said, taking another sip.

"Ah, here is a letter from your dear friend Count Drugeth." She waved it around. "Shall I open it for you?"

I propped a pillow behind my back. "Yes, yes, I want to hear what he has to say. Oh I hope it is agreeable news!"

She tore the envelope and unfolded the letter. Her eyes twitched back and forth as she silently read.

"You can read, can't you?" I asked.

"Of course, Milady."

"Then please humor me and do it aloud."

Dear Lady Lorant,

I will be traveling to Vienna on business and would very much enjoy engaging your delightful company over dinner. I believe I have knowledge you will be eager to learn and feel it is the kind of news, which is best delivered in person.

"John has good news! That can only mean one thing," I said.

"Yes, he says he has good news," the maid repeated.

She was getting on my nerves. If I didn't need her during my convalescing, I would have dismissed her immediately.

"Does he mention when he'll arrive?" I asked.

She presented me with the letter.

"Oh dear. What if I am not well by then?"

She stuffed another pillow behind my back. "This gives you incentive to follow the doctor's orders."

I scowled. She was right. If I wanted to be well when John arrived then I'd have to diligently drink my blasted tea and get plenty of rest.

"I'm also to tell you that a messenger sent over papers."

"What papers?" I asked.

"Papers to get your affairs in order."

"I'm not dying! I've merely got a cough," I said.

"No one believes you are dying. It is simply a precaution to ensure your estate is up to date and everything is how you wish."

"Bah! I'm old and sick and people want to make sure they get a piece before I meet my grave."

"People, Milady?"

"Those in my service, my patrons and charities, and anyone else who has been kind to me these past years."

The maid tidied up the room before clearing the tea tray. "Perhaps you should leave everything to Count Drugeth. You seem very fond of him," she teased.

"Mind your tongue," I scolded. I shooed her out the door. "And when you come back to irritate me some more, bring me my writing instruments and manuscript."

I was wholly aware I needed my rest, but if John was coming soon and bringing with him the good news, then I had to hold up my end of the bargain. But, what if it was not *the news* I was hoping for, what if John was coming to tell me something else? He would not dare bait me. He must know the only news I wished to hear was that of his engagement to Kate.

God willing, he'd better have severed his ties to that awful betrothed beast. I recalled the evening of our last outing. It had been the night of the performance; the same night John introduced me to Kate. Although not formally, John had also introduced me to the *other* woman pitted to be in his life. He had pointed out the plump Fanny Fugedy. She was purposefully wedged between her doting mother and a rising Hapsburg. The poor girl was frightfully homely and I could not help but feel sorry for the creature, but not enough to wish John be bound to share his life with her. And her mother! What a nightmare that woman must be! Of course, I was not friendly with the family, but I'd seen enough of their kind in my time to imagine just how they were; reliant on title and money to get whatever they wanted and whomever they wanted.

I made an aggressive attempt to clear my lungs. Time changed many things, but some things managed to remain the same despite progress, I thought. I shifted my weight, turning on my side to relieve the stiffness growing in my back. I was confounded about the concept of progress. I was pondering again. Still at my age I did not fully understand how a single event could have a tremendous effect when numerous attempts often had little impact. What set a situation apart and what separated the efforts? I shook my head, recalling the many schemes Elizabeth devised over the years. Some successful, but many were terrible failures that never came to be known or ended how we intended. I suppose that is the crutch of scheming; it is a play of wits met by counter strategies. Or, was it just luck?

I did not feel lucky lying in my bed, old and alone. I was somehow spared all these years, and for what? So I could wither with only my memories to keep me company, and oh what fond memories they were! It was natural to believe my being alive was to serve a greater purpose, but what if it was meaningless -- life that is? The thought was too much to bear. I was not ready to accept death was determined by chance; that our end was determined through no rhyme or reason and that I was simply the last flower to be randomly plucked from the earth. Even though it was the more plausible conclusion since I was the least superior and insignificant posy in the bunch, it was still too depressing to admit. Self-importance was all I had left to own, or at least the illusion of it, and I was not about to give it up or allow it to be taken away. Not yet, no, not just yet!

Charlie Courtland

Raid on the New Year

I am certain, Countess Bathory. She is the informant we've been looking for. She told Reverend Janos about the tunnel and led him to the entrance. She was able to get word to the reverend, telling him we were coming to inquire. She helped him flee so he could get his letter to the governor," Ficzko said, proudly. It had taken him a long while, but his persistence prevailed and finally he was able to provide his beloved countess with the name of the guilty party.

"What was her motive?" I asked.

Elizabeth threw a plate against the wall. The porcelain bits crashed to the floor. "I don't care about motive! Nothing the girl can say will spare her now. She's had her chance and refused to come forward and confess to her betrayal."

Elizabeth was unnerved. Everything was coming undone and the details of the mounding accusations against her were reaching the castle. Unbelievable testimonies were being heard in front of Parliament and with each lie spoken her future grew dimmer.

"She is the reason for bringing this all down upon my head!" Elizabeth wheeled around, her eyes full of rage and her fists balled by

433

her side. "She dares threaten me? Who is she to place my life in danger!"

When Elizabeth was worked into a tantrum she had the kind of voice that rumbled from the gut and boomed through the halls. Her words traveled far, reaching every ear of the lurking servants. I hated when she shouted like this, and even though I should have been used to it by now, the shrill made me tremble. I remained still except for the shaking of my hands, which I gripped tightly, folding them carefully on my lap. It'd do no good to protest. The girl was as good as dead.

Elizabeth dabbed the sweat beading on her brow. "Where is she now?"

Ficzko wrung his baby-sized hands. "Kata has the girl restrained in the washer room."

Without further delay, Elizabeth stormed out of the room. Of course, we all fell in line taking great care to match her pace as we rushed through the castle toward the room where the dirty laundry lay in sorted heaps.

Among the hanging sheets and beaten rugs was the girl. Stripped down with her hands tied behind her back, she awaited judgment. She was not frail like the others—she was a Croatian girl with a sturdy frame and healthy breasts. I always noticed, since my own breasts were inferior and my petite stature gave me a girlish appearance even in my advancing age. She whelped with embarrassment when we entered the room, rolling her shoulders and turning to the side to shield her privates from being viewed, but no position would hide her nakedness. It was pathetic to even try, and the poor posturing only seemed to enrage Elizabeth more. Without hearing a single plea, Elizabeth grabbed the first weapon available, a wooden club used to beat the dirt from the carpets.

She swung, delivering a harsh blow. The girl stumbled, but did not fall. Then another blow, then another and another. Elizabeth beat her with the club over and over until she could hardly lift the weapon from exhaustion. The smacking of flesh sounded like tenderizing meat and no matter how repulsive the scene got, I could not avert my eyes. I was stunned that the girl now beaten from head to toe refused to die. She clung to life mumbling what sounded like a prayer as Elizabeth paused to regain strength.

Elizabeth's dress was drenched in sweat and splattered with blood spray. She motioned for Kata to retrieve her a clean dress before she resumed delivering justice. She straightened her hair and ordered the girl be brought to her feet. The bruised and blooded Croat swayed on her hobbled limbs, her eyes swollen and nose crushed as she defied death. Elizabeth swung again, the blow sending blood spewing from the girl's gaping, puffy mouth. I thought that was it, that it must finally be over, but the girl still breathed. I'd never seen anything like it before; I'd never seen someone able to hold on to life for so long. I just wanted her to die—I just wanted it to be over. As long as she breathed, justice was not served.

I watched as the blows kept coming and the sound of smacking filled my ears. This pile of robust flesh was responsible for putting my own life in jeopardy. This singular being managed to bring trouble to our door making us vulnerable to the cruel world, our world that was very different from hers. How dare she, how dare she threaten and trouble me with fear! This was my home and this was my existence and how it was spent was not for her to decide. And now, because of her, I might lose the little I held dear and, because of her, the man I despised the most was coming. I'd have to curtsey beneath his smugness and honor him with polite grace while enduring his snide comments and demeaning slights. When all was said and done he'd muster the will to deliver his own judgment and sentence. It wouldn't be as humane as a beating or a slit to the throat. No, Thurzo would make us suffer long and hard. His justice would be much worse because we were certain to live through it.

"Why doesn't she die!" I screamed. "What is she hanging on for?"

Elizabeth stopped mid swing.

"Stop being so willful. There is nothing much here to live for so why don't you just die already!" I yelled at the girl.

The girl was so maimed that even if she wanted to provide an answer, she was incapable of forming a sound except for a low gurgling in her throat. If I had not heard the tiny groan I would have believed she were dead, but that damned rattle mocked me and I knew she was not yet finished. She hung on and clung with determination to life. I hated her bravery. I hated everything she stood for at that particular moment.

I pushed passed Ficzko and snatched a pair of scissors from the sewing table. He tried to prevent me, but I easily shoved his runt of a body out of my way. With the scissors raised above my head and firmly griped in my hand, I charged at the girl. Fueled by the anger of every injustice I suffered, I stabbed the Croat. I expelled the hatred I felt for everyone and unleashed my wrath repeatedly upon her mutilated flesh. With all my strength I forced the scissors into her skin and yanked them back out again, only to thrust them once more. Blood whipped from the sharpened tips and rained against the drying white sheets hanging overhead. I yelled for her to die and stabbed until I could no longer lift my arm high enough to deliver another blow. I collapsed on the floor, letting the scissors slip from my fingers and clank upon the stone.

"Just die…just die…" I whimpered.

I felt a hand on my shoulder. It was Elizabeth. She was offering consolation, or was it congratulations? There was a ringing in my ears and it drowned out the voices speaking behind me. I stumbled to my feet and wiped my bloodied hands on my soiled skirt. A pungent irony smell overwhelmed the air and I tasted salt on my dry lips.

I parted the lurking audience and in a daze walked to the safest place I knew, Nicholas waiting arms. I entered the room and crumbled against his chest. I sobbed, gripping the edge of his shirt in my clutched hands. I felt some relief by confessing to him what I had done and after some time my sobs dried and I was calm. I slipped out of my bloodied clothes and tossed them in the fire. The threads burned turning to ash. All evidence was history, and with each cleansing swipe of my bath cloth, so was the remaining trace of the Croatian girl. It was arrogant to think I could wash her existence so cleanly away. The memory of her will was permanently imprinted on my mind and the daringness of her effort to betray the countess forever changed the course of events. Through a single, insignificant being's actions our future was compromised. She had accomplished something in her life, albeit perhaps not what she wished, but her death was not in vain and she, whether I liked it or not, would not be forgotten.

The horrid scene disappeared beneath the veil of night. In the darkness I curled my leg around Nicholas as the winter air blew periodically, pressing its force across the courtyard. There was peacefulness in the rhythm of the wind and I did not mind the whistling sound it made when it squeezed through the small cracks in the door. I was exhausted and my limbs felt heavy and sore as I tried to sleep.

Nicholas sat up abruptly. His sudden movement startled me and I too, bolted upright.

"What is it?" I whispered.

"Did you hear something?" He was listening for a noise to repeat in the distance.

"It's just the wind," I said, relaxing a bit.

He did not settle, instead, he swung his feet off the bed and planted them on the floor.

"You're scaring me," I said, tugging at his arm.

"Shhh! I'm trying to listen."

I moved away and leaned against the wall. All I heard was the wind.

Nicholas dressed quickly and went to the door. He eased it open a slight crack and pressed his face to the edge.

I wanted to ask what he saw, but I knew it best to remain quiet.

Carefully, he shut the door and backed away without making a sound.

"Get dressed," he whispered.

My arms were instantly covered in goose flesh and my hairs stood straight up. Seeing Nicholas on guard made me immediately alert. I scrambled to my clothes and layered them on for warmth. He tossed me my boots and I laced them quickly. Together we left his quarters and slithered in the familiar shadows looming near the main house. In the distance I saw the faint flicker of torchlight and heard what I thought was the crunching sound of footsteps in the snow. Whomever it was moved stealthy towards the castle, rapidly approaching.

Nicholas was squeezing my hand as he protectively led me away from the barracks. A few more guards emerged and motioned to Nicholas to join them.

"What is going on?" a man asked.

"I am not certain," Nicholas answered.

"Should I sound the alarm?"

Before Nicholas could answer, another guard came running through the snow towards us. I recognized him as a tower guard. "It is not an enemy army," he said waving his arms.

The tension in Nicholas's grip loosened and my fingers tingled.

"How'd they penetrate the gate?" Nicholas asked, watching the flashes of light cross the courtyard just along the horizon.

"We lifted it for them."

"Upon whose order?"

The man pulled Nicholas away by the arm. "Upon Count Thurzo's, under the order of his majesty."

Hearing the utterance of Count Thurzo's name sent my pulse racing.

"Our own people are raiding the castle. We are to stand down until ordered otherwise."

"Nicholas! I have to get to Elizabeth," I said, shoving by the men gathering in front of me.

He grabbed a hold of me by the waist. "No, you must stay here."

"But, I must warn her…"

The booming impact of the breaking down of the front door killed the peaceful night.

"It's too late, they are in," Nicholas said, turning his attention in the direction of the main house.

The rest of the party moved quickly through the courtyard and disappeared through the grand entryway of the castle. Some of the men stayed behind to guard the exit while others rushed around the back to secure other means of escape.

"What is going to happen?" I cried. The sight was frightening and I was terribly worried.

"I'm not sure. It depends on what they are looking for and what they will find," Nicholas said. He was intently watching the raid from the safe distance of the archway leading to the guard quarters.

I had a good idea of what they were looking for, and the nervous twinge pinging in the pit of my stomach suggested they'd find it. I had to stop them, and if I couldn't, the least I could do was get to Elizabeth. I broke free of Nicholas's protective hold and ran along the path leading to the kitchen door.

"No, Amara...wait," I heard Nicholas call. He was taking chase and I knew it was only a matter of time before he'd catch me.

"Let me go, Nicholas," I cried, feeling his footsteps closing in on me.

He tackled me and together we tumbled and rolled in the snow. "It's for your own good," he huffed, pinning me to the ground.

As I lay panting in the snow I heard the shouts of the men raiding the castle.

"It is secure!" a man shouted.

"Stay still," Nicholas whispered.

Tears streamed down my cheeks and the cold dampness was spreading through the wool of my overcoat. Nicholas helped me up from the ground. Just then a bright light flashed in my face.

"Who goes there?" a man called out.

Nicholas brushed the snow from his arms and stood at attention. "It is I, Commander of the Guard."

"And who is with you?"

"Lady Lorant. She has been under my personal protection."

"She is not staying in the castle?"

"No, she is not."

"And she has no knowledge of the happenings within the walls?"

"No, she does not. As you can see she is going towards the castle, not away from it," Nicholas said.

"Why is the lady out at this hour?"

"She was startled by the intrusion and is concerned about the mistress. She wishes to know what is happening."

"Count Thurzo is raiding the castle as ordered by the royal investigation committee in reaction to the accusations presented recently to Parliament."

"Perhaps, I can speak to Count Thurzo?" I interrupted.

Nicholas buttoned his lip. I knew he wanted to protest, but was well aware he'd never do it in front of the other soldier.

The man escorted us through the shattered door of the main entrance. The halls were lined with men standing guard while others rummaged through Elizabeth's things in various rooms. He inquired to the whereabouts of Count Thurzo and after several gestures we were instructed to proceed toward the servants dwellings. Nausea climbed in my throat as we approached the doorway leading to the laundry room.

Standing amid the slaughtered body and rancid spray of blood speckling the ruined sheets was Count Thurzo. He held a torch to the indiscernible face of the Croat, and upon hearing our approaching footsteps rose to greet us.

"You can imagine my surprise when I stumbled over this in the dark," he said, referring to the corpse on the ground.

The guards had Kata bound and held on the other side of the room.

"What did the girl do to deserve such punishment?" Count Thurzo asked.

Nicholas pressed his hand against my side. It was his way of signaling me to remain silent.

"She stole a pear," Kata offered.

"A pear?"

"Yes, she stole a pear and many other things from Countess Bathory."

"Ah, I see." He turned the torch on me, illuminating my disinterested expression.

I gave the smallest curtsey.

The soldier who found us in the courtyard stepped forward and informed Count Thurzo that I was not staying in the castle and had no knowledge of the activities.

"Lucky for you, I already know this. I was informed before I arrived that you are no longer residing in the main house, but have chosen the comfort of a house near the guard quarters."

"You know?" I asked, surprised.

"Well of course. You didn't think your husband would let that detail go unknown, did you? When Draco heard of the accusations he was quick to write that he had removed you from the household. He was adamant about insisting that you had no involvement in the bizarre practices of the countess."

I thought I was going to be sick. Draco knew I was living with Nicholas in the guard quarters. Perhaps, this was why he delayed his visit. He knew if he came I would return to my chambers and would be suspected during the raid. I was overcome with guilt. By staying away he was protecting me, even if it meant in the interim he was losing me. I had taken his avoidance as selfishness, but it was a sacrifice.

Count Thurzo aimed his light behind me. "Where's that beast that is always trailing behind you?" He was referring to my wolf, Lyk.

"He is at my home in the guard quarter," I said. My answer providing further proof that I truly did not reside at the castle.

Count Thurzo turned his light back on the twisted lump of flesh lying on the floor. "Is there something wrong with the dungeon?" he asked.

"I wouldn't know," I answered.

Kata tried to step forward, but the restraints prevented her from doing so. "It's in terrible ruins, and quite a ways down. It's not fit for keeping."

"Not fit for a prisoner?" he asked.

"It's in ruins," she repeated.

I knew what she was doing. She was trying her best to keep Count Thurzo away from the dungeon, the workshop, and the tunnels leading to the monastery.

"Well that is something I must see with my own eyes! A dungeon not fit for a prisoner," he laughed.

The other men in the room chuckled as well.

I opted to stay behind, but Count Thurzo was not about to let me out of his sight. Reluctantly, I followed the party into the kitchen and to the door that lead to the descending staircase. I took a torch from the wall and began the grueling journey of 150 feet below the earth. With each step, the damp air brought with it a chill. The fetid stench of the narrowing passage conjured displeasing memories. The rot was an ill sign and my heart sank with the anticipation of mortal disaster. I knew the smell well, it was decay mingled with the scent of herbs and boiling potions.

Once at the bottom of the stairs, Count Thurzo paused. He sniffed the stale air. "Good lord, what is that smell?"

Several other men sniffed, they were all trying to distinguish what the rank odor was and where it was coming from. I pulled a handkerchief from my pocket and held it to my nose. I had to play along as if I were offended and quite unfamiliar with the place.

"This is no place for a lady," Nicholas begged.

"Nonsense! Every woman should see this so they will know where they do not wish to end up." Count Thurzo motioned for a group of men to go toward the dungeons, then he turned in the opposite direction. "I wonder what is this way?" he said, waving a man ahead.

Nicholas sensed my growing tension.

"Brace yourself, this is not going to be pleasant," I whispered. I was praying Elizabeth's henchman tipped her off and everything had been stashed away. However, the dead body in the laundry led me to believe she had been caught very much by surprise. Now, all I could hope for was that she'd escaped and was far away somewhere safe.

We had reached the end and were standing face-to-face with an iron-spiked door. Count Thurzo twisted the latch and threw it open.

Crouched over a stool was a woman. She turned hissing at the intruders who threatened her private space. "You will pay for this intrusion," she shouted. Her hair hung in a frenzied tangle down her back and her hands were covered in mashed herbs that she'd been kneading in a bowl.

"Oh on the contrary, Countess. May I remind you I am the Palatine Governor and I have come to deliver justice to these accursed walls."

Thurzo's appointed authorities pushed their way in swarming the space and surveying the scene. The carnage dusted in cinder ash littered the floor and bottles of mysterious fluids crowded the shelves.

"I demand to know what you are conjuring!" Count Thurzo asked, eyeing the bowls of potions sitting on the worktable.

"I'd offer you a taste, but I'm afraid you'd refuse."

"Take her into custody. I want her locked in her chamber and the entire castle searched."

Elizabeth screamed and fought as the men grabbed her by the arms and forced her from the workshop.

"You are fortunate it was I who came instead of the king himself!" Count Thurzo shouted after her. He took out a handkerchief and wiped the perspiration from his forehead. He walked over to a bowl and stuck his finger in the dark liquid. He held it up, shoving his finger beneath a guard's nose. "What is this?"

The man sniffed and shook his head. "I believe it is blood."

Appalled, Count Thurzo wiped his finger with his handkerchief and tossed it on the floor.

Elizabeth was taken to her room and locked inside. The rest of her entourage including Erzsi and Ficzko were rounded up and put under arrest. They were shackled and stuffed in holding wagons and swept down the mountain before the break of dawn. I was ordered to return to my quarters and wait for further instruction. Nicholas followed shortly, and informed me I was to remain with him until word was received from my husband. This was the end. This was the last time I'd see Elizabeth. I could not imagine how she would triumph. There was not a card left in her hand to play – it was finally over.

Nicholas sat in his chair with one leg draped over the other and his arms folded across his chest. The pulsing in his clenched jaw was a sure sign of his irritation and his posturing indicated he was not going to budge until I explained. He was waiting for answers and despite my distress I was going to have to give them to him.

"It's not exactly how it seems," I began. "The mess in the laundry room, well, I did that." I paced across the floor. "Elizabeth started it, but by using a club...I'm afraid I'm the one who finished it." I bit my thumbnail. "I killed her with scissors."

I expected shock, but Nicholas managed to maintain the same stern look so I continued. "I was in no condition to clean it up. You saw me. I was dazed—I've confessed all this to you. You'd think the servants would do their job, but I guess they had better things to do this evening. I can't believe Kata left that mess," I mumbled.

Nicholas shifted uncomfortably in his seat.

I put my hands on my hips. "That girl, she was the person who told the reverend about the tunnels under the monastery and spoke of misdoings in the castle which got him poking around. If it weren't for her, the reverend would never have found the tomb and the pine crates and he certainly would not have discovered the remains." I shut up. I remembered Nicholas had no idea what I was rambling on about, but it was too late, I'd already said too much.

I sighed. "Remember the Turks, the soldiers that came here long ago?"

Nicholas nodded. Of course he did. That wasn't a scene a person soon forgot.

I explained how I found the passage and tomb beneath the monastery. I even confessed finding the spikes and maps along with stacks of pine wood coffins.

"Tepes must have hid supplies and possessions below the monastery. It makes sense, and it fits with what we know about his tactics." He tapped his chin. "And you discovered this bit of treasure?"

I shrugged.

"Men have been looking for ages and it's been here the entire time?"

I shrugged again. "You know how Elizabeth was upset by the denial of her deed, well, she decided she'd store some of the Turk's remains just in case she needed evidence as a bargaining chip...the pine boxes were empty, so she stuck the bodies in there."

"How many?"

"I told her to get rid of them, but I doubt she listened. She never listens to me even when she knows I'm right and look where it's got her!"

"How many, Amara?"

"Nine, maybe more. Surely, it can be explained. They are Turks, after all, even though you can't really tell that anymore."

Now it was Nicholas's turn to sigh. He was thinking the same thing I originally thought. It didn't really matter if they were Turks. Count Thurzo could say they were the bodies of anyone and no one could attest or disprove the validity of the claim.

"Elizabeth's pleasure chamber looks different than I last remember. What is she doing down there?" he asked.

"It's scientific. She's attempting to discover a recipe that will slow aging. She's working on a beauty potion."

"The blood was not blood?"

I winced. "That I'm not sure of. It very well could be. Erzsi led her to believe virgin blood is the key ingredient to solving the riddle of the aging process."

"Virgin blood?" he asked, astonished.

"Noble virgin blood to be precise." I put up my hand to stop him from speaking. I knew what he was about to ask.

"She didn't kill those girls. They offered small amounts of blood in return for her kindness and advantage. It was an *arrangement* of sorts. Well, at least that is what she thought, but the first group got squeamish and ran off." I sat on the bed and folded my legs in a blanket. "Erzsi decided it was best not to use true noble girls, so she had Ficzko fetch common girls from the villages. They were washed and dressed and passed off to Elizabeth as noble subjects. The plan worked. The peasant girls were much more docile and willing to indulge the countess."

"Humm…I get the feeling there is more."

I explained how some of the girls were not healthy and got sick or died from infection.

I tugged the blanket up under my chin. "Maybe we should go away tonight. What if Count Thurzo changes his mind and decides I am involved and should be punished. I am just as guilty, but under the law do not have the same protection."

"Nothing is going to happen to you."

I expressed my objection and the more I talked, the more I worked myself into hysterics. I couldn't rely on Count Thurzo keeping his word. He'd change it just as suddenly as a spring wind if it benefited.

Nicholas listened, quite unmoved by my protest.

At first I was too self absorbed by my own concern to notice his lack of interest.

"Wait, how do you know nothing is going to happen to me?" I said after I calmed down.

"Count Thurzo said your husband wrote."

"And that is good enough for you? You trust him?"

Now it was Nicholas's turn to feel uncomfortable.

I crossed my arms. "Nicholas, you better speak now or I swear!"

"Let's just say Draco and I have an *arrangement* of our own."

"You have his blessing?" I asked.

"In a manner of speaking..." Nicholas began.

I choked out a sob. I clapped a hand over my mouth. The thought of Draco knowing was one thing, but the idea of him agreeing was quite another. The rejection burned straight through and the reality of my childish little fantasy came crashing down. Did no one love me for me? Nicholas was a hired suitor, or worse yet, he'd been *ordered* to do what he did by a superior officer. It had all been a dramatic seduction, or rather an incredible farce that I fell headlong into.

"I loved you," I said, the words rolling pathetically off my tongue.

"You say it as if it is in the past."

"Don't play me a bigger fool!"

"Please, let me explain...I've wanted to for so long, but I just didn't know how," he said.

I wanted to scream, I wanted to punch and kick, but all I did was sit stupidly on the bed.

"Draco knew what was going on by the letters you sent. He was concerned you'd be swallowed up in it. He couldn't be here to protect you, so he asked if I would keep you safe and close. He knew my proximity might stir feelings, but he was willing to take the risk if it meant ensuring your safety—we are trying to preserve your life."

"Why didn't he just take me away?"

"Removing you from Elizabeth's company would draw attention. Believe it or not, he didn't want anything to happen to her either."

"This can not be real. This is not happening," I said.

Nicholas joined me on the bed and took my hand in his. "What I feel for you is very real. Draco had a right to be concerned. I did become attached. I have feelings for you…my love is real and I am so sorry this *is* happening. If I could change things somehow, I would, but we must move forward from here. This is not the time to dwell or argue. I think it is best if we stick together." He spoke like a true soldier by determining it was necessary to unite forces to provide a strong front. However, two people holding hands provided a meek barrier when pitted against a sea of governmental powers and a book of laws. Even with Draco on my side and his influence with the king, I was easily sacrificial. The Bathory's would toss as many bodies forward in order to retain their property holdings, preserve their good name and please the king.

I should have stormed out. I should have rejected them all and defended my bruised heart, but I was tired…exhausted and shamefully felt I had no other place to run.

"What is to become of me?" I asked. My head fell against Nicholas firm shoulder.

"I will stay with you. I suppose Draco will make arrangements and when you leave, I presume I will go too."

"And Elizabeth?"

"Her family will take care of her. Perhaps you can find some consolation in the notion you are finally free," he added.

I didn't feel free. I felt more trapped and alone than ever. Nothing belonged to me, there was nothing I determined or possessed, not even my secret love. The sparing of my life was irrelevant. I thought of the Croatian girl who had fought so hard to remain in this world. She braved it all on her own and had lost in the end, but at least she had tried. I wrapped my arms around my knees and hugged them to my chest. I was ashamed. I thought I had defied convention and taken charge of my meager position, but to my surprise someone else had been pulling the puppet strings all along.

"I am a hideous burden," I said.

Nicholas kissed my forehead. "You are an exotic rare flower worth worshipping for eternity."

He meant this as a sincere compliment, but given my mood I was less than flattered. It was true, I was from a far away place, and I had been striking and colorful. It was difficult for me to thrive in the suffocating surroundings of nobility, but I was not exotic or particularly interesting and valuable. I was rare, by the thinnest definition. It was my husband who I owed that to. He was the unique asset—he was the unique breed in the king's precious collection. I was a woman in late bloom, my petals browning around the edges and the attractiveness of my body withering with each passing year. I closed my eyes picturing an eccentric, exotic plant trapped under glass in the middle of a hot house. It was there to be admired and revered, but did it miss its natural environment?

Instead of a pedestal on display, I saw an ugly glass dome trapped behind more ugly iron paned glass through which the cream of society pressed their perfect faces against. How I resented the illusive eyes and puckered lips of all those awful painted people marveling at my imaged flower. They snickered about the glorious wonder and greedily schemed about how to get one for themselves.

Abstract thoughts fragmented through my mind. The illusion was an illusion, and what I thought was up, was now down, but it was not just the people, it was also the landscape. It too was meant to elude. The pretty houses and gated garden with framed hothouse filled with oddities aided as a distraction to hide the ugliness of our way of life. It was all a ridiculous disguise, a bunch of fluff to conceal the bars on the windows put there to prevent enemies from getting in, and woman from getting out. I wanted to pick up a rock and smash my imagined scene and free the captive flower from its keeper. I wanted to smash it to pieces and watch it rain, for I'd always known it was an illusion, I'd seen it all for what it was including the ugliness. Perhaps that is why Elizabeth preferred Cachtice to the other places; it was the truest of illusions. It was as real as it got.

448

I thought my instinct was to fight, but at the moment all I wanted to do was surrender, so that is what I did. I surrendered to the fate I was dealt and the circumstances placed before me. Everything was already in motion and spinning well ahead of me. I was a fool running behind trying to catch up, to catch my breath, but I'd never be able too. I'd never break free or take hold, so I did what fate knew I would, I surrendered—or was I merely cracking?

"What now?" I asked, defeated. The fight was gone and my shoulders slumped under the heaviness I carried.

Nicholas looked through the glassy water filling my eyes. He was not marveling at what he saw, he was reaching out to cherish me in an entirely different way. I saw that now, and I believed every word he spoke that night to me—I had too. What other choice did I have? So when I finally gave in, it was to him.

In the Interest of Justice

The trial began on January 2, 1611. The gallery was jammed with eager ears waiting to savor every last shocking detail of the clan's gruesome practices. Given the rumors surrounding the case, Elizabeth was referred to by her adversaries as the 'Blood Countess' and kept from the proceedings.

Despite the spectacle and the overwhelming demand to get a glimpse of the infamous countess, Count Thurzo managed to secretly arrange that Elizabeth not be brought to a public trial. I was not privy to the particulars, but was informed Elizabeth was to be tried purely on a criminal basis and the charges against her would not include: vampirism, witchcraft or practicing paganism. Those titles were reserved and pinned on her cohorts. It did not matter whether it was true or not. It was merely out of consideration for the family. They had worked tirelessly, intervening on her behalf, which was primarily attributed to their self-serving character. The family flew into a writing campaign requesting leniency and begged that the charges against the countess be lessened. Dearest Paul even pleaded for Elizabeth's release since he was the rightful heir and had the most to lose if the court ruled against his mother. Count Thurzo ensured everyone that the charges against Elizabeth would be reduced and, as a result, property would not be confiscated – but nothing could be done about the debt. It was a compromise. The family maintained their holdings and, with it, Count Thurzo got his adjacent estates while the king was free of his debt to the family. All the monies loaned to him by Francis were erased. No one was ecstatic, but everyone was satisfied – well, everyone except Elizabeth, but her happiness did not much matter.

Seeing how someone had to be held accountable for the brutal acts, who better to blame than Elizabeth's most loyal followers. Those without title or influence were disposable and would appease the audience by serving justice. Besides, they were an odd little bunch snatched from the edges of society and their very appearance spooked the more civilized. No longer under Elizabeth's protection, the foursome was fed to the God fearing elite who were only too happy to purge the earth of the heathens.

Oddly, given the mounting evidence available for display, including the skeletal remains found in the pine coffins, the most damning evidence presented was a bound journal discovered conveniently stashed in Elizabeth's chest of drawers. Scribbled on the pages was a detailed list and registered account of subjects and results. It was a log of experimentation that often ended in death and was no different from a medical record, but to the jury it was proof of ritualistic murder. I did not see how they made the leap from a list of symptoms, treatments and observations to satanic practice, but they did. If this were truly the case, then every doctor and scientist was the Devil and should be burned. I learned it did not matter what was written, it only mattered what they saw or wanted to believe. I could draw the sign of a cross on a blank page and a man could claim I was a saint or another could state I was a sinner mocking the church for my own pleasure. There was no real justice—it was a dangerous game and we were out of turns and Elizabeth's cronies were powerless pawns taking the fall.

The testimonies of her accomplices were recorded and their sentences pronounced. Erzsi was accused and found guilty of unlawfully disposing bodies for a fee. For her heinous act, she was sentenced to death. The witch screamed and hurled curses when she was dragged from the gallery to an awaiting cell. Her outburst frightened the audience and many ran to the local church to be blessed before returning home.

Kata and Dorothea were found guilty of practicing pagan rituals and sentenced to have all their fingers torn out. Since their hands were their instruments of evil, it was necessary to sever them from their bodies. Without fingers, the pair could do no more harm to the innocent and unassuming. A public executioner armed with red-hot pincers ripped the women's fingers from their hands and dropped them one by one into a bronze pot. Their cries were lost in the whooping and hollering of the crowd gathering in the city square. If they survived, then it was by God's mercy and their lives would be spared, but mercy never came. The women bled profusely from the wounds and when all was drained, they collapsed on the stage.

After a monumental speech about sin, the governor ordered their bodies be tossed on the pyre. However, he acted too hastily by assuming they were dead when in fact, Kata and Dorothea were merely passed out from loss of blood and when their flesh hit the flames the women thrashed. Engulfed by fire and screaming, they burned alive and turned into a heap of ash. Again, it was evident to everyone the women had indeed been witches – because a righteous person could not bleed and return to life. No, it was obvious that only the damned could conjure such a scene.

Lastly, Elizabeth's little pet, her beloved dwarf Ficzko was brought forward. He was despised most of all because his appearance was hideous and twisted. He was a mutation of God's creation and did not deserve to exist in the first place. His head was placed on the chopping block and, with a swift swing of the executioner's axe, he was decapitated. As a precaution the governor ordered his blood be drained and his tiny body burned. All his parts were separated so there'd be no chance that the dwarf demon might rise again.

I stood on a balcony overlooking the city square and wondered how it was I had escaped. Draco was watching from his post while Nicholas secured my carriage. I was there to witness, like all the other lords and ladies, when in truth I should have been

Charlie Courtland

burned and tossed aside, but God was merciful and through his grace I had been spared.

Count Thurzo stepped forward on the stage and took a parchment roll from his pocket. He carefully untied the ribbon and unfolded the judgment. I held my breath. Although she denied the charges made against her and all requests to make her plea before Parliament where rejected, Elizabeth was found guilty of lesser crimes and a sentence was about to be delivered.

Thurzo cleared his throat and waited for the clamoring of the crowd to die down. "Countess Elizabeth Bathory!" he boasted. Heads turned and the crowd murmured. I half expected to see my mistress emerge from the shadows, but after several moments she did not appear.

"You are like a wild animal," he boomed. A hush fell over the shuffling crowd. "You are in the last months of your life and a jury has determined you do not deserve to breathe the air on this earth, nor shall you be allowed to view the light of our dear Lord. It is in our judgment that you shall disappear from this world and shall never reappear in it again. The shadows will envelop you and you will be given time to repent your bestial life. Countess Elizabeth Bathory, the court condemns you to a life of imprisonment in your own castle."

I gasped. Sentenced to spending the remaindered of her life at Cachtice? How was this any different? She'd already been sentenced to do that! I scoffed. "Not such a terrible punishment," I said, leaning towards the lord standing beside me. "I do not much care for the place, but the countess is content at Cachtice."

"I imagine she will not approve of the renovations which are planned," he snickered.

"Renovations?" I asked.

He put a gloved hand to the side of his mouth. "A crew of stonemasons are walling up a room in the tower. That is where she will remain until she dies."

"She will not be allowed to roam the grounds?" I asked, shocked.

"Oh heavens no! She is condemned to a cell in her own ruined castle. Dreadful, isn't it! From my understanding a room at the king's prison would provide better accommodations."

I gripped the man's sleeve. "How do you know this?" I asked.

The lord's hat was tipped to shade his eyes and face. His mouth was hidden beneath a curling moustache and pointed beard. He gestured for me to follow him to a private place behind a column. Something about the man was familiar. Was it the curling moustache? Perhaps it was in the eyes.

"Tell me, tell me how you know this!" I said, in a stern, but low voice.

He pushed the brim of his hat off his forehead. "I got word from Anna. She's been writing often and insisted I come."

I took a closer look. "Lord Buckley? Is it you?" I asked, shocked.

"In disguise," he answered, with a curt little bow. "Now, shhhh! Before someone hears you." He glanced around, but no one was paying much attention.

I stifled a laugh. "You look just like Vlad Tepes with that moustache and pointy beard," I teased.

He cocked a silly smile. "I thought it befitting of the occasion."

I turned serious again. "Anna is in touch?"

"Ah, she is a cunning woman. A perfect go-between able to play both sides," he said, proudly.

"Oh, that is much too dangerous. You should never allow her to do such a thing."

"As if I could stop her. She is her mother's daughter and evidently she's got a bit of my blood in her too." He shrugged.

I wondered if he were referring to his actual blood or the blood of the character he was portraying. Either way, it was undeniable.

"Now what?" I asked. I eyed a couple passing. They were engaged in polite conversation and did not give us a second look.

Lord Buckley offered me his arm. "I'm going to the party. Care to join me?"

"What? Going to a party!"

"Well, I didn't get all dressed up for nothing – this is an execution after all, there is always a party to follow."

"You can't be serious?" I asked.

"Oh you know me better than that! Of course I am serious. Besides, there is no better place to scheme than at a party." He leaned near my ear and whispered, "Everyone knows that."

"You have a plan then?" I wrapped my arm around his and began strolling towards court.

"There is always a *plan*, my dear. The difficulty is in the execution."

I giggled. It could not be helped. It was just like Lord Buckley to make a play on words, especially at a time like this. I gave him a good squeeze. "Why are you doing this?" I asked.

"As a favor to my daughter."

"Ah! It is for Anna then? We took a turn by the fountain. "You do know Elizabeth hates you?" I reminded.

"Nonsense! The woman adores me. Why else would she go to such lengths to make me miserable?"

"Did you marry?"

He stopped and adjusted his hat again. "I've got my eye on a wealthy countess," he said with a wink.

***

Lord Buckley collected intelligence while Anna and her husband mingled among the politicians. We agreed to meet in secret after everyone was asleep and compare what we'd learned that day, piecing the information together like a spotty puzzle with holes and missing edges. There was a picture, but it was unclear and imperfect. We knew the order was to wall up a tower at Cachtice. We just did not know when the transfer was to occur and who would be in attendance. We determined Anna would be responsible for acquiring the information since she was the eldest daughter and her inquiry would raise the least concern.

"Do you think they will let all of us attend to say our good-byes?" I asked.

"The family will be allowed and I suppose Draco and me can participate since we are part of the royal guard, but the rest of you will need to be in disguise," Nicholas said.

"What about me? How am I to get close enough?" I asked.

Nicholas shook his head. "I'm afraid they will not let you – someone else will have to switch places and take up your task."

"I can't ask anyone else to do what I must!" I said.

Every player in the room glanced from one person to the other.

Anna stepped forward. "I will do it," she said.

"Oh no, Anna, I can't ask you to do it."

Anna walked over and took my hands in hers. She looked straight into my eyes and held me there. "Remember what mother once said? She told me self-preservation can be a dirty chore and, in the absence of my father, the welfare of the family and the burden of taking care fell upon her."

I remembered that night. The night Anna discovered Elizabeth's workshop and witnessed the justice being delivered. How could I forget the young girl crouched in the iron cage swinging from the chain attached to the ceiling? The crackling of the girl's bones and raining of blood pattering on the floor was scorched in my memory.

"I was just a girl at the time and I was frightened that I'd never be as strong as mother; that if the time should come I'd never be able to protect my family like she was capable of doing."

I pressed her hand between mine. "Oh, Anna, you shouldn't have too."

"You told me that when the time came that I must find the courage or I would die. You said that I would not survive in this land if I were not willing to do what I must."

"What I said was much too harsh," I answered. "I'd no right to speak those words to you."

"You spoke the truth, Amara, and I respect you for that. Now, the time has come and I must find the courage or my mother will die. I am not willing to let that happen. Not yet. I won't let her down – she's fought too long and hard to be forgotten and left to rot in some damp stone cell."

"It is settled then," Nicholas said.

"No, I can't let her do this," I protested.

"We have no choice," Anna said.

"It will change you forever. You'll never be the same—never again," I pleaded.

"I have the courage. It is in my blood to do so and to find the will to help my family and save my people. It is my destiny, I understand that now."

"It is not your destiny! Your destiny is to live civilized in marriage and have children and drink tea like every other high-born noble woman."

Anna shook her head in disagreement rejecting the path I was desperately pushing her down.

"Let me try. Let me try to get close," I begged.

"We can't risk failing," Nicholas urged.

I hated knowing he was right, and I didn't want to admit it. I didn't want to put Anna in any kind of danger. Worse yet, I didn't want her to live with the burden and experience and the change that would occur inside her heart. A person could not commit such acts and return unchanged. It was impossible. I was already damaged. I should be the one to endure the final chore. It was my duty, my responsibility to carry it out, not Anna's. "I will not hear of this!" I shouted.

Anna dropped my hand. "It has already been decided and the wheels are in motion," she said.

I rubbed my temple. The pounding in my head was excruciating and I could not concentrate. There had to be another way, there just had to be!

Nicholas poured himself a drink. "We are out of time. I've received word we leave tomorrow for Cachtice."

"Tomorrow?" I asked, surprised.

"The lack of notice is quite deliberate. Count Thurzo sprung it on us to ensure we'd have little time to think of anything clever. He knows we remain loyal to Elizabeth and is doing everything possible to make certain we are docile."

"It is settled then. We will go forward with the plan," Anna replied. The sternness in her voice was demanding and orderly. She was ready to defend her family and was determined to prove she had the courage to do so.

The following day the carriages moved out. The family including Katelin, Anna and Count Zrinsky lead by Draco's intimate guard followed Count Thurzo toward Cachtice. Lord Buckley discretely went merrily on his way while Nicholas and I lingered, waiting for an opportune moment to switch carriages and change clothes so we could pursue the party.

I was terribly nervous because Elizabeth and I had never depended on so many for help before and, in order for our scheme to succeed, everyone had to execute perfectly; the timing had to be precise, the cues flawless and the portrayals believable. If one person faltered, it was over. I did not like the intangibles. I knew enough to know a person could not plan for everything, could not control every aspect of the game and therefore, nothing was absolute.

The Last Act

D isguised as common folk, Nicholas and I casually sauntered into the tavern. Sitting at a corner table was a well-dressed man dripping his charm on an unassuming woman. Her black hair was wrapped tightly in a bun and pinned neatly at the nape of her neck. Across the room I spied two ladies sharing a meal. They appeared to be mother and daughter and when I passed by, the older woman slipped me a note.

Once seated at our table, I read the note and then slide it across to Nicholas. Everything was going to plan. We ordered a drink and I gulped mine down with a startling eagerness – it was liquid courage and I needed to calm my shaky nerves. I gestured to the barmaid to bring me another and, like the previous drink, I downed it and slammed the glass on the table. That's what common folk did when they drank—they slammed things down with vigor and made crude exclamations. I wanted to fit in, so I played up the part.

I watched as the well-dressed man paid his bill and escorted the woman from the tavern. The mother and daughter followed, trailing several minutes behind. Nicholas tossed some coins on our table and slid his chair out.

"It's time," Nicholas said.

I kept my head down as we exited the establishment.

"Lord Buckley has done well," Nicholas said, as he unhitched the horse. "And it appears the others have come through."

Everyone was going through the proper motions, a unison cast executing to perfection. Even though our movements appeared blasé, they were deliberate and calculated. The mother and daughter's carriage rolled past and veered along the determined route. I mounted my horse and gave it a good kick. Riding together and carefully pursuing Lord Buckley's unmarked carriage, we turned up the road leading to Cachtice. Before we crested the horizon and came into the view of the standing guards in the tower, we slowed. Lord Buckley's carriage was pulled over on the side of the road and he was leaning against the wheel with his arms crossed.

"This is as far as I go," he called as we came to a halt.

"And the woman?" Nicholas asked. He dismounted his horse and walked over to the door of the carriage and peered inside.

"She's groggy, but she'll do. Ursula loaned us a dress. She thinks it will fit the woman," Lord Buckley answered.

"And they'll be waiting at the rendezvous point?" I asked.

Lord Buckley nodded.

Nicholas opened the carriage door and slung the drugged woman over his shoulder and carried her to the horse. With Lord Buckley's help, the men lifted the unsuspecting woman onto the horse and secured her in front of Nicholas. I stuffed Ursula's borrowed dress in my satchel and tied it to my back.

"Good luck," Lord Buckley shouted. He disappeared inside the carriage and, as it turned around, he stuck his arm out the window and waved his handkerchief as if he were a turncoat surrendering. I returned his farewell wave, but I doubted he paid much attention.

Together, we raced through the woods and across the pasture leading to the rear of the castle. I knew if we followed the course, we'd go undetected and should arrive under the cover of the overgrowth near an unguarded gate. Just to make certain we were not discovered, Draco took an extra precaution and instructed all soldiers to stand look out at the iron front and scouting towers. All their attention was being paid to the face of the castle and little regard was being given to the rear.

We tied the horses to a tree and Nicholas flung the woman over his shoulder and carried her through the back gate. Waiting on the other side was Draco. His hand twitched on the handle of his board sword as he surveyed the foliage threatening the alley near the castle wall.

"Quickly now, there is not much time," he whispered, as he waved us around the corner.

Thankfully there were few servants and most of the ceremonial parade was taking place in the main courtyard.

"Katelin has already been granted her final visit, now it is Anna's turn. We must hurry," Draco said.

We trailed behind him along the planned route to the small room. It was there that Nicholas and I hurriedly redressed the woman in Ursula's borrowed finery.

"Don't fasten it all the way up, she won't be in it long," I said. I unpinned her glossy black hair and combed it straight allowing it to hang around her drooping face. It was remarkable how much she resembled Elizabeth. Lord Buckley had exceeded my expectations and lured a stunning double into our devious trap. I slapped at the woman's face trying to revive her just enough so she could stumble along on her own. She moaned, as her head lulled to and fro, much like Elizabeth's had on her wedding day. Only there was no chapel waiting or eager groom, but a walled up cell with a poor view.

I hung back as Nicholas clumsily fumbled beneath her weight. He and Draco moved her through the corridor and around the corner. After they were out of sight, I edged closer to see if I could get a better look. Nicholas was hidden in the shadows with the woman slumping against his side. The sound of clanking boots and petite heels tapping the stone neared and within minutes I spotted Draco escorting Anna to the room followed by the prying eyes of Count Thurzo. They disappeared inside and the hall went silent except for the murmuring moans of the stirring woman. I saw Nicholas clamp his hand over her mouth and whisper something in her ear. If any man could put a lady at ease, it was Nicholas. His seductive tone was soothing and hypnotic and for the briefest second I was jealous.

Count Thurzo was the first to emerge. He slammed the door behind him and without much ceremony strutted toward the staircase leading to the main courtyard. Next, Draco exited along with several attending guards. Two of them paused outside the door ready to take up their post, but Draco instructed them to move further down the passage to give the royal family proper privacy. One of the men hesitated, noting Draco's orders did not follow protocol, but after receiving a stern look from his commander, the man did as he was told and retreated to his newly assigned position.

I fought the urge to race forward and bust into the room. Instead, I held my position and watched as Nicholas carried the half-dressed woman to the door. I heard it squeak open and gently latch shut. For what seemed an eternity the hall was quite and all I heard was the pumping of blood through my pulsating temple. Finally, Nicholas came out with the woman still dressed in Ursula's gown pinned closely to his side. The couple hurried along the passage and rounded the corner to where I was waiting.

"Hurry!" Nicholas ordered as the three of us scampered beneath the protective canopy enclosing the alley and to the back gate where our horses were tied.

I threw my arms around Elizabeth and hugged her tightly. "Are you all right?" I asked, positively out of breath.

"Yes, I think so," she said, trying to get some air into her own lungs.

"What took so long?" I asked Nicholas, as I swung my leg over my horse.

"We had some difficulty switching dresses."

"And Anna? Will she be able to manage?" A surge of panic rose in my chest as I thought about leaving her alone with the imposter. "What if she is discovered?"

Nicholas pulled on the reins turning the horses around.

I hesitated. "I don't think I can do it. I don't think I can just leave her," I said.

Elizabeth wrapped her arms around Nicholas's waist. "She can do this, Amara. You must believe in her. She's amazing. You

should have seen her. You'd be so proud. Our Anna cut out the woman's tongue. Slit it clean from her mouth in a single stroke!"
"She did what?" I asked.
"We must go now!" Nicholas urged.
"The woman won't be able to talk, nor scream or do anything to protest what has been done to her," Elizabeth explained. She was most impressed with her daughter's scruples. "They'll think she is ill and gone mad...or rather they'll think I've become ill and gone mad," Elizabeth laughed, as Nicholas snapped the reins.

Our horses galloped over the trail and along the path leading to the edge of the pasture. Before we crested the hill I paused and took a final look at Cachtice. From this vantage, it stood magnificently over the sleepy village nestled below. Built high above the other peaks on an impenetrable bed of tough limestone was a huge stone tower completely void of windows. In addition, and as part of the recent renovations, four gallows posted upright at the corners. There were not a hundred stakes impaled with the bodies of the enemy, but gallows imposed the same fright. It spoke to all who approached. The gruesome display was to symbolize to the people that justice was served. The Blood Countess was entombed in the tower where the light of the Lord would never shine again. Although her neck did not swing from the beams erected on her behalf, her life was taken, and no one would ever lay eyes on the monster again.

The final rays of the day broke through the trees and, as Elizabeth gripped Nicholas, the wind blew the silver streaked tresses of her ebony hair away from her face. I saw her as I always had; a Magyar warrior strong and wild. She was legendary in her own right, but not for the reasons she deserved.

"We still have a long journey ahead," Nicholas called out, his voice carrying before fading away. "We're not out of the woods yet. Come, Amara, we have much road to cover."

We traveled most of the night. When dawn broke we were exhausted, but had made it safely to the rendezvous. Waiting there for us was the Lavender Lady, Ursula and napping separately in his carriage was Lord Buckley.

"What are they doing here?" Elizabeth snapped, surprised by the presence of the two women and Lord Buckley.

"We couldn't have managed without their help," I said, wearily. The Lavender Lady had no expectation of loyalty to the countess and, truthfully, I quite anticipated her to reject my desperate request. I was not eager to trust an outsider, but considering the situation I felt I was left with little choice. Anna had assured me repeatedly that the women were exceptional.

Ursula handed me a clean pair of clothes and allowed me to change inside her carriage. Nicholas disappeared into the woods and dressed in his formal attire.

"I've secured rooms at a nearby inn. We can't stay long, but we should be able to get some rest and a bite to eat while we wait for the others to arrive," the Lavender Lady said.

Elizabeth edged closer, her face softening with curiosity. "Why are you helping me?" she asked, most sincere.

The Lavender Lady glanced at her daughter before returning her full attention to Elizabeth. "We are both women of circumstance. To hate you, to turn my back on you is the same as turning my back on myself, or on my beautiful daughter for that matter. Our daughters are friends and, most importantly, we are women."

"But, what I did to you, you must despise me. How many times have you wished me dead?" Elizabeth asked.

"What I did, I did to myself. I made my choices and suffered the consequences. It could have been much worse, but you were merciful."

"Merciful?" Elizabeth asked, surprised. This was not a term often associated with the countess' character.

"You gave me something you never had: a choice. I see now that it was the greatest gift, above money and marriage or fancy title." She reached for Elizabeth's hand. "Come now, we are both free."

Just then, as if on cue, Lord Buckley stirred. He put a hand to his mouth, covering a yawn. After wetting his lips, he smiled. Seeing Elizabeth he said, "Darling, you've made it! I'm so happy to see you in one piece." He glimpsed with indifference at the gathering faces, "And where's my lovely daughter?"

"Ha! Your daughter! What do you know of her? So, it was you who put her up to this?" Elizabeth asked, angrily.

He pretended like her words did not injure. "You should know best, my love. I haven't the least influence to put her up to anything."

"You didn't stop her."

"As if it would do any good to try. Both you and I know it would be a wasted effort."

"Now is not the time to bicker," Nicholas scolded as he tied the horses in line with those pulling the carriages. "Get in. We must be moving." He hurried us inside the carriages and secured the door.

I was hardly seated when the dratted thing jerked nearly sending me tumbling to the floor. I scooted over on the bench to give the other passengers room as our driver dropped behind Lord Buckley's inconspicuous coach. At a distance we trailed as we made our journey to the quaint inn slumbering in an unassuming village. Once we arrived, we agreed to take the liberty of dining privately in our room to prevent any of the patrons from recognizing someone in our party. It was a preventive measure and one we all thought was highly necessary.

The first to appear at the inn was Anna and her husband, Count Zrinsky. The clinking of nails on the floorboards outside the door alerted my attention. I stiffened, my head cocked to the side as I listened to the stirring sounds on the other side of the wall. When the door opened, the fuzzy face of my beloved wolf poked around the frame and his wet nose sniffed the air.

"Lyk!" I shrieked. I rushed over to him and threw my arms around his warm neck.

Following behind was Anna, a big smile pasted across her face. "I discovered this little stow away in my carriage when I left Cachtice. He was waiting patiently on the seat with his bag packed," she kidded.

"The ghastly beast panted in my face the entire way here," Count Zrinsky complained.

I grabbed Anna by the arm and yanked her to the sofa. "Tell us everything."

"She performed remarkably," Count Zrinsky boasted.

Anna blushed. "It was most frightening, but I think we managed to pull it off."

"Your mother says you cut out the woman's tongue?" I asked, seriously. I hated imagining Anna having to execute such a drastic deed.

"It had to be done. She was coming to and I couldn't risk her screaming or talking."

"How did you explain the blood?" I asked. Certainly there was blood. I'd witnessed enough abuse to know how these things went.

Just then, Draco entered the room. His black cape was covered in a fresh coat of dust from riding hard along a rutted trail. "She told everyone Elizabeth was ill, throwing up blood in fact, and was delirious given her current state and well, the prospect of spending her days in a walled up chamber," he said, as he swept across the room.

"It was very believable," Anna said, beaming at Elizabeth.

Draco looked at all the faces assembled in the room. "It appears we are all here. I'm pleased to see everyone has made it thus far, safely."

Nicholas flinched and took a step away from me.

"What about Katelin and her George?" Elizabeth asked. Elizabeth always referred to Count Drugeth's son as *her* George so he would not be confused with *my* George.

"Oh Mama, we sent them home. It is best that Katelin returns to Humenne. I only came this far to make sure all was well and to deliver Lyk to Amara. I too must return home as soon as possible.

"And Paul, where is Paul?" Elizabeth asked.

"He refused to come. He believes in your innocence and is doing everything he can to clear your name," Anna said.

"Somehow you must get word to him that I am fine," she said.

"For your protection, I think it is best if Paul is kept in the dark for now. His genuine campaign works in our favor and dispels any suspicion."

Poor Paul, I thought. It wasn't fair for his sisters to leave him out like that, but I did sympathize with Anna's plan. It was the smartest way to handle the situation.

Lord Buckley peeled his false beard from his chin. He rubbed the angry red mark blemishing his sore skin. "Dreaded disguise," he mumbled.

"I don't see why he has to be here," Elizabeth replied, referring to Lord Buckley.

"I was under the impression you might have missed me," he said.

"Bah! Why don't you go back to your Italian whore," she snapped.

"Mother, please," Anna begged.

Elizabeth crossed her arms and turned up her nose.

"Has everyone forgotten the task at hand?" I asked. There was a brief murmuring about the room. "We leave within the hour," I continued.

Our things were gathered and Anna and Count Zrinsky said their good-byes. Ursula was to go with Anna while her mother, the Lavender Lady, accompanied Elizabeth and me on the second leg of the journey. Shortly thereafter, the travel party boarded into separate carriages and Draco followed on horseback.

"You must hate separating from your daughter," I said to the Lavender Lady, attempting to make conversation.

"It is time. Anna is a trusted companion and promises to look after Ursula during her courtship."

"She is to be married?" I asked.

"Yes, to a wealthy gentleman. Count Zrinsky introduced the couple."

I nodded. "Will you live with them after they are wed?"

"Oh no, I wouldn't think of intruding on the newlyweds. Other arrangements have been made on my behalf."

Elizabeth ignored our conversation for a time, but when there was a natural pause she asked, "Did you love him, Francis that is?"

The Lavender Lady blushed. "I did, very much. And, did you?" she asked politely in return.

"No, not at all," admitted Elizabeth.

"I'm sorry then for you and I, and I suppose for him as well."

"Did you know he was killed by a whore? Stabbed to death in his own room."

I could see the harsh truth caused the Lavender Lady pain.

"No, I'm afraid I was never told what really happened."

"She came to me in Vienna. She tried to extort money from me after his death." Elizabeth looked away from the window and turned directly to face the Lavender Lady. "You should know I avenged his wrongful death and killed her. Even though I did not love him, he deserved better than to be stabbed by a whore."

The Lavender Lady smiled. "Thank you. That was most kind. I imagine he is very sorry not to be around to hear you tell the tale. He was fond of revenge."

Elizabeth chuckled. "That he was."

The journey took longer than I remembered and the anticipation of arriving at the port was eating away at my patience. Before we made the last stretch of the trip we decided to stop to lunch and to switch out horses. We had only been back on the road for nearly an hour when I heard the driver shout something to Draco. Up ahead there was a commotion and he was asking if we should turn around.

"What is he saying?" the Lavender Lady asked.

"Something about a skirmish."

"We're not well guarded," she said.

"These are peaceful times. We shouldn't worry."

"Times in this region are never peaceful," Elizabeth said, concerned.

The noise was growing louder and the thundering of hooves drew closer. I yanked back the curtain and watched as clouds of dust rolled past.

"Why now? We are almost to the port. I can see the sea on the horizon," I said, irritated.

Men were yelling and the carriage jerked as the driver tried to calm the harnessed horses. When we came to an abrupt halt, I unlatched the door and darted from the carriage. In the chaos I could hear Lyk snarling and growling.

"Get back here!" Nicholas shouted.

Charlie Courtland

Draco chased some of the men off, but a few were still trying to hold their ground against him. Lyk was snapping at the horses' heels and leaping about as they tried to stomp him.

"He's going to get trampled!" I cried. Instinctively, I ran toward him.

I could not discern the calls above the shouts and growls, and through the dust and thrashing of the snorting horses I became disoriented.

"Lyk! Draco!" I shouted. I beat my hands through the air trying to clear the way, but the kicked up dirt was creating a haze.

Hearing my voice, Draco lost concentration and let his defense drop.

"No!" I cried.

A red stain spread across his uniform. He grunted as he lunged at his enemy. The man swung and missed and Draco swiftly returned the blow, hitting his target head on. The man shouted something foreign and retreated into the woods.

I ran toward Draco and Lyk who was still growling and leaping about like a wild beast.

"Get her out of here!" Draco ordered Nicholas.

I felt hands on my shoulders. I was being tugged backward to the carriage. Men circled in the distance determining whether to flee or attack again.

I doubled over under the force of my protector who was trying to restrain me and make me follow him to the carriage. "Lyk, come! Come now!" I cried. I grabbed Nicholas's sleeve. "Draco is injured. It looks serious." I fought my way loose and again, ran toward Draco and Lyk. "You're hurt. We need to get help," I called to my husband.

"Damn it man, do your job and get them the hell out of here!" Draco said. He wasn't talking to me. He kept his attention focused on Nicholas.

Nicholas grabbed me again and this time used greater force to get me to obey. "Get back in the carriage. It is for your own good," he said, through gritted teeth.

"Retrieve Lyk, please," I begged. I couldn't stand the thought of leaving him behind.

469

Nicholas shoved me in the carriage and slammed the door. I watched as he raced across the road to where Lyk was stalking about on guard and viciously waiting another attack against his family.

It was chaos. The horses didn't understand what was going on and instinctively feared the snapping wolf pouncing around their hooves. The driver was whipping and yelling to keep them under control, but they stomped angrily at the ground pawing at the road.

Nicholas had hold of Lyk and it was taking every bit of masculine strength to secure the animal and coerce him toward the carriage. As soon as he neared the temperamental horses Lyk reacted and threaten them by barring his canine teeth. Nicholas lost control and his hand caught in Lyk's collar as the wolf sprang at the legs of the horse. The horse retaliated and flung Lyk away by kicking him in the side. He rolled, whining a humiliating cry as he toppled a few feet away. Nicholas tried to scramble to his feet to avoid the hammering of hooves by his head. A horse bucked and when it came down a foot caught a piece of Nicholas snapping something in his leg.

Seeing the struggle, Lord Buckley bolted from his carriage and made a dash to rescue Nicholas before he was crushed to death. He pulled him free and flung his arm over his shoulder. Nicholas wasn't moving his leg. It hung lifeless with his foot pointing in the wrong direction. By now, our driver had jumped down from his perch and was gingerly approaching Lyk who was whining and curled up in a ball on the side of the road. Lord Buckley got Nicholas into the carriage and then hurried to help the driver with Lyk. They loaded him into the cabin and slammed the door. With a snap of the reins we were rumbling towards the port where a ship was anchored.

I clung to Nicholas who was covered in sweat and dirt as he panted half slumped against the seat. I wanted to comfort him but I was terrified I'd cause more pain.

"Is it broken?" I asked.

Nicholas used his hands to lift the burden of his leg. "Oww! Damn hell, it is. It is broken."

"Who were those men?" I asked. I was too frightened to cry. I could not conceive what I'd just witnessed; the attack, the blood, the crushing of bones through the tangle of dust and cries.

"Raiders. They were very organized. They must wait for travelers heading to port and take them by surprise."

"Where is Draco? We need to stop and get him help. He is bleeding badly from his side."

Nicholas pressed his head against the back of the seat and closed his eyes. "He is gone. I am to take it from here." He grimaced, "But what good am I now." He tried to move his leg. A deep angry noise rose from his throat.

It scared me. I'd never heard him make that sound before and I didn't like it at all.

"Gone?" I asked, shyly. "Again."

"He can make it to a nearby military camp. They have supplies there…it is his best chance to survive."

I was hoping the wound looked worse than it was. "Is it serious?" I asked. I was shaking badly.

Nicholas shook his head. "I don't know, but it doesn't look good. There was a lot of blood. I think he got a sword in the side."

"And you? What about you?" I asked. I reached out to touch his leg but withdrew knowing my touch would only cause more pain.

"I'm not dead. I do think it is best if I get the leg set." He stared at his foot. "That doesn't look right," he said, giving a nod toward his foot. He was beginning to shiver.

I could see the ships and hear the gulls circling overhead. "Hang on. We're almost there," I assured him.

I was the first to jump out when the carriage came to a halt. Elizabeth and the Lavender Lady followed me to Lord Buckley's carriage.

"How is he?" I asked, through the window.

Lord Buckley eased open the door and carefully stepped over the fuzzy ball breathing shallowly on the floor.

"He's hurt, but I don't know how terribly. I think it is his ribs. Poor boy took a beastly kick in the gut."

A couple of dockworkers approached and offered their services for a small fee. Elizabeth gladly pressed some coins in their hands and instructed the men to carry Lyk and aid Nicholas up the plank of the ship. Their things were already being loaded and I was eager to join Nicholas in the cabin. I started after him and took up his other arm, securing it around my shoulder.

"What are you doing?" he asked.

"Be quiet. I'm getting you stowed on the ship."

Sitting in the distance was a clean, black carriage. A man emerged and stood waiting for a sign; some kind of acknowledgement that he should approach.

"Given the circumstances, the plan has changed," Nicholas informed me. He gestured to the approaching man.

"Oh no! No, no, no! I'm going with you!"

Nicholas paused. "You can't. You must go back and carry out Draco's arrangement for his wife – otherwise, Count Thurzo will come looking and you'll lead him right to her." Nicholas tipped his chin to Elizabeth and the Lavender Lady who were boarding the ship.

"But we are to stay together, you and me. That was the plan. I'm not leaving without you...I'm not going alone." I caught a sob in my throat.

Nicholas waved for the man to come closer. As he neared I recognized the tailored cut of his clothes and gracefulness of his walk.

"There's been a change of plan," Nicholas called out. "We ran into an unforeseen complication up the road. I'm afraid we got tangled in a bit of a skirmish. Draco suffered an injury, but was well enough to ride to a nearby military camp. I think my leg is broke and Lyk is hurt as well, but the ladies are fine – that is what is important."

My George did not utter a single word. He kept his eyes locked on mine the entire time. He was saying so much with that look that it hurt deep inside like the tearing opening of an old wound.

"Go now. Make sure she gets to Vienna safely. In Draco's absence, I will continue on with the countess." Nicholas kissed my forehead. "Don't worry. I will take care of them and myself too. I just need some time to heal. Now go with George – he's got you from here."

George reached out. I didn't want to go. I wanted to stay with Nicholas, but I knew nothing went according to plan. Life was unpredictable. No matter how carefully constructed, the unforeseen happened. It was Fate's way of punishing us for meddling. Had I really believed it would let us off so easily? I took George's hand and followed him to the carriage. I didn't look back. I couldn't or I would have lost my nerve.

I told myself when he was healed Nicholas would return to me and we would laugh again at our little adventure. For now, I found solace in the knowledge they were alive and very close to being out of harms way. All they had to do was contact Issacher and get to Brenta. No one would ever find them there. No one but us knew about the secret place built long ago for Vlad's son. He had never used it, but it hadn't gone to waste. An ancestor was adopting the hidden estate locked away deep in the heart of the marsh on the fringe of Venice. On the edge of society Elizabeth would live the rest of her days accompanied by the Lavender Lady who had traded her own dreams for her daughter's future. It was a mother's sacrifice and it was her penance to serve. Even if Elizabeth did not like the Lavender Lady, she respected her for the choices she'd made and continued to make for her child. I knew in time they'd discover a common ground and settle in and eventually accept the mutual admiration they felt for one another; just like Elizabeth and I had done so long ago at Sarvar.

I sat apart from George, never speaking a word as we rode toward Vienna. The only thing that connected us was our hands stretched across the seat and our fingers entwined with each other. He knew better than to speak, for there was nothing left to say. He'd given me all he could and, in the end, had done his duty.

Behind us the port disappeared and the woods thickened as we rolled toward Vienna and back to civilized city life. My things had been sent ahead and I was given permission to reside in the townhouse as long as I liked. It was a concession by the Bathory family for my cooperation—it was a bribe to silence me from spewing the truth about what occurred during all the years I spent in Elizabeth's company. Even though their lies were more damning and sinful, they made certain it reflected only upon her. All the darkness was to be cast on Elizabeth and the family was unyielding when it came to being drug into the light and tarnished by the glare of excusing eyes. It was the way it was; a room of mirrors bouncing images off one another and upon one another.

When we arrived, George and I entered through the back door so we would not disturb the servants or arouse the curiosity of the neighbors. I changed out of my clothes and washed the grime from my skin before tossing the torn remains of my dirtied dress in the lit hearth. George changed out of his traveling clothes and neatly folded them upon the chair. He began to make up the sofa while I turned back the covers on the bed.

"Will you sleep here?" I asked.

He hesitated. "Are you sure that is what you want?" he asked. His voice was soft and caressing – formal like I remembered and it soothed my anxious nerves. I knew he'd do anything for me. Well, anything he was capable of doing.

"I don't want to be alone. Not tonight, anyways." It was going to hurt to feel him beside me while knowing Draco was dying on a cot in some camp, and Nicholas writhed in agony with his leg set in a splint. They all suffered because of me. Selfishly, all I wanted was a warm body to fill the empty space and ease my guilt.

He joined me in the bed and rested on his back while I wrapped myself around his form and laid an arm across his chest.

"I can't stay long," he said.

"I know," I whispered. The surrender in my voice was apparent.

I believe he sensed while lying there that he no longer possessed all my heart – it was fractured in tiny pieces, each chunk belonging to another and leaving him with only a small portion to cling to.

"In time you will get use to the surroundings. You will form new attachments and find a way to endure the circumstances you're faced with. You always do," he said, tenderly.

I was not sure if he was talking to me or to himself.

"That's the worst thing about people. They can convince themselves to get used to anything," I said, wearily.

Charlie Courtland

My Condolences, My Beloved

Present Day: 1628 Vienna

My coughing fits were worsening and no matter how much tea I drank, my throat remained scratchy and dry.

"Open the curtains," I croaked.

The maid set down her book and secured the heavy velvet drapes by looping them behind the gold ornate hooks.

St. Augustine towered above everything else. The light reflected off the carved bodies of innocent angels as the weathered bronze bell remained idle in the tower. Pigeons cooed and bobbed their heads as they surveyed the street from the rooftop for bits of food littering the walk.

"Dirty, filthy, disease ridden birds," I said. "Rats with wings, that's all they are."

"You mean the pigeons? I think they're kind of pretty. Look how the sun plays with the iridescent colors of blue and green on their feathers. Surely, you can appreciate the beauty of the colors and how the Lord shines on all his creatures?" the nursemaid said.

475

"There's nothing beautiful about their runny yellow waste splattering on your hat when you're walking beneath."

She ignored my comment and resumed reading her book. That's what she did when she tired of my complaining.

I didn't take offense. I wasn't really interested in having a conversation with the woman anyways. I had better things to do; larger tasks to tackle like completing my story before John arrived. I dipped my pen and set it to the final pages of my memoir.

I never saw Draco alive again, I wrote. His wound was deep and he suffered through infection before succumbing to death. His body was returned to the king's castle and buried with great ceremony beside other fallen comrades. I said my peace while wearing my widow's black and returned to the comfort of my townhouse. Out of respect, I did not pack my things and disappear to Venice. I figured I owed Draco that much. Besides I did not wish to put anyone else at further risk, so I remained alone in the city. After all, he had given his life to save us and I could not bring myself to disrespect his noble sacrifice.

Through an elaborate coded message, I learned Nicholas's injury was severe and the doctor's were unable to save most of his leg. They cut it off from the knee down and he hobbled around the grounds of Brenta with the aid of a crutch. Lyk was his constant companion and although he fully recovered, I couldn't take away Nicholas's protective guide. I knew Lyk's place was in the country. It was where he'd be most happy and free to roam, even if it was in domestic captivity.

In an exchange of complicated codes, I wrote often to my friends about my life in the city, including my cat and my daily walks to the Café Sevilen Khan. I discussed my garden club and the acquaintances I made and complained about the neighbors and the noise and those horrid bells of St. Augustine. Each time I received a response, I prayed it would announce Nicholas was coming, but even though he tried to be encouraging, in time I finally realized that he'd never be able to make the trip to the city – he was too crippled and I sensed was greatly ashamed of his deformity. Still, I could not prevent daydreaming about the day, nor could I stop watching from behind the lace curtain of my drawing room window with the hope of seeing his carriage roll up. If only I could see him one last time, to let him know how much he meant to me and to kiss him goodbye, but that was not in the scheme, it was not to be.

***

Over the span of the next four years Katelin's husband George visited the muted imposter walled up in the tower at Cachtice. He was determined to keep up appearances for the sake of all our safety. He delivered food and often read books or shared bits of gossip. However, it was not enough and in the end and without light, the woman who we kidnapped died slowly and for the most part alone in the maddening silence while the real Elizabeth caged in an airy range wandered along the marshy boarders and strolled, masked through the streets of Venice during carnival with the Lavender Lady as her companion. Similarly, the light never shone on her face and as far as the world was concerned she no longer existed. In fact, Elizabeth Bathory didn't. She was a ghost haunting the bogs of Brenta and on occasion visited Issacher's kin in the ghetto under an assumed name. She was a mystery to most people and despite her thirst for adventure and science, she maintained a distance and curbed her practices. By this stage of her life, she was not well and it took much of her energy to keep up any charade. Most of the time, she opted to remain at the estate and enjoy the company of her trusted rescuers and the portraits of her infamous ancestors who looked proudly upon her from the decorated walls.

***

It was not until the 31st of July 1614 when a curious guard approached the cell at Cachtice, that the final curtain fell. Out of boredom, a fellow solider dared him to get a glimpse of the Blood Countess who was rumored to be dying and in her last days. Even at the age of fifty-four, Elizabeth was believed to be one of the most beautiful women in all of Europe and after a lusty bet, the guard wagered to prove it so with his own eyes. When he peeked through the door slot used to slide food through, he noticed there was no movement inside. He cocked his head so he could see more of the room and there, lying face down on the bed was the imposter countess. Priests were called and when the doors were unlocked and the woman examined, it was announced the Blood Countess was officially dead. Her appearance was shocking and the deterioration she suffered from lack of nourishment and light was startling. She was no longer the vibrant beauty everyone remembered, but was a withered bag of bones with ratty hair, wrinkled skin and black gums.

Without further ado and in the vein of tradition, stories spread reaching the most remote places in the country. People were speaking ill, saying Elizabeth died by starvation – she starved because she was denied virgin blood. Some even accused poor George of sneaking drops of blood in her food when he visited, but claimed the amount was not enough – that she hungered for more and in the end shrieked with pain as her youth escaped from her body and the spell she had cast to keep her seductive allure was indeed what cursed her to death.

Not wanting to be bothered, Count Thurzo requested the body be buried in the yard of a local church, but the townspeople's abhorrently squawked at the idea and refused to allow the evil flesh to be placed in blessed ground. It was disrespectful and many feared the corpse would taint the surrounding graves and possibly infect the living. The concerns were heard in front of a council and finally it was determined the body would be sent and buried in the town of Esced. It was only fitting that the Blood Countess return to the original place of her birth. It was the place from which she rose, and it would be the place where she'd finally be put to rest. To ensure she would not escape death, a priest drove a stake through her heart pinning her corpse to the ground for all eternity.

The ceremony was appalling and if it had been the real Elizabeth I would have grieved profusely at the mistreatment of her body, but instead I stood beside her children unmoved by the occasion and in wonderment of the tradition that was hereafter common practice – anyone determined to die unnaturally would be staked to the ground. This would prevent them from rising and preying on the innocent. The priest announced there was evidence that the Countess Bathory was responsible for unleashing evil upon the region. By allowing dark practices in her castle, she released a curse upon her people. This evil attacked the most vulnerable and was highly contagious if proper precautions were not taken.

He bowed his head, "I fear the curse cannot be undone by any other means."

Oh how pitifully sad the old priest looked and I truly think he believed what he said. He listened to confession and naively assumed people were innately honest and that man was merciful and reasonable, but I knew differently. I stared at the dead woman with the wooden stake driven through her chest and sympathized. It was terrible, what man did to her – it was inexcusable, but what was worse is that God allowed it to happen in the first place.

The priest made the sign of the cross, and together we uttered a final prayer. I squeezed the girls' hands and gave Paul a pat on the shoulder.

I turned away from the plot and walked to the carriage. A slight breeze came from the north and with it carried a chill, which shook me. It was over. Her life was done and, with it, a legend born.

Sixteen Hundred and Thirty-Seven

There was something mysterious about the breeze toying with the hanging branches of the foliage along the bog. The rustle of the leaves mimicked words, and I swore I heard people speaking in the distance, but I knew we were alone. I squeezed Kate's hand as we walked across the grounds. It was a delightful day and we were both enjoying watching young Georgy play up ahead. He loved this place. He loved to visit and hear the stories of his ancestors.

"Ah! To be so free," Kate laughed, as her son tumbled over the grass.

I paused and placed a protective hand over Kate's belly. "Are you feeling well? Shall we continue on?" I asked.

"Don't be silly, John. I feel fine."

I had placed Rosalyn, the caretaker's daughter in charge of maintaining the estate and requested the gate remain unlocked for our convenience. Together, we strolled along the tiered, mossy terrace and by the enormous statues lining the pathway. Kate called them the overseers. The marbled, weathered Gods frozen in time and damaged by the elements embodied the obscurity of the place. They hauntingly enhanced the ageless history which waited, isolated from the rest of the world. We crossed the lawn and entered through the garden gate. Just beyond grew an ancient apple tree that still bloomed, and on occasion if conditions were ideal, produced edible fruit.

"Come Georgy!" Kate called to our son.

He came bounding through the gate and halted by our side.

"May I go see?" he asked.

"Yes, of course," I urged.

Although an ordinary child might fear this place, he was born from the bravest of lines, albeit secretive, and was most courageous. I smiled as I watched him race towards his favorite, an exquisite rendering of a wolf howling at the night moon.

"He cries a warning to all that approach," I said, taking the opportunity to teach the lad.

"He does not flinch in the least," Kate said, proudly.

"He has no reason to be frightened. He's heard the tale and to him the wolf is a friend, a fierce companion and protector."

Kate nodded. "Perspective and balance, much like this enchanting place."

"Oh Mama, come see the royal guard." Georgy paused beside the chiseled form of the soldier. The artist's efforts were obviously focused on depicting the subject's penetrating eyes and Kate wondered if Lady Lorant had overseen the specifics. The stone eyes were intent on watching the horizon as the soldier stood with one hand on a sword and the other on his heart.

"He is very brave," Georgy said in awe. He knelt and touched the soft grass growing around the heavy stone. "Who is buried here Papa?"

"Ah, this is Nicholas Kosovich. He is the keeper of the watch."

"He is the man who lost his leg when he was saving the countess?" Georgy asked.

I nodded. "Without him, we would not be standing here, or anywhere, for that matter."

My son hurried to the neighboring grave marked by a sculptured woman sitting in a flowing gown, her head bowed and admiring the babe cradled in her arms. The ground around her monument was thick with lavender and the fragrance was overwhelming. Georgy touched the light purple blooms. "Lavender," he said sucking in a deep breath.

Kate turned. Her favorite had always been the unbelievable and most seductive piece demanding attention in the very center of the garden. From the first moment she stepped foot on the marshy retreat of Brenta she'd found herself drawn to the black raven surrounded by hundreds of white rose buds. The contrast was harsh, but striking and the expanse of the bird's wings signified great power. It was as if it was trying to take flight, but sadly unable to soar. The wing's fought to free the stone grounding it to the earth, but also spread as if they were protecting all those circling, bowing in services to the unlikely power. "Ah, there she is. The elusive woman," she said, breathlessly. She approached cautiously, her hand lifting, reaching out to touch the coolness and feel the rough cuts left behind by the chisel. "I wish I would have known her."

I patted the manuscript tucked beneath my arm. "My dear, you do know her – as well as anyone can." I had spent many hours reading the gift Lady Lorant sent. And as I promised her, I shared the tale with my family. The history bound together and penned by her hand would remain a secret, and this place, Brenta, forever a sanctuary of peace hidden from the outside world.

Kate hooked her arm around mine and together we paid our respects to the last curiosity in the garden, a graceful swan with its neck bobbing delicately before the sprawled raven.

"She did her duty," Kate said, her eyes filling with tears. "And you did right by listening to her – even if everyone said she was mad." She shook her head. "Mad? How can they say such things?"

I tightened my grip on Kate's arm. She had only known Lady Lorant a short while, but in the time they spent together Kate had become very attached and grew to love her more than she was prepared to accept. The passing of her friend was difficult and the rumors she overheard during tea and at garden parties sparked indignation. She did not like the gossip about the countess or Lady Lorant. Madness? That is what she overheard when she eavesdropped on the snickering women. What did they know of madness or mistreatment? Nothing! "She was an extraordinary woman," I said. Our history would have been much different if it had not been for her. I cannot bare to think what my life might be like if I hadn't taken her advice." I paused. "I suppose I would have followed my grandfather and lingered down a path full of regret and misery."

"But you didn't. That is what is important. You changed the course and by doing so you give hope to Georgy," Kate said.

I opened the bound pages of the manuscript and thumbed through the chapters of history. I unfolded the maps tucked in the back, and moved aside the slip of paper containing the account number of D. Sepet in Venice. On the last page was Lady Lorant's will and testament. In it she requested that I return her to Brenta so she could be put to rest beside her family.

"It's difficult to imagine any of it ever happened, but yet my eyes are not sewn shut. How can I deny what is right here in front of me?" I said. "No matter how many times I stand in this garden, I still find it overwhelming and difficult to absorb – the story I read over and over and the people who rest here beneath the stone statues and among the fragrant flowers, it's remarkable. Just look at this gathering; such a small and unassuming group. But yet...they did not know what they did, or the course they changed." I glanced at Kate, "Or did they?"

"Do any of us?" she asked. She plucked a white rose from a bush and placed it on Raphael's grave marker. "Do you think there really is a vial of blood buried beneath?"

Often I had wondered the same thing. "I have no reason to think otherwise," I said. My eyes wandered across the scenery. "All this makes a person question the written record of history and the validity of it all. As I stand here with this book in hand I cannot help but feel more confused about what I know." I turned and faced Kate. "What is truth? Our heroes and monsters are hardly opposites, much like that which determines the definition of love and hate. What I love, another may hate and what I hold dear, someone else despises." I sighed. "What account is absolute?" I kicked the ground. "What is concrete, what is to be believed?" I had so many questions, and yet when I sought answers, I was left with only more questions.

"I suppose most of history holds both truths and lies. She placed her hand on my chest. "The rest of what you need to know is in here." She then moved her hand and touched my face. "And what you can not feel in your heart, you will question with your mind, and if you follow history's lesson you will discover the truth," Kate answered, wisely.

Charlie Courtland

Author Note

Erzsébet Báthory was born in 1560 at the castle of Ecsed in Hungary. The Bathory family was a wealthy and powerful Protestant family. Members included: war heroes, a cardinal and the future King of Poland. However, the family tree also had a shady side, and their defects were believed to be the sad consequence of constant intermarriage. The less reputable half included an uncle who practiced rituals of satanic worship, and Aunt Klara, a notorious bi-sexual who enjoyed torturing her servants. Erzsébet's own brother Stephan was a drunk and a lecher. Many members of the Countess's family suffered from epilepsy, madness and other psychological disturbances. As a child, Erzsébet threw frequent fits, which might have been seizures or a psychologically disorder. It was reported that she would easily be overcome with rage and lash out with uncontrollable and often, severely harmful behavior.

At the age of six Erzsébet witnessed an event that possibly triggered her future habits. A band of gypsies visited the Bathory home. During their stay, one of the men was accused of selling his children to the Turks. With no evidence besides the word of gossiping royals, the gypsy was declared guilty by Erzsébet's father and sentenced to death.

Also during her eleventh year, Erzsébet became engaged to Ferenc Nadasdy, the 'Black Lord' of Hungary. He had a reputation for being a cruel and ruthless warrior, which made him a prize asset of the crown.

At a young age, Erzsébet was sent away and was surprisingly, and for the most part, left unsupervised. During one of her unattended excursions, she met a local peasant, Laszlo Bende. She was smitten and continued a secret romance with the boy. Unfortunately, this lead to a pregnancy and urgency by her family to cover up the incident and rush a marriage to Ferenc. Erzsébet gave birth in secrecy and was forced to leave the child with an adoptive family.

On May 8, 1575, at the age of fifteen, Erzsébet married the

twenty-one year old Ferenc Nadasdy, at the Varanno Castle. Since Ferenc was a solider and the leader of the 'Unholy or Black Quintet,' he spent very little time with his new bride. In his absence, Erzsébet relished her freedom, power and ran the estate with an iron hand, often personally delivering torture as punishment.

In 1585 Erzsebét gave birth to her daughter, Anna, and over the following nine years two more girls were born, Ursula and Katherina. However, it is speculated that Ursula died as a baby. Finally, in 1598, Erzsébet gave birth to her only son, Paul. With the heir born, the family was satisfied.

However, Erzsébet grew bored and restless so she decided to visit her aunt, Countess Klara Bathory. It is rumored that during these visits, and through the urging of her aunt, Erzsébet participated in orgies and bondage. She also developed an interest in the occult. Soon thereafter, she became associated with Dorothea Szantes, a black magic witch who encouraged Erzséebet's sadistic tendencies and helped her refine acts and devices of torture.

In 1603, Ferenc became ill. He fought for his life and held on until January 4, 1604. Accounts suggest he was poisoned by an enemy spy or his wife, while others think he was stabbed by a scorned harlot.

Four weeks later, Erzsebét moved to a townhouse in Vienna. Also sometime during this year, Erzsebét added another member to her intimate circle, Anna Darvulia. The woman claimed to have been in the service of Queen Catherine de'Medici and was familiar with potions that prevented aging and enhanced beauty.

One day, Erzsébet lashed out at a servant girl and slapped her violently across the face. The assault produced a splattering of blood. Thereafter, the Countess was convinced that the spot where the blood touched her skin appeared more youthful. She concluded that the ancient claim that the taking of another's blood could result in the absorption of that person's physical or spiritual qualities was true.

Eager for more blood, Erzsébet recruited the help of her faithful servants, a dwarf named Ficzko, and her old wet nurse, Ilona, along with Dorothea to kidnap and kill more young girls. This continued for nearly ten years.

Eventually Darvulia went blind and died. Without her trusted chemist, Erzsebét found herself aging again. Seeking opportunity a sorceress by the name of Erzsi Majorova appeared on Erzsébet's doorstep. In order to gain the Countess's trust Erzsi added a spin to Darvulia's take on eternal potions. She told Erzsébet that virginal victims must be of noble birth. The purer the substance, the better the benefits. However, getting noble girls was problematic so Erzsébet's crew procured peasant girls and before presenting them to their mistress, they made the girls wash, scour and dress in finery.

Erzsébet's lavish hobby and beauty potions created an enormous drain on her finances. She was always complaining about money and demanding a larger allowance. When she was refused, she had no other choice, but to sell two of her estates. This alerted the family and they called a meeting. During this meeting, the men agreed that it was time the widowed countess be sent to a convent to live out her remaining days. However, just days before the plan could be carried out, the Bathory family learned that the Impre Megyert had registered a formal complaint against Erzsébet with the Hungarian Parliament. For three days, the Parliament would listen to testimonies and accusations against the Countess.

From March through July of 1610, testimonies of witnesses were recorded. Some think it was the crown's interest in Erzsébet's property holdings that inspired the trial. At this time, if a noble was found guilty all their property would be confiscated and most important all the claims to debt, which the crown might owe to a certain noble family (which they did), was void.

On the night of December 30, 1610, Castle Cachtice (located in Csejte) was raided. The investigation was lead by Count Thurzo and his men. It was noted that a soldier discovered a body of a young girl that appeared to be cut and torn. The search continued leading the party down 150 stairs into a damp dungeon where they found Erzsébet. She was immediately taken into custody.

Erzsébet's trial began on January 2, 1611. When the public learned of the accusations against the Countess they labeled her the, 'Blood Countess.' The story grew more and more fantastic making it difficult to know what was true and what was silly folklore and superstition. Gossip spread from every mouth about bathing in

487

blood, draining blood and drinking blood – and forevermore, the association with vampirism and the Countess Bathory was born.

Erzsébet was condemned to a life of imprisonment. It is recorded that on July 13, 1614, Countess Erzsébet Bathory dictated her will and testament. She left everything to her children. Countess Erzsébet Bathory was supposed to be buried at the local town church, but the townspeople rallied and refused. Instead, her body was reportedly sent to the town of Ecsed, the original home of Erzsébet and where she spent her brief childhood.

Most characters in the story are based on historical people. They were either known family members or those likely to have crossed paths with the Countess during her lifetime.

Although reports have labeled Erzsébet Bathory as the most prolific female serial killer in history, evidence of her alleged crimes is scarce and her guilt an ongoing topic of debate.

About the Author

Charlie Courtland

The author writes under the nom de plume, Charlie Courtland. She graduated from the University of Washington with a B.A. in English Literature with an emphasis on creative writing, and a minor in Criminology. She was born in Michigan and currently resides in the Seattle area with her husband and two children.

Website and Blogs

http://ccourtland.blogspot.com
http://www.charliecourtland.com
http://www.bitsyblingbooks.com

Facebook Fan Page

http://www.facebook.com/charliecourtland

Made in the USA
Charleston, SC
15 September 2010